The Fathers' Sins

Happy Reading - Enjoy -

Adriana Parrinello

First published by Dog Ear Publishing
4010 W. 86th Street, Ste H
Indianapolis, IN 46268
www.dogearpublishing.net

ISBN: 978-1-4575-2867-5

This book is printed on acid-free paper.

Printed in the United States of America

Dedications:

- *To my husband, Matteo—for your support in helping with the kids while I pursued my dream.*

- *To my boys, Mario, Nino, and Matteo—you are the reasons I live.*

- *To my nieces, Josie and Maria—you are my muse.*

Prologue

He drove the beat-up pickup as fast as he could without drawing too much attention. His heart raced in his chest with a thumping sound that resounded in his ears. The adrenaline rush—something he totally missed. It had been too long since he felt this excited—this happy. Now that he had more money than he'd ever dreamed, he was going to make something of himself. This was the dawn he'd been anticipating—the opportunity to flee from a loser town with all its hillbillies.

He would show them.

He made a quick right and held fast to the brown paper bag filled with cold hard cash. Opening it, he inhaled deeply. *Ha!* He laughed out loud at how slick he'd been. They'd *never* suspect him! He had proved himself loyal, jumped at every beck-and-call, did *whatever* they asked, and they grew to trust him. But because they wouldn't give him what he merited, he took it. He'd duped them and he *would* get away with it.

He let out a whoop and threw a hand in the air. In just a few minutes, he'd arrive home to his girls. He'd scoop them up, snatch a few belongings, and head for Mexico!

He couldn't wait to see the look on their faces when he told them they were leaving. It would be hard for them to adapt to their new lives, but it was for their own good. One day . . . they would possibly even thank him. If they wanted to live in comfort, sacrifices had to be made—*big sacrifices.*

For a split second, he thought of his dead wife Cara and shivered. The mere thought of her sent a rush of blood to his face and stinging to his eyes. When it came to her, he had failed in an immeasurable way. He suddenly questioned if he was still screwing up. Yet, just as swiftly, the doubt departed. The plan was set in motion and there was *no* turning back.

He considered God. Cara talked about Him unceasingly. She said that God would forgive him . . . *if* he was repentant. Still, even if God *would* pardon him, he didn't need God now. He could manage life all on his own!

CHAPTER 1

The End of a New Beginning

December 14, 1973
Brewerton, NY

Laura played with the zipper of her shabby winter coat, pondering what on Earth had gotten into her father. It was so unlike him to show affection—even more unlike him to be in a good mood.

A blast of gunfire suddenly exploded, shaking the house. The earsplitting bang startled her and she screamed.

"What the heck was that?" she cried, as she quickly grasped her baby sister, Sabrina, who stood at her flank.

The child let out a whimper and instantly clenched her leg.

"Pop?" Laura asked again.

Matthew Duke Marcs reached behind his cloak and withdrew a handgun. Laura's eyes protruded at the sight of the large piece of metal. She wasn't even aware her father owned a gun. She watched in horror as he sprinted toward the front door.

"Stay here!" he barked. "Don't move."

With a tremor she called to him, "No, Pop. Don't go out there!"

Sabrina squeezed Laura's leg even tighter.

He gave her a look of alarm. "I gotta. Ya sista's out there." He glanced out the front window. His face turned ashen. He slowly backed away from the door.

Laura felt a weakness that literally brought her to her knees. Sabrina still stood beside her, now grappling for her neck. "What is it?" Laura's voice quivered.

"Laura, run. RUN!" He raced back toward them, guarding them with his body. He turned around, aiming his gun back toward the door. The door was kicked open. "NO . . ." His voice was silenced by the resonant blare of a gun.

Bullets scoured across the small cabin. Laura's instinct was to cover Sabrina, but her body seemed to move in slow motion as it hit the floor from the force of her father's body moving to shield her. The blow seemed to suck the breath from her lungs and Laura struggled to take in air. A spray of warmth splattered her face. Her head hit the floor, cushioned by the frayed carpet. Still, she felt her eyes fly open with the jolt. It took only that instant to see that the gunman sported a hat on his head and had a black mole under his eye. Laura's eyes quickly closed in fright as he advanced near where she lay. She held her breath and waited.

It was quiet now, except for the fading of scuttling feet.

Her head spun in circles. Holding her breath, she felt as though her lungs would burst. Suddenly, blackness engulfed her.

* * *

Laura dreamt, as she lay on the cold cabin floor. The day played back like a film in her mind . . .

Would winter ever go away? The snow, the freezing temps, the icy winds. Unfortunately, in the northern state of New York, winter seemed to never end. If you didn't like it, you moved. If you were too poor to move, you lived with it.

Yeah, gotta live with it. Laura bent forward to carefully wrap a pink scarf around Sabrina's dainty neck. She rose, stared out the dirty window of their secluded cabin, and shuddered. Everything beyond the wooden cabin door was frozen solid—everything but the distant sun that shone occasionally between clouds in the overcast sky. Now Laura sighed. She was a sucker for Sabrina. She would even tolerate subzero temps. Yet, the thought of exiting their warm house seemed worse than death.

Laura smiled at Sabrina's face and bent again to help her with her mittens. Of the three sisters, Laura and Sabrina had the closest resemblance. They both shared the same golden-brown hair of their mother. They both had her greenish hazel eyes and round heart shaped face.

Patty, the eldest, had the dark alluring features of their father. Her shiny black hair was long and curled at the ends. She had his blue eyes and his straight bony nose. Her high cheekbones gave her face a strong, yet refined look. *But unlike him, Patty was caring.* Unfortunately, it was uncommon for her to express her softer side, except to Sabrina.

The little girl was truly the only light in Patty and Laura's lives—certainly the only thing they lived for. *If only their momma had survived her delivery.* Life would've been so diverse—better. But it wasn't . . . and the heartbreak was more than Laura could sometimes bear.

Growing up the past four years without her had been grueling. Two teenage girls, nurturing a baby alone with a father who was rarely present. He'd show up in the evening, bring home food, check on things, and then retire to bed . . . or the bar.

Then suddenly, one day, he began to transform. He acquired a job he was actually able to maintain. More importantly, after years of alcoholism, he'd sobered up. Laura wondered who had helped him to climb back on the wagon. Patty said it wasn't important. The small refrigerator he recently purchased held fresh milk, eggs, bread, and a few other items. Their four cupboards weren't full, but had pasta and other dry foods they used to prepare their meals. Occasionally, he even brought home fresh meat.

In addition to the food that he purchased, he labored on the cabin—reinforcing loose floorboards and caulking the outer walls to keep the warmth in during winter months. He repaired and re-shingled the roof that was dilapidated in some areas. At last, he installed electricity. He even made sure they were wearing warm clothes.

Laura snapped out of her daydream and helped put on Sabrina's boots. After bundling up her own jacket and putting on her boots, Laura reached for Sabrina's hand and followed Patty out the door and into the bitter winter.

Instantly, the northern gusts rattled the fragile door and Laura quickly closed it. The girls scurried out into the snow. For a brief moment, the sun emerged and it's rays hit Laura's face. She took in the warmth and glanced around in wonder at how their property looked like a wintry wonderland.

Despite the depreciated cabin, the patch of land they lived on was breathtaking. A few acres of the property, where the cabin sat and vegetables were tilled, were naked. The rest of the land enfolding them was thick in woodland. Large oak, pine, and birch trees seemed to safeguard the home. During the spring and summer months, wild flowers bloomed, filling the air with a sweet fragrance. The land ran free with savage grasses and drifting hills.

A nearby spring was their only amusement. The girls had the path to the spring memorized after making hundreds of trips throughout the year. They swam in it and even bathed in it. The tall pine trees surrounding part of the spring gave them the privacy they needed.

In contrast, throughout the winter months, the hostile winds froze the clear water and dropped the temperature below human resistance. The cold left nothing thawed in its wake.

Laura huddled into her winter jacket and jumped in place to maintain warmth. Patty dove in and began making a snowball. Sabrina tumbled onto the puffs of snow and made angels. Her eyes seemed to light up as she rolled around, scattering flakes everywhere.

Laura felt a slight pang in her heart. The melancholy she felt moments ago returned. She thought of her momma again. *If only they'd had enough time to get help. If only their father wouldn't have walked out and left them alone. But no, he had to be drunk. He had to desert them.*

Laura shook her head to purge her mind of the hate she felt increasing inside her. Sometimes, she feared its depths would consume her. She closed her eyes, blocking out the painful memories. *Why was it on her mind so much that day?* She had long since gone through the grieving process. Still, the loss of their mother had left a scar so deep, Laura understood that she'd never truly heal. It was as though they lost their mother and their childhood in one repugnant moment.

Patty was only 12 and Laura 10, at the time of her death. Both girls withstood more responsibilities than others their age. It wasn't easy to do ordinary chores since they wanted for normal comforts. Ultimately, hard times were ever present while good times were sporadic. Therefore, little indulgences like playing in the snow *(even if they were freezing)* weren't taken for granted. *No,* Laura took these moments and engraved them on her heart.

She watched Sabrina for a while as she played. She looked so sweet with her reddening cheeks. Her curly hair bounced, while the three attempted to build a snowman that eventually ended up in a snowball battle. Snowballs flew across the shoveled path from one bank of snow to the other.

Laura studied Patty who packed the snow tightly into a ball. Her heart warmed to see her older sister smiling for a change. It seemed, lately, that all Patty did was complain and her mood swings were growing increasingly inconsistent. Laura prayed Patty wouldn't abandon them as she threatened to do so many times. Laura also prayed it was just teenage hormones triggering Patty's unpredictability.

At last, unable to endure the cold any longer, she called out, "Okay Sabrina, we should go in now. My toes are numb!" She smiled softly at her, assisting her from the snow pile, while she brushed off her back.

They all returned to the home and removed their wet coats, hanging them on the wall hooks, right of the door. They set their boots near the wood stove, also to the right of the room, to dry. Laura helped Sabrina put on another pair of dry pants and socks. She took the damp clothing to hang them over a chair near the stove fire.

Patty abruptly approached and irritably tore the wet clothing from her hands. "I got these. Go change outta your wet pants," she commanded.

"I can handle it," Laura argued, yanking the clothes back out of Patty's hands.

Sabrina ignored the argument. "Laura, let's play dollies." She clapped her hands with excitement.

"Sure," Laura grinned. Turning to Patty, she snapped, "Fine! You got it," She thrust the wet clothes back into her hands. "Don't say I don't try to help."

Sabrina bounced toward a basket, near the couch where they kept a few toys. She played unobtrusively to herself on the carpet, while Laura swiftly changed out of her wet pants. She brought them to the iron stove, which emitted a toasty heat.

"Yup! That's what I thought. Go play with your dolls," Patty mocked. She walked past Sabrina and Laura who had joined her on the carpet.

"You know! I'm just trying to keep her busy," Laura frowned.

"Whatever! You always find a way to get outta doing work," she yelled back.

Laura pitied Patty, for most of the responsibilities fell to her. At an age when young people were socializing with friends, Patty had to stay home and care for a family. Because of this, school wasn't an option. Of course, the school board couldn't protest when Patty no longer showed up for classes. It wasn't uncommon for kids to drop out of high school at 16 in their small town.

Laura replied, "I'm not looking for excuses. I'm taking care of Sabrina, so that's one less thing you need to do. *Sorry!*"

Patty glared out the small cabin window as she worked to wash a couple of dirty dishes over a bucket of cold water. She let out a huff, "Yeah, well, so am I. I'm sorry that I was born into this pitiful family. Sorry, I can't get outta this stinkin' hole we call our house. One of these days I'm going to disappear."

Laura rolled her eyes, exhausted from hearing Patty's idle threats.

"Heads up everyone, good old 'Pop' is home early," Patty announced.

Laura overheard the old pick-up sputtering up the gravel driveway. She rose and peered out the front window, watching as her father hastily exited the truck and sprang into the cabin. His face looked perplexed and slightly red.

"Girls!" he bellowed upon entering. He had a brown paper bag clasped in his arms. His eyes connected with Laura's and he gave her a rare smile. Caught off guard, Laura was hesitant to respond.

"Listen up," he stated in his thick Brooklyn accent. He placed the brown paper bag on the table, put his key in his pocket, and clapped his hands together nervously. "I know this is sudden, but we're leavin' town in a hurry. Gatha togetha a few things. I've got boxes in the truck ta throw ya stuff into." Laura and Patty remained still, uncertain of what they'd just heard. "Come on, girls. Let's move. We ain't got foreva. It's time ta roll!" He gave them a wink.

Patty and Laura looked at one another with uncertainty. *Leaving?* They'd never left the cabin to go *anywhere*. Aside from school and church, during the time in which their mother was living, they only knew of their poor home. The infrequent occasions they went shopping for 'girl's stuff' (bras, underwear, and other necessities their father certainly wouldn't purchase) was nothing to consider. In the 14 years of Laura's life, she'd never recalled a vacation or even a visit with family or friends. *Now, they were suddenly leaving town?* Laura felt excited and at the same time alarmed.

"Where we going?" she asked.

"Yeah," Patty inquired, "And why are we leaving so fast?" They looked at their father skeptically. Laura gazed into his blue eyes. Although he appeared frazzled and hurried, she thought he looked rather handsome dressed in black dress pants and a dark-blue turtleneck. The long wool coat he wore floated behind him, as he walked past them, seized the paper bag off the table, and rushed into his bedroom.

"Just do as I say," he shouted through the open doorway. "I'll explain in the truck. Patty, run outside and grab those boxes." He abruptly closed the door. Patty shook her head and gave Laura another puzzled look before tugging on her coat and boots to rush out the door at his command.

After a few moments, he stalked back into the kitchen, now with a briefcase in his hands. He glared at Laura who stood in the center of the kitchen in a stupor. He impatiently ran a hand through the mass of black hair on his head and put the briefcase down. His hard face softened. Slowing his pace, he gently grabbed her shoulders.

"Look, I know all ya life, ya neva known nothin' but this rotten, stinkin' cabin. But afta taday, I promise ya a different life, one filled with nice things and more money than we've eva had. I haven't given ya any reason ta trust me in the past. But I have a plan and now ya have ta try."

He unpredictably kissed her cheek and encouraged her to collect Sabrina and their things. Laura was speechless at his expression of tenderness. She glanced back and watched, while he picked up the briefcase again and headed out the door. Just that moment, Patty returned with the boxes.

Before long, the boxes were packed with their clothing, shoes, and other necessities. The simple home didn't take long to empty as even the dark paneled walls were barely adorned. The two small bedrooms were all but naked, except for the sagging mattresses they used as beds and a weathered dresser per room. Left in the kitchen and family room, was the table with its mismatched chairs and the timeworn couch with the springs penetrating the cushion covers. If it was true that they were moving on to a finer life, Laura certainly wouldn't miss the poverty they dwelled in.

Her father returned from outside empty-handed and helped pack a few other items. As Patty and Laura boxed their last things, he made trips to and from the truck. While he was outside, Patty suddenly gasped.

"What is it?" Laura asked.

"I almost forgot. I've got to go down to the spring," she whispered, glancing at the wood door, careful not to let him overhear.

"Why? What's at the spring?"

"In our tree house, I hid the locket Momma gave me for safe keeping. I can't leave it there. It's all I have left to remember her by." Patty dashed out the door.

"Where ya goin'?" bellowed their father upon reentered the home.

"I'll be right back. Going to the outhouse."

He picked up a box and questioned, "Couldn't hold it any longa?"

"I'm sure she'll be back in a second," Laura stated. She took hold of Sabrina's jacket and stepped to the couch where the child noiselessly played. "Come on, Sabrina. Let's go."

"Where are we gonna go?" she whispered in a tiny voice.

"Daddy will tell us in the truck. Let's hurry. We don't want to make him mad." Laura slipped Sabrina's arms into the humid coat, giving her back the doll to hold. She zipped it up, and then pulled on her own.

*   *   *

When Laura came to, her ears buzzed with a high pitch until, slowly, it began to diminish. Suddenly, the silence in the room was deafening. *What had happened?* A cold breeze blew in, chilling her. Then . . . feeling like an atomic bomb went off in her chest, she remembered. The scene recapped in her mind. Her father's scream still rang in her ears.

"Oh Jesus," she prayed, feeling a crushing heaviness to her mid-section.

Slowly, her eyes opened. Her stomach tightened, her mouth opened in a silent scream. Her father's body covered her chest, pinning her to the floor. Sabrina's body lay lifeless beside hers. Underneath the doll she held, a hole in her jacket oozed dark crimson blood.

"NO!" Laura suddenly cried out. She struggled to move her father's immobile body from hers. Finding a strength she didn't know she contained, she pushed at him and jumped to her knees. "No, Sabrina!" She gathered her tiny wrist into her trembling hand and felt for a pulse. Her own heart pounded so forcefully, she couldn't feel Sabrina's. *It couldn't be.*

Laura quickly unzipped Sabrina's jacket and began applying pressure to the wound. She prayed she could recall the first-aid class she took in seventh grade. She pressed her ear to Sabrina's chest and listened. Still, she struggled to hear a heartbeat. Laura immediately began working furiously to try to revive her, breathing small breaths into her mouth, and gently applying compressions to her chest. But still there was no sign of life in her.

Tears fell from her eyes. She unwillingly came to the reality that Sabrina wasn't responding. Still, Laura worked until she was certain she'd broken some of Sabrina's ribs with the weight of the compressions.

"Sabrina! Come back to me!" she screamed. But Sabrina was gone, never to return. Laura broke down and sobbed, collecting Sabrina's lifeless body into her arms. She let out a scream that pierced her own ears. She lifted Sabrina, determined to get her help. *It couldn't be too late! It just couldn't!*

She ran with her to the opened door in an attempt to get to the truck and into town. It was at that moment that she realized she needed the keys. Laura turned around, while holding her bloody sister, and recognized for the first time her father's body, riddled with bullet wounds. She carried Sabrina back to the carpet and laid her down.

Laura trembled with terror. Fear rooted her a few feet from his body. He was staring blankly at the ceiling.

"Pop?" she whispered. "Can you hear me? Please, wake up. We need to get Sabrina to the hospital." Laura wiped the tears from her face. She whimpered softly. Stretching over to touch his shoulders, she slightly shook him. He was so still. Moving a little closer, she gazed into his vacant eyes. He died saving her. He had jumped in the path of the fleeting bullets.

Suddenly, she cried out in anguish, "Pop! Please, wake up!" She let the tears fall from her eyes, while she clasped her heaving chest. The pain she felt was the all too familiar agony she suffered the night her mother died.

The loss of Sabrina would be more than she fathomed she could bear. She gathered the child's limp body into her arms. Rocking her sweet baby, she brushed Sabrina's curls back. She held her head and kissed her soft cheek. Dazed, she sat with the quiet bodies. Time seemed to suspend and she felt the blood drain from her face. The tears finally stopped. Her body felt cold, immovable.

Was this real? She closed her eyes and opened them again. It was real. They were dead and suddenly her emotions ran wild. She felt she wanted to beat her chest, tear out her hair, hit, scream, DIE! She'd never get to hear Sabrina's voice or see her beautiful bright eyes again.

She thought of her feelings for her father. She harbored so much anger in her heart toward him and now he was dead. *Why didn't she ever forgive him? Why didn't she ever tell him that she loved him?* Laura felt out of control—absolute panic at what had actually transpired, rage for those who did this, and a fear that she was left all alone.

It finally occurred to her—the chance of Patty's survival. It was probable that the gunman failed to hit Patty, just as he failed to hit her. She hugged Sabrina, kissing her little face for the last time, while she laid her down next to her father. Turning to him, she touched his face tenderly, kissing his cheek. A sob caught in her throat. Tearing herself away from their broken bodies, Laura gathered her wits to exit the cabin.

She searched the cabin in confusion for her boots, finally remembering she'd placed them near the wood stove. Tossing them on, she entered the nearly darkened forest. Laura recognized the land proficiently and knew where to find Patty. Running on unsteady legs, she entered the deep woods and down the familiar trail. Tears blinded her vision. Her heart thumped violently in her ears, drowning out the sound of the howling wind. Her entire body quivered and she wondered if she was going into shock. Her mind swirled in circles repeating the killings over and over. She couldn't have been the only one to survive.

"Patty!" Laura shouted in a hoarse voice. "Patty, where are you?" She staggered through the drifts of snow toward the path leading to their spring. She cursed the darkness that slowed her haste. Stumbling over something soft, she collapsed to the cold earth. It was Patty. The red saturated snow beneath her confirmed Laura's most grave fear.

She raised trembling hands to her mouth, holding her breath until her lungs burned with fire. She took in a gasp of cold air and released a piercing scream. Falling to her knees, she cried out.

"PATTY, NO!" She shook her head in defeat. Stricken, she surrendered to her grief. Fresh tears rolled down her face. Her body trembled like a leaf in the vehement wind.

She remained on the ground for a while. When the iciness began to penetrate, Laura rose to her numbing feet, struggling to maintain her balance. *Her* eyes were now vacant, *her* body cold. Aimlessly, she wandered through the old trail in shock. Somewhere inside, something screamed to get help. *What was she to do?* The closest telephone was miles away.

The beat-up pickup came to her mind. She could drive it into town. It was worth the effort to go back to the cabin. She tried to shake off the shock and focus on the trail. Willing her body to move faster, she retraced her steps toward the cabin.

Still a ways from the cabin, Laura heard a scurrying nearby that stopped her heart cold. Fear closed off her airway, nearly choking her. Instantly, she was racing through the woods, no longer on the trail. Her blood pumped forcefully through her veins. Her instincts kicked in and Laura ran for her life. Yet, in spite of her ability to find her way through the property with ease, Laura soon grasped that she was lost.

She stopped to catch her breath. Her face felt cold and her hands had lost feeling. She realized she couldn't last outdoors much longer. The dark forest was thick. She struggled to locate something familiar, but cursed fate again for allowing night to fall too quickly. Glancing back, she had lost her pursuer. She continued to run, until she came upon an opening—an extended drainage ditch. The wind whipped her long hair, while she darted down the channel, near the opening of the drain. With the moonlight as her guide, Laura studied the sewer, barred with rusted iron. Within the drain, she detected a dry area in which she could hide.

As luck would have it, a few of the bars were missing near the lower end where a shallow stream of icy water shimmered. She tiptoed through the ice-covered water and walked into the drain. Laura panted for air. Tears filled her eyes. She crumbled against the concrete wall and down to the ground, where she silently sobbed.

She closed her stinging eyes. The horror of the murders gripped her with a monstrous fear.

In all her terror and grief, she didn't hear the labored breathing straightaway. A chill ran down her spine and she sensed a presence. She lifted her head and strained to see in the darkness. The brilliance of the snow and the gleaming moonlight reflected the silhouette of a man.

CHAPTER 2

Tony

Despite the tunnel's darkness, Laura noticed his build. He was tall and broad. He wore dark clothing, making it more difficult to see him. He took a step closer. She opened her mouth to scream. With an instant reflex, he cupped his hand over her mouth. Laura struggled to release herself from his grip, until his soft voice reached her ears.

"Please," he whispered. "Don't scream. I'm not gonna hurt you." With his face only inches from hers and her eyes now adjusted to the blackness, she could see his strong facial traits. His chin was squared and his jaw firm. His face looked prickly with stubble from a few days without a razor. He wore a black knit hat over thick, wavy hair. His eyelashes were full and long and his eyes large and warm. They looked upon her with kindness and she felt herself slightly relax. His hand fell from her lips.

She gasped in the murky air and immediately asked, "Who are you?" her chest heaving in fright.

"My name is Tony Warren," he answered, still crouched on the ground, inches from her trembling body. "Who are you?" he asked in return.

"My name is Laura," she whispered, gathering her courage. "Look, I don't know what you know, but something terrible has happened. I need to get to the police."

The young man looked at her curiously. His eyebrows knit together with worry. "Good luck with that. They're awfully preoccupied right now. Why? What happened?"

"My family . . ." Unable to finish her sentence, Laura burst into tears.

"Were they hurt in the raids?" Tony probed.

Laura shook her head.

"I'm sure you've heard. It's all over the news. The raids?" he repeated.

"What you're talking about?" she finally managed.

11

"It's happening everywhere. People are looting, killing. It's crazy."

"Why?"

"Vietnam."

"But the war ended. Our troops are on their way out," Laura protested.

"Most of our troops are still there! They're slowly leaking them out. The country is outraged because they want our soldiers home. The government's doing nothing to get our POWs to safety and get our men home. Rioters are protesting for their immediate return! They are threatening to destroy every town, every city, until our soldiers are back on U.S. soil! Ironic, isn't it, how they cry for peace and protest by looting and killing?" he added. Finally looking her over, he asked, "Where you hurt in the riots?"

Her lower lip began to quiver, "You can't understand the horror I just witnessed. They were killed! My family! Murdered . . ."

Tony suddenly stood. His gloved hand came to his forehead in disbelief. "Oh God! I'm so sorry." It appeared he struggled with his emotions. "Believe it or not, I do understand," his voice broke. "I also witnessed the deaths of my family members, years ago."

Laura flinched at his words. The ache in the sound of his voice was unmistakable. Her curiosity was now aroused. Fiddling with a button on her dirty coat, she whispered, "I'm sorry." Pausing a moment to reflect on the agony in her soul, she continued, "This is just so unreal. It's so hard to believe they're . . . gone! *Because of rioting?*" Her face fell into her hands. She couldn't help but to unleash her frustrations in the form of more tears. Her head bobbed, as her body shook with uncontrollable sobs.

Tony seemed to find his voice. "Again, I'm so sorry. I saw you here by yourself and I thought I might be able to help. It's so scary out there. You shouldn't be alone." Bending back down, he reached out and touched her shoulder. "Were you hurt? Are you okay? You have blood on your face and hands."

Laura raised her head. She eyed the man before her and shook her head furiously. "No! I'll never be okay! This couldn't have happened at a worse time. We were ready to embark on the first—the very first adventure of our dreaded boring lives. We were packing to leave town. Pop was saying words Patty, my sister, and I have been dreaming of all of our lives. All of a sudden . . . the gun . . . bullets . . ."

Laura stood to compose herself. Her head began to spin again. Her breath came in short puffs. She felt her lungs screaming out for air. She tried to breathe. Reaching out for a hand . . .

* * *

This couldn't be happening! Not again! Tony caught the fragile girl in his arms. Her thin coat was wet and she felt cold to his touch. He squatted to the ground, holding her, while pulling an extra jacket from out of the large camping backpack he carried. He wrapped it over her shoulders and then looked at her face. A blast of cold air blew a wavy strand of her brown hair over her eyes. He reached over and touched her face as he brushed it back. He felt his heart wrench.

Why? Why did fathers' let bad things happen to their little girls? He hated that this young girl was left unprotected and vulnerable. He couldn't let her go defenseless. He'd have to take over . . . take control . . . take care of her.

He studied her face. She was in shock. She looked so innocent, yet worn. Her eyes were closed, causing her long lashes to touch her cheeks. Her face was red from the cold and irritated with tears. Yet, as his eyes fell upon her mouth, he found that her lips were perfect.

Trying not to let her beauty distract him, he rubbed her arms. She was nearly frozen. He pressed her closer to him to promote warmth. Tony felt an anger rise within him. *How could it be that this had happened to her? He had to make it right. He had to fix the wrong!* He was determined.

"Laura, wake up," he whispered. He gently tapped her cold cheek.

Her eyes fluttered a moment. "Pop?"

"It's me . . . Tony." Her eyes opened and once again, she captivated him. "I'm sorry," Tony breathed. "You passed out." His arms held her to him, even as he knelt on the cold concrete. She tried to regain her poise, but failed. "No, don't…" he suggested in a hoarse voice. ". . . Don't get up or you'll get dizzy, again." He secured his hold on her. "Are you okay?" he asked.

Laura looked up at his face. "Never again," she cried. A tear rolled from the corner of her eye. Tony watched it trickle into the mass of hair on her head.

"I know it feels that way. Here . . . let me help." They rose to their feet. He clutched her shoulders to help steady her. "Better?" he smiled.

"Thank you," she nodded.

"Have you eaten today?"

"Not hungry, thanks."

Tony adjusted the extra jacket over her shoulders. He then opened his large backpack and rummaged to find a flashlight and a snack bar for her. After checking the batteries, the light instantly beamed. He unwrapped the bar and handed it to her.

"Eat anyway," he suggested.

"No thanks," she refused.

Tony insisted. "You should eat it. It will give you strength."

She thanked him and took hold of the bar, but left it uneaten. Gazing at Laura, he saw the questioning look on her face, while she stared at the bag. "This?" he asked, pointing to it. "Long story. If you've got the time . . ."

"Actually, I should find my way back home and call the police. I left my family…"

"NO! You can't go back!" Tony exploded. Panic erupted within him. *He had to convince her!* "You're still in danger! You don't know if they'll come back after you!" he exclaimed.

"I can't just leave their bodies…"

"You have to! You can't help them! I'm sorry, but it's too late for them. You can only save yourself right now. Going back is too risky. They will kill you, too," he added.

"What do I do?" she asked near panic.

"Don't worry. You're safe here, for now," he coerced. She pressed her back against the concrete wall and slid down. Tony studied her a moment. With the beam of the flashlight, he could better see the details of Laura's face. She had a dainty nose that was perfect in proportion with her brilliantly round hazel eyes. Her cheekbones were high and her lips were full and red. The mass of rich brown hair had bronze and golden strands flowing through it and though it was disheveled from the snarling winds, it fell perfectly around her small face. Still, seeing the blood all over her jacket and some splattered onto her cheeks brought him back to a crude reality.

"Why are you here?" Laura questioned, snapping him out of his earnest gaze.

Tony cleared his throat. "It's a long story."

"What happened to you and why did you follow me in here," she bluntly asked.

"Fine, I'll tell you. Can I sit next to you?"

Laura shrugged her shoulders, "Whatever."

Tony knew that the girl was nervous and suspicious. He couldn't explain the way he felt an immediate attachment to her. He wanted her to like him and he wanted her to trust him in return. *She just had to.*

He sat next to Laura. "Well," he began, "As I told you before, I was orphaned too." He stared out into the winter before them. In a more serious tone, he proceeded. "My family and I, we lived in Syracuse," he stated. "I was 14 at the time—the oldest brother of three girls and a little boy. My mother was a good person. My father . . . not so good. But he was a hard worker and he tried to provide for our family." His voice faded out. Once again, he felt a numbing pain in his chest—the ache that seemed to never subside.

"It was June 3, 1968. Everyone was sleeping in bed but me. I couldn't fall asleep. Vincey, my little brother, and I shared a bed together.

"Anyway, I was restless. When I finally started to doze, I heard noises in the house. At first, I thought it was a dream and I fell back asleep. Not more than a few minutes later, I began coughing and smelled something burning. I opened my eyes to find the room was clouded with smoke.

"I woke Vincey. I told him to cover his mouth with the sheets and stay low. I got up and ran to the door. Not knowing any better, I touched the doorknob and burned my hand." He pulled the glove from his hand to display the burn. Laura looked at his hand. Fear unfolded across her face.

Tony continued, "I knew the fire was outside my door and if I opened it, it'd be the death of us both. I had no choice but to save Vincey and myself. Smoke blurred my vision, but I opened the window. Vincey had inhaled too much and passed out. I clutched my brother's lifeless little body and jumped out. Thankfully, we lived in a single-story home." Tony swallowed. His heart raced in his chest even as he told the story. For, no matter how many times he relived it, the vivid memories brought the raw emotions right back to the surface.

"What happened to Vincey, Tony?" Laura asked. She wiped the tears that slid down her face. She reached out and touched his hand.

Tony felt a surge of energy shoot through his hand at her touch. He held her gaze. Her eyes were warm and filled with understanding and compassion. He smiled, as a tear fell from the side of his eye upon recollecting the ugliest moment of his life.

"He died . . ." Tony sniffled and wiped the tear away. He rose from the cold concrete and paced the sewer ground. His breath became heavy and he was desperate to keep his cool, while a mere conversation of the dreaded night transported him to a murky, dismal place he didn't care to be.

"Do you know how the fire started?" Laura asked.

He looked at her for a long moment, meditating on her question. He was tense and angered and he knew he needed to restrain his rage, or lose control. Taking a deep breath, he suddenly eased. He stopped pacing and stood before her. Crouching down, he met her eyes. "My father fell asleep with a cigarette in his hand. I'm lucky I got out alive." He stood again and leaned against the cold wall. His strong arms locked across his chest. Laura rose as well and faced him as he spoke. "Outside, I ran to my sisters' bedroom window. I broke it to get to them. Flames burst out, hurling me off my feet and knocking me out. When I awoke, the fire department had arrived and everyone was dead but me."

"You had to have been devastated." She stared at him—mesmerized by his tale.

"Devastated? That's not the word. *I lost it.* I couldn't accept it. Same as you, I kept praying that it was only a dream. But it wasn't and the truth was ugly to live with.

"At first, they brought me to the hospital. They tended to the bump on my head, my burns, and scratches. They gave me a few breathing treatments to clear my blackened lungs. The next thing I knew, the cops were questioning me. They found it odd that I was the only one who'd survived. Especially when they discovered that my father had a $500,000 life insurance policy, with his children listed as beneficiaries. They began to suspect me."

Laura gasped, "I can't believe it!"

"Well, believe it. They held me until they investigated further. There was no evidence supporting their theory and when they found the cigarette that started the fire, they released me. From there, I was placed in foster care. I went from home to home and believe me when I say, it was a terrible experience. People who foster kids are supposed to take care of them. I ended up with parents who were only in it for the money. I lived in conditions I wouldn't expect a dog to live in. One home used me to do hard labor on their property. When I complained to Social Services, they moved me into another home. It was like being a nomad. I had no place I could call home.

"Finally, two years after the fire, they placed me in the care of the last foster parents I'd know. They were an older couple, good Christians. They loved me, but I was afraid to let them in. I knew that at 18, I was out the door and I didn't want to go through the pain of losing them, too. I promised myself then, to never let another person close to my heart again. I said my goodbyes and moved out. They were nice enough to give me some cash, since I'm unable to collect on my inheritance until I'm 25. The life insurance money went into a trust fund for me for when I come of age.

"Well," Tony continued, "In California, my mom's only sister had recently passed away and her husband, my Uncle Frank, was left all alone, as they were never able to have children. I contacted him after my family died. After losing my Aunt Margherita to cancer, he decided to move to New York to be with me and start over himself. He's my only living relative. He's helping me get back on my feet."

Laura breathed a long sad sigh. She whispered, "At least you have your Uncle Frank."

"Yeah, he's cool. He won't hound me to do this or that. He lets me make decisions for myself, yet gently guides me. But today, I feel like I failed him. When all the riots broke out, he told me to leave town and look for refuge north of Cicero where we live. I didn't want to abandon him." Tony paused with a concerned look. "He urged me take what I needed to survive and run. He would have come if it weren't for his bad bronchitis.

"So I did as he said and grabbed his camping backpack. I filled it with some stuff and took off. I left his apartment building and was running down a back alley, when a couple of thugs eyed my backpack. I knew they were looking to take it. They chased me down the alley, through the center of town!" he explained, his voice heightening in excitement. "People were being beaten in the streets, homeowners fought to keep their homes from being destroyed, cops were everywhere, but they were all preoccupied with the nightmare unfolding before my eyes. I ran across Brewerton Road and entered the woods. That's when I finally lost them.

"As I deepened my run through the woods, looking for safety, I saw your little cabin. I was about to approach the door to ask for refuge, when I heard a scream and then sobbing. I stopped and listened. Your wails sent chills down my spine. I finally spotted you hovering over someone lying very still. As I moved toward you, you rose and began to walk toward me. You walked right past me, without even noticing I was there. You looked so horrified. I wanted to help you, so I followed. But not before I stepped over the body and checked for a pulse." The tears slowly slipped down Laura's solemn face.

"Suddenly, you were running frantically through the brush. I realized you thought I was chasing you, and I knew that if I called out, I'd only scare you more and possibly draw attention to us. That's when I followed you here. I'm sorry if I scared you. When I saw you enter the sewer, I knew you had found a good hideout. Little did I know that we might actually be able to help each other." He looked down at her concerned face and smiled.

Laura sniffled, then questioned. "How's that? I've nothing to offer you," she whispered in a nasally voice.

"Maybe you do."

"Like?"

"How about your friendship? I watch your back—you watch mine. It's very dangerous out there. Another pair of eyes can spare both our lives."

Laura said nothing.

Tony's mind raced to keep her interested. "Laura," he stated, "I know you barely know me but I'd hate to see you have to deal with this alone. Let me help you."

"Tony, I don't know." Another tear formed and slipped down her cheek.

"We'll set out, take the first bus out of town, to safety. I'll do whatever it takes to protect us."

Tony could see the uncertainty in Laura's eyes. At last, she spoke. "I guess I don't have any other choice. I wouldn't even know where to start. If I go into town, I'm scared for my life. I'd need to go to a police station and report the murder of my family. What would happen to me from there?"

"I don't know what you'll come against in town. You shouldn't go without protection. If by some miracle you got to the police safely, you'd most likely be put in foster care." He paused a moment and added, "I wasn't lying to you. It's not all it's cracked up to be. Take it from someone who has been there. Do you have other family or friends willing to take you in?"

"No, I have no family. What else can I do?" she questioned, her eyes searching his for an answer.

"Let's get out of this sewer, for starters, and find a temporary shelter until we can get you help." Laura fought tears. Tony's heart felt heavy. "Look, you do what your heart tells you to do. If you decide to come with me, we'll take things one day at a time. When all goes back to normal, you can report your family's death. If you decide to go on your own, know my prayers are with you. I hope you get to safety."

She looked up into his face. For a moment, the tears seemed to halt. Her eyes were red-rimmed and looked drained. "You think we can make the reports afterward?" she questioned. Tony nodded in agreement. Her eyes grazed the smelly drain and then fell back upon him. She finally seemed persuaded. "When the raids are over, you promise to help get me to the police?"

"Absolutely."

Laura seemed to be considering him. "Okay . . . I'm putting my trust in you. Please, don't let me down."

"I won't," Tony smiled. "Here," he handed her the flashlight. "Shine in here. We're gonna need to keep you warm."

She eyeballed the backpack with question. "Well good God, what do you have in there?"

"All sorts of stuff." He kneeled down and opened the pack. "Let's see— hats, gloves, scarves. Canned foods, dried foods, plastic-ware, and a can opener, of course," he smiled. She smiled in return. She was breathtaking. He tried to concentrate. "I also brought water, a few simple tools, this flashlight, a first-aid kit, a few of my own personal belongs. That's about it."

"Seriously?" Laura remarked.

"Everything but the kitchen sink," he added. Laura let another smile fall across her face. He sifted through the bag and pulled out a snack bar for himself. "Eat," he ordered.

Laura bit into the snack bar he had given her and ate it heartily. She glanced up at Tony, who was openly watching her. She crumpled the wrapping nervously and peeked at him again. Still, he stared. Her eyes shifted a moment, until she looked flustered

"What?" she finally asked.

"Sorry, I don't mean to stare. I'm curious. How old are you?" He finally asked the question that had been badgering him from the start.

"Fourteen."

He shook his head. "Wow."

"Well, what about you?"

"I'm 19."

"Well, you don't look your age, either," she stated, matter-of-factly.

Tony smiled. A gust of wind blew in, chilling him. It was time they left and found shelter. "Well," he continued, "You ready to face the cold again?"

"Not really." She rubbed her hands together.

Tony approached Laura. "Me neither, but we must. It's gonna be brutal out there. Wear this jacket over yours. I know it's big, but it'll do the job. Keep your body moving. The wind will lower our body temperatures if we don't keep our blood circulating. Stay close to me. Try to keep up, okay?" He searched her eyes, while handed her a warm scarf and an extra pair of gloves.

At last, Laura seemed to gather her nerve and answered, "Okay Tony. Let's go."

He squeezed her hand and whispered, "I promise, I'll help you." Laura squeezed his hand in return.

Tony's heart warmed. He felt a healing begin within him that he didn't expected to *ever* feel. It appeared a new start to finally releasing the pain he had been sustaining for a long, long time. A pain so severe and so injurious no one man could contain it alone. Not even a man as potent as Tony Warren.

CHAPTER 3

Orphans

Tony released Laura's hand. She nervously stepped back. Her heart fluttered from Tony's touch. In school, boys had flirted with her often, yet it had never affected her in this way. It was something in Tony's touch that made her edgy—nervous. Something about the way he looked at her that made her pulse race.

She stuffed her arms through the jacket sleeves and looked away. "I'm so scared," she shivered.

"Don't worry. I'll be right by your side," Tony said.

"Thanks," she added.

He nodded in reply. The flashlight flickered causing a disruption. Tony looked out into the night. He grasped the flashlight. "I'll hold this and carry the bag with our stuff."

Our stuff? Why was this guy so eager to share his things with her? Didn't her father always argue that people didn't do good things, unless they had an ulterior motive? Was he right? What could this Tony want from her in return? Laura was near panic at the crazy thoughts that either the devil or common sense planted in her mind. She'd try to keep her distance and not let his good looks cloud her judgment.

Laura took hold of herself, said a silent prayer, and followed Tony between the drain bars into the bitter cold. As they exited the stench-filled sewer, it amazed her how much colder the open skies truly were. The wicked wind blew with full force, sending daggers through her.

They ran up the hill of the ditch and continued alongside the woods. "If we head away from town, we're more likely to remain safe," Tony spoke over the howling winds. Then reaching for Laura's hand, they ran into the forest.

"Why are we going into the woods? Isn't it easier to walk on open land?" Laura's voice bounced as they ran.

"Sure, it'd be easier to walk through, but we're more likely to be seen. Besides, the wind will kill us. At least in the woods, the trees will somewhat shield us," Tony explained.

"Oh yeah, I never thought of that." Her breath came heavy with exertion. She thought a moment and asked again. "What happens if we're seen?"

Tony stopped, his chest heaving. He stared her in the eyes. "Laura," concern emitted from his voice, "If rioters find us, we may be as good as dead. Their curiosity of the bag will surely lure them to steal the backpack and even kill us. I don't want to take that chance. Do you?"

She looked up at the man before her. So far, he'd been consoling and helpful. Laura liked him, too much for her own good. And though she was afraid and felt she needed to keep her guard up, she decided that she didn't want to be separated from him. Not yet, anyway.

"No, Tony. I don't want to take that chance." She thought a moment. Tears filled the rims of her eyes. "Please bear with me. I'm so scared."

"Trust me. Trust God. I don't know if you believe in Him, but I do and I believe He put you in my path for a reason. I know you don't know me. I can't say I blame you for being scared. But, have faith." The wind crackled around them. "Come on," he urged, reaching out his hand. Laura willingly took hold of it.

They trekked through the night with the moon as their guide. Occasionally, they'd stop for water. They ran past an abandoned house, rotted and collapsing. Laura wished they could stop to rest, even considered entering the old house for warmth.

Inevitably, she grew fatigued and weary. "Wait," she cried out. Her body felt numb and ached as it had never ached before. Tony stopped and ran back a few steps to her. They were both panting.

"If I'm running too fast, just say so. I'll slow down. It's just that this bag is getting heavy." Tony patted her on the back. "You okay?"

Laura swallowed hard. Her throat felt dry and ached. "Yeah, I need to rest a second. I can't feel my feet."

"I know. I'm sorry. It's just too cold. If only we could find an old shed, a barn, *anything*! I was considering that old deteriorated house, but it's not safe."

"At this point, I'd stay anywhere." She rubbed her gloved hands together to promote warmth. Laura closed her eyes, pushing out the thought of little Sabrina, Patty, and her father lying dead. She couldn't let herself feel the pain again, especially not at that moment.

"Ready?" Tony asked, disrupting her thoughts.

Distraught as she was, Laura smiled at him. "Yeah, I'm ready now."

They continued on, dodging broken tree limbs and jumping snow banks. The wind never ceased, making their journey all the more difficult. Soon, she lost hope again. Cold and hungry, tired and listless, they stumbled through the wilderness. Neither one spoke.

Laura felt her tears begin to swell. The horrid nightmare of the day seemed to drag on endlessly. Visions of what happened to her family never left her sight. She swallowed the protrusion in her throat and carried on.

As she walked behind Tony, something caught her eye. Behind a string of trees, Laura spotted a house. She stopped and glared at it for a second. Tony turned around and noticed her curiously staring. "What is it?" he asked.

"Look, behind those trees."

They ran past the trees, setting their eyes on a boarded up home, in the center of a small opening in the forest. "What do you think?" Laura asked in excitement.

"I don't know. Come on." He reached for her hand and the two found new energy as they ran up the rickety porch steps to the boarded door. Tony ran his gloved hand over the boards.

"Well?" Laura anxiously asked.

Tony was silent a moment.

"Looks abandoned," Laura added

"Can we really be this lucky?" He smiled, handing her the flashlight. "Hold that a second."

Laura aimed the light, while Tony searched the bag. He pulled out a hammer.

"You have a hammer in the backpack?" Laura flatly asked.

"Honestly, I don't know how this was even in here. Remember, this is my Uncle Frank's camping backpack. Maybe he used it to put his tent together. You know, pound the stakes into the ground?" Laura looked at him questioningly. She'd never been camping but guessed that he was right. She moved to his left and Tony began to pry the wood from the door. "Stand back," he warned.

Tony piled the boards on the porch floor. He then placed the hammer back in the sack in exchange for a flat screwdriver. His hands seemed to shake in apprehension. He nudged the lock with it until at last, the door began to prod open.

He pressed his weight into the door and the lock gave way. The door slowly opened. Tony turned around and faced Laura, while placing the screwdriver back in the pack.

"After you, milady," he stated and opened the door wide for her to enter.

"Wild horses couldn't stop me!" Laura accepted Tony's hand and followed him into the dark home.

*   *   *

Tony led the way into the darkness. With the flashlight burning, they found themselves in the living room. They walked through it, and then spotted an entrance to another room.

"We gotta find the fuse box or some candles," Tony whispered. He found a light switch and flicked it a couple times. "The power is off."

The entrance led them into the kitchen. To the left was a door. Tony led Laura toward it. "I'd guess that the fuse box is in the basement," he whispered. "Let's check this door." He looked down at her face shadowed with fear. "You scared?"

"We shouldn't do this," she whispered. "We're breaking and entering!"

"Laura, the house is boarded up. Don't be afraid," he encouraged.

"I am afraid," she admitted. She reached for *his* hand this time and shivered as Tony pulled her closer.

"Laura, no one else is here. There's nothing to be afraid of." He paused, "But I sure am glad you're here with me."

He felt the girl's horror and grief. He knew what was in store for her. For now, she appeared to be blocking out the sadness. But he knew, *oh*, how well he knew that one could only do that for so long. He looked at her with compassion. Tony felt comforted by the thought that she wouldn't have to endure her grief alone.

She tugged on his arm, snapping him back to reality. He placed his hand on the doorknob and turned it. Immediately behind the door were steep steps that ended at the concrete floor of the basement. He inhaled the humid air and descended the stairway, holding Laura close. The steps creaked beneath their feet.

Upon reaching the bottom, Tony flashed the light before them. Considering the home's size, the basement was small. Its four walls made an exact square, with two small windows. Dozens of boxes were piled up against the far wall, facing the stairway. Laura curiously walked forward and picked up a stray empty box. She looked at Tony questioningly.

He shrugged his shoulders. "Strange."

"Yeah, I say we find that fuse box for now and investigate later." She hugged herself. "This place gives me the creeps."

"Ditto," Tony replied. He flashed the light around until he spotted a steel box on the left corner of the far wall. Together they walked toward it, brushing spider webs away as they went. He dusted the box with his gloved hand and pried it open, exposing the energy switches. As Laura held the flashlight, Tony flipped the controls. "That'll do it."

"Thank God," Laura sighed, meeting Tony's gaze. Suddenly, they both sprinted for the stairway, jumping a few steps at a time. Reaching the top, they entered the kitchen, and Tony closed the basement door, laughing.

"Glad that's over with?" he teased.

"I didn't see you taking your time climbing the steps," she taunted back.

Tony laughed again and turned the light switch on. The small kitchen light blazed above the table. They froze for a moment, taking in the kitchen and its beauty. Even in the dark, it was obvious that it was fully furnished, but nothing prepared them for the colorful décor and style. The entire kitchen was finished in oak cabinets and baby blue countertop. The walls were painted a bright yellow. The curtains were a sheer blue material coordinating with the light fixture and the counter. Even the yellow stove and refrigerator matched. Finally, the oak table and chairs that completed the look, was set in the middle of the room.

Laura eyed the faucet, then glanced down at her blood stained hands. She turned the knob and water flushed from the nozzle. She gasped, "We always wanted running water, but we had to settle for the well. Pop always promised . . ." Her voice crackled, as she scrubbed off the dried blood. The troubled look in her eyes was enough for Tony to realize he needed to step in.

"Well, now you got all the running water you need. For now, to be safe, let's shut this window shade. I don't want anyone to see the lights on in here." He reached across the sink to the window, pressing his body lightly to hers, while he pulled the shade down. He quickly backed away to stay focused. "Hey, come on. Let's see what else we find."

Laura turned off the faucet and shook the water from her hands. Tony grabbed her damp hand and led her to another doorway, right of the basement door. They entered a small laundry room, complete with a washer and dryer. It even had a hamper for dirty clothes still sitting on the floor.

Laura shook her head again. "Why is this house all boarded up and abandoned, when it's still equipped with everything?"

"It's possible this is a vacation home."

"If it's a vacation home, then why board it up?"

"Who knows? For now, let's take advantage of a warm place with all the luxuries." He watched the girl before him. He liked the way she chewed on her lower lip, when she was in deep thought.

She walked out of the kitchen and back into the living room, shutting the light off in one room and turning it on in the other. Tony followed, almost in a trance, loving the curious way she looked at everything.

The beautiful chandelier, with little sparkling crystals, lit the elegant room. Again, Tony closed the curtains to keep any light from penetrating. The furniture was covered with sheets. With Tony's help, Laura lifted the dusty sheets from the furniture, exposing a navy blue French-style sofa, love seat, and chair. The coffee table and lamp tables matched, all centered precisely, facing the large fireplace and cherry wood mantle. Everything flowed together with the Oriental rug and draperies.

"Want to go see what's upstairs?"

"Sure," she walked past the fireplace and laughed. "This sure beats our old wood stove." Laura stopped in her tracks. Her smile faded quickly.

Tony stood at her side. "Hey, it's all right to cry," he soothed.

She nodded and let out a long sigh. "I still can't believe it." Choking back a sob, the river of tears rushed forward. "Oh, Tony, this pain is killing me," she whispered.

His chest tightened in anxiety for her. "Laura, this is going to be the hardest time you'll ever have to endure. But somehow, the pain does ease. It won't be for a while. You'll wake up for days, months, still stunned by it all. All I can tell you is that I'm here for you. You don't have to do it alone."

She sobbed, at last releasing what had been manifesting all night. Tony didn't know if it was too bold of him to pull her into his arms. He longed to comfort her in some way. So not to scare her, he rubbed her back softly. Underneath his hand, he felt her tremble and shiver.

He lifted her chin so their eyes could meet. "You up to checking out the rest of this place? Maybe it'll take your mind off things a little while longer."

She sniffed and nodded. Again, he took hold of her hand and led her through the living room to a door, beneath the second floor stairs, across from the fireplace. They discovered a half bath, decorated in peach and blue pastels.

From there, they ascended the stairway to the second floor. Laura stopped. "Tony?"

He stopped also, "Yeah?"

"Why us? My father had nothing of value," she whispered.

He sat on the carpeted step and pulled her down next to him. "Only God knows that answer."

"Well, who's to say that the looters won't find *us* here?"

"It's very possible. That's why I'm trying to keep all the lights off. I don't want to take any chances. Luckily, we're surrounded by forest," he explained.

"But Tony, our cabin was in the woods, too."

He thought for a moment. The house was quiet, but for the buzzing of electricity. "Laura, is there any open land near your house?"

"Well, yeah. I lived right near a spring and Pop had a patch of farm land where we grew crops."

"Well, there you go. The open land made the home easier to find. Shoot, you and I barely found this house. Don't worry." He brushed away the tear that trickled down her cheek. "Thank God I found you," he whispered. He finally leaned over and pulled her into his arms.

"Thank God," she whispered, briefly returning his hug. Once again, the two continued ascending the stairway to the second floor.

*   *   *

They entered the hallway, using the flashlight to keep from turning on too many lights. To the left of the stairway was a full bath. It was decorated in browns, complete with shower and tub. It even had a laundry chute that led to the laundry room beneath them.

Between the bathroom and the first bedroom was a large linen closet. They briefly examined the closet, finding it contained sheets and blankets for a bed and undergarments for both men and women, still in the original packages.

The following door to the left of the hall, was the first bedroom. It was unfurnished. Tony entered and searched the closet. It held modern clothing for girls, from toddler sizes to young adult sizes. Beneath the clothing, a shoe rack with a variety of different shoe sizes also for girls. Next to the shoe rack, Tony discovered a few sleeping bags.

"Weird, isn't this?" he questioned.

"They must've had a lot of girls living here. But where are the beds?"

"Perhaps they used the sleeping bags?" Tony assumed.

"Could be," Laura guessed.

"These will come in handy," he stated with a nod.

Laura looked up at her rescuer. He was an angel. He'd taken her under his wing, shared his food, found her a place to rest, and risked his life to help her. The best part of it all was that he had expected nothing from her.

She prayed he wasn't too good to be true. For now, she didn't know how she'd ever thank him.

They exited the bedroom and walked back into the hallway. At last, opposite the first bedroom door, was the master bedroom. Laura flashed the light on and gasped. The room was painted with a soft pink hue. The bed, dresser, and nightstands were made of a fine mahogany. The canopy above the bed matched the soft pink curtains and carpet. The bed itself was placed in the middle of the large room, centered between two windows. Next to each side of the bed were the nightstands. Both with a beautiful antique lamp and crème shade. Laura had never seen anything like it. The room was lovely.

Within the closet, left of the door, they found more men's and women's clothing. They gazed at one another confused. They had truly lucked out.

"Wow," she breathed. Laura walked to the bed and touched the pink and crème bedspread. "Look at this place. It's amazing—like they never left. How could these people up and abandon this? It's not right, us coming in here and using their things. We should get out of here." Suddenly, she gasped. "Tony, what if the owners come back?"

"Laura, let me remind you—the doors were boarded up. Maybe they left in a hurry and this stuff means nothing to them. When your life is at stake, who cares about materialistic things?"

"Yeah, but . . ."

"No buts. Stop thinking negatively. We've nowhere else to go. Do you want to go back outside?" he quizzed. Laura shook her head. "I've turned the heat up, so when the house warms up, we can take all these layers of clothes off. We'll eat something, wash up, and finally get some rest."

She felt exhausted. Her legs and arms still ached, yet Tony's energy helped to boost her.

"Come on, lazy bones," he tugged at her arm and pulled her into another quick hug. "You saved our lives tonight by finding this house. I owe *you*!"

Laura blushed. Her hands fell onto his arms. She felt them flexing as he held her. Heat flushed her face, changing it different shades of pink. "I don't think so," she whispered. "You saved *me*."

"Well, we're even then!" he smiled. "Come on. Let's get something to eat," he suggested, as he exited the room and jogged down the stairs. Laura turned the lights off and chased after him.

Tony and Laura sat at the kitchen table. Having used the bowls in the cupboards, Laura reached out and began to gather Tony's dirty dish. "Hey, sit down. I got it. You're tired. It's late and you're falling asleep in your pork and beans."

Laura rose from her seat, when it suddenly struck her that there was one bed and two of them. She blushed with embarrassment. Flustered, she didn't know how to approach the subject. She watched Tony, as he walked to the sink and then through the kitchen, checking the locks on the back door and windows. He paused and stood before her.

"Don't worry. I'll sleep on the couch."

Laura stood in shock. "How did you . . ."

He smiled, creasing the dimple in his cheek. "You're too cute," he teased, with a laugh.

"Don't laugh at me."

"I'm sorry. I shouldn't, but it's true." They exited the kitchen and sat on the velvety couch in the living room.

CHAPTER 4

Enduring

"Look, I'm not gonna lie. I don't know you and I'm not exactly comfortable with having to share the bed. But it doesn't make sense to have you sleep down here. Besides . . . I must confess, I'd feel more safe knowing you were with me upstairs," Laura admitted.

"Are you sure? I mean, I agree. I certainly don't want to make you feel uncomfortable. I'd be fine here on the couch. Or I could grab a sleeping bag from the spare and sleep in there. But if you need me near because you're scared, I'll be there."

"Do you mind sleeping on the sleeping bag in the same room with me?" she asked.

"No problem. You don't have to be alone. Go on up. I'm gonna lock up and shut off the lights." He rose from the couch. "Oh, and just use the clothes we found in the closets, if you want to shower and change."

She glanced down at him, while climbing the stairs. Nodding, she quickly returned her attention to the second level of the house. In the linen closet, she came upon a white flannel nightgown, with little pink flowers and grasped a package of women's underwear. Still, she felt hesitant using the homeowner's things. She stepped into the master bedroom and took off Tony's coat, as the temperature was finally more comfortable. Glancing down at her bloodstained jacket, she gasped. Laura closed her eyes, leaned her head back, and forced down the urge to scream. She raised her hands to her face, desperate to maintain control.

Immediately, she peeled away her soiled coat and clothes, and threw them in the corner with disgust. She felt dirty and though she was tired, Laura needed to wash. In her bra and panties, she opened the bedroom door. Peeking out, she saw that Tony was out of sight. She made a dash for the bathroom, twisting the doorknob, too late to grasp that Tony had had the same notion. Laura let out a small scream after taking in Tony standing in the bathroom with only a small towel wrapped around his waist.

*   *   *

Tony turned around in shock. He gazed at Laura in her underwear, the flannel nightgown in her trembling hands, barely covering her body.

"Laura," his lips held a grin. The look on her face held a million words. He felt the urge to laugh, but didn't. He knew she was already horribly humiliated.

"Tony," she stumbled, trying to hide her nakedness with the nightgown. "I thought you said you were gonna lock up the house?"

"I did. I figured I'd jump in the shower and then go to bed." He tried to keep his eyes on hers, but couldn't. He swallowed, "Were you gonna wash up, too?"

Tony saw her blush again, as she quickly backed away. "Yeah . . . I'll wait 'til you're through." With her eyes focused at his chest, she bumped into the side of the bedroom door and dropped the nightgown.

Tony's face flushed. She picked up the gown and ran into the bedroom, shutting the door behind her. He snickered to himself and closed the bathroom door. Turning the shower water on, he stifled a laugh. *What was wrong with him, anyway?* Something about her made his heart burn. *Hope it's the pork and beans.* He laughed again, as he jumped in the shower.

*   *   *

Laura leaned behind the closed door and cursed herself. She heard the shower water turn on. Covering her face in her hands, she didn't know whether to laugh or cry. Gathering a hold of her emotions, she looked around the room. She turned on the dim lamps and turned the chandelier off. Sifting through the closet, she withdrew a robe and put it on. Laura then turned over the bed and set it with fresh linens. She found a sleeping bag for Tony and laid it on the floor, next to the bed.

Finally, she sat at the vanity in the far corner, right of the door, and stared at her reflection in the mirror. Her face was still speckled with dried blood. Underneath the grime, her skin flushed with humiliation. She looked away. *So stupid! This isn't home, where you don't knock and don't worry about walking in on someone who expects privacy. Tony is a man.* A man she hardly knew.

Tony . . . no wonder he could sustain hauling the backpack that entire way. She blushed again at the thought of his toned chest and arms. Her cheeks burned. Laura decided she was being ridiculous. Yet, sitting at the vanity, she mulled the scene over in her head with a blush. She prayed he'd stay in the shower forever.

Inevitably, the water turned off. Her heart began to pound. Tony would walk through the door any minute. She struggled to tame her hair, wanting to appear unruffled.

From in the bedroom, Laura heard the bathroom door. Seconds later, Tony knocked. "Hey Laura, did you fall asleep? May I come in?"

She cleared her throat and called out, "Sure, Tony. Come on in." Tony stepped into the room with only a pair of men's long-john underwear on. Both the wavy brown hair on his head and chest were still moist. Laura caught a gasp in her throat but managed a smile. He walked over to the sleeping bag, while throwing on a crisp white T-shirt. His demeanor was cool and collected.

"Boy that felt good." He sat on the sleeping bag and stretched his legs before him, as he spoke. "Hope I didn't use up all the hot water." He gave a sly smile, laughter unmistakably in his eyes. He grabbed a pillow off the bed and made himself comfortable.

"I'm sure you didn't. And if you did, I'm used to cold baths." She bit down on her lower lip. Tony's eyes shot up and met hers. Her face flushed. "The well water was always cold when we washed up, and I'm used to it being chilly." She stuttered a moment. "W-w-we used to have to warm it up on the stove." Gulping, she hoped to save herself. Shaking her head, she pointed toward the door. "I'll go." Laura picked up the dirty laundry in the corner.

"Yes, you better," Tony was openly smiling now. "Oh, and Laura?" he teased. She kept her back to him. "Try not to bump into anything on your way out."

She stormed out of the bedroom and into the bathroom, his laughter following her. Deliberately, she took a long shower, in hopes of finding Tony asleep when she returned. She opened the package of underwear and changed into a pair. They fit perfectly. Laura put the nightgown on, which also fit, and stared at the foggy mirror. She'd never taken a shower before and wanted to savor every moment—the smell of her hair and the softness of her skin. Tony's body soap seemed to remove every last remain of her cabin life. After brushing her teeth with a new toothbrush, she found in the bathroom cabinet, she took a hairbrush and mechanically worked on the tangles in her hair.

Laura's mind wandered and she closed her eyes tightly. *No!* She refused to think about the day's happenings. She didn't want to feel. Sleep was all she desired. She dried her hair with a towel again, re-brushed it, and exited the bathroom. The nightgown clung to her damp body.

To her surprise, Tony was curled up on his side, in the sleeping bag, and appeared fast asleep. A small smile played on his lips. She made her way to the bed. Climbing in, she reached over, and turned off the lamp.

*   *   *

Tony sensed her frustration. He held in his laughter. With all the fun he was having, he didn't stop to realize that it was possible she was suppressing her pain. His smile vanished. It was okay to try to distract her, but she had to be screaming inside. He rolled onto his back and looked at her in the darkness. She seemed calm. Her shoulders rose and fell rhythmically.

Suddenly, his heart felt heavy. He knew too well, what she was going to be feeling when reality would sink in. He closed his heavy eyes.

*   *   *

At long last, sleep found its way, but so did the nightmares.

Back in the cabin, Laura frantically hunted through the home in search of Sabrina. She called out to her. She checked out back. Through the woods and to the spring, she cried out to her. "*Sabrina, Sabrina!*" Too dark—it was too dark to see. She ran toward the beach. The water suddenly rose and splashed the shore in high waves. Laura felt herself being pulled into the water. She struggled to keep her head above. She screamed in terror as the black water swallowed her up.

"Help!" She sat up in the center of the bed. Perspiration and tears left her face damp. Tony struggled to his feet and sat on the bed. He wrapped his arms around her. Laura was sobbing aloud.

"It's okay," Tony soothed.

"Tony, I want Sabrina," she cried. "I was all alone. I couldn't find her. I'm all alone without them, Tony. I'm all alone."

Tony held her. He smoothed her hair and rubbed her back, as she cried. "No, no, you're not alone. I promise I won't let you go through this alone."

She sobbed in his arms until she cried herself to sleep. Welcoming the darkness didn't stop the despairing nightmares from returning.

This time the dream was more vivid.

Laura was home. Sabrina played in the corner with her doll. Patty read a book on the sofa and Matt was in the kitchen with Cara. *Momma! She was alive!* Laura raced for the kitchen. She tripped and fell to the floor. Unable to get back up, she called out, "*Momma! Help me!*" Cara looked at her daughter. Tears filled her eyes. Soon the room stretched a mile long. Cara began to vanish. Laura struggled to get up. She stretched out her arms and felt somebody. She pulled them into her embrace. His face so close to hers, she spotted the dark mole under his eye.

Laura cried out, "NO!"

She was still in Tony's arms. They sat up in the bed and gently he rocked her until her cries subsided.

"I'll be right back," Tony whispered. He rose from the bed and turned on the lamp.

Seconds later, he returned. In one hand he held a little pill and in the other, a glass of water. "Here, take this sleeping pill. I usually take it for *my* insomnia." She looked at him, unable to comprehend. "It's a sleep disorder I have. Some nights, when I can't fall asleep, I take a couple. It'll help you rest." He offered her the pill. Willingly, she swallowed it with the water.

Tony reached for the light but Laura stopped his hand. "Please, can you keep it on?"

"Okay. Do you want me to stay next to you?"

"Please. I'm so scared."

He snuggled under the covers, next to her. "Go on, close your eyes. I'll be right here if you need me."

Laura reclined next to him. She tucked the covers under her chin and smiled at Tony. "Thanks, for everything. Sorry, I was such a dunce earlier."

Tony's face lit up. "Oh, that? I should have locked the door. I'm sorry for teasing you. Now go to sleep!" he ordered. He reached over under the covers and squeezed her hand a quick moment.

Laura flushed at his touch. She pushed the nightmares from her mind and focused on Tony. He was compassionate, handsome, and funny. He was someone she could easily get used to being with.

Her body began to relax and drowsiness seized her.

* * *

Until the sun's rays penetrated through the pink curtains and into Laura's eyes, she'd been resting peacefully. She squeezed her lids tight, but the sun was persistent. She tried to place an arm over her face, but it felt heavy. Grunting, she peeped through a crack of her eye. Immediately her eyes flew open.

Tony's face was two inches from hers. She was sleeping on her back and Tony on his stomach. His right arm was thrown over her chest and arms. She felt the warmth of his body on her skin and shuddered.

How'd this happen? She tried to be careful and stay on her side. Yet, she had rolled over into his arms. Slowly, she moved out from under his arm, without waking him. Still in a deep sleep, he moved even closer to her. She caught a gasp about to escape her lips.

He mumbled something in his sleep. She remained silent. He rolled over, this time opposite of her and suddenly tumbled to the floor. Laura screamed, as she glanced over the edge of the bed. Tony nervously scrambled to his feet.

"What the . . .?" He looked at Laura.

This time, Laura withheld her laughter. "Tony, you fell," she stated.

"Man!"

"Are you okay?" she asked, nearly giggling.

"I think so." He scratched his forehead and ran his fingers through his tousled hair. Finally, he smiled and let out a laugh. "Talk about clumsy."

"Guess I'm not the only one," she teased.

Tony laughed aloud. "Tell you what, smarty-pants. Why don't I make the bed and you go change. We'll go downstairs and get some breakfast." He gave her a wink.

Self-consciously, she matted down her disheveled hair, "Sounds good." She straightened the wrinkled nightgown and walked toward the door. Giving him a devilish grin, she asked, "More pork and beans?"

Tony laughed again. He slowly made his way to block the doorway and folded his arms across his broad chest. "Aren't we the sarcastic one this morning? You leave that up to me." He stared into her eyes, whispering, "Now go get dressed, clumsy."

She childishly stuck out her tongue and skipped past him, out of the bedroom, and into the bathroom. Tony's laughter followed her.

They washed their faces and dressed. Laura and Tony both used the clothes that best fit them from the closet. Together they entered the blue kitchen. Tony opened a small box of dry cereal and they ate in silence.

When she finished, Laura rose from the table and walked to the kitchen window. She raised the shade and peeked through a crack in the board. The sun shone brightly on the newly fallen snow. She gazed over the backyard, curiously. Tony walked up beside her, his chest gently brushed her back.

"Looks like it snowed some more as we slept," he said.

Laura answered, "It's a good thing we found this place, or we'd have been frozen like icicles."

"That's for sure. I was so tired last night, I would've walked right past this place. Thanks to you, we slept in a warm bed."

They both stared out the crack in the boarded window. Looking down, she whispered, "Sorry, if I kept you up last night."

Tony sighed. "Why do you keep apologizing?" he whispered with concern.

"I kept having those stupid nightmares."

"It's normal."

"This all seems like a bad dream. I wanted so bad to wake up this morning and be in that crumbling cabin. Please, don't get me wrong. I'm thankful we found this beautiful place. And you—you've been great."

Tony put his hands on her shoulders. "I know what you're feeling."

Laura turned around to face him. "Tony?" Tears glistened in her eyes. "How do I go on? It doesn't seem right! I just go on living while they're dead?" She shook her head back and forth trying to push the ugly images away.

"Laura, you're going to have to. You've no choice. I know my words are harsh. But they're true. It'll feel as though nothing will make it easier. All you can do is keep busy. Cry when you need to cry, scream when you need to scream. Just don't bottle it up. It kills you if you do."

She fell limply in his arms. Her shoulders shook in grief and anguish. "Tony, I need to cry," she bawled. "I need to cry."

"Then cry."

"I want to hit, kick, scream! I'm so angry! They shouldn't have killed little Sabrina. She was just a baby!" she uttered in despair. "And how was it that I was spared? How?"

As the tears coursed down her cheeks, they coursed down Tony's as well. "Laura, do you believe in Jesus? Are you a Christian?"

She nodded, then sniffled before she answered, "Yes. My mother was a devout Christian. She raised us as believers."

"Then know in your heart that Jesus is right here. He knows you're hurting. Let Him help you carry this cross. He's all you need. That's who helped me through my tough times. He can help you through yours, too."

"Why didn't He stop them, then? Why didn't God stop that man from killing my family?"

"I don't know. I believe sometimes the devil wins the battle, but God *always* wins the war. Jesus made sure that you wouldn't be alone and led me into the woods. He helped us find this place for shelter. He'll never give you what you can't handle." Tony soothed her back with his hands.

Laura cried out, "Well, I can't handle this, Tony! I miss them so much."

"Hey, look at me." He gently clasped her face in his hands. "You'll be strong, because you *are*. Don't grieve without hope. You'll hold her again. When you're old and gray, one day, you'll join Sabrina, Patty, and your father. For now, you'll survive. It's going to be hard. But in time, the pain gets better. Meanwhile, you have me to lean on and Jesus to help heal you. Don't you trust in Him?"

Laura wiped the tears from her face. Deep in her heart, she could see how God was working to help her through. The simple fact that Tony happened to find her when he did, was a very obvious plan of God's. "Of course I do. Momma always said that Jesus would never leave us nor forsake us."

"That's right. So we must believe that, because He promised it." Tony's expression was serious. Laura was caught off guard by his show of strength and deep faith. He let his arm fall from her shoulder to point out the crack in the boarded window. "Hey, see that road behind those trees, out there?"

Laura strained to see through the small crack. "Yeah, what about it?"

"Let's put on our coats, go out back, and check the perimeter around us. Then we'll take a walk down that road and see where it leads. That'll keep your mind occupied for a while."

She took in a deep breath and released it slowly, "Sounds good. I'll get the coat you lent me." She exited the kitchen and walked into the living room.

"I'm right behind you," Tony shouted.

Laura turned around and watched Tony put the bowls in the sink. A tear froze in her eye. She *was* thankful that Jesus brought Tony to her. He was wonderful. He was there for her . . . *but for how long?*

He stopped midway and caught her gaze. He stared back at her. Mesmerized, she watched him walk to her.

Grasping her hands, he whispered, "Laura, I'm here for you." She closed her eyes and felt his lips gently kiss her forehead. He pulled her into his embrace. Laura's head spun.

CHAPTER 5

The Pains of Survival

They left the warm home and carefully descended the glossy porch steps. Walking through the deep snow, they entered the backyard.

Laura glanced back and studied the outside of the home, for the first time, in daylight. The exterior vinyl siding was painted a light green color. The windowsills and casings were painted brown, along with the shutters. The house was an old Victorian colonial. Nevertheless, it seemed well cared for.

In the yard, there was a distinctly large maple amongst the other standing timber. Its thick, long gray branches scraped against the side of the home, as the glacial winds blew through it. Laura shivered at the eerie sound. She watched Tony walk toward a shed to the left of the enormous tree.

He trudged through the thick snow and made his way to the unstable shed. He tried the handle, but it was jammed. "Should I open it?" he called out to Laura.

"Well, it doesn't look sturdy." She shrugged her shoulders and gave him a weak smile.

He gave it one more push. "I guess we'll have to wait until spring to see what's inside."

His words jolted her like a bolt of lightning.

"Spring?" she questioned.

"Yeah, I've been thinking. The house is obviously abandoned. It's well hidden in the woods, so it's safe. It almost doesn't make sense to leave."

Laura still considered this. *Should she go to the police? If so, with whom would she stay? Would her mother's parents take her in?* It wasn't likely, from what she'd heard of them through her mother. If they did, they'd be the same as complete strangers. *And would she want to be any place else other than with Tony?* He promised to help her. He promised he'd be there.

37

Laura was still undecided. She'd stay with Tony, for now, and when things calmed down, she'd go to the police and report the murders of her family. *But it wouldn't take until spring for the riots to end, would it?* She gazed out at him, as he waited for her reply. "I think you're right, Tony. It seems we're safe here," she called out. "We'll stay just a few more days."

"Okay." He wrestled with the door and finally gave up. "Forget it! It's frozen shut!" He kicked the door in frustration.

"Let it go. It's not important," Laura insisted. "Come on," she called to him. "What's this?" She pointed to a large wooden box, with a door. It was attached to the house, directly under the back door porch.

As they approached the wooden box, Tony guessed, "I bet it leads to the basement."

"Yeah, but I don't remember seeing any doors in the basement." Laura tried opening the door. "It's locked."

"It must be a storm cellar," Tony guessed again.

Laura shrugged, "Who knows?" She shivered and hugged herself.

"Cold?" Tony asked.

"A little."

"We can go back in if you want."

"No, it's all right," Laura said. "Let's take advantage of the sun. We couldn't pick a better day to take that walk. Come on." She tugged at his hand.

"You're right. Let's see how close we are to civilization."

Letting his hand go, they headed back toward the front of the house and began their hike down the snow-packed trail. In the daylight, the woods gleamed in shimmering crystals of ice.

They walked in silence. She drifted off into thought. She smiled, remembering the day prior, when Sabrina played in the snow. She could still hear her laughter. A tear streamed down her cheek.

"Hey look!" Tony's timing was perfect. He pointed to a street up ahead. "Come on." They began running toward the street and soon found themselves near the city of Cicero. They walked another half mile before coming to a cross road named Factory Street. They'd actually traveled across town during the prior night's trek. Tony guessed that they journeyed nearly five miles.

"Wait!" He pulled Laura behind a parked vehicle, stooping behind the tire. He placed a finger to his lips to silence her.

With fear in her eyes, Laura looked at Tony. "Why, what did I do?" she whispered.

"Shh! It's not what you did, but what they'll do *to you*." He pointed to a group of men who stood in front of the door of a supermarket named 'Grillo's'." They all wore long dark cloaks and Fedora-like hats. Laura froze. She remembered the man who murdered her family. The hat he wore was similar to the hats these men were wearing.

She watched them fidget nervously. One said to the other, a cigarette hanging from his lip, "What's takin' so long, man. We should make a run for it."

"Shut up. Gino knows what he's doin'."

Another man exited the store. A hat concealed his face. "*Niente!*" he shouted, speaking a foreign language. He tossed an apple to the one with the cigarette and shouted, "Let's go, the pigs are comin'!" They quickly scattered, entering a long black vehicle parked in front. The tires squealed and the car drove off.

"What's going on?" Laura whispered.

"Looters. They probably robbed the market."

"Those hats . . ." Before Laura could complete her sentence, Tony grabbed her gloved hand, and to her dismay, ran toward the store.

"Wait, what are you doing?" she screeched.

"Follow me." He ran across the street and into the store. The place was both deserted and destroyed. Food was scattered everywhere. Soda cans rolled across the shiny linoleum floor. A vegetable rack was completely tipped over and tomatoes and potatoes rolled freely. Tony ran behind the register and kneeled before an unconscious man. He put his head to his chest, without touching him. He seemed to sigh in relief, stood, and suddenly grabbed a grocery bag.

"He's gonna be okay. It's just a bump on his head. Come on, Laura, help me." Tony was immediately running throughout the store, filling the bag with miscellaneous groceries.

Laura glared at him in shock. When he ran past her, she seized his arm. "What are you doing?"

He brushed her hand off. "We've got to hurry." He noticed her pause. "Laura, trust me!"

Her heart filled with fear. *What had she gotten herself into?* Perhaps Tony wasn't what she believed him to be. She watched him run about filling two large grocery bags. He passed the register and quickly withdrew a five-dollar bill from the wallet in his back pocket. He tossed it at the counter and ran to the doors. He shouted, "Come on Laura. Let's go!"

"I can't believe you're doing this!" She stood rooted in the center of the small market.

Tony ran back to her in frustration. Putting down the bags, he picked her up and threw her over his shoulder. Grasping the bag handles, he ran out the door.

At first, the shock of it left her astonished. She let Tony carry her and was silent, as he ran onto the salted streets and back onto the hidden path leading to the abandoned house.

"Let me down!" she finally screamed. Tony continued to run on the hard-packed snow. "Put me down, this instant!" She shouted as she pounded his buttocks.

"Will you stop it? What's wrong with you?" Dropping the bag handles, he plopped her down, steadying her with his hands.

She stared at him in disbelief. "What's wrong with *me*? I can't believe you stole from that poor man! They left him for dead. Not to mention how you carried me off like a cave man." She took a deep breath, glaring at him through suspicious eyes. Her fists were firmly planted onto her hips.

*   *   *

Tony tried to keep the smile from forming on his lips. She looked adorable when she was angry. Yet, he needed to calm her. "Laura, look," he started, "I know it's wrong . . ."

"Yes, it was!" she interrupted. "All those talks about Jesus, and then this?"

Tony frowned, realizing how truly serious she was. "Laura, please let me finish." He grabbed the bags and began walking. "You need to understand something. We're in the middle of mass chaos! What do you think those looters were doing? It's not every day that men like *that* steal from small grocers. They were taking advantage of the situation. No, it's not right what I did. Five dollars is certainly not going to cover the amount of groceries I just took. But I made a promise that I'm going to keep. I have to take care of you, first and foremost. If it means stealing, then I'll steal."

He looked down at Laura, who had softened up and was now reaching for one of the bags. He gave her the lighter of the two and smiled. She timidly looked down.

Tony continued to speak when she didn't respond. "Look, until things blow over with these raids, we're gonna have to do what it takes to survive. It won't be easy. If it's possible, I'll return to that man and repay him. I'll get in touch with Uncle Frank as soon as possible and he will help us. We won't need to resort to this to eat." Still Laura walked with her head down, appearing to be listening intently.

"I have some money," added Tony. "But I'll use it when we absolutely need it. If we stay in the house for however long you decide, we don't know if we're going to start getting electric or gas bills. If we do, we'll have to pay them or we'll lose those luxuries. I have to be smart about these things. That's why I saw an opportunity and took advantage. I know Jesus will forgive me because it's sheer survival at this point. I wouldn't be doing that under normal circumstances. I hope *you* can understand and forgive me, too."

He watched her carefully as he spoke. She hid her face from him, concealing her fears. Tony shifted the bag to his left arm and touched her face with his right hand. He forced her to look at him. Tears filled her eyes, but remained in place. He put his arm around her as they walked.

"Please say something. You know, before you came along, I didn't care what happened to me. But now that you're in my life, I'm cautious of every step. I want to be sure that you're taken care of." He wiped a tear that lazily rolled down her cheek.

He felt the tears burning his own lids. He thought of all the years that he'd spent alone since his family passed. How hard he fought to not get attached to friends or foster parents. Now, in two short days, he'd felt his heart open up and all the fight diminished.

Laura finally threw her arms around him, dropping the bag to their feet. She sobbed in his arms, snuggling her face into his neck. He knew her pain. He understood it. Tony let out the breath he'd been holding. Having her look upon him with love was all that mattered to him now.

"Laura, I won't ever let anyone hurt you again." He held her to his chest with all his strength.

* * *

Why did she ever doubt him? She squeezed him tighter giving a small prayer to God in thanksgiving. They picked up the grocery bags and continued the trek back to the house. When they reached the house, Laura unpacked the stolen groceries, while Tony started dinner.

When they finished preparing, they sat at the table. After a quick prayer for forgiveness and thanksgiving, they ate. Between bites, they talked. "Laura," Tony said, "Uncle Frank *will* help us. If you decide to stay, there will be two things we'll need to discuss. The first thing I wanted to mention was your wanting to report the death of your family, and the other is that I think it's best you don't go back to school."

Wiping her lips with a napkin, she replied, "I know why you wouldn't want me to report my family's murders. They'll know that I'm orphaned and I'll end up in Foster care. I don't think I want that either. But I want to seek justice for their deaths. I can't live with myself knowing that their killer never paid for what he did." Laura's cheeks blushed with anger.

"But don't you understand the penalty you'll have to pay to seek justice? That means more pain and heartache for you. Let God be the judge and don't worry, he'll get his just pay. If you can't let go and forgive, you'll never heal. Trust God to bring your family's murderer to justice. Unless, you don't *want* to stay here, then that's a different story. If not, I do understand. I'm still a stranger to you."

"Tony, it's not that. You should know that by now. I trust you more than I trust myself, right now. But I do understand that you're right. I don't want our friendship to end. I like you." Laura cast her eyes downward, embarrassed by her own openness.

"Likewise. So far, I really like your company," he said with a grin.

"I don't know why. I've been a horrible mess."

"That's to be expected."

Laura held his gaze. A rush of emotion filled her smiling eyes. Changing the subject, to keep her face from burning a deeper shade of rose, she began, "As for school, if I stay, I'm not worried. Christmas break will be starting soon and I won't have to go back 'til after the New Year."

"Well, I was thinking more along the lines of you no longer attending."

Laura choked on her soup. "What? You mean drop out?"

"They'll find out you're an underage orphan. It'll be the same as if you go to the authorities. You'll still be looking at foster care."

"That's true. I guess I feel like I should be continuing my studies. I'm really good in English and Algebra."

Tony thought intently for a moment. "If you stay, I could buy you books that could teach you English, Algebra, and whatever other subjects you want."

"You'd do that?" she questioned with a smile.

"I solemnly swear." He crossed his heart with his finger. "When you're old enough," he added, "You can always go back to school to get your GED."

Laura contemplated everything. "I have a lot to think about," she admitted.

"I understand. Meanwhile, I've got to get in touch with my uncle and see what's going on. I don't know what has even become of him. I pray he's safe."

Another thought jostled her. "Tony, if I stay. How do we support ourselves?"

"I'll get a job, as soon as possible," he immediately answered.

"How will you get to and from work?"

"I'll cross that bridge when I get there. We'll need money to live and I'm not about to let you starve because I've got to walk a mile or two."

She shook her head in understanding. He was right again. If she finally decided to stay, maybe it was best that she stayed hidden at the house. While he was gone at work, she'd study in her free time and maintain the house for him, too. Her real worry was cooking. That had always been Patty's job. *Oh*, how she wished she had paid attention when Patty tried to teach her.

Tony interrupted her thoughts. "All right, what's going through your head now?"

"Tony, if I stay . . . while you go off to work, I'd take care of things here."

"That'd be great," Tony admitted.

"I just don't know how to cook," she confessed.

He burst into laughter. "You can't cook? Don't you worry. I'll teach you!" He patted her hand from across the table and continued laughing.

* * *

As Tony had promised, he snuck into town the next day and got in touch with his Uncle Frank. He returned to report that Uncle Frank had remained hidden during the raids and was safe. Tony explained to him how he found Laura and wanted to foster her.

That night, Uncle Frank came to the house to meet Laura. He seemed a kind man. She liked his big brown eyes, bushy eyebrows, and amazingly thick mustache.

"I understand you're still contemplating going to the authorities," he mentioned, while sitting at the kitchen table with them, after a meal.

"I don't want to burden anyone," Laura stated.

"Well, if you're worried about burdening us, don't! Tony feels a responsibility to care for you and frankly, so do I."

"Where will we live?" Laura questioned.

"I recommend you both hiding out here, for now. I'll see what I can find out about this homeowner. If they've truly abandoned their home, perhaps I can buy it off the city. If it's not for sale, we'll figure something else out. For now, if you're not comfortable with the set up here, just say the word. We can set up another bed in the spare bedroom and Tony can sleep there."

"That's not even my worry. Having him near me is actually very reassuring because I've been having such horrible nightmares. My worry, I guess, is that I feel like I just left my family to rot out in the cold. They received no proper burials, and their murderer got off scot-free."

Uncle Frank nodded in understanding. "In regards to the murderer, if you go to the authorities to seek justice you won't be able to remain here. They *will* put you in foster care. I'd try to win custody over you, but you're not my relative. Chances are . . . we'd lose you the same. If you should decide to stay and not go to the authorities, I can promise you this: we will give your family a proper burial, I will be here for you as a father-figure, and we will care for you as a family member."

"Just like that?" she asked. "Just because you feel obligated? I've got to do something in return. Cook, clean, work—something!"

"You don't have to do anything," Uncle Frank assured.

Tony pressed his elbow into Uncle Frank's. "Let's at least get a hot meal, every night, out of this," he whispered loud enough for Laura to here.

Laura let a smile fall over her face. Uncle Frank's grin widened. "He's always talking about eating, this one," he grumbled while pointing a thumb to Tony.

"As long as you teach me, I'd be happy to cook. I'll clean and wash your clothes. That will be the least I could do," Laura replied.

"So, you'll stay?" Uncle Frank pressed.

Laura slowly nodded. "Yes, I'll stay. I appreciate everything you both are doing for me. I don't know how I'll ever thank you."

"Well, I'll be up in your business, all the time," Uncle Frank warned. "I won't be living here with you both, if we get the house. I will stay in my apartment for my own reasons. I do, however, expect Tony to take responsibility when I'm not here. And that doesn't mean that I won't be here daily. I want to make sure you continue to learn and that you're both living a God revering life. Meaning, I *will* be bringing Tony's bedroom set to put in the spare for him to sleep in. It's only right that you get your own private room."

"Well, that's more than I had at home," Laura confessed. "Again, thank you!" She stood and extended her hand. Uncle Frank stood and accepted her handshake. He even pulled her into a bear hug. Laura's eyes filled with tears of gratitude.

* · * *

After a few days, Uncle Frank informed them that the raids were controlled and the state of New York, along with the rest of the country, began to resume normality. He also came to find that owner of 'Grillo's', who had been assaulted, was left with a serious concussion, indefinitely hindering him from running his store. The man put his store up for sale, at once, opening up the opportunity for Uncle Frank to start his own market.

Uncle Frank offered Tony a job managing it. Before long, Tony was bringing in a paycheck that not only covered their grocery bills, but also the bills that began arriving to a P.O. Box that Tony set up at the local post office. The strangest part was that the bills were coming in under the name of a 'Maria Fontana.'

Uncle Frank took this information and did further investigating. He discovered that the original homeowner of the 'abandoned house' was deceased and the property was never claimed. He went through the necessary legal action and purchased the property along with the home for Tony and Laura to live in.

Tony's bedroom set was brought from Uncle Frank's apartment to the house, and set up in the spare bedroom. The first few nights, Tony tried sleeping separate from Laura. But Laura despaired, for the nightmares continued and Tony found himself sleeping next to her more often than not. Eventually, it became their secret that Laura shared her bed with Tony, for no other reason than to have him near during her darkest hours.

She felt beyond blessed to be 'unofficially' adopted by Tony and Uncle Frank. They made her feel like part of their family. Uncle Frank's presence added warmth to the house. He helped them in so many ways. First, he assisted Tony with the tear down of the boards on the windows and then he helped with the maintenance to the old house.

As he had promised, regarding the bodies of her deceased family, one warmer day, a few weeks after the murders, he and Tony found their way back to the cabin and did as she asked. They took the remains of her family members and buried them next to one another under a tree, near the vegetable garden Laura used to till. The next day, Tony and Uncle Frank brought her there to pay her final respects to her family. Returning to the scene of the crime, Laura sunk to a new low. It took much coercing, on both Tony and Uncle Frank's part, to get her to leave their graves.

Back at the 'abandoned' house, Laura's only consolation was in her new friends. Even the house had become more than a shelter, but a place of belonging—a place to call 'home'. They rearranged things to their liking, making it their own.

By the time spring rolled around, Tony and Laura became as close as any two friends could be. In the mornings, they ate breakfast together before Tony would leave for work. In her free time, Laura would read and study the books he purchased for her. After work, he and Uncle Frank would come home to dinner, Uncle Frank would then retire to his apartment, and Tony and Laura would spend their evenings going over the books together. He also read from a Bible and together they learned more about God. Some evenings, Tony would sit with Laura and listen to her speak of the family she had lost. He'd comfort her in her grief.

But as Tony had said, with time the pain lessened. Nightmares did occasionally haunt her, but the memories of the hard times began to diminish and the few good ones remained. At times, it still ached her to have to move on, but she persevered.

Soon time carried the friends into the warm summer season. Tony and Laura's feelings began to grow as grapes on a vine, rooting deep into their hearts. Hearts, which they had both feared would never love again, began to melt. They were the best of friends and before long, they were more.

Laura was happy with her new life. She grew accustomed to doing the cooking and the cleaning. Tony was a wonderfully patient teacher. His cooking skills soon began to rub off and she learned to prepare remarkable meals. Uncle Frank complimented and lifted Laura's esteem. He was always there to be sure she was well cared for and that she continued her studies with Tony.

After her 16th birthday, almost two years later, Tony declared his love for Laura. Sitting on a blanket of leaves under the large maple tree in the yard, he gave her a first kiss. The long awaited kiss was the start of a love neither one would soon ever forget.

Before long, another year passed. Laura turned 17 and Tony almost 22. She developed into a full-figured, yet petite, woman and Tony was more a man, with wider shoulders, and strong arms and legs. Their love continued to blossom until he finally proposed, promising a life of love and happiness. They vowed to get married and spend the rest of their lives together.

CHAPTER 6

Moments to Cherish

November 1976

Winter's cold whip lashed out against the house. The home huddled against the monstrous forest north of the small town of Cicero. The snow continued to fall, as it hadn't in years. Banking high against the house's exterior, it took on as another wall. Not a wall of soft white clouds, but one of hard ice and snow. Not only did it cause the house to feel colder, but the retched snow also provoked the feeling of imprisonment, at least to Laura who, with worry, continued to peer out the living room window.

She hoped Tony's figure would soon emerge from the stilling darkness. She knew the storm was the reason for his delay. Every day at exactly seven-thirty, he'd stroll through the door in eagerness to spend the rest of the evening with her. It had become a ritual. Tony would open the door, give her a whistle, and she'd run into his embrace.

Yet, an ominous presence seemed to hover over her that day and that disturbed her. She glanced at the new watch Tony had given her for her 17th birthday. Eight-thirty-five. Panic continued to disrupt her train of thought. It was Thanksgiving Day and after a full day of cooking, she wasn't about to let the ugly weather spoil it.

She spent hours preparing the turkey roasting in the oven, along with the fixings to go with it. Not to mention all the time she'd spent pampering herself to look beautiful for Tony.

As she stood in the window awaiting his arrival, she felt so grateful for the way she instantly bonded with him. The way he opened up to her, that first night, telling her his story of the pain he'd suffered, at the loss of his family, as well. Laura pondered on that for a moment. That was the only time he'd ever really spoke of his family. She wondered why he never opened up about life before the horrible fire.

What had it been like for him during the years he grew up? And better still, why hadn't she thought of asking him before? Laura felt guilt rip through her. She didn't want her relationship with Tony to be one-sided. She promised to make it a point to talk to him about his life, his past, and his family, prior to the fire.

She paced the living room floor, hesitating to peer through the window, time and again. Her new dress swayed as she stepped into the bathroom to look at her reflection. She had pulled her hair up into a twist and added a slight touch of color to her cheeks and lips. Her eyes were lined in brown and laced with a light-blue color to match her dress. She adjusted the bodice that was cut a little lower than most dresses she owned. She felt sensual in the dress he had purchased for her. All the clothes she had were clothes Tony had purchased. In fact, everything she owned, he bought for her.

Laura lovingly gazed at the beautiful solitaire diamond ring he had also given her that past summer. She loved it. He had picked it out, as well.

It was a rare occasion when Laura could actually depart from the house to go shopping or for any reason. She considered this some more. *Why did he always give her a hard time about going into the city?* She understood she needed to turn 18 first. She understood his fear of them being separated. *But who would find out she was an orphan unless she told them?* She knew better than to say anything. Laura decided to raise the subject up to him. *If only he'd get home!*

She exited the bathroom, checking on the turkey again. Turning the oven back on low, she sighed. She wished he'd connected the phone line he kept promising her. At least she'd be able to call the grocery store to see what time he'd left. She made another mental note.

Footsteps suddenly approached outside on the porch. She wiped her hands on the dishrag and ran into the living room to open the door. In the blistering cold, Tony stood frozen to his very core. Laura gasped at the sight of him. He stood with his gloved hands in his coat pockets. His boots left a trail in the icy white snow that had piled up on the porch steps.

"Oh, Tony!" She pulled him in the door, shutting out the freezing air. She immediately began to take off the wet layers of clothing.

He shivered at her touch when she ran her warm fingers threw his icicled hair. "Oh!" he moaned. Leaving him in his T-shirt and jeans, she piled the mountain of wet clothes onto the carpet and helped him over to the roaring fire she'd built.

"Our next purchase is a truck," he grumbled.

"No, our next purchase is a phone. I've been worried sick about you! Sit here and I'll get you a warm sweater." She threw a blanket over his shoulders and dashed up the stairs, tumbled through his drawers, and pulled out his warmest sweater. On her way down, she reached into the bathroom and snatched a dry towel. She quickened her pace until she knelt before him and helped put his sweater on. She towel-dried his hair and looked at him with concerned eyes.

"Tony, where's Uncle Frank? Why didn't he drive you? You could've froze to death." She rubbed his ice-like hands between her soft fingers, trying to promote some warmth.

He held his eyes closed. His chin quivered as spoke, "The storm is so bad. He couldn't pull the truck out of the parking lot, let alone get it through the woods."

"You should have just stayed there!" she suggested, pulling the blanket up over his shoulders again.

He opened his eyes and watched as she blew warmth onto his hands. "Wow," he whispered with a smirk, admiring her. "And leave this beautiful creature all alone on Thanksgiving Day? No way. Come here."

Still on her knees before him, she bent forward and kissed his blue lips. Her mouth melted his. She let his hands go and draped her arms around his stiff neck, massaging it as the kiss lingered on his softening lips. "Oh sweet Jesus, you feel good," he whispered.

She hugged him. "I'm glad you're home. Come on, I think you should go upstairs and take a nice hot shower before dinner."

"You're right." He tried to rise from the chair. He glanced up at Laura, who stood to assist him. "I think I'm stuck," he cried. She burst into laughter, as she placed her arm under his to help lift his stiffened body. She giggled all the way up the stairway at how awkwardly he walked.

"Laura, it's not funny," he sniveled. "I can't move." A smile played on his lips.

"I know. I know," she cooed. She aided him into the bathroom, removed the blanket from his shoulders, and turned to go.

"Laura, I think I'm going to need your help." He stood in the center of the bathroom, unable to lift his arms on his own.

She smiled at him, as she walked back into the bathroom, placing the blanket on the counter. They had grown accustomed to seeing one another in their swimsuits and the rare occasion of a glance in undergarments. But they respected one another's privacy and kept their distance, just to avoid temptation.

She helped to remove his sweater, then his T-shirt. His toned chest sent shivers up her spine. She ran her hands across his warm chest. He pulled her closer and whispered that he loved her. He brought his lips to hers and gave her a slow kiss. The kiss deepened and this time *she* began to melt. His hands traveled up and down her back. Laura quivered. His touch was magical, his masculinity undeniable.

The temptation to fall into sin was ever present, but they managed to remain pure. Laura dreamed every day of becoming his wife and wanted nothing more than to be his. But, their strong moral beliefs had kept them from crossing the line. She loved him for that. They believed that sex was only meant for married couples. Even three months prior, when they officially became engaged, they promised to wait for their wedding night.

Now, their kiss became more passionate and he pushed her body against the bathroom wall. She reeled at his touch. She embraced him harder, running her hands over his back. He seemed to stagger from her reaction. With no hesitation, he bent over and gracefully picked her up, carrying her into her bedroom.

He set her on the bed. She reached out and pulled him to her. He stopped in mid-air and sniffed. "Laura, is something burning?"

She gasped, "Oh no, my turkey!" She jumped off the bed and ran down the stairs, Tony's laughter following.

"I'm gonna take a cold, I mean, hot shower while you fix that," he shouted from the second floor.

Laura cursed herself for having forgotten the turkey, and further more for not running from the bathroom at the mere sight of him. She frantically fanned the smoke. Luckily, the turkey itself didn't burn, but the juice had started to dry up. With oven mittens on, Laura reached into the smoke and withdrew the bird. She carried the large pot to the table and decided she'd carve the turkey when Tony was through showering. Impatiently, she sat at the table, listening to the storm blowing outside.

Finally, she heard him slowly descend the stairs. Outside, the wind continued to howl violently. Suddenly, the lights flickered and went out.

"Tony?" Laura cried. She rose from the chair in fear. "Tony?"

"I'm right here. I'm coming." The fire in the living room fireplace gave a soft enough glow to guide Tony into the kitchen. He reached out into the darkness and she felt his hand pull her to him. She embraced him.

"What happened?" she cried.

"The storm. Here, follow me." She trailed after him into the living room where he lit two candles sitting on the mantle. Reaching for Laura's hand again, he led her back into the kitchen.

"Looks as though we'll be eating by candlelight tonight," he smiled reassuringly.

She sighed in relief when he hugged her. "I knew this evening wasn't going to go as planned," she managed in a small voice.

"Come on, Laura. Look how romantic this is." He helped her into a chair and from behind, whispered into her ear. "Thanks for warming me up, earlier."

She blushed, as he sat in the chair next to her. He watched as Laura gracefully carved the steaming turkey and placed a large piece on his plate. "If it's dry, add some gravy." She smiled widely at her masterpiece. They said a prayer and Tony nodded with approval after taking his first bite.

Dinner proceeded with light conversation, which helped to ease some of Laura's fears. By the time the meal was over, she felt herself again and began to enjoy the evening. Despite the lack of lighting in the kitchen, Tony and Laura cleared the table and stored away the leftovers, saving some for Uncle Frank. Tony gathered the candelabras and hand-in-hand, they entered the living room. He placed the candles back onto the mantle and clenched the iron poker to revive the dying flames.

Laura peered over his shoulder, as he poked at the stronger blazing timber. His cologne filled her nostrils and she nearly careened in delight. She placed her arm around his lazed shoulders and began rubbing them. "The house will get cold fast, without the furnace. It's a good thing we have so much firewood, thanks to you. This fire feels good, huh?" she asked.

Tony put the poker back into its place and turned to face her. "Not as good as you in my arms." He gave her a soft kiss, making her heart flutter. She enclosed her slim arms around his waist, hugging him with all her strength.

"What's that for?" he asked.

"Cause, when I woke up this morning I felt the day wasn't going to go as planned. The devil knows he's done all he could to sour my day. First, the storm. Then, you being late and practically freezing to death. And finally, let's not forget my burning turkey. Now the lights went out . . . and yet, you saved the day. You've made this night magical."

"Well, if I've truly saved the day, as you put it, that's the least I could do after all the hard work you put into dinner."

"It was good?

"Delicious. But not quite as good as the dessert I'm holding right here," he teased while nuzzling her neck. Laura giggled. He kissed her again.

She felt the blood rise to her cheeks. *He could drive a girl insane.* They stumbled to the couch and sat. The kiss strengthened. Laura no longer knew if it was the fire that was burning her face or the heat that came from his touch. She heard a soft moan escape her own lips, not even realizing she'd made the sound.

*　　*　　*

Her little moans were driving him mad. He didn't want to stop touching her, feeling her. She felt so warm over the cotton dress.

"Laura, we have to stop."

"I know, but I can't."

"Laura," he pulled her slightly away.

"But, I love you and we're going to be married soon."

"We always said we'd wait. We have to, baby. I don't want this to be something we're going to regret."

"Tony, I wouldn't regret it."

He sighed, brushing back a loose strand of her hair. "Laura, you're so beautiful, so sensual. I couldn't ask for a better wife. But I don't want to lose you. I'm not gonna jinx this."

"You're right. You always are." She smiled back at him. Lifting her hand, she ran her fingers through his sandy hair. He shivered.

Tony reached for her hand and kissed the palm of it. Slowly, he bent forward and kissed her. His lips lingered on hers for a moment and he paused.

"I'm gonna turn the bed down and come right back." He rose from the couch leaving Laura alone to her thoughts. When he returned, minutes later, he sat on the rug next to where Laura now huddled in a blanket. She smiled at him.

"Thanks for bringing me back to reality. Sometimes it's so hard to resist you," she whispered.

"You think it's easy for me? I have to talk myself out of it every minute we're together. Why do you think I walk away? Giving us a few minutes alone helps to clear our heads. Looks like I'm going to be doing an awful lot of walking!" They laughed in unison. In a more serious tone, he added, "You know, if we keep this up we'll never be able to resist. We either move the wedding date up or break our own rules. I don't want us to fail, not when we've held out this long. I mean, not only would we sin—you could get pregnant. That's not a risk we can take. We're in no way ready for a family."

Laura shook her head in agreement. "Tony, I know that you're right. Sometimes, it's so hard to stay away. There are moments that I don't care if it's wrong. Once I'm away from the temptation, that's when I thank God we were able to stop." She gazed into his eyes, tears filling hers. "I just want you to know, I've never loved so completely. You're my world. If you took me right now, I wouldn't stop you. That's how much I love you."

Tears brimmed Tony's eyes, as well. He looked down guiltily, unable to keep her gaze. "I don't deserve you," he stated.

"That's ridiculous. If anything, you're too good for me. I cannot return to you what you've given me. Not just financially, but spiritually, emotionally." She lifted her finger and forced his chin up so their eyes could meet. "Why would you say that?"

Tony rubbed his face with his hand and finally looked into her eyes. "You think *I* saved *you* that night when I found you in the woods. The truth is . . . *you* saved *me*. Once I laid eyes on you, I fell like a ton of bricks." He cast his eyes downward again. "I don't deserve you because . . ." Tony paused a long moment. Laura waited. "Because, I was selfish," he finally added. He raised his voice a slight notch, sounding angry with himself. "I wanted you all to myself. I didn't want you to go to the police because I was afraid I'd never see you again. So you've had to live the last three years trapped in this house, you quit school—which you loved . . ."

"Oh yeah, you really twisted my arm," Laura interrupted. "Tony, this is where I want to be. Don't think for a second that I'd be happier anywhere else. I love you." She leaned forward and kissed him again.

Tony responded, kissing her in return. When the kiss ended, she pulled the blanket off herself and draped it around the both of them. She kissed his cheek and now nuzzled *her* face in *his* neck. She wrapped her arms around him, holding him tightly. "Let's just lie here before we go upstairs to bed."

Tony enfolded his arms around her and they spooned near the fire. Before long, both began to doze. Sometime close to midnight, Tony awoke. He could feel her warm body pressing against his. His hand caressed her arm. Laura turned and, in her slumber, pulled him closer. He looked at her face as she slept. Her lips were slightly parted and he kissed them. Very quietly, he lifted her off the cozy rug and carried her up to bed.

* * *

Sometime in the middle of the night, Laura awoke to the lashing winds beating against the old house. Remembering the conversation she shared with Tony, she turned over to face him. The bed was empty.

"Tony?" She rose from the bed feeling a deep chill. Finding her way to the closet, she pulled out her robe and descended the dark steps. From the bottom of the stairway, she saw a light glow coming from a candle in the kitchen.

She walked toward the soft flame. She heard sobbing and quickened her pace. In the kitchen, Tony sat at the table, his face in his hands as he cried.

"Tony," she whispered, "What's the matter?"

Startled, he looked up and tried to compose himself. "Oh, hey, it's nothing. I'm okay."

"Tony Warren, I know you. Now, tell me why you're crying?"

He stood and reached for her hands. He pulled out a chair and made her sit. "Laura, I need to talk to you. It's important."

Something inside of her screamed, as she looked at the seriousness in his face. Something told her to run—to not listen to whatever it was he was about to say. But she remained sitting, frozen with fear. For Tony to cry, something had to be wrong.

CHAPTER 7

Darkened Dreams

"Laura, what I'm about to tell you may change us, forever."

"Then I don't want to know. Tony, please, I know you're feeling guilty about the school thing and about my being stuck in this house all day. Please know that I'm where I want to be. Nothing's more important than our love. Nothing will change that."

"Laura, yes it will."

"Then I don't want to know," she cried.

"Please, listen to me," he pleaded.

"NO! I don't want to know. I don't want what we have to change." Tears began to heat her face.

"Please, don't cry. I never wanted to hurt you. Laura, I love you!" His fist angrily pounded the table.

Laura jumped, but with a voice just above a whisper, she stated, "I love you too, Tony. You've never hurt me."

His head hung low, "I have."

Her voice rose now. Tony glanced up. "NO! You took me in. You fed me, taught me, loved me. You NEVER hurt me." She stood from the chair and stormed from the kitchen and into the living room.

Laura stared into the amber ashes of the fireplace and trembled. Her heart pounded in her chest, causing it to ache. Tony quietly approached her, placed the candle on the mantle, and rested a hand on her shoulder, turning her to face him. Tears coursed down her cheeks.

"Why are you doing this?" she cried.

"You need to know the truth." His face was solemn.

"I don't want to lose you. I couldn't bear it if I lost you. Please, don't try to find a way out."

"Is that what you think? I'll never leave you!" Tears filled his eyes.

"Promise?" She wiped her tears and kissed him.

He nodded. "I love you, Laura. More than mere words can describe. But after what you said tonight I can't live with myself anymore."

"Why? What did I say?"

"That you were willing to give yourself so completely to me. I've been taking advantage of you. Now, it's time you knew the truth about me."

"It doesn't matter, Tony. Whatever it is, it doesn't matter."

Tony sighed again. They walked up to her bedroom and went back to sleep.

The next morning, Tony awoke early and left for work without waking her. Throughout the day, she repeated the happenings of the evening before in her mind. She couldn't imagine what was so important that he needed to tell her. Laura decided that if it meant changing their beautiful life, then she never wanted to know.

Unable to concentrate on any studying, she collected the books from the kitchen table and put them away. Trying to occupy her mind with other things, she went outside to shovel the snow off the porch. Still unable to stop thinking of Tony, she sat on the couch, in a blanket, and stared into the large fire she kept burning as the power had yet to return.

Laura recalled how close they came to making love and shivered. He was so beautiful and the love they shared was like nothing she could've imagined. Yet, deep inside of her, something was telling her that Tony wasn't himself. Something in his eyes told Laura he was different.

At last, seven-thirty rolled around and Tony arrived. The power had returned and Laura was able to warm up leftovers from the day before. When the living room door opened and Tony whistled, she peered through the kitchen doorway and greeted him cheerfully.

"Finally, you're home," said Laura. She kissed him warmly. He grabbed and squeezed her.

"I've missed you today," said Tony, his voice low.

She groaned, "I missed you, too." She returned his hug and kiss. "Come and eat. I'm sure you're hungry." Tony removed his coat and boots and they entered the kitchen. He was happy to see that the electricity had returned. "How bad is it out there?" she asked.

Tony let out a long sigh. "You wouldn't believe how much snow is out there. Poor Uncle Frank had to sleep at the store last night. He couldn't get his truck out of the parking lot. The whole city is at a standstill," he replied.

"Where is he? Did he drive you home?" Laura poured Tony a glass of cola.

"I had to walk home. The snow is just too deep. Uncle is staying late to stock up on inventory since the place was nearly bared before the storm hit. He won't be coming to dinner again tonight." He thanked her for the drink, downing half of it in one gulp.

"Did you give him the leftovers from yesterday?"

"He polished them off by lunchtime. He couldn't stop raving about your cooking."

"Oh, come on. You're just saying that." Laura blushed at the praises.

Tony crossed his heart and raised his right hand. "Swear." They laughed while Laura served their meal. They ate in a comfortable silence. After dinner, they rested before the fire and snuggled. A few questions nagged at Laura and she wanted to somehow broach the subject.

"Tony," Laura whispered.

"Hmm?"

"Talk to me."

He peered at her questioningly, "About . . . ?"

"Tell me more about what your life was like growing up with a big warm family." She smiled at him lazily.

Tony let out a huff. "Warm?"

"Well, that's the impression I got."

Tony wiggled around to find a more comfortable position. "Do we really need to talk about it? I don't like to think back—too painful."

"Painful? Why?"

Tony squirmed some more, almost annoyed. "Honestly, Laura . . . I'm enjoying our time here on the couch too much to start thinking back on a dark time in my life."

Laura was almost confused. She assumed his life at home was pleasant, if not every child's dream. She pushed a little more. "I must confess, Tony. I'm curious about your family. I've just about spilled every thought and memory to you about my life, yet you rarely ever bring anything up about yours."

Tony ran a hand through his disheveled hair. He let out another frustrated sigh. "It was a long time ago and frankly, there's not much to tell. Honestly, my childhood is like one big blur, anyway. Maybe it's best that way. I'm happier now than I've ever been. Why conjure up unhappy feelings and memories?"

Now Laura was even more curious. *What had made his childhood so unhappy?* Just one last push, "Was it your dad who made things unpleasant for you? Kind of like mine?"

This time Tony's annoyance was evident. He struggled to sit up. His demeanor completely changing. "Laura . . . look. I don't want to be rude, but there's nothing to tell. My father was a miserable man who was selfish and without morals. He had no respect for women, was a liar, and an egotistical pig! Yes, in many ways he was like your father –only worse. Your dad had an addiction that drove him to selfishness. My father was just plain self-centered. He thought only of himself and his needs, his wants. I don't like to talk about him because I vowed a long time ago to be the exact opposite of him."

Laura sat stunned by Tony's sudden outburst. "I'm sorry. I didn't mean to push. I never knew you felt that way. Don't get upset. It's just that . . . as well as I feel I know you, I've never heard you talk about your years growing up." She ran a gentle hand over his shoulders and she felt him immediately relax under her touch.

He looked at her and let a small smile fall on his lips. "It's okay."

Laura yawned and whispered, "Come on, let's go to bed. You gotta wake up early for work tomorrow."

She paused a moment, remembering one of the things she wanted to ask. "Speaking of which," she continued, "I was serious about hooking up that phone line. It's not as if the bill's going to be huge. I have nowhere to call but the grocery store, which is a local call. Do you think we can get one?"

"Laura," his face grew serious again.

"Oh, and is it okay if I come see you at the store tomorrow? I'd like to get out this week."

Tony's face paled. His eyes filled with concern. "Laura, that's precisely what I want to talk to you about. I can't let you do that unless I tell you everything. Do you understand now? I need to tell you. I knew the day would come when you wouldn't want to stay locked up here anymore."

Now they stood in the living room, inches apart. Laura extended her arms and held him by the waist. Calmly, she said, "Tony, I told you last night to drop that subject. Just answer my question."

Tony looked lovingly upon her and placed his hands on her face, opening his mouth to begin to speak.

"Stop. Don't say it, Tony." Laura again whispered.

Tony's face turned red and he tore his hands from her face, breaking away from her hold. He stormed away, then turned around and stalked back. "Laura, listen! Don't make me angry! You're acting like a child. Now, I'm going to tell you everything if it kills me. You can't go into town and you never will, unless we move and leave New York, forever."

"I know why," she blurted. "You're afraid someone's going to find out I'm an orphan and take me away from you. You're afraid that . . ."

"No, it's not only that. It's more than that. You're in danger! Laura . . . Laura there were no raids. I lied to you. I told you there were raids so you'd be scared to go into town and would have no real choice but to stay with me."

Laura froze, as the words began to sink in. "What? What do you mean, 'no raids'?

"From the moment I saw you, I wanted to help you. I felt a sense of obligation to see to it that you'd be all right. I didn't want you going through the heartache and pain that comes with the orphanages and foster families. I figured if I told you that riots and raids were the cause of your family's death, you wouldn't venture into the city to seek help. You'd stay with me. It was after I got to know you that it became more than just an obligation to care for you. I was falling in love and wanted to keep you close to protect and love you. But the raids were part of a big lie I'd created."

Laura's mind raced. *Was this what all the fuss was about?* Then she recalled something. "What about the next day, when we went to the market and those looters raided the store. What was that all about?"

"That's what I need to tell you more about. They were looking . . ."

Laura wasn't listening. Her mind was elsewhere, when she interrupted him once again. "Is that the big secret?" she asked.

"No, there's more . . ."

"Wait a second, if rioters didn't kill my family, then who did?"

A stretch of silence left Laura's heart racing. Tony turned and looked away. His shoulders collapsed in defeat. "Tony, do you know who killed my family?" Another long silence passed and Laura grew more concerned. A fear gripped her. "Tony, it wasn't by chance that you were in the woods and found me there, was it? Do you know who killed my family?" Tony's shoulders shook with sudden sobs. He hid his face from her. Laura touched his shoulder lovingly. "Tony?" He didn't answer. The fear that swept over Laura made her legs tremble.

At first, he didn't respond. He slowly turned to face her. Tony's red face was streaked with tears. When he finally spoke, his voice was barely audible. "Yes, I think I know who killed your family."

Laura could taste the vomit that threatened to explode from her queasy stomach. "Who, Tony?" She waited in anticipation.

Suddenly, his gaze became a glare. His face contorted. A rage seemed to seethe from within. He looked at her through acrimonious eyes. Something had clicked. The man in front of her wasn't the man she loved.

"Tony," she almost backed away. "What is it?"

"*NOTHING!*" He screamed.

Laura jumped at the outburst. Confused and stunned, she questioningly gazed at him.

"*STOP LOOKING AT ME!*" he shouted again.

She jumped again. Her voice whispered, "Tony, what's wrong?"

"I'll tell you what's wrong. YOU! I'm sick of you!"

Laura stood in shock. Something *was* wrong. This wasn't her Tony. Yet . . . it was. Suddenly angry, she stalked past him toward the staircase. "Maybe you need some time alone."

"You're not going anywhere." In two large strides, Tony seized her arm forcefully. Laura slipped and fell to the floor.

She gasped, horrified and in disbelief. Tony would never hurt her. Tony had never laid a finger on her, except in love. In that brief moment, she concluded that something had gone terribly wrong. She lay on the floor allowing fear to restrain her.

"You think I'm gonna let you walk on out of here and walk right into their trap, huh? Well, you've got another thing coming, lady! Get up!"

She dared to speak to him. In a calm and soothing voice, she pleaded with him. "Tony, what's the matter? What are you talking about?"

"*SHUT UP!* I don't want to hear you anymore. Now, I told you to *GET UP!*" His hands shook, as he demanded her to rise.

Laura slowly rose to her feet and backed away from him. *She must get through to him.* "Tony, let's go upstairs and go to bed," she said calmly. "We can forget this ugly moment ever happened."

"Stop telling me what to do! I should've finished this when I had the chance. Get over here." His eyes were wild. He ruthlessly grabbed her and pulled her into a fierce grip.

"Tony, I know you don't mean any of this. You'd never hurt me."

"Tony's a coward—a good-for-nothing coward!" He grazed over her with his eyes, looking longingly at her.

Laura froze. "No," she whispered. Before Laura could respond, he pushed her. Laura screamed and stumbled to the floor. "No!" she screamed.

"Don't move. *Do you GOT THAT?*" he challenged.

Laura shook her head in fright. Tears streamed down her cheeks. "You promised to never hurt me," she whispered. "Why are you hurting me? You're not this cruel."

Suddenly, he seized her forearms, lifting her completely off the floor. Laura screamed as he roared words she couldn't make out. The look in his eyes was petrifying. He was crazed with anger.

"Cruel?" he bellowed. "You come from the creator of cruel! You're the spawn of cruel. If I hadn't taken over and done what I did, he'd still be torturing that loser."

He was mad! *What was he talking about?* Laura was confused by his words. She wrestled with him, trying to escape his clutches, but he was so much bigger, stronger. "Tony what are you talking about? You're delirious. Please," she pleaded, "Stop! I'm begging you."

"Yes!" he spat. "Beg me to stop and I won't. Just like him, I won't!" He tightened his grip and threw her to the floor again. She struggled to get back up, but seconds later, his hard body pinned hers to the floor. She screamed, but her pleas fell upon deaf ears.

Savagely, Tony tore at her sweater. For a moment, she was stunned, unable to accept that he was seemingly trying to force his way with her. Her instincts finally kicked in. If she didn't defend herself, something horrible was going to happen. Suddenly, she beat at his chest, striking him. But he simply clasped both her hands above her head, with one hand.

With his free hand, he held her chin. "Stop fighting me!" He forced a kiss.

Laura tried to scream, but the horror of what was happening left her dazed. "*TONY!*" she shouted.

He froze. His eyes locked with hers.

"Don't do this," she whispered. "You don't want to do this."

He remained frozen, his body still pinning hers to the floor. She'd done it. Somehow, she reached her Tony. Tears began to brim in his eyelids. Without warning, he released a scream so horrifying that she'd not soon forget. Laura tried to embrace him, to comfort him. In all the confusion, she knew something was seriously wrong.

He rolled off her and onto the floor next to her. He beat at his head and cried out like a mad man. Laura embraced him, kissed him, and soothed him, telling him that it would be okay and that she'd help him. But he suddenly stiffened in her arms and abruptly stopped.

"NO!" he shouted. "I won't let this happen. You're not gonna weasel your way outta this," he cursed aloud. "*I HATE YOU, ANTONIO!*"

Laura watched, as he struggled within himself. She didn't know what to do to get through to him. She trembled beside him, gently touching his leg, until his evil glare raised the lump back in her throat. Her hand instinctively moved away. She opened her mouth to scream, but he quickly clasped his hand over it.

"Shut up. Don't scream." Laura stopped moving and pleaded with her eyes. Unexpectedly, he got up, all the while keeping his hands on her. "Now, you're going to do whatever I tell you."

Laura played along long enough to rise from the floor. He released her and she dashed for the front door. He ran to catch her, clenching her arm and pulling her to him. She cried out in frustration. He turned her around to face him, shaking her like mad. Laura lifted her leg and kicked him in the groin. He hollered in pain. She pushed him hard, knocking him to the ground. He let her go and she ran into the bathroom, locking the door behind her.

In the darkness, she toiled for the light switch, breathing hard and fast. Finding it, she shrieked at the sight of her reflection. Blood oozed from her lip and her hair was disheveled. *What had happened?* Sobbing uncontrollably, she ran the water to wash her bloody face.

Outside the door, she heard his footsteps racing toward the bathroom. Reassuring herself, she checked the lock. She waited while no sound came from the other side. Startling her, he punched the door.

"Let me in! It's your fault this happened. Your fault! You had to talk about him didn't you? You're just so nosey. What went on in that house is nobody's business. Nobody's!" Again, he pounded on the door in a rage.

Laura placed her hands over her ears to stop the noise, but only added to it with her own screams. The harder she screamed, the harder he pounded on the door. Suddenly, there was silence. She tried to calm herself. *This was madness. He was talking madness.*

Unexpectedly, one by one, the hinges of the door began to fall loose. A panic rose in her and she felt a scream in her throat. "No . . . No! Tony, stop this!" she yelled.

"It'll all be over shortly." His eerie voice traveled to her ears and she searched the bathroom for some kind of protection. *Nothing!* She turned the light off, in hopes of throwing him off. Perhaps she could dash out before he had a chance to grab her. The door fell open.

She crouched down and made a run for it. His hand grazed her back as she slipped past him into the kitchen. He was immediately behind her. The back exterior door was far out of reach. She'd never make it. She took a hard left and grasped at the basement doorknob. She quickly turned it and opened the door, slamming it into Tony's body. His body mass flung forward into her and suddenly Laura was falling. A terrible scream pierced the air. She felt a sharp blow knock the breath from her lungs, while darkness consumed her.

*   *   *

A deafening siren echoed in Laura's ears. At first, it increased higher, but slowly it began to fade. Her body ached and she was aware of why. She knew where she was and, even worse, she knew how she got there. Laura prayed for God to take her, so to not face the reality of what had happened. She drifted into a restless sleep.

A searing pain eventually woke Laura to an ugly world she refused to accept. Still, she had to help herself. She opened her eyes.

The smell of the musty basement filled her senses. She cringed. She had truly fallen down the flight of stairs. Hesitantly, she shifted her eyes to her mangled body. She glanced at her left arm beneath her, closing her eyes in disgust. Swollen, it was twisted in an odd position.

Putting herself in a sitting position, she cried out in pain. Laura caught her breath, while holding her broken arm. She tore a piece of her tattered sweater off and stuffed it into her mouth, biting down hard. Tightening her stomach muscles, Laura twisted her left arm into place. Her bones crunched at the motion. Instantly, the blood rushed back into her fingers. Tears spilled from her eyes as she cried out in agony—the fabric muffling her screams. She pulled it out and hurled forth what was left of her dinner.

She wiped her mouth and her tears, gasping at the sight of blood all over her hands. Her eyebrow was cut and throbbing. The retched taste of dried blood gagged her again. She spit onto the cold cement. With her heart pounding in her ears, she gathered her courage and tried to stand. A sharp pain traveled up her leg from her ankle. Her eyes grazed her leg to find her ankle swollen the size of a small cantaloupe. Laura moaned at the pain. Even her ribs ached.

Tearing her eyes away from her broken body, she glared up the stairway at the closed door. *Where was he? How could he have left her this way?* Her anger flared. Leaving through the front door meant risking a chance of an encounter with him. Laura decided to find another way out. Glancing back around the small basement, she grazed the room for another escape. Aside from an old trunk they used to store old clothes in, boxes piled up against the far wall were the only contents of the basement. She tried to focus. It suddenly struck her that the boxes could be her escape. She'd pile them under the window, somehow break it, and dig through the snow to freedom. Before she began her plan, she slowly hobbled to the trunk.

She'd use some old clothes to keep warm, for her escape. Using her strong hand, she lifted the lid covered in dust. Laura slowly removed her tattered sweater. The pain was enough to make her head feel light. She sat on the chest and also peeled off her skirt. She replaced her clothes with an older sweater and a pair of frayed jeans. Digging through the piles of clothing, she came across a blouse and wrapped it around her broken arm, tying the sleeves around her neck as a sling. She tightly wrapped her swollen ankle as well. Finally, she took out her outdated coat, one of Tony's old winter boots for her swollen ankle, and her old boot for her other foot.

Then slowly, she began. Laura stacked the boxes, filled with the clothes they found in the closets that they didn't want, and placing them beneath one of the windows. She made them form a stairway, to easily climb. She prayed it would hold her weight. Half way through her plan, when most of the boxes were in place, she came across a few boxes that contained large pieces of metal too heavy for her to lift. She struggled with the first one but managed to drag it to the side. She gasped when her eyes fell upon an opening behind it.

Her heart began to pound loudly. It was a hidden room, and if her calculations were correct, it led to the storm cellar in the backyard.

With renewed hope, Laura began dragging the heavy boxes out of the way. It was as she had suspected—the storm cellar. Tears stung her eyes. She was going to get away, after all.

Before entering the hole, Laura glanced down at her hand in the sling. The small solitaire diamond seemed to shine even in the gloom of the basement. She wiggled it free and angrily threw it across the basement at the stairs. From there, she began to prepare herself for the ruthless cold. Laura slipped on the coat. She slid her swollen foot into Tony's boot, the other in hers. Sliding passed the mass of boxes, Laura entered the hidden room.

CHAPTER 8

Even Free, There's No Escape

She inched through the tight hole, holding her broken arm tightly to her chest. From above she could feel the chilling temperature creep down. She shivered, whispering a small prayer for strength. In the darkness of the storm cellar, she found a ladder. She felt the first step and securely placed her strong foot on the wood. The second step was difficult for her, but she managed to climb.

At last, she reached the top of the ladder. Her hand traveled up to the wooden door. It was barred with a piece of wood. She cursed, knowing that even if she could remove it, the weight of the snow would be too heavy to push.

Feeling defeated, she began to silently sob. "Oh God," she cried. "Please help me." She lifted her right arm and began pulling the bar out of its prongs. Without warning, the heft of the snow began to cave the wooden door inward. Laura hovered quickly. The hard packed snow hit her back, knocking her off the ladder and onto the basement floor with a thud. She felt a pain shoot through her arm as she hit the floor. Laura screamed out, immediately smacking her hand over her mouth to prevent Tony from hearing her cries. She was so close to getting away.

She slowly and painfully rose from the floor. She brushed at the snow that covered her. Laura looked up at the door that now swung freely from its hinges. The westerly winds blew more snow in, its flakes falling gently onto her cheeks. Tears fell from her eyes again. God had heard her.

Laura attempted to climb the ladder again, pulling herself out onto the cold ground. She was finally free. Now she'd do what she should've done three years prior. The police station would be her final destination. She glanced up at the sky. The sun had yet to rise. Examining the grounds, she saw no sign of Tony. As quickly as her swollen ankle would allow, she hopped alongside the house, across the lengthy front yard, and to the dirt road.

Laura sobbed, while the pain in her heart seemed to crush her very soul. So many incredible memories passed before her, as she left the house she had grown to love, along with the man living in it. Wondering how she found herself in the predicament she was in, she cried with abandonment.

Still, she continued her escape down the snowy road, occasionally falling, for the snow was nearly two feet deep. She trudged along, ignoring the wind's cold whip that numbed her completely. Determination assisted her until she ultimately reached town, passing Uncle Frank's closed store.

Laura prayed Cicero's police department was near. She hoped to find it quickly. Her ankle throbbed painfully. Her body shook violently.

Panicking, she glanced around. Every shop and store was closed. Even the gas stations seemed deserted. More tears fell from her eyes. Though she'd freed herself from the basement, she was still unable to escape the nightmare. She limped down Crabtree Lane until she reached Brewerton Road. Making a left, she walked aimlessly. So forsaken and pained, Laura suddenly decided that she didn't care whether she lived or died.

Yet, as a blue and white car with lights on the roof turned into a far off parking lot to her left, her hope was renewed. Laura took a deep breath, and despite her ankle, despite her desire to give up, she ran. The wind beat her face and whipped her hair. She felt frozen down to her very core. Tingling everywhere, she couldn't bear the pain any longer.

At last, she reached the building with a sign above labeling it, 'Cicero Police.' Sobbing hysterically, she climbed the stoop and stumbled in through the front doors. Laura cried out one last time, then lost all consciousness and fell to the floor.

*   *   *

Chief of Police Massimo Desanti leaned on the front desk of an officer as they spoke. The front doors swung open and he glanced up. A young woman, in a coat much too small and wearing two different boots, entered and fell to the cold wet floor. He rushed to the young woman. Feeling for a pulse, he sighed in relief. One look at the broken girl told him instantly that she needed medical attention.

"Quick," he bellowed. "Call EMS!" Gently, he picked up her frail body and carried her into the warm lounge. "Get me blankets, Manelli!" he ordered. The rookie ran from the lounge, returning seconds later with two wool blankets.

The chief leaned over the frozen girl, examining her closely. She had a gash in her right eyebrow, needing to be stitched. Her small face was covered in dried blood and her lips were blue from the cold and swollen with small cuts. His nervous hands worked the coat. His eyes fell upon her arm in the makeshift sling.

He removed the coat and wrapped the warm blankets around her. He also removed the larger boot, only to find her swollen ankle. He couldn't believe what he was seeing.

"How is she, sir?" Manelli asked.

"Bad!" he roared. "I don't know who did this, but when I get my hands on the animal, I'm gonna kill him!" Angrily, he glanced at the two other officers who crowded them to take a better look. "Where's that ambulance?" he screamed.

He shook his head, as he examined her bruised body. He knew too well what battered women looked like. He was thankful to have been at the station extra early. Unbeknownst to him, he was meant to be there when the young woman literally fell through the station doors.

When the ambulance arrived moments later, they laid her listless body on the stretcher and rolled her into the van. With the lights flashing and the sirens sounding, the ambulance rushed her to the closest hospital in Syracuse.

Chief Desanti ran to his desk as he barked orders at his men. He reached for his pistol and secured it into the harness around his shoulder, running from the building to his squad car. At an abounding speed, he caught up with the ambulance. He was determined to handle *this* case personally.

The paramedics wheeled the girl directly into the emergency room and quickly began to cut off her clothes. The doctors rushed back and forth. It was evident that her arm was severely fractured and that it was even possible that she was bleeding internally.

A surgeon questioned the chief. "Do we have a family member we can call? Anyone who'll sign the consent forms to perform whatever medical procedures she may need?"

"None. No identification on her. I'm having my men run a search to see if anyone missing fits her description. So far, we haven't come up with anything."

Dr. David Stewart shook his head. "We're going to give her the medical attention she needs. Surgery is most likely a necessity. The longer we wait, the more serious her condition could become."

Massimo cussed. "Do what you gotta do. We can't lose her!" He stalked off into the waiting room, reaching for his radio.

There was still no word on the girl's identity. Massimo decided to wait for her to wake so he could question her himself. He paced the waiting room, every so often checking with the station to see how things were running. He ordered the young rookie, Peter Manelli, to form a small team of men together. They were to search the town for any clues that might lead to the mysterious girl and who had caused her those injuries.

Two hours later, the doctor appeared in the waiting room. Beads of perspiration were still wet on his face. Massimo jumped up from the stiff chair and ran to him.

"Well?"

The doctor sighed. "Well," he began, "She's out of the woods. First, we managed to regulate her body temperature in time to operate. She was nearly hypothermic. The x ray's confirmed a break in the arm. From the looks of it, she must have been pushed off something. At the break, small fragments of the bone chipped off. We came to the conclusion that the bone had to have been twisted, broken, and snapped back into place. She had to have repositioned the arm herself." The doctor shook his head.

Massimo cursed again, shaking his head.

"So, we realigned the bone, strengthening it with a few screws, and set the cast. It should heal with no problems. I do have some good news. Though she did break a rib, she has no internal bleeding, which was our first and most important concern." The doctor wiped his brow with a hanky as he spoke. "We wrapped her ankle tightly. X rays confirmed no breaks. Of course, she'll still need to stay off it for a while. She does not have a concussion. Still, we'll be monitoring her. She's going to be okay. But she'll definitely wake up feeling as though a truck ran her over."

"Thank you, doctor." Massimo shook the doctor's hand, but quickly excused himself. Finding his way to the nurses' station, he asked if he could see the young woman. They pointed the direction of her room as they watched him with curious eyes.

Massimo found his way down the corridor to her room. He held his breath as he walked in. They cleaned the dried blood from her face, exposing the black and blue bruises she bore. Half her head was bandaged up from the blow to her head and they had brushed her brown hair away from her fragile face. He couldn't tear his eyes away from her. Somehow, he found a seat next to her bed, closed his eyes, and swallowed hard.

Patiently, Massimo Desanti waited for her to awaken. Occasionally, he left for a coffee or to radio the station. Despite their efforts, they still had been unable to identify the girl. Restlessly, he strolled back into her room and placed himself back onto the vinyl chair. Looking at his watch, he sighed heavily. It was nearly ten o'clock. It had already been two hours since she had come out of surgery and still she lay asleep.

He rubbed his eye and yawned. Soon, Massimo's eyelids began to grow heavy, and for a moment, he closed them. His mind still raced, continuing to repeat the morning's happenings. Deep in thought, he barely heard the girl beginning to stir. Suddenly, his skin prickled and he opened his eyes.

Her eyes were deep and fear was etched within them. She was staring right at him.

He smiled, finally finding his voice, "Hi there. How ya feelin'?" Massimo held his breath as he waited for a response.

*   *   *

Laura looked at the man before her dressed in a wrinkled suit and crooked tie. She groggily gazed around the hospital room. She had made it to safety. She sighed in relief, forgetting that the man had asked her a question.

"It's all right. I'm here to help you," he continued.

Laura's stomach suddenly ached. What had happened, at last, began to penetrate.

"If you can tell me your name, sweetie," he urged.

Laura looked at the attractive man before her. Another handsome face. She immediately made a promise to never trust another. She opened her mouth to speak, but a sob escaped and the dam holding back her tears was broken.

"Oh God," she whispered between breaths. "I . . . I don't know what to do . . ." She tried to sit up, but the man gently stopped her. He quickly stepped out to get help.

Moments later, a doctor entered the room with a nurse behind him. "I see you're finally awake. How do you feel?"

Laura shook her head in 'no'.

"It's going to be all right, honey. This is Chief of Police Massimo Desanti, I'm Dr. Stewart, and this is Mary, your RN. You're at St. Joseph's Hospital in Syracuse. Now, lay back down. You just had surgery on your arm and you're weak." He took a breath and reassured her. "We just need a few questions answered."

Laura looked at the people around her. She had to trust them. She had no one else. The chief looked as though he was genuinely concerned, as well as the doctor and nurse. She gazed carefully at the woman who quietly checked Laura's pulse with warm fingers. She lovingly brushed back Laura's hair and smiled. The gentle feel of the nurse's touched felt maternal and Laura longed for her mother.

"It's all gonna be jus' fine, sugar," she whispered.

More tears swelled in Laura's eyes, falling down her cheeks.

"Let me help you." The young chief cut in. "I want to find who did this and make sure they can't do it to you, or anyone, ever again. Tell us your name and how this happened."

Laura cautiously peered into the man's eyes. *He seemed sincere.* Yet, a part of her wanted to protect Tony. She couldn't understand what had happened. If something was wrong, she didn't want him to go to jail because of her. But he did what he did. The proof was right before her eyes. Struggling for a decision, she decided that if Tony needed help, these people could help her to help him.

"Take your time, sugar," the nurse encouraged. Laura managed to smile. The doctor and the chief both sighed in relief.

Laura cleared her throat and began. "My . . . My name is . . . Laura Ann Marcs."

"Hi Laura," Massimo said as he extended his right hand. Hesitantly, Laura shook it. He smiled back and continued. "Now I certainly don't expect you to call me by any other name, but Sam. That's my nickname."

Laura nodded, while the nurse and doctor grinned. "Thank you," she whispered.

The chief continued, "Please tell me how this happened to you." He paused a moment, glancing at the doctor and nurse. They immediately made themselves scarce.

"Laura," the doctor interrupted, "We'll leave you to the chief, here. If you need anything, if you're in any pain, press this button." He pointed to the call button on her bed rail and patted her lightly on the shoulder. He followed the nurse out of the room.

"Okay," began Massimo, "Just so you know, you're okay. You have no internal injuries and they operated on your arm. Your leg is sprained and you broke a rib, but they stitched your cuts and physically you're going to be okay. You just need to heal. The question is—how are you emotionally? I'll call your parents and let them know you're gonna be all right. Then we'll find who did this. For starters, where do you live?"

Laura swallowed as she nervously played with her hands. "I live on Crabtree Lane."

"You live there with your parents?" he asked.

Laura took a deep breath. "No. My mother died when I was ten. The rest of my family was killed, three years ago."

"Killed?"

"Yes, killed."

"How?"

"I don't know. That's how this whole mess started." Laura felt her heart begin to thump harder.

"I'm sorry, honey. You lost me. Can you start over?" Massimo encouraged.

"It's a very long story," she warned.

"I've got all day."

"When I was 14, I lived with my father, Matthew Duke Marcs, and my sisters, Patty and Sabrina. We lived off a dirt road that didn't even have a name. I know that it ended right into Mud Mill Road."

"Yes, Mud Mill," Massimo reaffirmed.

"Anyway, our mother died giving birth to Sabrina, my baby sister. In December of 1973, just as we were packing up our things to move out of town, a man broke through our door and began shooting. Somehow, everyone was killed, but me. I managed to escape and hid in a large drainage ditch. That's where I met him."

"Who?" Massimo continued to scribble into a notebook as she spoke.

"Tony, my fiancé. We need to get him help. Something is wrong with him," she insisted.

"What is Tony's last name?"

"Warren."

"So you happened to meet him on the night your family was murdered? You didn't think that was coincidental?" Massimo pressed.

"He told me that the Vietnam War had caused rioting and raids throughout the states. And that somebody probably killed my family to steal from us. I was skeptical at first, but having no one else to believe and nowhere else to go, I trusted him. I later found out that the story about the raids was a lie. I'll get to that part in a moment."

Massimo smiled at her. "Go on."

"Well, we needed to find a shelter. We walked for miles." She paused a moment and added. "I hope I won't get in trouble by telling you this."

Massimo snickered, "Don't worry. I've no intentions of putting *you* in jail."

"Okay, the house we live in . . . we found it abandoned—all boarded up."

Massimo jotted a note onto his pad. Distracted by the information she'd given him, he tried to respond to her concern. "Um . . . What puzzles me is that the original owners never showed up?"

"Apparently they were deceased. The original bills came in the name of a 'Maria Fontana' or something of that nature. I'm not sure. I only know that we found it abandoned and that after some negotiating with the city, we were able to purchase it. I guess it sounds kind of crazy, now that I think about it."

"Not crazy. Fishy is more like it," Massimo stated. "I just can't figure this out."

"There isn't much to figure out. Tony was orphaned at a young age, too. He didn't have anyone and neither did I. I lived three of the happiest years of my life in that house, until last night." A shadow fell over her face, darkening her eyes.

"What happened to you, Laura?"

"He insisted on telling me something. Something that he claimed would change our relationship forever. I told him I didn't want to know. I simply wanted to get out of the house more. For the three years I lived there, I barely left. I stopped going to school and went into town with him very rarely. Tony convinced me that it would be too risky and that someone could've found out I was orphaned and still under 18. That meant that we'd be separated and that they'd take me away.

"So he tutored me at home. But, it got to the point that I couldn't stay in that house anymore. I wanted to get out more. Even living in the shack with my family, I went to school and socialized with other human beings. I needed to be around other people again.

"When I mentioned this, he became sad and said he had to tell me something that would change us. He said that in order for me to have more liberty, we needed to leave New York forever. I didn't want to change our life together. I loved him and loved being with him. I simply wanted to get out more." She gazed into the ceiling, her eyes filling with tears. "You know, we were going to get married next year?"

A tear trickled down her face. She wiped it away angrily, as Massimo watched on sympathetically. "If you guys were so happy, why did this happen?"

"I don't know," Laura cried. "He insisted on telling me whatever it was he needed to say. That's when he told me that the story about the raids was a lie. Naturally, when I heard this, I put two and two together. 'If my family wasn't killed by rioters, then who killed them?' I asked him. That's when it happened. Before my eyes, he became this dangerous, angry man. He'd never raised his voice to me. Suddenly, he started screaming things to me I didn't understand. Something is wrong." Laura took a deep breath, accepting the tissue that Massimo offered.

"Do you still want to go on?" he asked.

"Yes, maybe you can help him. Chief D . . ."

"Sam."

"Sam," she continued. "I don't know what happened last night. In all the years I was with him, I'd never seen him angry. I'm worried about him. I think he needs help, because something went wrong. Something went terribly wrong. He would've never treated me like he did. But...he hurt me!" she cried. "He broke my heart." Laura sobbed.

*   *   *

Massimo rose from his chair and ached for the broken girl. He hesitantly put his arm around her, afraid to press his luck. But Laura didn't protest. She leaned on his shoulder and cried.

He'd made up his mind. No matter how much she wanted to protect this 'Tony', he was going to get him. The whole incident didn't sound right and he was going to find the underlying reason. No matter what it took.

CHAPTER 9

And Justice for All

When Laura gathered her emotions, Massimo sat back down. His eyes looked tired and his hair ruffled. By this time, his tie was thrown over the back of his chair and the top button of his wrinkled shirt was undone. The lines of stress were apparent on his forehead as he spoke.

"Now, I don't want to insist, and please tell me if I am, but I need you to tell me all that you remember. You said he was lying about the raids and you asked him who killed your family. That's when you said something went wrong. Is that correct?" Massimo Desanti scribbled something on his notepad as he spoke.

Laura shook her head solemnly. "Yes," her voice barely above a whisper.

He didn't want to push the already fragile girl, but he needed to complete the statement and find this 'Tony' character. He gave her an encouraging smile. "Please, continue." Massimo watched, as she gazed down at her broken arm.

She sighed, "Well, he got angry and violent. I could tell from the look on his face that he wasn't right. I tried to back away. He started throwing me around. When I fought back, he got meaner. He pinned me to the floor, he almost forced himself upon me, but I called out his name and finally reached him. He was going through something. I'd almost say a battle. He loosened his grip and I escaped. I tried to run after kicking him . . . you know, where it hurts men most. We struggled and I managed to get out of his grasp. I ran into the bathroom for safety, but it didn't help. He loosened the pins in the door. I was able to get away from him and ran into the kitchen. That's when I made the stupid mistake of opening the basement door. Somehow, it smacked into Tony, Tony fell into me, and the next thing I knew, I was laying on the basement floor."

Laura paused a moment.

"Are you okay?" Massimo asked. "Are you in any pain? Do you want me to call the doctor?" He seemed concerned by the look on her face.

"My arm hurts, but I want to finish telling you this." She tried to make herself more comfortable on the bed and gasped in pain.

"Please don't move. I'll help." Massimo put the pad of paper down and helped adjust her pillows and her blanket. "Do you need a glass of water?" He offered her the cup on the nightstand.

Laura drank and then continued to explain to the chief how she'd found the hidden room that led to the storm cellar doorway in the yard. He carefully listened as she explained the rest of what had happened. He shook his head and stared at her in disbelief.

"It's a miracle you're alive." Massimo gently squeezed her good hand in reassurance. "One last question. It's somewhat personal, but I need to know, because it's possible he's been breaking the law all this time. We're you two intimate?"

"No," Laura immediately stated. "We wanted to wait until we were married."

"Okay, Laura, I've got to do some things now. But I'll be back."

"Wait!" she cried out. "What're you going to do to him?"

"Laura, what Tony did to you . . . whether you want to accept it or not . . . he broke the law. If he needs help, then he'll certainly get it where he's going. When I return, I'll explain everything that will happen to you. Don't worry. Meanwhile, one of my men is posted outside your door. If this 'Tony' is still in his crazy mind set, there's no telling what he may do. You concentrate on resting, and I'll take care of things from here."

"But, what will happen to him? Please, tell me," she pleaded.

"I'm gonna do some investigating. I'm going to run a trace and see if Tony has a record. Then I'm going to go from there. Chances are, he'll be arrested and questioned. From there, it's questionable." The chief paused a moment. "Thank you, Laura. You've given me all I need to get to the bottom of this. See you soon." Massimo walked out of the room.

"Wait, Chief?" Laura shouted.

He walked back in the doorway, "Yes?"

"If you find him, please don't hurt him. He needs help. If you can, please help him."

Massimo nodded, then walked away amazed. The poor girl had definitely been played for a fool. The thought of someone taking advantage of this innocent person enraged him. He was going to find this monster if it was the last thing he did.

* * *

Laura watched Massimo wave to her and stalk out of the hospital room. Her nerves felt raw and she began to shake. She buzzed the nurse. Moments later, Mary entered.

"Hey there, what can I do for you?" she asked.

"I don't know. Look," she showed the woman her trembling hands.

"It's gonna be all right. I'll be right back with a sedative to help calm you." She walked back out, leaving Laura trembling in her bed.

She rested her head on the soft pillow and closed her eyes. Visions of the night before forced her eyes open. It still shocked her that Tony had done this. Not her Tony. Not the Tony who saved her from a life of tears, pain, poverty, and of broken dreams. Not the Tony who had swept her completely off her feet into a world of love and magical memories.

Her body shook uncontrollably at the thought of losing another loved one. *Why?* She sobbed unrestrained, until the nurse returned and quickly injected the sedative into her I.V.

Slowly, she felt the drug begin to do its job. At last, she found a place where no pain existed.

*   *   *

Massimo literally ran down the corridors of the hospital to get to his vehicle. As he turned down a hallway, he nearly collided with favorite rookie, Manelli.

"Manelli, I was just about to call you. Are any of the others with you?"

"Yes, sir. Miller and I drove down here together, sir. We hadn't heard from you."

"Yeah, well I've been busy. Where's Miller?"

"On his way up, sir. There he is." Manelli pointed down the hallway.

Massimo spotted the slow-moving figure. He waved his hand at him, and Miller picked up his pace until he reached them.

"Miller, I want you to stand outside the young woman's door until I can get someone posted there, permanently. No one, I repeat, no one is to go into her room but her doctor and the nurses. She may still be in danger and I'm not going to take any chances with this guy."

"Manelli, you come with me. We got work to do."

The chief and Manelli rushed out of the hospital doors directly to his squad car. He cursed the weather as he scrapped the newly fallen snow from his vehicle's windshield. He thought of Laura and thanked God that she'd escaped the house in time, for another storm was about to blow in.

As he squealed his tires onto the icy road, Massimo called the station on his radio. "Desanti, over."

"Yes, Chief?" the dispatcher at the station replied.

"I've got some information on the young lady we brought into the hospital. First, I need someone assigned to her room, pronto! I have Miller there for now, but I want him back at the station, doing what he does best, answering phones."

Manelli's chuckle quickly faded at the seriousness of Massimo's face. Massimo continued. "First, run a check on the girl and see what we find. Her name is Laura Marcs. M-A-R-C-S. Her father's name is Matthew Duke Marcs. They lived in a cabin off a dirt road, near Mud Mill Road. The street does not have a name. Are you writing this all down?" Massimo shouted, as he drove steadily down the snowy street.

"Yes, sir, Chief," the voice echoed back. "Go on, we'll get Ballard and Fliger on that, immediately. I'll assign Callo to the hospital."

"Good. Let Ballard and Fliger know I want them to go to the cabin and see what they find."

"Sir, if it's a dirt road and the weather's this bad . . ."

"I don't care if there's a blizzard! If you need to get the city's four-by-four pickups, then do it! Just follow my orders!" Massimo screamed into the receiver. "Tell my men to be prepared. There may be corpses in the cabin. According to the girl, her family was murdered there three years ago. Who knows what they'll find." Massimo looked over at Manelli, who now listened intently. "You won't believe what this guy pulled," he whispered to him.

"Sir, are you still there? Over . . ." the dispatcher shouted back.

"Yeah, I'm here. Okay, have those guys run the check on the girl's family and scope out the cabin. In the meantime, I need you to run a few other checks. See what you find on the name, 'Tony Warren'." Massimo gave him a brief description of Tony, including his age and a few other details Laura gave him.

"Oh, also run a check on the name Maria Fontana. Possibly the previous owner of the home Laura's been living in. Find out what the causes of death were. Over . . ."

"Got it. Is there anything else, sir?" the voice sang through the static of the radio.

"Hell, I'm far from done here, man! I've got Manelli here with me, but I'm going to need two of my best men. I'm going in to find this guy. I want to go to the Crabtree Lane house. We're sure to find him there. Oh, and in case he gives me a problem, get me a warrant to search the house. I'm on my way in. Over and out . . ."

Massimo slammed the receiver down. The window wipers continued to career back and forth, brushing the snow from side to side. "Darn weather!" he blasted.

The rest of the trip back to the station was quiet. Manelli seemed thankful as they arrived and parked the squad car. Massimo rushed into the building, with him close at his heels. They entered his office and discussed a few plans on how to arrest Tony. Massimo sat back in his chair and took a sip of the coffee his secretary had brought in. It was bitter and hot, just the way he liked it. After an hour, Officer Hilton, the dispatcher whom he'd spoken with over the radio, quickly ran to greet him in his office.

"Sir," he shouted as he waved a few papers in the air. "I think we found something."

"It better be good." Massimo snapped.

"Oh, it is. We ran those checks. On the girl, her father wasn't exactly your average 'Joe'. He worked different jobs here and there. He never kept a job longer than a couple of weeks. Apparently, he was continually fired for drinking on the job and was always late or absent. He even got in trouble with the law for a few things. Nothing major, a few brawls at the bar, a couple driving while intoxicated, speeding, and other moving violations. Let's just say he had a problem."

"I get the picture. Get to the point, Hilton." Massimo's patience began to wear.

"Yes sir. Let's see. We have record of employment on him up until October of '71. After that, it's as though he fell off the face of the earth."

"That's 'cause he did. But wait, that was five years ago. Laura said her family was killed in December of 1973."

"Sir, perhaps he wasn't employed legitimately, if at all."

"It's possible." Massimo jotted another note on his notepad and said, "Okay, what else?"

"The young lady, Miss Laura, was reported missing by the school board at Cicero-North High. Apparently, the school board became concerned when the girl no longer attended classes. A missing persons report was filed, but nothing was ever heard of her again. We spoke to the principal of the school and he stated that it wasn't uncommon for the girls to miss school. Patty Marcs dropped out of high school at age 16."

"What else?" Massimo barked.

"Okay, here's the doozy. Ballard and Fliger just radioed in. No bodies were found at the cabin. It was as if the murders never occurred. No evidence to back up Ms. Laura's story about their murders."

Massimo reclined in his leather chair and ran his fidgety fingers through his already messy hair. He blew the air from his lungs loudly and suddenly pounded his fists on the desk. "What does this all mean? I believe the girl is telling the truth. He must have gotten rid of the evidence. It's too cold and the ground is too frozen to search the vicinity for bodies now. But come spring, we'll find them. What did you find on Mr. Tony Warren?"

"Tony Warren. Clean as a whistle. Nothing on him. He's never been in trouble with the law. He's been working at Blandino's Market for the past three years. I don't get it," Hilton exclaimed.

Massimo scratched his head. He sighed deeply and asked, "What about the owner of the house, Maria Fontana?"

"Oh, yes!" Hilton stated. "I almost forgot. Get this . . . Fontana is her maiden name. Her married name was Giacalone. She's been dead for more than six years. Cause of death, killed in a house fire with the rest of her family, except one child, who moved to California. Yet, she's still listed as the owner of the house."

Massimo stood and paced the small cluttered office. He held the half-empty mug of coffee in his hand and stopped to sip it. "Too many missing pieces of the puzzle," he argued. "Let's do this. Let's get the warrant for the house on Crabtree Lane and if he's not there then we'll head over to Blandino's Market and question Blandino himself. Maybe he can feed us some info on this punk."

With that, he summoned for the warrant and together with Manelli and the two other police officers, exited the station. As the lights blazed and the sirens blared, the squad vehicle moved with velocity. Wind and snow swirled around the car as it passed through the city streets. Massimo steered the vehicle into the Town Clerk's parking lot and changed vehicles immediately. He signed the necessary paperwork with the township and he and his men climbed into the four-by-four trucks and maneuvered the vehicles back onto the main road.

They turned onto left on Crabtree Lane, the snow crunching under the weight of the vehicles. It was with much difficulty that they finally found the trail that led to the house. They left the vehicles a few hundred yards away and exited. Massimo gripped his gun with his gloved hand and signaled to the men to silently surround the house. He walked around to the side of the home and spotted the storm cellar Laura spoke of that had allowed her escape. He looked for any sign of her flight, but the gusting winds had long since covered any footprints she may have made climbing out.

He walked back around to the front and ascended the rickety porch steps. He knocked on the door. He waited a moment and again signaled to his men that he was entering. He reached for the knob. The door was locked. He stepped back, lifted his large boot, and kicked the front door open. He aimed his gun as he slowly entered. Manelli covered his back, but no one appeared to be home.

Massimo gave the sign for two of his men to search the second floor. He and Manelli would search the main floor. They walked through the living room. Massimo slipped into the bathroom. The sink was splattered with blood, presumably Laura's.

They stealthily tiptoed into the kitchen with guns raised and muscles tense. The door to the basement was locked and barricaded with a chair. Massimo's face reddened with anger. He threw the chair out of the way in fury. After opening the door, he turned on the light and spotted the sticky blood at the bottom of the staircase, as well as the evidence of the nausea that came with a broken bone. They descended. The temperature in the basement dropped and Massimo saw where Laura had made her escape.

"Boss, check this out." Manelli called. He was peeking into the small hole Laura had escaped from.

Massimo stalked over. They both peered into the storm cellar. Snow and wind blew through the open doors. On the floor was the ice and heavy snow that had caved the door inward.

From up the stairs, the two other officers called down, "Chief, all is clear. The house is empty."

"Same here. Let's hit the store." Massimo jogged up the steps two at a time. His men followed him back outside and into their trucks. They drove back down Crabtree Lane. Making a right, they sped into Blandino's Market parking lot. Massimo huddled against the wind as he explained to his men their next moves. "Morgan and Lansing cover all the exterior entranceways. If you notice any disturbance inside, radio for back up. There's no way he's getting out of here, if he's in there at all. Manelli, you back me." They all nodded in agreement and took their positions.

Massimo and Manelli entered the store. They looked around the nearly empty market and spotted two men, one older, one younger, chatting behind the deli counter. Massimo's eyes clashed with the younger one's before he slipped away into the back room.

Massimo and Manelli approached the counter. The short older man nodded at them and smiled. "How may I help you, gentleman?"

"I'm Chief Desanti from the Cicero Police Department." He flashed his badge, as Manelli flashed his. "We're under the understanding that a Tony Warren is employed here. Are we correct?"

80

"What if he is?" the man asked. "What do you want with him?"

"I have a warrant here for his arrest for the aggregated assault and battery of Miss Laura Ann Marcs. Is he here?" Massimo's voice was cold and to the point.

The man's face paled. "What? That's ludicrous!"

Massimo stared the man down. "You gonna tell me where he is or do I need to arrest you for aiding and abetting?"

The shorter man stood his ground and faced the large chief. "Now hold your horses there. Do you have a warrant to search my store? What proof do you have?"

Through clenched teeth, Massimo seethed, "Miss Marcs appeared at the police station doorstep this morning at 6 A.M. She was nearly raped and badly hurt. She underwent surgery for a severely fractured arm. Not to mention, a broken rib, stitches, and a sprained ankle. Now I'm done stalling here. I assume you're Frank Blandino?" Massimo questioned.

"I am." Frank stated.

"Well, Mr. Blandino. Unless you want to be charged with aiding and abetting or obstructing justice, you better get his rear out here, now!" The chief began raising his voice.

"All right, I'll see what I can do," Frank said, near a whisper.

Moments later, Tony appeared with Frank. He seemed to talk nervously as he tried to explain what it was the police had told Frank about Laura. When he discovered that Massimo was still standing behind the counter, he froze. Tony glanced at Frank in anger, and then glared at the police officers. Suddenly, he dashed into the back room.

Tony ran quickly, but Massimo was quicker. He hurdled the counter top with Manelli close at his heels. They cornered Tony, who tried to escape. Massimo pushed him against the wall of the back room with his massive body. They struggled a moment, and finally, both Massimo and Manelli tackled him to the ground.

Massimo questioned, "I take it you're Tony Warren?" He pulled a pair of cuffs from his pocket and roughly placed them on Tony's wrists. "Well Mr. Warren, your running days are over." They dragged Tony to his feet. "What's the matter? You're not gonna ask why you're being arrested?"

They hauled him out of the back room and into the front of the store. "I didn't do anything!" Tony shouted in a rage. "Let me go," he protested.

"Does Laura Marcs ring a bell? Remember the woman you're supposedly so in love with? The one you hurt. You're going to jail for a long time, buddy."

They crossed the deli counter and Tony spat at Frank. "You!" he screamed. "You set me up. You told me they left!"

"Tony, please!" Mr. Blandino pleaded. "I'll get you a good lawyer. I promise." He shouted after them as the chief dragged Tony out of the front doors.

"You're going to pay for this, old man. You're going to pay!"

"Shut up!" Massimo spit the words out with venom. "The only one who's going to pay, is you! Now get in the car!"

Manelli began reading him his rights. Tony was placed in one of the two squad cars at the scene, and hauled off to the station. Massimo stood outside and watched as the vehicle drove away with Tony inside.

"Great job, sir." Manelli complimented. "I can't believe he tried to make a run for it. He had no chance against you, sir."

"When I get through with him, he's gonna wish he never laid eyes on that girl." Massimo jumped into his vehicle. The sirens shrilled across the quiet street, assuring the chief that Tony would no longer be a threat to society.

CHAPTER 10

The Belfords

Laura relaxed in the hospital bed staring at the ceiling. She prayed to God and asked Him if her life would continually be a tragedy. Numb and tired, she closed her eyes. Images of Tony flashed before her. She thought of his warm smile, his soft touch. She wondered what would become of him. She had gone over it in her mind repeatedly and still couldn't understand what it was that made him lose control.

She sighed and forced herself not to think of him. Laura glanced at the clock. It was six-thirty in the evening. Moments later, she heard a rap at the door and Massimo entered. His stubbly face smiled warmly, yet was unable to conceal the concern in his eyes. "Hi there. You okay?"

"I'm okay. Come on in."

"I wanted to keep you up-to-date on what's happening."

Laura's eyes lit up. She slowly sat up in her bed. "Fill me in."

Massimo sat and flipped open a notebook. "My men went to your old home. The cabin was empty. No sign of the deceased bodies of your family. In fact, the cabin was wiped clean."

"Wiped clean? What do you mean?"

"The evidence was disposed of. I'm still going to have forensics comb over the place. Come spring, we'll scavenge the premises and see if we can find any sign of their bodies."

"Well, the bodies wouldn't be in the cabin. The bodies are buried underneath a maple tree, next to the garden. Their remains should be there. I saw the graves myself, when Tony brought me there once to pay my final respects."

"Laura, you don't seem to understand. There is no evidence that even proves the killings happened. Like the cabin was scrubbed clean. No gun powder residue, no blood, not a hair follicle. We'll look for the bodies later. But that's not the point."

"Are you saying these people are professionals or something?" Laura shook her head. She was so puzzled and confused. Nothing made sense anymore.

"Precisely!" When she didn't question him further, Massimo continued. "We went to the house on Crabtree Lane and everything was as you said, though Tony was nowhere to be found. He had locked the basement door and barricaded it with a chair.

"Meanwhile, after running a few checks, we came to find that Tony has had no prior record. He's clean. It boggles my mind, but he has not even had so much as a moving violation. As for the deceased woman's name you gave us that appeared on the bills, well, for one: it was her maiden name; and two: the woman is *still* the owner of the home. Tony never purchased the house.

"Anyway, our only choice was to follow up at Blandino's Market. When we arrived, we spotted two men and confronted them. To make a long story short, we had a little struggle and arrested Tony. When we questioned him at the scene, he denied everything. Says he never laid a finger on you.

"When we arrived at the station, he was all frazzled and said he had no idea what we were talking about. He said he wanted to know where you were. I told him you were severely injured and in the hospital. Suddenly, he's putting on this act and he's all upset and crying that you were hurt. He even insisted on seeing you."

Laura began to cry.

"Please," Massimo pleaded. "Don't cry. Don't let this con fool you. I'm sorry, Laura. I know you believed him to be good. But if this guy is so nice, then why has he been lying to you and why did he do this to you?"

"I don't know," she responded. "I can't believe he never loved me. He had to."

"It's possible. But I still can't help feeling that there's something more. For now, you need to move on. An arraignment will be held in a few days. At the pretrial, Tony's going to either plead guilty or not. If he pleads guilty, things will go smooth and easy. He'll be tried and sentenced and he'll do time. If not, well . . . let's hope he does the right thing."

Laura thanked Massimo for his help and watched him exit her room. She closed her eyes and let her tears flow freely. The thought of Tony spending time in jail made her want to hurl.

Suddenly, it hit her. *Why was she feeling guilty?* She didn't put him in this dilemma. Laura became angry. He'd ruined their life together. He'd lied to her and he'd hurt her. Perhaps Massimo was right. Anger replaced the ache in her heart. She wiped the tears from her cheeks and made a promise to pick up the pieces, once again, and move on.

The following days for Laura however, weren't quite so easy. Still recovering in the hospital, she was weakened from continual nightmares and her recovery was slow. The only light in her life was the kindness portrayed by Massimo. Chief Desanti was a wonderful friend. He visited her often and even went as far as setting up a donation fund for her medical expenses. Generous people all over town donated and some even gave gifts. One family in particular, the pastor of her mother's church, came to visit her in the hospital. They brought her flowers and their hopeful words. Laura was astounded at their charity.

Within a few days, they'd gathered enough money to pay for most of her expenses. She later came to find that Massimo had paid a generous sum as well. She began to feel optimistic of her future. A few days later, the day of the pretrial, Massimo came by and informed her that Tony had pleaded guilty. His sentencing would be in a few weeks. That day, her feelings were erratic. She was upset to the point of needing sedation. After visiting with a psychiatrist, she began to understand that it would be a long healing process for her.

At last, the day of her discharge arrived. Massimo entered her room. He gave her a brief hug. "You're looking wonderful today!" He cheerfully stated.

Laura blushed. She had taken extra special care with her hair and makeup, hoping to lift her self-confidence. "Thanks." She sat in a chair, holding her broken arm, and sighed. "Chief, what's going to happen to me?"

"Laura, your psychiatrist says the best thing is to find yourself a home, full of loving people, who'll care for you. Therefore, the courts have decided that foster care is in your best interest. You're going to stay in a home a couple hundred miles from here. It's a wonderful place. I've checked into it myself. You'll be living with other girls your age and will be homeschooled. You'll be much better off there. This way you have a chance of getting adopted before you're 18 and starting over with a new family." She looked at him skeptically. "Trust me," he reassured.

*　　*　　*

Later that evening, Massimo's Volkswagen Beetle scurried down Interstate 90 heading east. Laura sat in the cramped vehicle, trying not to feel anxious. She glanced at the fogged window to her right, wiping it with her free hand. The roadway sped by, taking her farther away from the only place she'd ever called home. Brewerton was going to be but a distant memory. She shook her head to rid the melancholy thoughts. She glanced down at the purse in her lap. It was one of the gifts that had been given to her by the generous people of that little town—the town she was born in and grew up in. Now she was leaving and she was leaving alone.

With the exception of Massimo. Not only did he offer to pay a large sum of her medical expenses, but also took a day off to drive her to her new home. Laura looked at his side profile, watching him concentrate on the road ahead of them. He stole a glance at her and smiled reassuringly. "You nervous?" he asked.

"Yes," she simply stated.

"Well, don't be. You're going to be all right. Hopefully, a wonderful family will adopt you and you'll never be alone again. As for these foster parents, they have been fostering kids for 20 years. Bill is a pastor of a local church and his wife, Hannah, stays home to help with the foster children. I believe they are currently fostering three other girls. They have a large, respectable home on a couple acres of land, just near a large canal. I know you'll love it. You're gonna be fine!" Massimo reached over and patted her hand.

"Okay, so where is this place, anyway?" she asked, her curiosity finally aroused.

"In Little Falls. The way I drive, we'll be there in less than an hour."

"Just because you're a cop, that doesn't mean you can break the rules," she teased.

"You're right. I should be a model citizen," he cracked with a smile.

"What made you want to become a cop?" she curiously asked.

"Well, honestly?" he questioned.

She nodded.

"I grew up in a home with an abusive stepfather. Almost all of my childhood I watched him beat my mom. One day he went too far and killed her."

Laura gasped, the tears filled her eyes. "Oh, Chief, I'm so sorry!"

He reached over and placed his hand over hers. "Don't cry. It's okay. God has a reason for everything. Had those terrible things not happened, I would've never become a cop. Now, I'm stopping crime on a daily basis and fulfilling my purpose in life. That's why you can never give up. God has a plan for you, too, Laura. You have a chance to start your life over and make something of yourself. Do it!" He smiled and said, "Now, let's not talk about sad things anymore. Deal?" he extended his free hand.

Shyly, Laura took it and smiled back, "Deal." The rest of the drive was silent, but comfortable. They stopped for a bite to eat and then continued on their trek. Within the hour, they entered the city of Little Falls. They passed houses and medical buildings; pizza parlors and clubs; drugstores and gas stations.

Finally, they drove past a large gate and up a curving driveway. Massimo helped Laura with the small suitcase he'd given her. Together they ascended the porch steps shoveled clean from snow. Still limping from her sprained ankle, Laura leaned on her crutch. Massimo raised his hand to knock, but the stained-glass door was opened before he had a chance.

A tall woman wearing a gray dress greeted them. "Ah, Chief Desanti, please come in. This must be Laura," she assumed. "How do you do? I'm Hannah Belford."

"Nice to meet you," Laura responded. She shook the woman's cold hand. Gazing around the foyer in awe, Laura turned her attention to the house. It was large, yet cozy, as Massimo had said. The coffee-colored walls were decorated with pictures of smiling faces. To the left was the double doorway of a small library. Its wooden trim work was cherry-red covered with many books. Laura finally felt excited. She tried to focus on Mrs. Belford and Massimo.

They were led into the office to the right of the front door where they sat at the mahogany desk to sign some paperwork.

"Thank you so kindly, Chief. I'm sure Laura is thankful for the generosity you've shown her." Her gaze held Laura's.

Laura understood her insinuation. She stuttered, "O-o-of course, I am."

"Well, there's no need for thanks. It's my pleasure." Massimo patted Laura's shoulder comfortingly.

Mrs. Belford pursed her wiry lips together in a smile. "Well then, she should get along fine here."

After a brief tour of the first floor, Massimo turned and faced Laura. "I've got to be on my way, now." Laura's face crumbled. "Mrs. Belford, I'd like a moment alone with Laura. We'll step out the front doors. It was a pleasure to meet you and thank you. Please take care of our girl." He pumped the woman's hand vigorously and exited the home with Laura's hand in his.

The cold wind whipped Laura's hair and face, freezing the tears in the corner of her eyes. Massimo reached for her face and kissed her forehead. "I believe in you. You be strong and make a good life for yourself. Always remember to follow your heart. Okay?" Laura nodded. "May I keep in touch with you?"

"Definitely!" She smiled to cover the sadness she felt. He handed her his card. She took it happily. "Thank you for *everything!* I'll never be able to repay you for your generosity."

"I never asked for anything in return. Only that you take care of yourself." He extended his arm and Laura, still holding her crutch, clumsily embraced him. "Goodbye," she whispered.

"Goodbye." He quickly descended the steps and entered his vehicle. Laura watched it drive away. Feeling the cold penetrate her coat, she reentered the house.

Mrs. Belford was startled at the doors opening and Laura observed that she'd been peeking out the window. "Oh, you startled me." A hand held her heaving chest.

"I'm sorry, Mrs. Belford."

"Very well. I'll help you with your luggage. Follow me. I'll be showing you to your room, which you'll be sharing nicely with three other young women. They're around your age. You should get along very well." Her sentence felt more like an order than a suggestion.

Laura hobbled through the short corridor that led to a flight of stairs. She climbed the carpeted steps. To the left, a hallway led to two doors.

"Your room is the second on the right." At last, Mrs. Belford came to a halt at the door. She rapped on it and abruptly opened it.

The three young women were scattered about the large room, each engrossed in what seemed their schoolwork. Mrs. Belford stood in the doorway and clapped her hands sternly. "Excuse me! It would be most polite of you girls to greet your new roommate." Her voice was cold.

The first girl rose from the twin-sized bunk bed. "Well, why didn't you say so?" She peeked around the older woman's torso and reached for Laura's good arm, dragging her further into the room. "Hi," she announced, "I'm Tammy Springer." Laura smiled back at the girl with bushy eyebrows and bright brown eyes. Her pretty features hid behind large framed glasses. "You're going to share a closet and bunk with me."

"I'm Laura. It's nice to meet you." The shorter girl shook Laura's hand heartily.

"All right, Tam! Don't take her arm off," replied another. This girl was stunning in appearance. She kept her long blond locks tied in a ponytail and her green eyes shone as brilliant emeralds. Sauntering over to Laura— her tall slim figure swaying with each step—she introduced herself with an extended hand.

"I'm Barbara Brooks. You may call me Barb." She took a few steps back and allowed the third girl to present herself.

She had bright red hair, piled on her head in ballerina bun. Her fair white skin showed a faint sign of freckles. Angela was also taller and very slim, though her figure was quite fuller. She smiled at Laura with happy blue eyes.

"Hi Laura, I'm Angela Ventiglia. It's nice to finally meet you. We've heard a great deal about . . ." Barb quickly jabbed Angela with her elbow. "What I mean is . . ."

"Don't worry, Angela." Laura chuckled in spite of herself, not wanting Angela to feel uncomfortable.

"Well then," interrupted Mrs. Belford. "Now that the introductions have all been made, my work is done. Tamela, I expect you to show Laura around the house and make her feel as comfortable as possible. Make sure you show her the bathroom and . . ."

"I know, Mrs. Belford," she reassured the older woman as she walked her to the door. When the door was closed, Tammy fell against it and sighed. "My God, I thought she'd never leave," she whispered.

"Tell me about it, that old coot always overstays her welcome." Barb walked over to her bunk and plopped down. "Well, I hope you like it here, Laura. So far the three of us get along great."

Laura felt threatened, but quickly recovered. "Oh, don't worry. I'm pretty easy going." She smiled at them, feeling all eyes on her. She reached for her luggage with her good arm.

"Oh, here," Tammy offered. "You can put that here for now." Laura watched the small girl struggle with the luggage as she placed it on the bunk bed on the left side of the room. Between the two bunk beds, which were placed on opposite sides of the room, was a round table with four chairs. Next to each of the beds were large dressers. Tammy opened the top three drawers to her dresser and offered to help Laura unpack.

Tammy was sweet and helpful. She was quick to make Laura feel at home. Laura was already fond of her. "And here's the 'john'," Tammy stated as she walked her back into the hallway to the door next to their room.

Tammy opened the door. The sink was cluttered with makeup and hairsprays, labeled and placed in a compartment for each individual girl. "You can put your makeup and things in the empty bin," Tammy invited.

"Thanks." Laura glanced around and exited the small bathroom. In the bedroom, she found Angela humming a song on a portable radio and Barb painting her long nails on her bed.

"So," Angela spoke first. She turned the radio down. "You're from Brewerton? Isn't it in like the boonies?"

Laura nodded shyly. "It's . . . well, I guess you can say that it's nice and quiet. I liked it." Laura felt reluctant to speak of her past. "We have all weekend to talk about it," Laura added. "I'm really tired tonight."

"Yeah, Ang," began Barb. "Don't pressure her. She'll talk when she's ready."

Laura jumped in. "Well, I don't feel pressured. I understand your curiosity about me. It's still hard to talk about . . . things. And like I said, I'm feeling a little tired." She busied herself with unpacking to conceal her quivering chin and tear-filled eyes.

"That's fine," Barb added.

Laura nodded and smiled. "I just need some sleep. I've had a long day." The girls agreed and decided to turn in as well.

Meanwhile, Tammy gave Laura a rundown of the schedule the girls were kept on. They were homeschooled daily. No makeup or nail polish was to be worn during school hours. After school, they were to do homework until dinner.

After dinner and during their spare time, they could exercise in the small gym in the basement. When weather permitted, they were allowed in the yard to play basketball or volleyball, where nets were set up for each. When one wanted quiet time, the library was always available. It even had a typewriter they could use.

Tammy explained all this while they unpacked Laura's bag and then undressed for bed. Laura tried to remember it all and prayed she'd get used to the routine fast. When, at last, the lights were out and Laura was in her bed, she felt the emotions of the day begin to press. She tried to muffle her cries. Tammy suddenly reached down and patted her shoulders.

"Laura, what's the matter?" she softly asked.

Laura tried to speak, but couldn't. Her emotions were raw and she felt as though she'd burst. Trying to shut the faucet of tears off seemed near impossible. She needed a friend—not a nurse, not a cop, but a friend—a sister. Much like the one she should have been closer with—Patty.

"I'm sorry. I don't mean to keep you up." Laura felt another surge of tears burst from her soul.

"My God, Laura. What can I do to help?" Tammy sincerely asked.

"Hey, you two. What's going on?" Barb flipped the light switch on. All three of the girls looked at Laura in anticipation. They immediately appeared to understand her emotional outburst.

"I'm sorry, guys." Laura sat up holding her cast and wiped her wet face with her free hand.

"Can we help?" Angela asked.

Tammy jumped off the top bunk and sat next to Laura. "You know, I didn't think it would be so hard to start my life over. The second I close my eyes, Tony's all I see."

"Tony's that jerk, right?" Angela asked.

"You see, that's just it. A part of me hates him. I feel as though he *is* a jerk. Yet, I can't stop loving the way we were before. I know you must think

I'm totally nuts. But I'm not. I feel so lost. I've no family and I lost the man I love to the monster he became. I know it wasn't my Tony who hurt me."

"You mean you didn't see who attacked you?" Barb's eyes bulged.

"Of course she saw, stupid. She means that it didn't feel like the same person she was in love with," Angela answered.

"Exactly. Tony would've never laid a finger on me before. We were so much in love. You should've seen what it was like on the day he proposed to me. It was Heaven." She paused a moment and glanced at Tammy's hands holding hers. "Now," she continued, "he's in jail and he's out of my life, forever."

"Well, you're not alone. You have us. We're your friends and whenever you need anything, the three of us will be here." Tammy gave Laura a tearful smile.

"You can count on me as a friend, Laura." Angela sat next to Laura and gave her a peck on the cheek.

"And me. We'll call ourselves 'The Four Musketeers'!" The four girls laughed at Barb's enthusiasm. "Welcome to our humble abode." Barb hugged Laura briefly, and then kissed both of her cheeks in a European fashion. "Some home, huh? What do you think?"

"So far, so good," Laura stated. The smile on her face was genuine and she felt happy that her new roommates had accepted her.

"Did you get a load of Belford? She's so mean! She has serious issues." Laura secretly agreed with Tammy's statement. "Nothing we ever do is good enough for that woman."

Laura thought for a moment. "One thing I did notice is that she's nosey. I caught her spying on my goodbye to Sam."

Barb asked, "Wait a minute. Who's Sam?"

"Sam is the Cicero Police Chief, Massimo Desanti. He's called Sam for short." Laura glanced around at the girls' giggling faces. "What? What's so funny?"

"We're nosey too," confessed Tammy. "We knew you were coming today and wanted to sneak a peek at you. We peeped through the window and saw you and the chief getting out of the car. Boy, that Chief Mattimo sure is cute!" she exclaimed.

"It's Massimo." Laura corrected with a giggle in her throat. "But don't worry, I still can't get it right and just call him 'Chief'." The four girls laughed in unison. Laura added, "I'm glad you guys are so nice. Thanks for cheering me up."

Tammy jumped back up onto her bed and said, "Well, let me tell you, girl. When I first came here it was no peaches and cream."

"Can of peaches!" Angela corrected.

"Whatever!" Tammy continued, "For starters, four years ago I was involved in a bad accident with my parents. A drunk driver hit us head-on and my parents were killed instantly. I was severely injured. The doctors thought I'd never walk again. But I showed them. I worked my tail off 'til I regained control in my muscles and nerves. Now I can do dances around those doctors. Two years later, when I was better, they put me here. I had no family willing to take me in. It was hard adjusting. I know just how you feel. Then I met these two clowns!" She gave a laugh at Barb and Angela's frowning faces.

"I'm sorry about your parents, Tammy. That's terrible," Laura stated.

Barb informed Laura of Angela's and her own story. "Ang has been here for three years, since her guardian passed away. I've been here two years. The sixth home since I was a baby."

"And you've been the luckiest. No family to get attached to. No one dying on you, breaking your heart," added Angela.

"Tell me about it," Tammy and Laura both said in unison. Suddenly, they burst into laughter. Moments later, thunderous footsteps were heard in the hallway.

"Shoot. It's Belford doing her 'lights out' walk-through! Everyone hit the sack. Someone get the lights," Barb ordered.

The lights went out and the girls jumped into their beds, all the while trying to muffle giggles. Without warning, the door was thrust open.

Silence.

Finally, Mrs. Belford shouted, "Good night, ladies. Mr. Belford just arrived home and needs peace and quiet. No talking!" She closed the door.

Barb was the first to speak, whispering, "Meanie." The group couldn't contain their giggles.

That evening was the start of a wonderful friendship between the four young women—one that slowly mended aching hearts and consoled their lonely souls.

CHAPTER 11

Sisters

Laura's relationship with the girls deepened. The four young women grew closer with each day. Not only did they share a room, but their feelings, their hopes, and their dreams. Tammy, Barb, and Angela grew to love Laura.

The Belfords were quite the 'trip,' as Tammy well put it. Though Mr. Belford was also rather stern, he warmed up to Laura quickly. His Godly words of wisdom gave Laura hope and inspired her to have a closer relationship with God.

Because Laura had missed years of schooling, she was immediately tested to determine what grade she'd be positioned in. She was placed in the eleventh grade instead of the twelfth, which would've fit her age range. What pleased Laura most was that her aptitude tests ranked high, meaning that all of her studying with Tony had been worth the while.

After a few weeks, Laura truly felt her life coming to order. The swelling in her ankle had diminished and in less than two weeks, the cast on her arm would be removed. Emotionally, she still longed for Tony's love and she prayed he was getting the help he needed.

Before long, months passed and they were into the new year. The young women spent nearly all of their time together, yet rarely disagreed or quarreled. Like mature adults, if something upset one, they simply discussed it until all was settled.

One February evening, they sat quietly in their room. They had finished their chores and their homework early. Tammy stretched out on her bunk, and let out an obnoxious yawn. "Oh boy!" she shouted. "I'm gonna die of boredom."

Laura looked up from her bunk and added, "Me too!" She looked at the other two girls across the small room. "Let's do something. If I keep reading like this, I'll be blind before I'm 30." The girls stared at her blankly.

"And what do you suppose we do different?" Angela snapped. "It's the same routine, day in and day out. Go to school, come back, eat dinner, and do homework. It's enough to drive us insane," she exclaimed.

Unexpectedly, Tammy sat up. Her eyes lit up as she shouted that she had a wonderful idea. "Oh no," continued Angela. "If your idea is anything like the one you and Laura had on Christmas, you can forget it! If Belford would've caught us, we'd have been scrubbing toilets for the rest of our lives. And all for a lousy pizza we never got to eat!" The girls all laughed as they reminisced of their first Christmas together.

"Oh, come on, girls. Where's your sense of adventure? I don't want only Laura and me to sneak out. I want us all to sneak out." Her face shone with anticipation.

"You're nuts!" Angela exclaimed. She jumped from her bunk and ran across the room to Laura's bed. "But I love it!"

"I think you're all nuts," Barb added.

"Oh, come on, Barb." Laura rose from her bunk and sat up next to Tammy as well. "We'll get all dazzled up and go into that café in town, by the pizzeria we went to on Christmas."

"And do what? Watch a bunch of old fogies dance to that jazz crap?" Barb asked.

"No silly! Why watch them dance when you can join them!" Tammy stood and walked to her dresser. "What can I wear?"

"Are you delirious?" Barb exclaimed. "This is crazy." She watched as everyone ran to their dressers and closets to rummage through their clothing. "Well, I guess I better come. I'm certainly not going to let the three of you go by yourselves. Lord knows how much trouble you may get yourselves into, if I don't come. If it weren't for my common sense and . . ." Someone threw a pillow at Barb as she rattled off. "Hey!"

They all laughed in excitement as they prepared themselves for their outing. Laura borrowed a jean mini-skirt from Angela and matched a red cowl-neck sweater with it. She styled her hair and applied her makeup anxiously. Tammy put on a pastel pink sweater dress, which fell well below the knees. The color did nothing for her complexion, but she didn't seem to notice. Angela pulled out a beautiful green cable-knit sweater that clung to her shapely curves and coordinated a cream wool skirt with green shoes to match. Barb wore a tighter black skirt and a blue butterfly-collar shirt. They all busied themselves with hair and makeup until, at last, they were ready.

At ten o'clock when the lights were out, the girls opened the small window, took out the screen, and began to climb down the rosebush lattice. "Oh man!" cried Barb. "I hope I don't fall. I'm afraid of heights."

"Don't look down," Tammy encouraged in whisper. "Just keep moving your foot from one bracket to the next and hold onto the gutter for support." Slowly, they descended the rickety lattice. Someone whispered to tell the last person down to keep the window slightly open.

Finally, the foursome was safely on the ground. They buried themselves in their coats for warmth and walked along the house in the dark of the night. Upon reaching the street, they quickened their pace until they began walking toward the city. Once they were out of earshot, they sighed with relief.

"How did you and Tammy do this for Christmas? My heart is pounding a mile a minute," blurted Barb. "I feel like an escaped convict."

"Aww, it was nothing," stated Laura as she glanced at Tammy. They both winked at one another. Especially when they had the trouble they did climbing back up the rosebush lattice, which resulted in them dropping the pizza and defeating the purpose of their escapade. But they said nothing, for it was worth the risk to get out and do what other teens did.

"You guys will be so glad we did this. Sometimes you have to go out and make your own fun," Tammy stated.

They walked along the salted streets that led them into the city of Little Falls. Despite the cold weather, the four young women were enjoying themselves. The main road was brightly lit with streetlights.

"Isn't this great?" Tammy shouted with excitement. Her nose was red from the cold. "Hey Laura, remember the pizza boy?"

"How can I forget?" Laura smiled at Tammy, recalling the cute boy behind the pizzeria counter. "Hey, there's the café. Come on!" Laura pointed in the direction of the small café, not two more blocks into town.

They hastened their speed until they stood before the café doors. Tammy stopped and pulled the girls aside a moment. Her warm breath hazed in the cold crisp air. "Okay, gang. Let's put on our mature faces and go in there and act like women. Now, how much money do we have? Let's not exceed our budget." Everyone opened their wallets and withdrew their allowance money.

They counted it. "Okay, we can only order one two-dollar drink, each. Nothing alcoholic, we don't need to get carded," Tammy ordered.

"Yeah! Like we're gonna drink alcohol." Ang smacked Tammy's arm. They laughed as they entered the doorway.

The café was dimly lit, giving it a cozy atmosphere. It was surprisingly busy. They walked toward the live band that played and found a booth in which to sit. "This place is so cool," shouted Barb over the loud music. "I'm glad we did this."

"Told ya!" Tammy screamed back as she wiped the fog from her ridged eyeglasses. "Do we know how to have fun or what?" The girls giggled with excitement. A waiter came to take their order. They all agreed on a soda. He nodded and walked away. They sat and waited for their drinks. Tammy swayed to the music. Soon, they all were enjoying the jazz band and the altered atmosphere. Moments later, the waiter arrived with their sodas and they drank with delight. The foursome let loose and began to finally enjoy their evening out.

A short while later, a few booths away, a group of younger men gazed at the girls. Barb glanced their way and noticed their stares. "Oh, my Lord," she tried not to shout. "Don't look now, but a group of guys at that booth to my right, are staring at us." All three girls instantly strained their necks to see the booth of on-looking men. "I said 'don't look now'!" she barked.

The men smiled at Laura's table. The girls smiled back. Moments later, two of them rose and began to strut toward their table. The girls panicked. "Here they come!" Tammy squealed, "And one's looking right at you, Laura."

Laura felt herself shrink. "Don't panic," she heard someone say. "What harm can a dance do?"

"But I don't want to dance with anyone," Laura cried. "I can't even bear the thought of being in anyone's arms, but Tony's." She couldn't believe the words had left her lips. She was still in love with him. She tried pushing the thought from her mind and concentrated on the situation at hand. But she just couldn't focus.

"Just one dance . . ." Tammy's voice trailed off. The men approached the table.

"Good evening, ladies," the taller of the two spoke in a voice low and deep. "How are you?" He stared at Laura's flustered, yet smiling, face. The girls felt too intimidated to even answer. Their only concern was Laura. Then, as if the band had synchronized their timing with his, they began playing a slow song. "You wanna dance?" He extended his hand across the table at Laura.

She swallowed the lump that rose in her throat. Glancing at the others, she saw their smiles of encouragement. Gathering her nerve, she told herself it was one dance and rose from her seat. The other man stayed and flirted with the girls.

He led her to the dance floor, where he placed his arms around her waist. Holding her body tightly to his chest, he began to slowly move. "What's your name, beautiful?" his breath hot on her face.

She swallowed again, turning her head from his face. Looking at her table of friends, Tammy gave her the 'okay' signal, while Ang and Barb chatted with the other stranger. Only this time, she wasn't feeling as encouraged as before.

"Laura," she managed.

"Hi, I'm Bob," he said. Suddenly, he pulled her even closer. Their hips swayed from side to side. Soon his hands began to rub her back, and moved lower and lower until his hand rested above her buttocks. Laura panicked—he had gone too far. She lifted his hand from her rear.

"Not so fresh," she sang.

"A little friendly touching. Relax and enjoy," he stated.

"Just keep your hands above my waist line."

He chuckled arrogantly. "No problem," he added with a wink.

"It's been real," Laura said, pulling away and walking across the dance floor back to her booth of friends. She wiggled past the stranger who caught her frustrated look. He waved goodbye and walked away. "Can we leave, please?" Laura whispered. Tammy had witnessed the man groping Laura and was glad that she had embarrassed him by dumping him at the dance floor.

"No problem, sister!" Tammy defensively added, "Let's get outta this joint." The girls arose from their seats and exited the smoke-filled café, passing the group of men as they left. Laura overheard Bob say to someone that he didn't know what her problem was. She rolled her eyes and shook her head in disgust.

Outside, Laura felt herself trembling. Tammy hugged her. "I'm sorry, Laura. I should've never encouraged you to dance with him. He didn't seem like such a creep."

"Tammy," Laura advised, "How many times have I told you? Never, and I mean never, trust a beautiful face." Laura shook her finger as she scolded her friend.

"Okay gang," Barb whispered. "I don't know about you, but I've had enough excitement for one night. Let's get out of here."

They all agreed and descended the stoop to head for home. They walked in the shadows along the road as quickly as they could. Soon they were all eager to get back to their confined home. At first, it seemed as though their walk back would remain silent. Until Angela spoke, breaking the hush.

"You know, if Belford caught us, we'd be dead!"

"Well, we are breaking the rules," Laura admitted.

"Still, I tell you, she's just looking for any excuse to yell at us," Ang argued.

"Yeah, she is tough. But it's for our own good. Whether we want to believe it or not," Laura reasoned.

"Are you kidding me? That old bag won't stop until she can punish us the way she really wants to," she exclaimed. "She has no compassion and no understanding. How can she claim to be a Christian?" Laura frowned at Ang and Ang questioned her. "What?"

"Yeah, so she's tough. That's her job."

"Baloney, she's our 'mother.' She needs to set an example for us. What kind of example is she setting, when she can't even show a little love and compassion?" said Ang. "Well . . ." she paused a moment, glancing at Tammy and Barb. "What do you two think?"

They both shrugged.

"Something must have happened to her to make her this way," Tammy guessed.

"Precisely my point," Laura quarreled. "We're no one to judge Mrs. Belford. Only Jesus can judge her."

The others listened intently to Laura's viewpoint. Barb rubbed her cold hands together, as she added, "Laura, you're right. If she can't show love and compassion for us, do we treat her the same way? No."

"I'll have to agree with her too, Barb," Tammy said. "Treat others as you want to be treated."

Ang gasped, "I can't believe you guys. She doesn't do that for us!"

"Look," continued Laura. "We're all entitled to our own opinions. I know she's been mean and cold to us. But do we really know what's going on in her life, in her heart?"

Nobody answered and the rest of the short walk home was in silence. The tension finally began to ease when they began climbing the lattice. Tammy was the first to begin ascending. Midway up, one of the hinges broke loose. Tammy let out a howl. "*Shh!*" they all hissed. She quickly mounted the rest and climbed safely into the window. Moments later, she peered out the window and gave the 'okay' sign to the others. "Coast's clear," she whispered.

Barb began to climb her way to the window. Laura reached for Angela's arm and held it. "Are you mad? You're too quiet." They watched Barb take baby-steps up the lattice.

"No, I just hate to admit when I'm wrong. I actually admire you for voicing your opinion. It takes guts." The girls hugged when they suddenly heard a loud screech. Barb had loosened another hinge and now hung in mid-air.

From in the window, Tammy tried reaching for the loose lattice. Barb held on for dear life, all the while Laura and Angela tried to keep from laughing. "Hang in there, Barb. I've got it," Tammy said, while she strained to reach the lattice, grasping it in time. Barb quickly ascended it and climbed through the window to safety.

"It's not funny!" she called out the window, while Ang and Laura began climbing up as well.

"Shh!" They muffled their giggles. Tammy tried quieting Barb, but she was furious.

"My life was in danger," she cried, "And all you could do is stand there laughing."

"Chill out, Barb. You're okay, now," Ang reassured as she replaced the screen and closed the window. "Man, it's cold."

Laura shuddered, "The room is freezing. We should've never left it open."

"Don't worry," assured Tammy. "It'll heat up, again."

Ultimately safe in their room, the girls relaxed and began undressing and preparing for bed. Angela washed her face in the bathroom, Tammy put her clothes away, and Laura was already under the covers. Barb still shook from her adventure. "So," Tammy whispered to Laura, "You and Ang okay?"

"Oh yeah. We had a difference of opinion. It doesn't mean we're angry with each other." Laura rustled her feet under the covers. "I'm still freezing."

Angela exited the bathroom and the girls all climbed into bed. In the darkness, they spoke of their little escapade. "Laura," Ang asked. "Who taught you all that . . . stuff?"

"What stuff?" Laura questioned.

"That God stuff? I mean, you're so kind to everyone. You even stick up for Mrs. Belford. I've even seen you talk about Tony with love in your eyes and he's put you through so much heartache."

"Ang, I do forgive Tony because I can't accept in my heart that he was in the right state of mind when he hurt me. Hey, if Jesus forgives me for my sins when I'm truly sorry for what I've done, shouldn't I love others the way He loves me? The same applies for Mrs. Belford.

"As for who taught me about God . . . well, the ironic part is, Tony did. So did my mom. She always taught me to 'treat others as I want to be treated'. That puts a lot into perspective for me. Sometimes," Laura stated with sadness in her voice, "I wish I would've listened better to what my mom used to tell Patty about boys. When I look back, I realize what a great role model Patty was for me. Guys were always flocking around her and she handled it with such control. I really miss her. Even if she was sometimes hard, she was very wise and always listened. Momma gave her some good insight."

"Like?" Tammy asked.

"Like . . . waiting 'til you're married to make love to someone."

"Laura," Barb interrupted, "You loved Tony. You were with him for three years, under the same roof, in the same bed. I'm surprised it never happened."

"It doesn't matter. We shared a bed, when he had a separate bed to sleep in. All making out with Tony did was make my bond with him even stronger. It made it all the harder when he hurt me. Just because we never made love, that doesn't mean that I should've allowed myself to get that close to him. If I hadn't, maybe my heart wouldn't still be breaking over him."

"I guess you have a good point. But don't kill yourself over it. God forgives you if you're truly sorry, right?" Ang asked.

"Yes," Laura simply stated. "That doesn't mean there's no consequence."

Laura lay restlessly. She stared at the ceiling. The events of the evening brought Tony to mind. *Would she ever stop thinking of him? When would the time come that she could really move on without him?*

The memory of their first kiss flashed through her mind. Her heart suddenly felt heavy. Only God could help her move on. To reassure herself, she put her hands together in prayer.

CHAPTER 12

Grisly Goodbyes

Three months later when May drifted in, so did more spring rain and gloom. The unforgettably long winter didn't want to retreat, leaving almost all of New York under clouds and wetness. But this made no difference for the foursome in the Belford foster home. They made having fun a habit. And though the evening out to the café was their last, they didn't let that stop them from enjoying one another's company.

At least until the dreaded day of May 10, 1977—a day the girls had been distressing over since they bonded in friendship. But what had happened was unavoidable and beyond their control. Matters were left in God's hands and the hands of a determined and bitter Mrs. Belford.

That morning, the young women walked down the stairway of the second floor. They discussed homework and exams. As they passed the front door, Tammy's eye caught sight of a handsome couple sitting behind the glass doors of Mrs. Belford's office. She gasped.

"What is it, Tammy?" Laura asked.

"It's them. They're back." Her face paled and she quickly raised the glasses on the bridge of her nose to see clearer.

"Who's back? What're you talking about?"

"Over nine months ago that couple came to meet me. They were looking to adopt me, but you know how long the process takes. Since I never heard anymore, I assumed they'd changed their mind."

No one could speak. They quickly walked back up the staircase and into their room in silence. Tammy threw her backpack onto her bed and glanced at Laura. Laura's eyes filled as she extended her arms to hug her dear friend.

"Don't worry! Remember, God's will, not ours. For the past few years, all we've wanted was a family to love. This may be your only chance. Don't let the fear of change stop you."

Tammy stiffly nodded, "If this is really it, I guess I shouldn't complain. Those people are nice. Yet, I can't even think about being without you." She let out a sob and ran to the bathroom.

Angela hugged Laura, who tried desperately to stifle her tears. "You'll still have us."

"I know and I'm so thankful for both of you." She reached for Barb's hand as well. "It's just that Tammy and I have gotten so close, the same way the two of you have always been. She's the sister I lost four years ago." They nodded in understanding.

The girls tried to go about their normal routine, but the tension was unmistakably there. Tammy walked around on eggshells, jumping at every sound. Rightly so, for without warning, the bedroom door was thrust open.

Mrs. Belford walked into the room. Her face was cold as ice, hard as flint.

"Clean up this room!" she bellowed. "You have visitors, Ms. Tamela, and I want all of you and this room to be in proper form." She pivoted and exited the room, slamming the door.

Staring at the closed door, Tammy stood in shock. The girls came around her and tried comforting her. Laura walked her to the table, and sat next to her. She tried hard to keep from breaking down. Once again, it was happening. She was being torn away from someone she loved.

The three girls felt helpless as they sat around the table staring blankly at the door. No one spoke. Moments later, a harsh knock startled them and the door was thrust open. Mrs. Belford entered. Her eyes swept the room. She glared angrily at the girls. At once, she put on her rehearsed smile and turned to the couple who stood in the doorway.

The woman had short dark hair, a startling pair of black eyes, and red painted lips. She was slender and petite and the most elegantly dressed lady Laura had seen. The man was tall and handsome. His light brown hair was feathered back fashionably, giving him a young appearance. His bright hazel eyes complimented his bearded face. He was also slender and fit and was dressed in a professional business suit. But Laura was familiar with these same characteristics—pleasing to the eye, but not pleasing to the soul. She eyed him skeptically, wondering what kind of father he would make.

"Please," Mrs. Belford interrupted her thinking. Her lips were tightened into a smile, "Do come in, and don't mind the mess. The girls just finished school and haven't had the chance to tidy up." The man led his wife into the room. They smiled at the four frightened girls. "As I'm sure you recall," Mrs. Belford continued, "This is Tamela."

On quavering legs, Tammy stood and greeted them. "Hello. I didn't think we'd meet again," she managed.

"Hi Tammy," the woman stated cheerfully. "It's wonderful to see you again." She gave Tammy a sincere hug. "You remember me, don't you? I'm Marlene and this is my husband John." Tammy slowly nodded.

"Shouldn't you introduce your friends?" Mrs. Belford ordered.

"Oh, yes. These are my best friends: Laura, Angela, and Barbara. They're like family to me," she added.

"It's nice to meet you all. It's comforting to know that you're so close." Marlene added.

After a moment of awkward silence, Mrs. Belford offered them a seat. The girls rose from the chairs and allowed the couple to sit with Tammy and Mrs. Belford. "Ladies, why don't you head to the library and start your schoolwork? Give the Knights some private time with Tamela," Mrs. Belford said.

"Please," Tammy pleaded. "Do you mind if they stay?"

"Whatever makes you happy, sweetie," John stated.

"Thank you."

Marlene Knight spoke again with the softest of voices. "The last time we met, we didn't get a chance to get to know one another. Let's do that today."

"Sure."

"Well, for starters," began John, "You know it's been nine months that we've been going through all the necessary paperwork for the adoption process."

"Yes," Tammy uttered. "I recognized you right away today, as you sat in the office."

"Oh, good. We'd hoped you'd remember us. We've been looking forward to this meeting. I hope you've been as well."

"I had no idea you were still interested."

"Mrs. Belford?" John asked in a stern voice. Laura wondered if they were about to see some of his true colors.

"Oh. Well, we don't like to give the children false hope," she stammered.

"But I thought it was policy to make the children aware of the status of their adoption," John pressed.

"Not necessarily," Mrs. Belford replied.

"Well, I'm sorry you weren't notified, Tammy. We were under the assumption that you were," Marlene said.

"That's okay. Maybe it was better this way," Tammy managed.

"Go ahead, dear. Tell Tammy our story," John encouraged. Laura was surprised to see the gentle manner with which he spoke to his wife.

"Where was I? Oh yes, anyway, John and I were married about 16 years ago. I was 28 and John was already 33."

"Nothing like giving away my age, dear," John smiled. Everyone giggled. Laura couldn't hide the smile on her lips.

"Sorry, honey. Anyway, we tried to conceive for almost ten years. I had three miscarriages within the first seven years. The last one caused major complications and I was forced to have a hysterectomy. We were devastated, of course. We tried concentrating on our business and it worked for a few years. But nothing could fill the gap in our hearts and the emptiness in our home. At this point, it didn't seem to make sense, me in my forties and John nearing his fifties, to adopt an infant. John and I consulted with our family. John has a younger brother who has two boys. We wanted advice from someone with teenagers. Since I'm an only child and both my parents are already gone, I really rely on John's family for support. After speaking with them, it was all set.

"That's when we began a search for foster children in the United States. When we came across your file and had heard of your terrible loss, we couldn't get you off our minds. We know we can be good parents to you. Would you give us a chance?"

Tammy took a chance and began *her* story. "I'm really sorry you've been through so much. I think I understand how you feel to want a family so badly. I feel the same way. After losing my parents in that accident, I didn't think I'd ever have the love of a family, again. I wish I'd died in that car crash, especially when none of my distant relatives were willing to take me in. Once I got here and met up with Ang, Barb, and recently with Laura, I began to feel as part of a family again. We love each other like sisters.

"Now, I don't know if I can bear the thought of losing them. I know you'd be wonderful parents, but it would be at the cost of my relationships with my sisters. I don't think I can do that." Tammy bowed her head and let the tears spill from her eyes.

Laura ran to her side and gently patted her back. "Please don't cry. It'll be okay," she encouraged in a whisper.

"Oh, John, I can't endure this heartbreak. What're we to do?" Marlene's eyes filled with tears.

"Ms. Tamela, you don't have a choice in the matter!" Mrs. Belford sternly proclaimed.

"Yes, she does, Mrs. Belford," John implored. "We'd never force her to come with us unwillingly. We'll simply adopt one of the other girls as well."

Both Mrs. Belford and Marlene's eyes lit up. "John, do you mean it?" Marlene stammered. Laura was also surprised.

"Absolutely! We have the money and the room. Now it's up to Mrs. Belford to do her part." He looked at her questioningly.

"Well, I don't foresee a problem. You've already been through most of the crucial procedure for Tammy's adoption. I may be able to push the paperwork along and have the adoption process hastened. In less than a month, or maybe two, we could have one of these fine young ladies ready for adoption."

"That's just what I wanted to hear, Mrs. Belford. A generous donation would be made in your honor if you stand by your word. The question is . . . who?"

The group of girls looked around to one another and then to Tammy, who had dried her pale face. Tammy, Laura, Barb, and Angela exchanged confused looks. *Who would be chosen?* They were all close.

Laura panicked a moment. She panicked for Tammy, fearful she might be moving into a home that might not love her the way she deserved. *Who were these people, seeking to adopt a young teen as opposed to a younger child? Were they looking more for someone who would get stuck caring for them as they aged? Or perhaps they were really looking to get some young girl who was old enough to be more a servant girl than a daughter?* Either way, she loved Tammy too much to let her get into this alone. Without being too obvious, she hoped to give Tammy a hint that she would take the chance and go with her. She kneeled down and clasped Tammy's hands.

"Whoever you choose as your sister, I want you to know that we all love you and none of us would feel hurt by your decision. You'll always be a sister to me."

"No," Tammy cried. "I can't make this decision. I love all of you the same. Sure, Laura and I have grown close because we bunk. But Barb has been orphaned most her life. I-I-I can't do it . . . I simply can't!"

"Well, then," Mrs. Belford interrupted, "Since you can't decide, may I suggest Ms. Laura? You claim to have grown close with her."

"If that's okay with both girls, we'd be blessed to have you both," Marlene stated. Tammy smiled. Laura choked back her fear and smiled at her reassuringly. Marlene's face lit up with glee. She stood and took the hands of the both of them. "You both would be the best thing that ever happened to us." She embraced them and turned to face Mrs. Belford. "When may we pick up our daughters?"

"I'll get on it as soon as possible. Once the approvals are made by the state, and the inspections pass to have Laura added to the household, it won't be long at all."

* * *

It took the paperwork process another two and a half months. Mrs. Belford said she had plenty of red tape to cut through to have the second adoption process go faster. By mid-July, the girls had grown accustomed to the idea of having to part. The date had been set for July 23.

The eve of the adoptions arrived. The mood was somber and no one spoke. Laura and Tammy's small luggage were already placed at the door. Tammy, Laura, Angela, and Barb sat at the table playing one last card game of Rummy. They sat in silence, all of them afraid to speak of what the next day would bring. The doorknob turned and Mr. and Mrs. Belford entered. They walked into the room, scrutinizing every inch of it. Mrs. Belford spotted the luggage at the door and smiled.

With a surprisingly gentle voice, she began, "Laura, Tammy?" The girls ignored her. "I know at times I've been hard. But I want you both to know that I've always wanted what's best for you and that I'll miss you both . . ."

Laura's blood nearly came to a boil. Unable to remain composed, she blurted, "You just couldn't wait until we all turned of age, could you? Did it ever occur to you that maybe we didn't want to be adopted? That maybe we wanted to all find a place of our own, and live like real sisters. How do we know what kind of people these are? What if they're not as nice as they seem?"

Mr. and Mrs. Belford seemed stunned by Laura's outburst. Her friends were as well.

Mr. Belford stepped forward. "That's no way to speak to my wife, Laura. We understand that you're upset, but we only want what's best for all of you."

Laura continued, "We don't know that for sure. I've been there when your own parent don't give a lick about you! What makes you think some stranger is going to love us? And what of Ang and Barb? What might this do to them?"

"Why do you think the adoption process takes so long, Laura? Did you think we would just throw you out to the wolves? We research each parent and both Marlene and John Knight are very reputable. They've been seeking adoption for quite some time. You are going to a good family!" Mr. Belford insisted.

Mrs. Belford stammered with the iciness back in her voice, "What I did, I did so you wouldn't be separated. If this is the thanks I get, well then . . ." she turned on her heel and left the room.

Mr. Belford shook his head in disappointment. "Despite what you think, we will miss you both." He turned and followed his wife out the door.

Dumbfounded, the girls looked at Laura. At last, they understood the capacity of love she felt for them. Recklessly, Barb began to cry. Angela joined in on the sobbing. Soon, they all howled. Laura began to laugh through her tears. The three stunned girls looked at her.

"What's so funny?" Barb nasally asked.

"What a bunch of babies." She willed her tears to stop, but they wouldn't. "I'm really going to miss you two." They embraced one another.

That night, after 'lights out,' Laura, Tammy, Barb, and Angela sat underneath the window and talked until the morning hours. They devoted one last night to dreams and fears and hopes and fantasies. When morning arrived, they were all physically and emotionally exhausted. Tammy and Laura prepared to leave, while Ang and Barb dressed and began their daily schedule. At last, the Knights arrived and it was time to go. The foursome walked down the stairs for the last time.

Upon reaching the foyer, Laura asked if the others might be able to join them outside. Despite the words said earlier, Mrs. Belford agreed. Outside, the sun's rays spilled across the front lawn. Laura closed her eyes and savored the warmth.

Meanwhile, John placed the luggage into a rusty old station wagon parked in the driveway. "Okay, ladies, we're all set." A smile played on his handsome face. He climbed the porch steps and joined the group. "Remember," he continued, "just because Tammy and Laura are leaving, that does not mean you four will never see one another again. Laura and Tammy will be able to visit here as often as you'd like." Everyone was thrilled to hear his words.

Laura turned to face Angela and Barb. "I promise I'll write you all the time. Let's never lose touch. I love you," she whispered to Ang and they hugged. "And you, Miss Barbara – I love you, too." They embraced.

Tammy said her goodbyes, as well. It was tear jerking to watch them part after so many years together. She even embraced Mr. and Mrs. Belford and bid them farewell. Laura reached for Tammy's hand and they descended the porch steps. John and Marlene followed.

Suddenly, Laura stopped. She couldn't leave knowing her last words to Mrs. Belford were so harsh. She turned to face her.

"Mrs. Belford?" Laura called. She ran back up the steps. "I can't leave without saying goodbye. I'm sorry."

"Oh dear." Hannah Belford blew her nose into the already wet hanky and smiled. "Say no more. I understand and I just want you to know that I'm happy you have found a family. I know they will be good to you!" She pulled Laura into a hug. "Goodbye, my dear. You need to run along. The Knights are waiting for you."

"Goodbye, Mrs. Belford. Thank you!"

"God bless you," she called out.

Laura hugged Mr. Belford and thanked him as well, then kissed Barb and Ang one last time, before she dashed down the steps. She took one last look back. It seemed like yesterday that she'd arrived with Massimo and now she was leaving with a built-in family. Thinking of Massimo, she made a mental note to contact him once she was settled.

A cool breeze crept down the nape of Laura's neck, sending a shiver down her spine. She waved to her friends as she entered the Oldsmobile station wagon. When the engine revved, she felt a pang in her stomach. This was it. She was starting over, yet again. A new life.

Would it be one that she'd always dreamed of? With a nice home, a father who would strive to make ends meet, a mother much similar to the one she'd lost, and a best friend for a sister? Would Laura go back to public school, meet new friends? Would her senior year be as great as she'd always hoped? Only time could tell.

Laura closed her eyes and said a quick prayer, hoping that the answers to all her questions would ultimately be . . . a resounding YES!

CHAPTER 13

Healing Hearts

The rusty old station wagon drove the new family east on Interstate 90 toward the city of Albany. Laura and Tammy stared excitedly out of the vehicle's windows. In the front, Marlene and John chatted, occasionally pointing out points of interest to the quiet girls in the back. An hour later, when they finally exited the dreadfully long highway, the girls sighed in relief. According to the signs, they were now heading south on Interstate 87. Minutes later, they exited that expressway and made a left onto a street that led them into a more urbanized area.

After a few more turns, they entered a small neighborhood of elegant homes. They passed a sign that read, 'Welcome' at the entrance. John slowly brought the vehicle to a halt at a stop sign.

"This is our community," Marlene merrily announced. "I hope you both like it here. John and I moved in about four months ago. We got tired of our small house and when we knew the adoption was near finalization, we purchased the home we'd been dreaming of." She giggled when she glanced at John and added, "Now all we need is a new car. This old thing can't last forever, hon." She patted her husband lovingly on the back.

"I know Mar, but you know how much I love this car." He gave the girls a quick glance and stated, "It was my father's, and after he passed away, I couldn't find the heart to sell it." Marlene and John exchanged glances. She shook her head at her husband's sentiment. "Would you like to walk the rest of the way?" he joked.

"You'd never!" Marlene gasped. She playfully slapped his forearm. Laura and Tammy couldn't help but laugh. It was evident that their new parents were still crazy for one another.

At long last, John maneuvered the old 'boat' into the driveway of their beautiful newly built home. "We're here," husband and wife sang. John pulled the vehicle into the side entrance garage.

The family stepped out of the vehicle following Marlene outside to the front of the house. Tammy and Laura gazed at the exterior of the home in awe. Marlene began the grand tour. "As you see, we just finished the landscape." The two nodded in approval. The white colonial home was enormous. She led them up the porch steps. "What do you think?" she asked.

"What do we think?" Tammy repeated. "It's beautiful."

Laura leaned up against one of the porch's two-story pillars and allowed her eyes to absorb the neat design of the landscape. Even the grass was perfect. This was just too good to be true.

"We'll go into the house from here," Marlene announced. She inserted the key and opened the front door. John rushed in with their luggage and placed them in the large foyer.

Tammy and Laura entered behind him. A colossal 'Welcome Home' sign hung from the second floor balcony. Tammy's eyes filled up. Laura still couldn't believe what she was seeing. They turned to their new parents and thanked them with emotion.

"Oh, quit your blubbering!" John cried, as he wiped his own eyes. He hugged them both as Tammy giggled with delight. Laura couldn't help but stiffen in his arms. She hated to admit that he did seem wonderfully humorous and easygoing. She prayed it was sincere.

At last, they gazed around the first floor, amazed at the home's elegance. It even smelled new with fresh paint and oak trim. Ahead was a grand staircase that proceeded to the second floor. To the left of the staircase was the living room. An archway separated the living room with a dining area near the back of the home. To the right of the staircase was a hallway leading to the kitchen, laundry, and garage. The first floor was painted in light shades of blue and a rich burgundy. The mahogany oak furniture and woodwork harmonized, giving the home a rich appearance.

John and Marlene continued to walk them through the house. They escorted them first through the living room. The corduroy blue couch and loveseat were arranged around a mammoth entertainment center, complete with a television, stereo, and a library of books, music albums, and eight-track tapes. Accompanying the couch, loveseat, and entertainment center were ornate end tables, duplicating the woodwork in the room. The finishing touch was a realistic artificial tree decorating the large bay window, draped in matching corduroy blue curtains.

Through the living room, they entered the dining room area. Laura had never seen such exquisite taste in decorating. The blue from the living room tied into the dining area as well. The redwood trim and furniture carried over. The dining table appeared at least eight feet long, with eight dining chairs. The table was set with eleven six-piece plate settings. It looked as though they were anticipating guests. Candles and flowers also decorated the table as centerpieces.

From the dining room, they entered the warm-hearted kitchen. Again, the blue and mahogany colors were worked into the décor. The kitchen even had a smaller breakfast nook overlooking a beautiful yard. Tammy and Laura both gaped in amazement.

As Marlene and John gave the tour, they made the girls feel welcome and comfortable. John offered them a drink.

"Actually," Tammy announced with a giggle, "I need a bathroom."

Marlene showed her to the bathroom right of the nook and returned. She sighed and then smiled at Laura, who still shook her head in amazement. "Do you really like it?"

"How can I not? If you could've seen the house . . ." she scoffed at her own words. "If you could even call it a house, the shack I lived in most of my life, was the size of this kitchen alone. This is truly beautiful, Mrs. . . ." Laura paused a moment. It dawned on her at that moment that she didn't know what to call her adoptive parents.

Marlene abruptly jumped in. "Oh, please. I don't want to seem too pushy, but we'd absolutely be honored if you'd call us 'Mom' and 'Dad'. That is, of course, if you feel comfortable doing so. Otherwise, call me 'Marlene'."

Laura gave Marlene a reassuring smile. "It may take a little getting used to, but I don't think that will be a problem at all." Marlene reached out and hugged Laura, who squeezed her back in return. "Thank you so much for adopting me too. Both Tammy and I just couldn't part. We've both lost too much." Marlene nodded in understanding.

John poured an iced tea for everyone and they chatted a few moments before they continued the tour of the home. Both Marlene and John mounted the staircase in the foyer, with Laura and Tammy following closely.

John placed the luggage in the hallway near two doors to the right. To the left was the master bedroom and bathroom. In John and Marlene's room, they had a rosewood bedroom set placed between two large windows that gave the room an airy feel. It was custom decorated in mauve hues, with a plush dark mauve carpet and light mauve sheers draping their canopy bed and windows. The room in its entirety was majestic.

Across from the master suite, were two additional bedrooms each equipped with a full-size bed, nightstand, dresser, and a vanity. The room closest to the stairway was decorated in a soft yellow and the other in a dusty green. Tammy bounced in excitement while Laura stood mesmerized by the enormity of it all.

"I don't believe we have our own rooms!" Tammy squealed in delight.

"Well, pick one!" Laura asked.

"It doesn't matter to me. I'm thankful just to have one." Everyone snickered at Tammy's melodrama.

Marlene stepped in. "May I give you my opinion?" Of course, the girls were happy to hear her view. "I see Tammy in the dusty green and Laura in the yellow. Tammy's full of life, which green is the color of. And Laura is full of sunshine, like the color of the sun. That's what I imagined when we decorated the rooms." It was settled.

Both Tammy and Laura beamed as they raced for their luggage and entered their rooms. Marlene and John stood in the doorway and admired the young women as they examined their bedrooms.

"You see," John continued, "It was perfect for us to adopt you both. We had the extra space and God has blessed us financially. Now we have a complete family. Something Marlene and I have been dreaming about since the moment we were married." They looked lovingly at one another and hugged. It would take some getting used to, seeing parents who expressed their love so openly.

Moments later, the doorbell rang. John scurried down the stairs to answer it. "Food's here," he shouted. The Knights had planned a 'Welcome Home' party for Tammy and Laura. Marlene called the girls down as she helped the caterer assemble the food on the counter. Like clockwork, the doorbell rang again and family and friends filled the home in anticipation.

"Laura, Tammy," John shouted as he waved a hand to have them come. "Let me introduce you. Joe, these are my girls, Laura and Tammy. Girls, this is my little brother, Joe, and my lovely sister-in-law, Bernadette."

"Oh, John, you're such a kiss-up," jested Bernadette. The young women shook hands happily. "Get used to this jokester. You're going to love him."

"We already do," Tammy exclaimed.

"And their sons, my favorite nephews . . ." John continued.

"You mean your only nephews," one proclaimed.

"No, my favorite nephews," he answered as he ruffled the hair of the boy who spoke. "This is Peter and this young man is Michael." The younger boys shook both Tammy and Laura's hands.

John and Marlene introduced them to another couple, who were their business partners and best friends, Marco and Paula Apolone. As they were about to sit for dinner, the doorbell rang once again, and a man dressed in priestly attire entered.

"Ah, Father Bill! I'm so glad you could make it. You're just in time." John introduced the man to the two girls and found a seat at the table. "Father, would you do the honors of a blessing?"

The young priest crossed himself and bowed his head in prayer. "Heavenly Father, we're delighted today to share in the homecoming of these two lovely ladies. We ask that You continually bless them with Your goodness and love. We pray for John and Marlene to be a strong, Christian influence in their lives. And that You bless this food, Lord, which comes from Your bounty. Through Christ Jesus, our Lord, Amen."

'Amen' was heard across the table and everyone began to eat. Laura watched as if from another world. *Was this truly happening?* A surge of thanksgiving poured into her heart. The family really did seem sincere. Tammy noticed tears in her eyes and also became emotional.

She stood in the midst of the passing of food and declared that she wanted to make a toast. Glasses rose as she began. "I think I can speak on both mine and Laura's behalf when I say this. But I don't think that either one of us could've imagined being a part of a family such as this. Sitting at this table amongst our new parents, family, and friends fills my heart with so much happiness. I don't know about you, Laur, but I never imagined I could find this, again. Thank you, Mom and Dad. May God bless you."

"Here, here," everyone cheered. Marlene's smile filled with gladness as she rose from her chair and embraced Tammy and then Laura. Everyone cheered to see the moving moment. The evening continued to flow with ease. After dinner, the group gathered in the living room where Uncle Joe and Aunt Bernadette, along with the Apolones, had gifts awaiting the girls.

Aunt Bernadette sat the two young women next to her on the couch and handed them each a small box and card. "This is too much," Laura began to protest. "You've all been too kind."

"You be quiet and open that gift, young lady. That's an order coming from your favorite Aunt Bernadette."

Laura and Tammy giggled as they opened their gifts. Both girls received a gold necklace with a charm divided in two that read, 'Sisters Forever'. They embraced Aunt Bernadette and Uncle Joe and immediately placed the necklaces on one another.

Mr. and Mrs. Apolone both handed them another gift. The girls scrambled to get the wrapping off. They gasped at the elegant watches.

Laura's memory flashed back to the year before, when Tony had given her a similar watch as a gift for her 17th birthday. Her heart ached a moment. Quickly recovering, she gave them thanks.

"So," Uncle Joe stated, "Did John and Marlene tell you how they came to meet, centuries ago?" The girls chuckled as they shook their heads. Before long, Joe began telling stories of times past. He had the group in a clamor.

"You should've seen the look on my brother's face when I introduced him to Marlene. My big brother needed to be scraped up off the floor."

"Oh, come on, Joe. Don't exaggerate," John begged.

"Exaggerate? You couldn't talk the first half-hour without stuttering or mumbling." Everyone laughed, including John.

"Well, with a knock-out like this, what did you expect?" John embraced his blushing wife. There was an 'aww' and someone yelled to have the wedding album pulled out. Before long, old photos were being passed around and Laura and Tammy got a closer look into their new parents' lives.

Uncle Joe and Mr. Apolone cracked jokes and helped to make the evening even more enjoyable. At one point, they cornered the girls and began giving them advice on how to handle John.

"Just bat your eyelashes and he'll melt like butter. It works for Marlene," Marco joked.

"Hey, I'm not that big of a push over," John defended.

"He's in denial," both Marco and Uncle Joe agreed, leaving Laura and Tammy in stitches.

Later, as the evening came to a close, the guests filed out. Tammy and Laura thanked them as they escorted them to the door. Alone, at last, Laura and Tammy entered the kitchen to help Marlene with the clean-up.

"Oh no! You two are exhausted. Let me and John clean up and you both go get ready for bed."

"No way, Mom. You did this for us. We can't leave you with this mess, no matter how tired we are," Tammy argued. They both insisted until Marlene gave in.

Before long, the first floor was back in order and Marlene and John nudged the girls up the staircase. They slowly ascended together. Tammy turned to Laura, "Aren't they incredible?"

"Too good to be true."

"Did you see that spread they put out?" Tammy's brown eyes bulged in exaggeration.

"Unbelievable. What did you think of our new extended family?"

Tammy smiled at the thought of Uncle Joe. "Uncle Joe's a riot. So is Mr. Apolone. Everyone was so nice—especially, Marlene and John. This *is* unreal," she whispered.

"My thoughts exactly!"

Tammy removed her glasses and yawned.

"Well," Laura continued, "This is my first night sleeping in a room all by myself. It feels weird. I'm gonna miss not seeing one of your body parts dangling from the bed above me."

They both giggled. Tammy extended her arms and hugged Laura. "This is the start of an awesome adventure. Between getting to know our new family, going to a new school, and having the freedom to live like normal kids. I'm in Heaven."

Laura nodded in agreement. "Me too. Goodnight. I love you, Tammy Knight!"

"I love you, Laura Knight." They giggled as they entered their individual rooms.

Laura quietly closed the door to her room. After unpacking her things and placing them in the closet and dresser drawers, she slipped into her pajamas and pulled back the bedspread. Even the sheets were matching, with adorable little yellow and green flowers floating on a pale yellow background. She slid between them and turned off the light. Despite the heat of the summer night, Laura pulled up the sheet. The air conditioned home was cool and refreshing in comparison to the upper level of the old abandoned house. A small shiver trickled down Laura's spine.

Laura closed her eyes and thought of Tony. She sighed at the memory of how things used to be. She missed the feel and scents of the old house. The way the house creaked and rattled on windier days. She was even homesick for the solitude she had grown to hate. Suddenly, Laura envisioned Tony's face, the touch of his hand, and his warm embrace. Her heart literally hurt at the thought of him. She ached to hear him whistle and missed the sound of his voice.

What was he doing that very moment? Did he ever think of her? Laura questioned why she was thinking of him, when she should be thinking of the start of her new life.

The new school would bring exciting activities, like drama, choir classes, and school dances with plenty of fresh faces to meet and boys to dance with. Yet, she was already making herself feel out of place. *Would she forever feel the guilt of betraying Tony, at the thought of moving on with someone else? Did she even want anybody else, was the bigger question?*

A lump formed in its normal place in Laura's throat. She rose from her bed and stole away into Tammy's room. Tammy was in bed, snuggled quietly under the covers. Laura patted her shoulder gently, whispering Tammy's name. She peeked through a crack in her eye. "Are you okay?" she asked Laura.

"I'm sorry to bother you. But I can't stop my mind from racing. As exhausted as I feel, I can't sleep. I got Tony on the brain."

"Oh no."

"Oh yes. I can't figure out why. Would you believe it if I told you that I'm homesick for him and the old house?"

"No, it doesn't surprise me. You lived there for a long time. But you have to forget him and start over. Now go back to your room and go to sleep."

"How?"

"Count sheep," Tammy suggested.

"That never works for me."

"Drink hot milk."

"I don't want John and Marlene to see that I'm still up."

"Then get back to your bed and say a prayer. Only Jesus can help *you*!" Tammy exclaimed.

Laura muffled a laugh. "You're right. I'll go talk to Jesus." Once again, in the privacy of her own room, Laura knelt before her bed in prayer.

"Lord, You know my lifelong prayer—to have a real family. I never dreamed I might actually have that again. Please let these people be everything they seem to be. After losing my family, I never thought I'd have a sister to be close with again, and now You've given me one in Tammy. I lost my mom at a tender age. Will Marlene be the mother I so long for? And what of John? My father wasn't much of a father, but I was devastated to lose him the same. Is this guy for real, Lord? Please let it be so.

"Thank You for forgiving my sins. Thank You for blessing me even when I don't deserve it. Lord, I even thank You for the time I shared with Tony. I'm grateful I was able to experience that kind of love. Despite what happened to us, Lord, I really love Tony. I pray You can help him. Whatever it is that's wrong with him, please heal him. If it's in Your holy will, please bring him back to me the way that he used to be. In Your precious name, I pray. Amen." She crossed herself and climbed into her brand new bed.

The crisp linens against her face were all Laura remembered, as sleep conquered all.

CHAPTER 14

Moving Forward, but Looking Back

Living with the Knights that first month couldn't have gone any smoother, despite Laura's reservations. She still couldn't bring herself to call them 'Mom and Dad', but felt herself growing closer. They really were turning out to be everything she'd hoped for.

John and Marlene lavished the young women with new clothing for both school and home. Whatever essentials they needed, they were given. At the end of August, they were enrolled in the nearby high school to finish off their senior year. They also began driver's training. John promised that as long as the girls showed responsibility and kept deserving grades that he'd, alas, break down and buy a new vehicle, giving them the station wagon to get to and from school in.

Meanwhile, in that first month, Laura followed through with her promise to telephone Massimo and tell him of her adoption. After some exploring, she found the card he'd given her and called. He was thrilled to hear from her and promised to visit her before the summer ended.

As the school year was about to begin, she received a call from him wanting to use a vacation day to pay her a visit. They set the date and Laura waited anxiously to meet with her friend.

On the day of his visit, Laura prepared in her mind questions to ask him. When he arrived, she smiled at the sight of the handsome man and escorted him in through the front door. She introduced him to the Knights and to Tammy. John guided them through the kitchen and out onto the concrete patio to enjoy the warm summer day.

"Since the two of you have some catching up to do, we'll be back in a while with some lemonade." Marlene, John, and Tammy re-entered the house, leaving Massimo and Laura to chat.

"Laura, this is beautiful. They seem nice. Are you happy here?"

"Yes, I haven't felt this complete, since . . . well, a while. They're unbelievably generous and more loving than I ever expected. Thank you for your help. Now I have a family for the rest of my life." She squeezed his hand gratefully.

"That's great. Tell me about your life," he encouraged. Laura spoke of the welcome home party the Knights had thrown them. She mentioned John's promise to give them his car as long as they upheld their grades. She went on to explain the extent at which these strangers were going through to please her and Tammy. Still, despite the positive turn out of the events of her life, Laura couldn't help but ultimately go to the one subject that constantly lurked in the back of her mind.

Her eyes suddenly darkened. "Chief, I have a question for you. Did you ever find my family's bodies?"

Massimo seemed to be expecting this question and his face grew serious. "Oddly enough, no. This spring, we searched those graves—nothing. They were never dug. Just the surface of the ground was scraped to make it appear as though the ground had been disturbed. So, we searched the entire area—still nothing. Forensics combed the house and perimeter. Clean as a whistle."

"Professionals?"

"Exactly. This wasn't your average whack-job. The people, or person, who did it, knew what they were doing. They covered up the murders so well, that if you hadn't witnessed them, we'd have never known. We even questioned Tony. He said that when he and his uncle, who later verified his story, arrived at the scene, the bodies were not there."

Laura contemplated his words. Before she could stop herself, not truly sure if she wanted to hear the answer, she asked, "Does he ever ask about me?"

Massimo lowered his gaze and nodded, "I figured you'd ask. Well, that's one of the reasons I drove out here today. You need to know what's happening with him."

Laura stiffened. "What is it, Chief?"

"Tony's up for parole in the next few weeks. Depending on the last ten months of his behavior, it's a possibility that he'll be released. I intend on being there for the hearing and doing everything necessary to have him stay in jail a while longer. There's just no justice if he walks so soon after what he did."

Laura hadn't allowed herself to think of the possibility of Tony's release. Massimo disrupted her thoughts. "And yes . . . he's still asking about you. He's still insisting that he talk to you. He wants to know what happened to you and where you are."

Laura's heart leapt. *Did he still care? Or was he still seeking to hurt her?* "Why?" she finally managed, her mouth dry.

"Apparently, he wants to explain things to you. Laura, I recommend that you stay far away from him. If by some chance he finds you, I advise you not to respond. He's a dangerous guy and I don't buy the innocent act he's playing right now. His good behavior has moved his parole date a few months sooner than I anticipated. I have to admit, I'm scared for you."

A light breeze blew through Laura's hair, almost caressing her face. Her summer dress ruffled in the breeze and she held it down with her hand. Her gaze was distant as she asked the ultimate question. "Is it possible he's sorry?"

"Who knows his heart? If you were my daughter or sister, I'd advise you not to chance it. Stay away, Laura."

Laura shook her head. She didn't know what to believe. Her heart told her to believe in Tony and that possibly they could reconcile. Her brain told her Hell would freeze over first.

"Let's get those drinks," she stated. "It's hot out here." They entered the house and joined the others. After the long drive, Marlene and John insisted Massimo stay for dinner and spend the evening with them. He did so and they had a pleasant night together.

When the clock chimed eight, Massimo arose and said his goodbyes. Laura walked him to the door. He waved a finger at her. "No sad faces, and heed my warnings. Will you promise to let me know if you need me? I know I'm far away, but you're never too far for me to help you."

"Thank you. I promise." She gave him a hug and watched as he entered his vehicle and drove away. Upon closing the front door, she let her face fall into her hands and cried. John, Marlene, and Tammy guided her back to the couch and encouraged her to speak. She told them what Massimo had said of Tony. They sat quietly as she let her feelings spill forward.

"I'm sorry, Laura, but I have to agree with Massimo. Tony has no business looking for you. He severed his ties to you the night he hurt you," John added.

Marlene and Tammy agreed with John. "Don't worry," Tammy consoled. "There's no way he can find out where you are. The adoption files are confidential."

If only she could be sure.

* * *

Laura tried to put the conversation with Massimo out of her mind. As school began, she applied herself to her studies and kept busy with after-school activities. Tammy saw to it that they were constantly volunteering for school functions, and Laura couldn't have been more grateful for the distractions.

On September 25, when Laura turned 18, the Knights gave her an intimate birthday party including Uncle Joe's family. The same weekend of her birthday, John drove the girls back to Little Falls to see Angela and Barb. They were able to spend an amazing afternoon together, filling one another in with details of the past two months apart.

A month later brought them into October. Both Laura and Tammy had already sent in their applications to the College of Albany. They waited anxiously for a reply, and were ecstatic to receive two forms of good news within weeks of each other. The first was their acceptance into the college, and a few short days later, the passing of their driver's training exam.

They burst through the front door, shouting for Marlene on the day of the exam. As they hung their jackets in the foyer closet, Marlene appeared. A seriousness held her expression. "Marlene, what is it?" Laura immediately asked.

"First, tell me . . . did you pass?" she inquired.

"Laura and I passed our driver's training exams!" Tammy screeched.

"Oh, girls, that's great. I'm so happy for you!" Marlene congratulated them both with a kiss.

Laura tugged at Marlene's arm and demanded to meet her eyes. "Okay, why the dismal look?"

Marlene reached for her hand and ushered her into the kitchen. On the table in the nook, was a pile of assorted mail. Marlene sifted through it and pulled out an envelope.

Laura's heart fell. Her knees weakened as she took hold of the letter, recognizing Tony's handwriting instantly. She stumbled into a chair and stared at the words he wrote on the envelope:

Ms. Laura Ann Marcs
46 Fairway Court
Albany, NY 12257

No return address on the envelope. "It's him, isn't it?" Marlene questioned.

Laura nodded.

"But how?" Tammy stammered. "How'd he find out where you live?"

"Frankly, it doesn't surprise me," Marlene stated. "There are plenty of ways he could've found out. I was just praying that he'd leave you alone."

"Are you going to open it?" Tammy asked.

"I have to," Laura hesitated. "I need to know what his plans are—where he stands." She stood from the chair, and in a daze, mounted the staircase to find her room.

"If you need us, we'll be right here for you," Marlene called after her.

She reached her bedroom, sat on her bed, and tore at the envelope. Her hands shook in apprehension.

October 24, 1977

My dearest Laura,

Where do I begin? There are so many things I need to say and am afraid I'll never get the chance. I'm happy to hear that you've been adopted into a wonderful family. You'll have to forgive my intrusion. But what I need to tell you can no longer wait. I'm being paroled soon. I don't expect you to come running into my arms. Although, I'll admit, I've dreamt about it a thousand-and-one times. The three years we shared together were magical, even if they were based on lies. The truth is, I've never loved another as I love you. It tears me apart to know that I've destroyed that. I don't think I'll ever forgive myself. Nor do I anticipate your forgiveness. What I did was unforgivable. But that's part of what needs to be explained. Please, give me that chance. Even if I know that we'll never be able to share again what we had, at least I'll know that you'll understand me better.

Every night I pray for God's blessings for you. I never wanted what happened to happen. And if all I'll have left is the memories, then that's okay. A love like ours is not something that happens to everyone. It was special. And I'll hold on to that for the rest of my life.

Will you give me the chance to explain? If you do decide to write me, please send me a letter at Uncle Frank's store and I'll be sure to get it. Thank you, Laura, for more things than I could ever list. Thank you for three amazing years, for your unconditional love, and for giving me a chance to redeem myself. (I pray your heart will give me this one last chance.) I truly miss you and love you.

Forever,

Tony

Laura clutched the letter to her heart and sobbed. *He always knew the right things to say!* It ached her to think that there was a possibility that he was truly sorry and that she was not giving him another chance. But the uncertainty of his actions all but left her with more doubts in him than she could concede. Those doubts fueled her anger.

She crumbled the letter into a ball and tossed it at her door. As much as she missed him, as much as she knew she still loved him, the scars were still too fresh and too deep. She exited her room and stalked back down the staircase and into the kitchen. Marlene and Tammy turned to see an angry Laura enter.

"Well, are we being nosey to ask what he had to say?" Tammy asked.

"Not at all. It's as Massimo said. He claims that he needs to explain. Well, you know what? I don't want to hear his excuses. I don't want to know what happened. If it hadn't been for that happening, I wouldn't have you both. So, God allows things to happen for the good of those who love Him and I believe that," she heaved. "And furthermore, I don't want to look back. I want to focus on now."

"That's my girl!" Marlene cheered. "I'm glad to hear you say that." She pulled Laura into her arms. Suddenly, Laura withered.

She let out a cry and asked, "But why does it still send my heart beating when I think of him? Why does he still haunt my dreams? Why can't I forget him?"

Laura sat on Marlene's lap. Marlene brushed back the hair from her face and cupped it in her hands. "Because you devoted three years of the most vulnerable time in your life to him. Because when you love, you give your whole heart." Laura cried in her arms. Marlene tried to soothe her.

Tammy tried as well. "Here, Laura." She offered her a glass of water. Laura took it and sat in a free chair. Marlene and Tammy surrounded her with their comforting words. "What will you do?" Tammy finally asked.

"I'm going to call Massimo. I'm going to ask him to tell Tony to leave me alone. Hopefully, he'll get the picture. If he loves me the way he says he does, then he'll let me be."

"Good thinking," Marlene encouraged.

Laura did exactly that. Later that afternoon, she placed the call to the Cicero Police Department. She was connected to his desk and moments later, his strong voice bellowed through the line.

After the initial "hellos," Laura quickly got to the point. "Chief, remember when we saw each other last, you made me promise to call you if I needed you. Well, I'm calling to take you up on that offer."

"Laura, anything. What is it?"

"You were right. Tony found out where I lived and mailed me a letter. I received it today."

"What! What did it say?"

"Just what you thought he'd say. He wants to explain things and is hoping I'll give him a chance. I need you to do me a favor."

"You name it."

"Please, go to him on my behalf and tell him to let me be. I don't want to know any reasons why, because it doesn't matter anymore. I'm here and I'm happy and I don't want to look back."

"No problem. I'll make it clear that you want nothing more to do with him."

"Thank you."

"Absolutely. Laura, thanks for calling me. I'll take care of everything." With that, they hung up.

At the nook table, Laura put her head down onto her arms and cried. She felt a warm hand on her shoulder. Wiping her tears, she looked into John's warm eyes. "You okay?" he asked.

"I will be. It may take a while, but I'll be fine."

"Hey, can we talk?" he asked.

Laura wondered where the conversation was heading. Reluctantly, she nodded.

John continued, as he sat next to her. "I'm not stupid. I could sense your skepticism of me from the get go. After understanding the childhood you had and the hardships you've undergone, I can easily see why you have a hard time trusting me as a man and as a father figure. I never expected you to trust so easily, but I hope that in time you will learn that I have no ulterior motive—that I really do just want to love you like a father. Whether you're ready or not, I'm here for you and always will be."

Laura felt a burning in her throat and succumbed to more tears. She allowed John to gather her into his arms, and after a genuine hug, he guided her into the living room with the rest of the family.

Laura anxiously waited for Massimo's call for the next few days. Four days after their conversation, he called and explained to Laura that he made the visit to the prison. Upon seeing the chief, Tony tried to refuse his visit. He was restrained and told to hear Massimo out. He told Tony about his conversation with Laura after she'd received his letter. Massimo described a sudden change in Tony's character. He said that Tony suddenly appeared colder. He listened to Massimo's plea to let her go, then leaned forward and whispered to him that he didn't care what Laura said. He said that he was being released in two weeks and no one could control him anymore. Massimo then warned Laura not to be left alone in the next few weeks.

She shared the account with her family. John vowed that he'd protect her. That night, after crawling into bed, Laura cried to herself. She couldn't understand how Tony could write such a moving letter one moment, to turn around and threaten her shortly afterward. She prayed for him that night. She asked God to help him. It seemed he was still not in the right frame of mind.

*   *   *

The week of Tony's parole, John talked to his partner and decided to take a small vacation from the financial firm. He took the girls out of school and flew them to Florida for a week. Laura was relieved to be out of New York, for the time being.

They spent seven wonderful days in Orlando, basking in the warm sun and touring Disney World and other theme parks.

Nevertheless, upon returning to New York, the change in weather and her continual worrying had weakened Laura's resistance. Two days after they arrived home, Laura came down with a fever and massive head and chest cold. She rested on the couch, trying desperately to breathe through her congested nose. That day, Tammy arrived home from school with

Laura's homework. Two more days out of school worried her teachers, and Tammy was asked to bring home the assignments Laura had missed. She went over the work with her and then left to allow her sister rest.

Laura rested her head and dwelled on her new family members. *Tammy was so wonderful. She was devoted and loyal, too.* They were best friends, through and through. They shared classes together, finished driver's training together, and now they even shared John's old car together. It was rare if they argued, and when they did, it was because Tammy would yell at Laura to forget Tony. Otherwise, sharing and giving came easy for them.

Meanwhile, Marlene rattled away in the kitchen, preparing dinner. Since the girls had moved in, Marlene no longer worked, wanting to devote her time to her family. Laura's bug gave her the perfect opportunity to make her famous chicken soup and see to it that Laura took her medication. She was fulfilling her lifelong dream of being a doting mother.

John arrived home from work early that day. He was harassing his wife in the kitchen, driving her insane with his jesting. It was amazing the way he supported his family in every way. He was a brilliant provider, branching his expertise in two different career fields. He was a financial planner by day and landlord of two apartment buildings and numerous rental homes by night. He worked hard to maintain their lifestyle and to give all of them his best. To Laura's surprise and delight, John *was*, by every means, a father. He was giving and loving, yet stern and wise. The three women looked forward to the evenings when he'd come home and stir up the household with his comical personality.

That was the only thing that could bring a smile to Laura's face as she rested on the couch and sulked in misery with a cold. John dawdled into the living room to check on her. He sat near her legs on the couch and whispered, "How's my doll?"

"Hey John," she tried to smile for him. "I can't even lift my head." Laura's voice was near hoarse from the sore throat and cough.

"We have to rebuild that immune system." He rubbed his bristly chin and thought. "You need rest, Marlene's chicken soup, and more rest."

Laura weakly smiled. "John? Did I thank you for that awesome vacation?"

"I'd say about five hundred and twenty times."

"I had the greatest time at Walt Disney World. Have I told you that it was my childhood wish come true?"

"About three hundred times."

"Well then, I'll tell you once more. Thank you." Laura closed her aching eyes. A smile remained on her lips.

"Get some rest." John patted her leg and left.

Laura took his advice and allowed herself to let go. Unluckily, she fell into a restless sleep. Her dreams haunted her with visions of Tony. She fretted in her slumber, unable to escape the darkness that seemed to surround her. Someone touched her. In the murkiness, she could not see who it was. "Laura," Tony's voice whispered. She awoke instantly. Her body was drenched in a sweat. She looked around the room disoriented. *Why was it so dark?* Fear engulfed her. Her breathing was still heavy. She tried to call out, but her voice failed. *Where had everyone gone?* Alarmed, she found herself all alone.

CHAPTER 15

The Ring

"Marlene? John?" Laura called out in a raspy voice. She coughed and winced at the burning in her chest. Her heart raced as she lay on the living room couch. Woken from a disturbing dream of Tony, she panicked at the thought of being alone.

The sound of footsteps descending the stairs gave her a sense of relief. "Right here," John called. "You finally woke up, huh? Sorry I left you in the dark, down here. But I know when I'm sick, even the light bothers me." He placed a gentle hand on her forehead. "Man, you're still on fire. Let me get you something."

Laura rested her heavy head on the pillow. Unable to raise her voice above a loud whisper, she asked where Marlene and Tammy were. John informed her that Tammy needed a few things for school and Marlene went with her to the store. He also reminded her that she missed dinner and that she needed to eat as soon as she felt up to it.

As Laura heard John rustling through the medicine cabinet, the telephone rang. He ran to the phone in the kitchen. "Hello," he answered slightly out of breath. "What? Who's this? How did you get my number? I see," he paused a moment. "Thanks for the tip."

Bringing her a glass of water with two pills, John sat next to Laura on the couch. "Laura, I have a small emergency at one of my rentals. It's strange. Someone called and said that they suspect one of the vacant condominiums has someone prowling around in it. They saw my sign out front and called it to warn me. I don't know what to do. I don't want to bring you there, in case there really is trouble. Yet, I don't want to leave you here alone." He looked lovingly into her eyes.

"John, call the police first and have them meet you there. Don't worry about me. I'll be fine. I'm sure Marlene and Tammy will be home shortly. Go take care of it. Just be sure the cops meet you there."

"Are you sure you'll be all right?"

"Positive. Do me a favor. Lock the doors and turn on some lights," she teased.

"I'll be back as soon as I can. Love you." He kissed her forehead and left.

Laura sat up on the couch. She reached for the remote control to the television and turned on the set. After taking the aspirins, she tried to focus on the tube before her. Tissue in one hand and the remote in the other, she sifted through the stations. Fifteen minutes after settling on a program she was enjoying, again, the telephone rang. Laura sighed and reluctantly rose to go to the kitchen. Her head was groggy and she held out a hand to steady herself. Midway there, the lights began to flicker. She hastened her speed, reaching for the phone in time before darkness fell across the house.

"Hello?"

"Laura . . ." Massimo's voice faded before Laura had a chance to speak.

"Chief? Hello? Chief . . . are you there?" The line died.

Laura's heart raced. It was too bizarre. She felt her way through the kitchen and into the dining room. She grabbed a candlestick off the dining room table and re-entered the kitchen. Fumbling through a drawer, she found a box of matches and lit the candle with quivering hands.

With the candlelight as her guide, she made her way back into the living room. She peered through the window sheers. Fear gripped her when she discovered the neighbor's homes buzzing with electricity. She steadied her balance, holding her spinning head. *What was happening?*

Taking a deep breath, she walked into the foyer and pulled her coat from the closet. Placing the candle on the small entryway table, she slipped it on, as well as her shoes. She braced herself to exit the house and run to a neighbor for help.

Laura rested her hand on the doorknob of the front door. The candle was still lighting her way. She opened the door. A cold fall breeze blew the flame out. Yet, Laura could still make out the familiar figure that stood at her door. She gasped.

Laura stumbled aback, unable to think clearly at who appeared before her. He entered the house. Immediately shutting the door, he grabbed her, and muffled any scream that formed in her throat with his hand.

"I've been waiting so long for this," Tony's voice said gruffly.

She closed her eyes and willed her heart to stop racing. She deliberated whether to embrace him or run from him. She opened her eyes to search his in the darkness. He wouldn't meet her gaze, though his face was close enough to hers that she could feel his breath on her cheek.

128

"Don't say a word," he warned. She shook her head in comprehension. "There's no one here to help you so don't bother to scream. I sent your new father in pursuit of a prowler, so before he realizes that he was set up, it'll be too late."

Laura's eyes instantly welled up in sadness. This wasn't her Tony. She ached inside for the man she used to love. She shook her head in no. He pushed her against the foyer wall with his chest, releasing his hand over her mouth. His body pinned hers. His hands held hers against the wall. His mouth suddenly met hers in a soft kiss. Her defenses seemed to dissolve in an instant. So desperate for his affection, she returned his kiss with passion.

Unexpectedly, Tony was responding to her, softening his hold over her. Her hands were released and she instinctively wrapped them around his neck, pulling him closer. Her heart pounded against her chest with a desire she feared she'd never feel again.

"Laura," he whispered longingly.

Laura melted in his embrace. She kissed him without restraint. "Oh God, Tony!" she cried as he held her gently to him.

"Oh, baby, I've missed you so much. I'm so sorry! I'm so sorry!" Tony suddenly cried.

"Don't cry. It's okay," she soothed.

He touched her face with tenderness. "God, I love you! I'm so sorry!"

Laura held his face in her hands. "Let it go! We'll get you help. We'll find out what's wrong with you and get you help," she promised.

"NO!" he suddenly shouted, pushing her roughly against the wall again.

"Please," she begged. "Tony, don't stop loving me."

"QUIET!"

"I know you never wanted to hurt me. Tony, you're good. You love me and I never stopped loving you!" she cried.

"NO!" he shouted. In a calmer voice, he affirmed, "Stop! It won't work."

Suddenly, he savagely kissed her, crushing her body under his weight. She tried with her might to reach him again, but he wouldn't allow it. When the kiss ended, she gasped for air, feeling her head starting to swoon.

"Please," she managed. "Tell me what went wrong?"

For a moment he softened, stepping back enough to let her move unhindered. Yet, so close that she could not escape his powerful hold. "Oh," he moaned. "It would take too long to explain it all. You're just like your father, always talking too much."

"My father? What're you talking about?"

"Shut up! Stop asking questions. I'm gonna finish what I came here to finish." He raised a fist to hit her.

She instinctively raised her hands to cover her face. Laura closed her eyes, waiting for the blow. But the blow never came. She opened her eyes and tried to make out the twisted expression on his face. In the darkness, a gleam of liquid spilled from his eye. He was struggling again. He couldn't do it. He couldn't hurt her. Her heart cheered.

She embraced him, kissed his face, and tried to soothe the sobs that began to escape his throat. Laura held him as his stiff body began to thaw in her arms. She let her own grief spill forward. In conclusion, she was finally able to admit to herself her undying love for him.

Tony stumbled to the ground. The tears poured from his eyes. She held him in her arms, wishing she could see him clearly to memorize his beautiful face, once again.

At last, she spoke. "Tony, I knew you couldn't hurt me. I know you love me."

Without warning, he hardened in her arms.

"Oh no, don't go there," she begged.

"Stop telling me what to do!" he raged. "I've gotta end this!"

Laura was so confused and increasingly growing more scared. She toppled backward trying to regain her footing before he could follow through with his threats. She rose to her feet in time to dash for the door. Tony grabbed her leg and tripped her. She screamed as they struggled. She wiggled from his grip, managing to regain her footing and jumped up the stairs to seek safety. Tony cursed as he made his way up the staircase behind her. Before reaching the top, he caught hold of her foot, once again. Laura struggled to free herself by kicking at his hands. She struck out with her foot and hit Tony in the chest. She screamed as she watched his silhouette fight to maintain balance and suddenly tumble backward down the stairs.

She waited a moment, heaving to catch her breath. His body appeared motionless at the bottom of the stairs. Holding herself firmly to the banister, she descended the staircase careful to walk far around his body as she exited the house for help. The tears coursed down her cheeks as she reached the end of the driveway in time to see Marlene and Tammy pulling in with the station wagon.

Both women quickly exited the car upon seeing Laura in her disheveled state.

"Laura, my God! What happened?" Marlene reached for her collapsing daughter.

"Tony! He's in the house. He attacked me. He . . ." Laura began to lose focus.

"Oh, Tammy. She's going to pass out. Help me get her in the car."

Laura shook her head as if to shake away the dizziness. Marlene and Tammy both assisted her into the vehicle. John's timing seemed impeccable as his vehicle screeched to a halt in the driveway. He stumbled out of the car in a panic. Marlene repeated Laura's explanation. Abruptly, John sprinted for the house. He entered the front door. Seconds later, he reappeared.

"He's gone! He set me up!" He raced to the car and looked Laura over with concern. "Did he touch you? Did he hurt you?"

"John, let's get her to the hospital. I'm afraid she's hurt," Marlene stated. They climbed into the station wagon and John raced to the hospital.

In the car, Laura tried explaining what had happened. Tammy sat with her in the back and held her sister's shoulders as she cried. Laura was in hysterics by the time she finished explaining. Both Marlene and Tammy cried with her. John's anger flared.

At last, they reached the hospital. John called the police and notified them that Tony had tried to hurt Laura. He asked them to place a call to Chief Desanti in Cicero and notify him of the attack. Meanwhile, after waiting in the emergency room for over a half-hour, Marlene and John began to grow impatient. Laura's fever hadn't yet subsided and she began to tremble. A nurse finally called them in.

Laura leaned on John as he guided her into the ER. A man, who introduced himself as Dr. Willows, and a young intern with a tag displaying 'Paul Roberts' as his name, listened carefully as Marlene explained what Laura had been through. After asking the family to exit the small curtained area, they thoroughly examined Laura.

The young intern called the family back in. He cleared his throat and began, "My name is Paul Roberts. I'm an intern here." He gave Laura a sweet smile as he spoke to her. "On behalf of Dr. Willows and myself, I'd like you to know that there's no real physical harm done. Aside from a little bruising, you appear to be okay. It's also apparent that you're fighting a serious bronchial infection. This is a real concern for us. Your oxygen intake is lower than it should be. If we're not careful, this can lead to pneumonia. We will be keeping you overnight for observation, Albuterol breathing treatments, and we'll begin administering intravenous antibiotics immediately." He turned to the family. "Emotionally, Laura's showing evident symptoms of shock: the glazed look in her eye, the shivers that don't seem to relinquish. This also concerns us. Her emotional state is definitely unstable. I think she needs a good night's rest in a place where she'll feel safe. I'm sure you've called the police department."

"Yes," John stated. "They're on their way."

"Good. At this time, we'll assign a room to her where she can get settled and rest. We'll be giving her a sedative to calm her. But before we do, we'll have a psychiatrist examine her and give us a better prognosis." He smiled kindly at Laura and patted her foot. "Don't worry about a thing. You're safe here. We'll take good care of you."

Laura smiled weakly, thanking him in return. He exited the small compartment.

Tammy sat next to her on a chair and gently stroked her hand. "I'm so sorry we left. My God, we were only gone for an hour." A tear lazily rolled down her cheek.

"It's my fault," John accused. "I should've never fallen for that stupid hoax. I knew it sounded fishy."

"Will you all please stop? It's nobody's fault. Not even Tony's," Laura wept.

"What? How can you defend him?" John's voice rose.

"John, you'll never understand! Not all of us have lived this plush life that you have lived. Tony had a hard life and as a result, something's really wrong. He was struggling in there. It's hard to explain, but I know he didn't want to hurt me, and I pushed him down the stairs." She placed her face in her hands and cried.

"Maybe you're right. I don't get it. How does a guy hurt a girl? There is no reason! So don't torture yourself for pushing him down the stairs. If he was seriously hurt, he would've still been there, and he wasn't. He was gone. That means that he's prowling about and possibly still trying to hurt you. I'm sorry but I'm not going to feel sorry for him. In fact, he better not come near you again."

Marlene gave John a sign to take his anger down a notch. Laura was sobbing uncontrollably again. She coughed and sputtered trying to get her words out. "I'm sorry. Marlene, don't be mad at John for wanting to defend me. I love him for that. But I can't explain what I experienced in there. Now I know for sure that something is truly wrong with him and I never gave him the chance to explain it to me. I was wrong. If I loved him, why didn't I ever let him say what he tried so many times to say? He wanted me to understand and I was too selfish."

Tammy embraced Laura and said, "Stop this. You're the victim here, not Tony. No matter what, there's no reason for him to attack you. I don't care what the circumstances are. If I know you, you've never been anything but loving to him."

"Tammy's right," Marlene encouraged, "Please stop blaming yourself. He's a sick man and that's nothing you can help."

"I love him," Laura cried. "I never stopped. I never will."

Marlene shook her head in sadness and no one spoke another negative word of him. Once Laura was admitted and transferred to her room, she appeared more relaxed. Before long, the psychiatrist entered the room wanting a few minutes alone with her. She preceded with a few psycho-analysis exams. After counseling Laura for a short while, she exited the room. From behind the partially opened door, Laura overheard the doctor give the Knights her perspective of Laura's condition.

"I'm Dr. Lori Janice," she announced. "I've talked with Laura. I'm afraid she may need to continue with therapy on a regular basis. She's been through quite an ordeal and I'm not just talking about what happened to her this evening. Laura has endured serious traumas, such as the loss of her original family, for starters. She was an eyewitness of their murders. Then the experience she underwent the first time around with Tony. After care-ful review of her past, the serious trauma she's survived will affect her everyday life if not treated. She's done a wonderful job on her own, but . . . it'll catch up to her.

"As for the condition she's in after tonight's occurrence, Laura's defi-nitely in shock. Still completely lucid in her mental state, but her mind can't completely comprehend, or should I say, accept what she's experi-enced. This makes it difficult for her to understand her feelings, because she's so torn between what she knows she should feel and what she actually feels. She's going to need time." The doctor then gave them her card and promised to keep them up to date on Laura's condition.

It seemed no more than a few moments later that the police arrived. Paul Roberts suggested that the Knights give their statement outside of the hospital room, but Laura insisted on hearing what the police had to say.

An older police officer gave them a report of what they discovered. After receiving John's telephone call, the police went to the Knight home and found definite evidence of tampering with the exterior electrical unit. The power company was called upon immediately to restore the problem so that the investigation could continue. In the home, there was no dam-age and all things appeared intact. They found the candlestick in the foyer and a sign of the struggle, but Tony was nowhere to be found. An APB was put out on him and the police were in pursuit as they spoke.

The officer stated that Laura would be under police protection for the night and at home, until further notice, per special request from Chief Massimo Desanti. According to the police officer, the chief was trying to contact Laura to warn her of Tony's release. Unfortunately, he had been too late.

A security guard was placed outside of Laura's hospital room. John insisted Marlene take Tammy home while he remained to keep an eye on Laura. In the meantime, Laura was given a sedative to help her rest. Tammy and Marlene reluctantly kissed Laura and John goodnight and left. John sat on the chair in Laura's hospital room and reached for her hand.

"I want to make you a promise that I'll always protect you," he whispered as he kissed her hand.

"Thank you. I'm so sorry for all this trouble. You got more than you bargained for when you adopted me."

"You're everything we could ask for in a daughter . . . and more. Don't be sorry. You've given us so much joy already."

"But, I'm such a mess."

"Shh." He soothed. "Don't think about anything. Just know that we love you."

Laura closed her eyes, feeling the sedative beginning to work. "I'm so tired."

"Rest," John whispered. "Just rest."

Laura felt his warm breath on her cheek as he kissed her tenderly, before she fell heavy with sleep.

*   *   *

Sometime later in the night, Laura thought she sensed a presence in her room. She knew that John hadn't left her side and so she slept in comfort. A familiar warm hand caressed her cheek. She tried to open her eyes to see who it was, but they were still too heavy.

"John?" she murmured.

"Shh," a voice hushed. "Rest and know that I'll always love you." A kiss warmed her lips.

Laura's heart felt happy and she smiled. She wanted to tell him that she loved him, too. She wanted to reach out and hold him. Her mind traveled back in time and she remembered sweet memories with him. His voice, that voice.

Her eyes instantly sprung open. It was Tony's voice. She glared around the room. No one was in sight, not even John.

"John?" Laura cried in a panic. "Where are you?" She threw the covers off and tried to rise from the hospital bed. Her vision blurred and she stopped to refocus. Laura pressed the nurse's button. She rested her head back on the pillow, her legs still dangling from the side of the bed.

Moments later, a nurse entered. "You shouldn't be getting out of bed, young lady. You've been heavily medicated," she reprimanded as she lifted Laura's legs and placed them back on the bed.

Laura frantically called for John. The nurse assured her he was probably in the bathroom or grabbing a coffee. Laura hysterically insisted that the nurse ask the guard in. He entered.

"Ma'am, your father stepped out for a quick cup of coffee in the cafeteria. He'll be right back," he guaranteed.

"Did someone come in here?" Laura asked.

"No ma'am. I've been outside your door all night, except for a few short breaks, which I let your father know of."

"Nobody's been in here?"

"No ma'am, I assure you."

"I could've sworn it was real," Laura shook her head in dismay.

"What was real, dear?" the nurse asked.

"I felt the presence of someone I know here."

"You were just dreaming, honey. Now close your eyes and get some rest. Your father will be back shortly."

Both the nurse and the security guard exited the room, leaving Laura to her thoughts. She glanced around the room, spying the clock. It was nearly midnight. Laura leaned back and rested her head. It must have been a dream. She pondered on it. He'd kissed her and promised to love her always. A lump rose in her throat and she tried not to cry. She needed to get it through her thick head that Tony wasn't the man he used to be.

Laura reached over to get the glass of water on the mobile tray next to her bed. Her heart skipped a beat as she focused on the shiny object next to her glass of water. She swallowed the protruding lump in her throat. It was the engagement ring Tony had given her so many months before. She clasped the ring. She was right. He'd been in the room.

Moments passed and finally John entered. He quickly sat beside her. "Laura, they told me you were looking for me. I ran to the cafeteria for a cup of coffee to keep me awake. What is it, honey?"

Laura's trembling hand held out the engagement ring. John looked at it, then to her, still not comprehending. "This was my engagement ring from Tony. I took it off and threw it in the basement the day I escaped the house. Earlier, I had a dream that Tony was here. I dreamed that he kissed me and promised to love me. When I realized that the dream was of him, I woke up thinking it was real. You had left to get coffee and I was frantic for you. I called the nurse and the security guard and they swore that no one had been in here but you. Yet, I found this by my glass of water. Tony really was here."

"That can't be," he protested. "You're being watched every minute."

"Then how do you explain this?"

John rushed from the bed to the door, demanding the officer explain how the ring appeared. The officer was baffled, stating that he had only left for a moment for a bathroom run, while John was gone.

"Well, in that moment, he could've killed my daughter. What kind of a security is this? My daughter's life's in your hands," John bellowed.

Ten minutes into a telephone discussion with the local police department, Massimo Desanti entered the room.

"Chief!" Laura exclaimed. "I'm glad to see you." She embraced her friend. "What're you doing here so late?"

Massimo shook John's hand, and after introducing himself to the guard as Police Chief of Cicero, he commanded him to exit the room. "I had a friend fly me in on his private jet to see you. I understand Tony was here about an hour ago?"

"Yes, the guard left his post for a moment and Tony snuck in. I just got done reaming out the Albany Police Department," John admitted

"Did they tell you what happened?"

"Tell me what?" John asked.

"I was just dispatched, by the locals. They spotted Tony Warren leaving the hospital around eleven with a van matching the description and plate of a van reported stolen earlier. He must've taken it prior to making his little stop here. As a security officer caught sight of him, Tony took off with it. They tailed him and began a chase. He managed to get onto the freeway and gain speed. They set up a roadblock and tried to trap him at one of the overpasses on Route 9. He was hell-bent on escaping and he ran the vehicle off the road. He lost control and went down the cliff. The vehicle plummeted to the bottom, hitting the rocks below. It blew up. The blast blew all the windows clear out of the van."

Laura gasped, placing a hand over her mouth. "NO!"

"Laura, I'm sorry, but I'm afraid he's dead. Though the blast sent a massive ball of fire into the air, we were able to recover a shoe, and bits and pieces of his clothing, which contained his blood. Forensics will verify that it's his DNA. It's indisputable. Tony's gone."

Laura clutched the ring even tighter and rolled over in the bed, turning away from both John and Massimo. Her mouth fell open in a silent scream. Once again, she had lost someone she loved to the clutches of death.

CHAPTER 16

Goodbye, Tony

The following morning, Laura lay lifeless in the hospital bed. She stared out the window, not really seeing beyond it. She felt dead inside. The only person she wanted to talk to was Jesus. John had stepped out, finally giving her a moment to really feel.

Questions rambled through her mind.

"Lord, why does it keep happening to me? I lost my baby, Sabrina, who my arms still ache for, my Momma, Patty, and Pop. Wasn't that enough? Wasn't that ENOUGH?"

A tear trickled down her exhausted eyes. She couldn't fathom that her Tony, good or bad, was gone. Despite the past year they had been separated, she still loved him. Now, he was no more. Her Tony—the funny, sensitive, passionate Tony—was gone.

"Lord, is he up there with You? Did he have a relationship with You as he appeared to? Will I see him someday, when it's my time? Please Lord, don't let his soul go to Hell."

Another tear spilled from her eye as she thought of the possibility of never laying eyes on him. *How was she going to pull through this?* When her family died, it was Tony who helped her. He had been her strength. Tony had been her rock.

"Lord, I can see there are two lessons to be learned here. One: Always give someone the chance to be forgiven. I should've known better, after Pop. I did it again with Tony. Forgive me, Lord.

"Two: I need to remember that You're all I need. From now on, I can't trust myself. You're infinite and I need to believe that You know what's best for me. So here I am, do with me as You please. All I ask is that You stop this heart from hurting . . ."

The previous evening's intern, Paul Roberts, interrupted Laura's prayer. "How's our girl?" his voice was above a whisper.

Laura could only nod.

"I know you've been through a lot. If I can help in any way, please say so." He reached under the blankets for her arm. Lifting her limp hand, he placed two fingers on her wrist and timed her pulse. Moments later, he made notes on her chart. "I'm going to check your eyes." He opened her lids with his fingers and flashed a light before them. She blinked. Her eyes were expressionless. "Didn't get much sleep last night, did you?" She lowered her eyes. "I hate to be a pain in your butt, but you shouldn't have fought the medication. It would've helped."

"I didn't fight it. Sleep just never came," she finally spoke.

"You could've called and we would've upped the dosage."

"What, so I can stop feeling? That's not going to happen," she added sarcastically.

Paul Roberts sat on her bed and lifted her lowered head with a gentle finger. He looked into her blank eyes, his face as serious as hers. "I understand your pain. I lost my fiancée two years ago to a car crash. It's unbearable. But here I am. I'm still standing. Some days you want to put your fist through a wall, other days you simply live. Bottom line is, you're young, and you've your whole life ahead of you. You have a wonderful family. What more can you ask for?"

Laura finally focused on the young man's face. *Where had he come from and how was it that he was actually making sense?*

"I love my family. They're the best thing that ever happened to me."

"Well, there you go. Your wonderful family is dying to come in. May they?"

Laura nodded. "Wait. I realize that you probably don't go around sharing that with your patients. I appreciate that you shared it with me, just to give me hope. Thank you."

"You're right. I rarely talk about her anymore. It's too hard. But when I look into your eyes, I see the same pain there that was in mine. If the least I can do is share my experience to help another, then why not. Good luck to you." With that, the charming doctor withdrew from the room.

The door was still open as he filed out and Tammy, Marlene, and John entered. Before wrenching her attention to Laura, Tammy waved to the doctor as he left. She smiled at Marlene, who smiled in return. Apparently, intern Paul Roberts caught the eyes of Tammy Knight.

Laura greeted her family dishearteningly. The tears began to flow. John had already explained to Marlene and Tammy what happened to Tony. The three were there to comfort her.

After another visit with the psychiatrist, Dr. Janice, and after Dr. Willow's approval, Laura was given the release to go home. They prescribed stronger medication for Laura's bronchial infection and additional medication to help her emotional get-through the next couple of nights. From there, they prescheduled Laura's next counseling appointment.

*   *   *

The following month didn't seem to get better for Laura. Though she was physically over her bronchial infection, her emotions were still erratic. She couldn't find it in her heart to put Tony's ring away. She felt as though she'd be saying goodbye to their love forever. She looped it onto the chain of the necklace Aunt Bernadette had given her and hid it near her heart. Meanwhile, the holiday season seemed to bring her down even further. It appeared as though her bout with depression would never refrain.

Laura tried to move forward. She and Tammy took classes in school that assisted them in finding part-time jobs, using their secretarial skills. Tammy was hired as a file clerk for an insurance company and Laura as an office worker in a law office. Straight from school, the girls would go to their new jobs and work a limit of four hours a day, five days per week.

John and Marlene were both excited for them and purchased an additional vehicle for Laura to use. The vehicle was an older model, but was perfect for getting around in.

At last, Christmas was around the corner. One particular evening, Laura and Tammy dared to head out in the bristling cold to go to a nearby mall for shopping. After a few purchases in the hustle and bustle of the mall, they decided to call it a 'day'. As they strolled through the massive entryway toward the doors, Tammy's eye caught a glimpse of the young intern, Paul Roberts.

"Laura, isn't that him?"

Laura squinted across the hallway trying to see passed the mass of people. As her eyes caught sight of him, he turned her way and smiled.

"Oh!" Tammy screeched. "He's coming."

"Will you calm down? It's just a guy."

"Just a guy? Come on, Laura. He's drop dead gorgeous! Admit it!"

"Okay, okay. So he's cute. What did I tell you about cute guys, anyway?" Laura warned.

"Shh. He's coming."

He approached the two and his smile widened. "Laura Knight and . . ."

"Tammy," Tammy offered.

"That's right, Tammy. How are you?" he grinned.

"Fine, thank you."

"Just fine," added Tammy.

"Let me guess, a little last-minute Christmas shopping?" He flashed a dazzling smile Tammy's way. She about melted.

"Oh yeah. Last-minute shopping," Tammy parroted.

Laura tried to contain her smile. Tammy was obviously wild about him. "How about you?" Laura asked.

"Well, I'm buying for my family back in Detroit. I'm going to fly west for a few days and spend time with the folk back home. I rarely get to see them anymore."

"Oh, are you originally from Detroit?" Laura asked.

"As a matter of fact, I am. Born and raised there almost all of my life, until I finished my degree at Michigan State University and got my internship here in Albany."

"That's interesting," Tammy flirted.

Paul smiled. Despite the noise of the busy mall, an awkward silence fell between them. Laura jumped in. "Well, we must be on our way."

"So soon?" Paul questioned.

"Well, we're not in that big of a rush, Laura," Tammy stated as her eyes bulged, giving Laura the signal.

Laura sighed and for Tammy's sake, gave in. "No, we don't have to rush. But I'm sure Paul has shopping to finish," Laura continued.

"I do, but it can wait. May I buy you a hot cocoa or a coffee?"

Before Laura could protest, Tammy agreed. They walked to a nearby café within the mall and sat at a small table. After placing their orders with the waitress, their awkward conversation continued.

"Laura, feeling better?" he asked.

"Thanks to God and Dr. Janice, I'm much better. Just taking it one day at a time."

"She's doing better than that. She got a co-op job working as a clerk for a lawyer. Our dad even got her a car," Tammy praised.

"That's great. Who's the lawyer?"

"Jasper Stone," Laura answered.

"Sounds familiar."

"Well, Tammy here is being too modest. She's doing just as good for herself. Her co-op class got her a job as a secretary for an insurance company. Hopefully, we'll both be able to stay on after graduation. At least until we go to college."

"That's great. Looks as though you both have a bright future ahead of you."

The conversation lingered a while longer. They drank their coffees and chatted lightly. For Laura, it seemed as though the discussion would never end. She felt uncomfortable under Paul's examining eye. At last, they rose from the table and said their goodbyes.

"Thank you for coffee, Paul. It was nice," Laura managed.

"Yes," Tammy winked at him. "The best coffee in town, not to mention the company."

Paul blushed and held a grin. "Thanks, same here. Hey Laura, maybe I'll come see you sometime at your office job. Perhaps, we can do lunch?"

Laura simply smiled, singing the word 'goodbye' as she gathered her shopping bags and purse and walked away. Tammy called out after her, as she smiled at Paul one last time before clumsily sprinting off to catch up to Laura.

"Laura!" she hollered. "Laura, did you hear what he said to you?"

Laura glanced at Tammy as she juggled the bags in hands. "Yes, I heard him."

"Why didn't you at least answer him?"

"I didn't know what to say."

"You could've said, heck yeah!"

Laura giggled. "Tammy, you're so funny. Why would you want me to say 'yes,' when you're the one with a crush on him?"

Tammy frowned, "Because it's obvious he's interested in you, not me."

"You don't know that." They exited the mall and entered the bitter cold of winter. Laura huddled deeper into her winter coat, walking even faster.

Tammy raced to keep up. "Come on," she continued. "Why would you say no to a guy like that? He's got the world at his feet. His head seems screwed on straight and he's a gentleman."

"Tammy, I'm far from ready. I still can't get Tony out of my mind. Nor do I want to. At least, not yet."

"Why are you still holding a torch for that guy?"

Laura came to a sudden halt. "I don't know. Please, just leave it alone." Suddenly, she began to stalk even faster, as she changed the subject. "You should go for Paul, since you think he's so wonderful. He won't take a second glance at me after getting to know you."

"Who are you kidding? You're beautiful. I'm just a clumsy frump."

Laura stopped in her tracks, again. The wind whipped at her long hair. "That's by far, the dumbest thing I've ever heard you say."

"Thanks."

"I'm serious. You're not frumpy. You're beautiful both inside and out."

"And that's exactly what beautiful people say to ugly people. 'That beauty comes from with-in'," she mimicked.

Laura turned on her heel and strode toward her car. "You're being ridiculous." She entered the key in the lock and opened the door. "Now get your rear in there, before I kick it."

Both girls broke into laughter. Laura started the ignition and began the drive home. "You know, if you want, I can help you learn to apply makeup. We can get your hair cut and styled differently and maybe you'll feel a little more confident about yourself."

"I don't know. I think I was made to look frumpy."

Laura raised her hand and smacked Tammy's forearm. "Stop that!" They both chuckled, but remained silent the return home.

In the next week, the Christmas holiday was at hand. Laura was happy to be a part of a loving Christian family who took the birth of Christ seriously. On Christmas Eve, the four went to midnight Mass at the Catholic Church nearby, singing and praising the newborn King. The following day, they joined Uncle Joe and Aunt Bernadette's family, and enjoyed a warm, joyous day.

Laura had a few weak moments, especially on Christmas Eve, but most of her grief was being expressed through the counseling sessions with Dr. Janice. The drive home from Uncle Joe's on Christmas night wasn't long, yet long enough for Laura's brain to start to wander.

She thought of Paul Roberts and wondered if he'd made it home to his family in Detroit. From there, her mind lingered to Massimo. She mulled over where he might have spent this holiday. Without warning, her mind wandered to Cicero and her Christmases there. She thought of Uncle Frank. She was sure he had been notified of Tony's death. *Now that he was all alone—no wife, no nephew—with whom did he spend his holiday?* Her heart ached for all his losses.

Laura looked lovingly upon her new family. She was blessed to have them. Her eyes fell on John. His strong facial features were relaxed as he skillfully maneuvered the vehicle with one hand and held Marlene's hand in the other. It was sweet how they still displayed their affection openly.

Marlene unexpectedly coughed, placing her hand over her mouth. The cough seemed to rattle her, until it finally came to a stop. She glanced at her hand and gasped.

"What is it, Mom?" Tammy asked.

Marlene wiped her hand with a tissue paper and quickly crumbled it. "I think I'm just catching a cold."

Something didn't sit right with Laura from there. She began observing her adoptive mother and this cough that she claimed was just a cold.

Though the next few weeks brought them into the New Year, Laura felt none of her New Year resolutions were sticking. She still dreamed of Tony, despite the counseling, despite her own will. As for moving forward, she lived every day as it came, not truly thinking ahead any further than she needed to.

One day in particular, she received a telephone call at her office job from Paul Roberts. He asked to take her out to lunch. Laura kindly gave him a few excuses and hung up the phone. A few weeks later, he tried again, to no avail.

Again, Laura refused.

Meanwhile, Marlene's cough hadn't yet diminished. For weeks, the family insisted she see a doctor. She set an appointment with a specialist that was still two weeks away. Her already frail body became even thinner. They grew more concerned with each day.

Early one February morning, two days prior to the appointment, Laura overheard Marlene coughing so hard in the bathroom, she could be heard clear across the house. Laura tapped on the bathroom door.

"Marlene? Are you all right?"

Tammy joined her, concern on both their faces. Laura knocked again. Marlene didn't respond. Both Laura and Tammy began to panic. "Mom? Open the door. Can you hear me?" They heard a low moan.

Laura dashed for the garage and rustled through John's toolbox. Finding a fine flat screwdriver, she raced for the bathroom. Her hand trembled as she worked the doorknob, finally getting it open. Marlene, white as a sheet, lay on the bathroom floor. The sink was full of blood. Marlene was in much worse condition than she let on.

Laura and Tammy called 911 and an ambulance arrived, rushing her to emergency.

Marlene was taken in immediately. Paul sprinted toward the girls upon seeing their arrival. Both Laura and Tammy cried as they explained the blood they discovered and Marlene's continuous cough the past two months. John arrived in time to hear what had happened. He was frantic with fear.

"Don't worry, Mr. Knight, Tammy, Laura. We'll find the underlying cause of this, as soon as possible. I'm going to take matters into my own hands and ask them if I can personally study her condition."

Laura reached for his hand and squeezed it. "Thank you." He nodded and left.

The three sat in the waiting room and prayed together as the doctors began their examination of Marlene. John wept bitterly, stating that he should've pushed her to go to the doctor sooner. Laura and Tammy tried to comfort him, but he was beside himself with fear.

The time passed sluggishly, as they paced the waiting room floor impatiently. Laura and Tammy both called the school and their employers and explained their situation. Before long, Uncle Joe arrived and waited with them, desperate to keep his big brother calm.

At last, Paul and Dr. Eric Stanley, Chief of Staff and head surgeon, appeared and directed them into the x ray waiting room. The four sat down and prepared themselves for the worst. Standing near the x ray results on the lighted wall, Dr. Stanley began his explanation.

"I'm afraid I don't have a good prognosis. After a series of x rays and ultrasounds, we've discovered a mass here in Marlene's left lung." He pointed at the darkened area of the x ray. "After careful consideration, we want to perform what we call a mediastinotomy. This procedure is performed by making a small incision in the chest, then inserting a scope to remove a tissue sample of her lung. From there, we recommend a CAT scan and/or a MRI to get a better picture of how serious this is and if, in fact, any other parts of her body show a similarity to what we see here. Most likely, we're looking at immediate surgery. The mass covering the lower third of her lung needs to be removed. For now, we can't say for sure how serious this is. But, it doesn't look good."

John leaned back in the chair, raising his hands to his face. He rubbed his face roughly, as if trying to remove the scene from before him. "Okay. Okay, let me get this straight. It's cancer?" he asked bluntly.

"I'm afraid so."

Tammy let out a sob. "Oh my God."

The tears dropped down onto John's cheeks. His face crumbled. He tried to compose himself but couldn't. Uncle Joe kept a gentle hand on his shoulder. Tammy hid her face, her shoulders rising and falling with sobs. Laura's breath became short. She stood from her chair, wanting to console her father. A heat rose to her neck and face. The room began to spin, a ringing pierced her inner ear, and darkness fell before her.

*   *   *

Laura rose from her chair. Paul noticed the color drain from her face. She called out for her father before nearly tumbling to the floor. He reached forward and caught hold of her. He barely struggled as his strong arms swept her up and gently placed her on the waiting room couch. Joe,

John, and Tammy rushed to her side, as Paul quickly dashed from the room for smelling salts. He returned moments later. They cleared the way for him and he gently lifted her head to wake her. Laura came to.

"What happened?" she groggily asked.

"You fainted," Paul stated. "Have you had anything to eat yet today?" Laura shook her head no. "It figures. You need to eat," he chastised.

Laura sat up, trying to regain her bearings.

"Are you okay, honey?" John questioned. "Don't worry everything is going to be okay. It just has to be." Father and daughter embraced, putting a lump in Paul's throat. "Hey, you called me 'Dad'."

She blinked to clear her vision and smiled at him. "That's 'cause you are."

He let out a cry and hugged her again.

They all exited the waiting room and, at last, decided it was time to tell Marlene what was to come. Paul stayed on, after Dr. Stanley left, explaining in detail the procedure and answering any additional questions the family had. He watched as they pulled together to comfort and lift Marlene. It amazed him the way the two adopted girls truly loved and cared for their parents as their parents cared for them. Something about them couldn't help but draw Paul to them. He chuckled to himself at that thought. That something was Laura. *Who was he kidding?* He couldn't take his eyes off her.

It was something in the way she talked, how she used her hands to communicate, and the way she smiled that made his heart skip a beat. Her golden-brown hair was always styled and she always appeared neat and intact. Her clothes complimented her perfect figure and her big hazel eyes seemed to shine. If only he could fill the emptiness he'd seen in them. If only she'd give him the time of day to do so. It was evident that he was attracted to her. He only hoped she felt the same.

*   *   *

That evening, as Tammy and Laura drove home together, they were silent. Laura couldn't speak of the unbelievable fear she felt in her heart for Marlene. As Tammy drove John's car, Laura closed her eyes and fought back the tears. She prayed some more.

"Lord, are You there? Because I can't seem to feel Your presence much these days. Everything's going so wrong. I see Your blessings every day and I thank You for them. But lately, Lord, I feel like I'm losing myself, bit by bit, each time someone I love is taken from my life. Please, Jesus, don't let my new mom die. You put her in my life for a reason. Now this? I don't understand. But I'm going to keep on trusting You. I'm going to count on You to take care of my new family. Because, of all the things that Momma ever taught me, the greatest was Your love for me. Thank You, Lord."

Laura opened her eyes and focused on the road before her. She had faith that God would help Marlene. She knew that she could trust Him to take care of her. Still, Laura couldn't shake the horrible fear she felt. It was the same fear she felt the night she lost her real mother. Laura remembered that night vividly. That memory remained engraved in her mind forever.

CHAPTER 17

Momma

The Old Cabin
February 21, 1969

Patty and I huddled together in our twin bed, trying to stay warm. The wood stove in the kitchen/family room could not compete against the rough Northern New York winters. In fact, our little cabin almost shuddered against the howling glacial winds.

I covered my ears with my hands to keep the shouting voices of both my mother and my father from penetrating.

"What were ya thinkin'?" he shouted.

"What was *I* thinkin'? I told ya a thousand times that we shouldn't. You were so drunk ya couldn't have stopped yaself if ya tried!" My mother, Cara, began to cry.

"Stop that. Ya know I hate it when ya cry."

"Matt, what're we gonna do? How are we gonna manage? Another mouth ta feed? We can't afford . . ." She broke down in tears once again. *Another mouth to feed? What was she talking about?*

"Isn't it you who always says 'have faith'. At this point, there's nothin' more we can do. Let's tell the girls. Maybe now they'll start pickin' up some of the slack 'round here."

"Matt, they'a still kids. What do you expect from 'em?" her Brooklyn accent still thick.

"At 10 and 12, they ain't no kids! I told ya a hundred times ta stop babyin' 'em, Cara. When ya gonna listen?"

Both Patty and I cringed at the sound of the chairs scrapping against the wood floor as both our father and mother arose. Pop's thunderous footsteps made their way toward our nine-by-nine bedroom. The flimsy door plunged open and in entered our despondent mother and aggravated father.

"I know yous still awake, so listen up. Me and ya ma have somethin' to tell yous."

More bad news? Pop had recently lost his job . . . again. That past week, he'd come home one evening in a drunken stupor, ranting and raving that he'd 'been canned'.

Momma was upset with him of course, saying something about how it wasn't fair that Patty and I had to go to school without a lunch. He didn't respond. He simply did what he did best and that was to walk out and leave the burden on my mother's shoulders.

Now, Momma sat at the foot of our bed. Her spiraling golden-brown locks bounced as she fidgeted with our blankets. "Girls, we have some news," she tried to compose her emotions, "But with it comes a bit of work and sacrifice." She looked at us each individually with a reassuring smile. "Momma's gonna have a baby."

It all made sense, now. Another mouth to feed would *indeed* be a problem. Patty and I sat up in our bed. "Don't worry, Momma," Patty uttered. "We'll manage. We always do."

Tears filled my mother's eyes. "That's right, Momma," I added. "Patty and I'll help you take care of it. It'll be like having a real doll."

Momma ruffled my already messy hair and smiled through her tears. "Oh, thank God for yous." She gathered us into her safe arms and squeezed us.

"All right," Pop's stern voice interrupted, "Here's the deal. I don't wanna see ya motha doin' all the work 'round here. I better not see yous standin' 'round here doin' nothin'. Yous ain't babies no more. That means, helpin' ya ma with the inside *and* outside work. Do I make myself clear?"

"Yes, sir," we chanted in unison.

"Fine. Now, go ta sleep." With that, he stalked back into the kitchen.

Momma tucked us back into bed. A tear slowly slid down her cheek. "I hate him, Momma," Patty whispered. "He's so mean to you. Blamin' you for this. Why do you put up with him?"

"Don't hate ya fatha, Patty. He's the only one you'll eva have. I pray that Jesus will help him ta turn his life around. You should pray for him, too."

"Forgive me for sayin' this, but he doesn't deserve your prayers."

"Patty! I don't eva wanna to hear ya say that, again," our mother scolded. "Ya fatha has made mistakes, but his heart is good and it's in the right place. If he'd just stop drinkin' he could pull himself togetha. I know it."

"I hope you're right, Momma."

"Me too," I added. Although I wasn't quite sure my mother felt that my father sobering up would ever happen. She kissed our cheeks and scurried out of the room.

*   *   *

The next seven months of my mother's pregnancy proceeded hastily. Day by day, we watched my mother's belly grow bigger. Likewise, our father's attitude grew meaner.

He claimed to search for jobs, as he was desperate to get his hands on anything. I later came to learn that my father was illiterate and that explained why he was never able to hold a job. When flowers began to blossom and spring was in the air, he farmed on our property. Selling the crops we tilled, saved us from near starvation.

Meanwhile, Patty and I finished off the school year in June, bringing us to the last months of Momma's pregnancy. Those last few weeks were difficult for her. The summer heat caused her ankles to swell, making it impossible to do any work. That's when Patty and I began to seriously take on the household chores. Momma taught us how to do everything. We cooked, we cleaned, we even farmed. She repeatedly reminded us of how proud she was of the hard work we endured. She always encouraged us.

It was rare to have a summer evening, the four of us. Most of the nights, our father would take what little money we had and spend it at the bar. Momma would always cover up for him. But Patty and I had grown to despise him. We were old enough to understand his selfishness. It was that understanding that made us question our mother's devotion to him.

One hot August night, we ate at the dinner table. Momma had gathered together a meager meal. Our father didn't seem pleased with it. He slammed his fork down on the table, causing us all to jump.

"This is pathetic," he seethed. We looked at him questioningly. "I'm so sick of lookin' at ya sad faces. I'm outta here." He abruptly pushed his chair back and stormed out the door. Momma struggled, as she got up from the chair and ran outside after him. Patty and I peered through the open kitchen window and watched as Momma held her stomach while catching up with him.

She waved her hands at him as she hollered. Her anger boiled over as never before. "For the past 13 years I've been prayin' ta see a change in ya. Every night when ya walk out on us ta spend our money on booze, I defend ya!" she screamed. "Well, no more! I won't do this no more. We're sufferin' because of ya. Ya refuse ta clean yaself up and take responsibility. Ya not the man I married, Matt."

Our father glared at her. This time, his angry dark eyes didn't stare her down. "You'a a loozza!" she spat. "And I hate what ya done ta me and I hate what ya doin' ta my girls. Is this the example ya promised ta set for 'em? My father was right. *You'a* the liar, not *him*."

Patty and I were astonished that he stood there and absorbed her harsh words—words that he definitely deserved. Momma continued, "Ya promised me the world and ya given me nothi' but heartache. My girls are the only things keepin' me here. Honestly, I'm startin' ta believe that it's in their best interest ta leave."

We watched in horror, as he lifted his hand and smacked our mother. Patty and I rushed out of the cabin door. Momma had her hand on her cheek. Tears instantly streaked her face.

Pop towered over her, pointing a finger in her face. "Shut up, Cara. Ya pushin' it!" Unaware that we were standing there, he struck her again.

"Stop!" I screamed. We ran toward her, but stopped midway.

His angry eyes came to focus on me. He took a step back from my mother who still resisted him. "Step down, Cara. Take ya place as the obedient wife, like ya always do." His voice deepened and growled, "Or I'll send ya reelin' back." He glanced at us once more and jumped in his old pick up, leaving my mother in a heap of tears.

Patty and I ran to Momma's side. The tears spilled from her eyes, but she remained strong in her stance. "Good for you, Momma. Are you okay?" Patty asked.

"I'll be fine." We walked her back into the cabin and helped her down on the couch. She patted the grungy pillow next to her, inviting us to sit. "I'm sorry I blew up like that. I couldn't hold it in no more. I'm also sorry ya had ta witness that ugly side of ya fatha."

"Is there any other side?" Patty asked.

"There used to be. When I married him, he wasn't the man ya see taday. He was kind and lovin'. He seemed ambitious and smart. He promised me the world. I hate ta say this, but I was stupid ta believe him. I was so captivated by his handsome face and by his hopes and dreams. I believed more in him than he believed in himself. Once he started drinkin', it was ova. He gave up, and I feel as though I'm about ta. All I've eva wanted was fa him ta clean up his act. Well, I told him tonight and just look where it got me. That's the first time he's eva hit me."

"I'm sorry, Mom. I hate him. I hate him for hittin' you. You're a wonderful wife and mother. He doesn't deserve you. You're way too good for him." Patty exclaimed in frustration.

Momma didn't defend him this time. She closed her tear-filled eyes and let them flow down her face. "The ironic part is that my family warned me. They told me not ta marry him. They told me ova and ova and I refused to see it."

"Momma," I asked. "Is that why you never talk about your family to us? We don't have grandmas and grandpas. All the kids at school do."

"Because it hurts me too much ta even think about 'em. We neva see anyone, because everyone disowned me when I married ya fatha. My fatha, your Nonno Nino, begged me not ta marry ya pop. It was almost as if he could foresee the future. He told me time and again, that if I married him I'd ruin my life."

"How'd he know?" Patty asked this time.

"Because, he figured ya fatha out. He sensed that ya fatha didn't have a hard workin' bone in his body. But most of all, ya grandpa didn't like him because he wasn't Sicilian."

"What's Sicilian?" I inquired.

"It's an island near Italy, stupid. That's where Nonno's from." Patty exclaimed.

"Patty, that's not nice. Don't call ya sista stupid," Momma chastised.

"Sorry."

"Nonno and Nonna moved to America from Sicily before I was born. We carried all our Sicilian traditions ova ta the States. I rememba speakin' Sicilian at home all the time. My motha was definitely the honorable, obedient wife, and a wonderful motha. My fatha was lovin', yet strict. But fa someone 'right off of the boat', he was a brilliant businessman. He was very powaful and had all kinds of connections."

"What do you mean," I asked.

"Let's just say, bad people were afraid of Nonno. I hate ta say it, but sometimes he stepped outside the law ta help a fellow Sicilian outta trouble. That's why otha families highly respected Pop and would come ta him fa advice. They'd borrow money from him, instead of a bank. He'd always give the less fortunate the benefit of the doubt. He was able ta do that because we was very wealthy.

"Yes, Nonno and Nonna was good to me. Now, when I look back at how my life was before ya fatha, I realize that I was livin' like a princess."

Momma struggled to her feet and led us into her bedroom. In her closet, under one of the loose floorboards, she withdrew a small box. She opened it up and exposed a beautiful gold locket. "This is 24-karat gold from Italy. Mom and Pop gave me this on my 16th birthday. I loved 'em so much, that I wanted ta honor them by puttin' *their* pictures in it."

Patty and I both had a chance to hold the locket in our hands. I looked at the pictures curiously. My grandfather looked strikingly handsome with a neatly trimmed mustache and big brown eyes. His brown hair was perfectly groomed and slicked back. Our mother was a replica of *her* mother. Her soft brown hair framed her round little face. It was wavy hair, like my mother's and like mine. Nonna's golden locks of hair were kept neatly tucked back with a beautiful decorative hair comb.

"Patty, you'a the oldest and I'm trustin' ya with this. If fa whateva reason somethin' should happen to me, ya are ta see ta it that this locket never falls inta ya fatha's hands. He'd hock it in a New York minute fa cheap beer and booze. Fa now, I'll keep it here." She placed it back under the loose board and led us back into the kitchen.

"Tell us more, Momma."

"Yeah, what happened next?"

After making herself comfortable on the couch again, she continued her story. "Pop was a good husband and fatha. But he had his rules. He was strict with me. Especially, because I was the only child, I was neva allowed to date. All my cousins' marriages were arranged ta otha good, respected Sicilians. Nonno always wanted us ta marry 'our kind', he'd say. I happened to meet ya fatha by chance. We met in secret, behind Pop's back. I fell fa him and his lies. He asked me to marry him.

"When I told my parents I wanted ta get married, they was devastated because he was an 'americano' and a 'punk', as Pop once put it. Pop was stubborn, but I was even more stubborn. He insisted I break it off, immediately. He even forced me ta take a trip ta Sicily ta try and forget him. But, as soon as I returned from Italy, we eloped. I left and got married at 18, without my family. I disgraced 'em. That's been the biggest regret of my life." Momma paused. Her eyes were distant as she recalled a past we never knew existed.

"After realizin' that they truly cut me from their lives, I was heartsick. I didn't really understand the seriousness of it. I thought, 'Oh, they'll fagive me—they'll neva disown me.' But they did. I was lost without 'em. I almost couldn't function. One night, one of my closest friends introduced me ta Jesus. I mean, I was raised Catholic. We'd go ta church on Sundays. But I never took the initiative ta get ta know God more, until I really needed Him.

"After losin' my family, I turned ta the church. That's how I became saved. I neva wanted ta lose my family. But when they wanted nothin' more ta do with me, the church embraced me. They taught me that Jesus loved me, no matter what decisions I made, good or bad. I learned that I needed ta be wiser in my decision makin' and I learned ta walk the straight and narrow path. As long as I repented of my sins and accepted Jesus as my Savior, then I was saved."

"Momma, you haven't talked to your family since you got married?" Patty questioned.

"Oh, I've tried a hundred times ta talk to 'em, in many different ways. I tried callin', I sent lettas, and I even sent my pastor ta try and persuade 'em ta give me anotha chance. My fatha said I broke their hearts and they wanted nothin' ta do with me. I miss 'em terribly." The tears swelled in her eyes. "It's days like taday, I wish I'd listened ta 'em. But when I look at my two beautiful girls, I wouldn't change my life fa anyone in the world. You'a everythin' ta me." She kissed us both. "Now do your old Ma a favor and wash those dinna dishes."

Patty and I did as she asked. Momma sat on, surely recollecting times of old. She dabbed her tears with a hanky. My heart went out to her. I thought of my grandparents and how unfair they were to her. *How could they go on not knowing about their only child?*

Momma blew her nose gently, as she cried to herself. I couldn't stand to see her so upset and distraught. As I was about to go to her, I heard her let out a yelp.

"Momma, what's wrong?"

"Oh Lord. Oh Lord!" she cried. "Patty, run and grab me a towel, quick." Patty dropped the dishrag and dashed from the kitchen into momma's bedroom to retrieve a towel from her dresser. She ran back and handed it to her.

"What happened, Momma?" she asked.

"Oh God! My wata broke."

"What does that mean?" I asked.

"That means the baby's comin'."

I began to panic. *Where was my father? How long would it take before he returned? Did Momma need to go to the hospital?*

"What're we going to do?" I cried.

Momma seemed lost in thought for a moment. She took a deep breath. I'll never forget the fear in her eyes that moment. "Girls, if ya fatha doesn't make it home in time ta take me ta the hospital, you'a gonna have ta help me deliva this baby."

Patty screeched, "How, Momma? You need a hospital. Laura and I don't know what the heck we're doin'. Let me run into town and find you some help."

"That's definitely an option, Patty. But it depends on how fast I go inta labor. Fa now, I need ya both ta help me."

We helped lift Momma from the couch and guided her into her bedroom. She raised her leg to climb the sagging mattress and buckled over in pain clutching her swollen belly. "Oh no!" she cried. She panted for air, until the pain eased. "Okay, check the clock, Pat. That was my first contraction. We'll see how far apart they come. In the meantime, ya girls need ta prepare a few things."

I reached for my mother's hand and squeezed it, all the while swallowing the lump in my throat to keep from crying. "Are you going to be okay, Momma?"

She smiled at me reassuringly. "Yes, baby. Pray that Jesus is with us and that He helps this baby ta come out safely. Okay?"

I nodded, unsure of what to do next. She pointed to the kitchen and began spouting orders. "Pat, I don't want ya goin' fa help. I have a feelin' this baby's gonna be here soona than we think. Sweetie, ya need ta listen carefully. Grab as many towels as ya can and bring 'em here. In the kitchen, get the scissors, a large bowl, and boil water in the largest pot we have. Laura, honey," she called me. "Outside, in the shed, you'll find the big wicka basket we use fa our laundry. We'll put a clean sheet and some blankets inside it. When the baby comes, *we'll lay it* in there. Next . . ." she stopped in mid-sentence and grabbed her belly. "Oh no, anotha contraction."

"Mom, it's only been three minutes," Patty cried.

"Okay. It's okay," Momma moaned. "We can do this, girls. I'm relyin' on ya. Go, do as I asked." After following through with her directions, we gathered together in the bedroom. Momma explained the birth process to us between contractions. She then ordered us to use the scissors and cut strips of cloth from an old sheet. She said we'd need them to stop the circulation of the umbilical cord in two places before cutting it. Next, we sterilized the scissors in the boiling water and poured the clean boiled water into the large bowl. All was ready. Patty and I, both, were nervous, yet excited to watch the birth of our baby brother or sister.

Momma's contractions began getting closer. The sweat beaded down her brow as she panted through each one. I opened all the windows to let the cool evening air in, but still the room was blisteringly hot. We tried to make her comfortable. Nevertheless, the closer the contractions came, the more our mother screamed in agony.

Hours slipped passed us. Momma was exhausted and began to despair. "Oh Jesus," she prayed aloud. "Somethin's wrong. Why isn't this baby comin' out? Please, don't let this baby die. Please, help my baby." Patty and I tried to calm her.

At that moment, we heard the door slam, as Momma began with another contraction. Patty stayed with Momma. I was determined to give my father a piece of my mind. I entered the kitchen and found him leaning on the counter, with his head in the trash.

"Are you sober enough to take your wife to the hospital? Momma is having the baby and it's not going well." He looked at me with vacant eyes. My words didn't seem to connect in his brain. "Pop, I said Momma's having the baby. We gotta get her to a hospital."

He turned back around and hurled into the trash. I was sickened by his drunkenness, nearly feeling the need to hurl myself. He turned around and tottered toward the front door. He was going to leave. He was going to desert us.

"Pop . . . Daddy wait!" I suddenly cried. "Momma needs you." I grabbed his forearm to stop him. His muscles constricted under the force of my hand. For the first time ever, I stood straight as I spoke to him. I looked him in the eye. "If you leave her, she'll die and I'll never forgive you! Help her!" I ordered. He pulled his arm away and turned his back on me. "*Don't go!*" I screamed. But the slamming of the cabin door silenced the urgency in my words.

Slowly, I felt the hot, stinging tears spill down my face. Tears I knew would burn in my heart, forever. I lowered my head in defeat.

Distracting my thoughts was another piercing scream coming from my helpless mother. "Laura!" Patty yelled. "Help me!"

I dashed for the bedroom in time to see Patty at our mother's feet. Momma's legs were spread open and though she had covered herself with a sheet, I could see the opening where the baby's head was coming out.

"Come on, Momma. Keep pushin'!" urged Patty. "The baby's right here."

Momma's face was drenched in sweat and red as she grimaced at the pain in her abdomen. She took a deep breath and pushed again. The baby's head finally came out, facing upward. Patty's hands trembled, as she wiped the baby's face with a warm wet rag. The baby let out a howl that sent a chill up my spine. Momma sobbed and pushed again.

Luckily, Patty was standing close by, for the baby nearly sprang from our mother's womb into her arms. "It's a girl!" Patty cried. We all cried tears of joy. Patty screamed for a towel and I quickly delivered. Momma had enough energy to give the last directions on how to tie and cut the cord, and then passed out in exhaustion.

Patty and I worked swiftly. I held the baby wrapped in the towel, as Patty tied the cord in two places and cut down the center with the sterilized scissors. Cautiously, we placed the baby on the bed and wiped the jelly and blood from her pink little body. She screamed in anger, as we cleaned her and wrapped her up in blankets for warmth. Patty carried her to the head of the bed.

"Momma, do you wanna hold your baby girl?" Patty asked.

Momma barely opened her eyes, but reached out to hold her. She whispered her thanks to Jesus and kissed her.

"What'll we name her?" I asked.

"Laura?" her voice hardly audible asked me.

"I like the name Sabrina."

"Well, since Patty got to pick out your name, Sabrina it is."

"Wow," I whispered. "Thanks."

Momma smiled at me. "Now, please," she whispered, "Take Sabrina and lay her down. Make sure ta hold her head. I'm not feelin' well."

We carried Sabrina to the basket and somehow managed to lay her in it. Patty and I both wanted to tend to Momma. We began cleaning her up, when we noticed the large amount of blood on the sheets beneath her. Patty tried stopping the blood, but it was impossible.

"Momma? Momma, can you hear me?" I called. She tried to focus on my face. Her eyes were rolling backward. Suddenly, I noticed her all too pale face. Her lips were turning white as well. "Momma, look at me. How do we stop the bleeding?"

She pulled my head close to her lips and whispered into my ear. "Take care of the baby. I love you." She leaned her head back down on the pillow and closed her eyes . . . forever.

"Oh God. No, Momma. Don't die."

"What?" Patty screamed. She jumped from the foot of the bed and pushed me out of the way. "What're you sayin'? She ain't dyin'." She shook our mother's shoulders. "Momma, Momma?"

Momma didn't respond. Her body was lifeless. At first, we didn't know what to do. Suddenly, it was as if little Sabrina felt the separation and began to wail. Patty and I were frantic. Thankfully, Momma had everything prepared for the coming baby and Patty was able to find a baby bottle and nipple. She quickly warmed up a bottle of regular milk and fed it to her. Sabrina took the bottle eagerly.

When, at last, she settled down, reality sunk in. We were grief-stricken at the loss of our mother. We stood near her body, unable to part from her. I rested my head on her chest and begged her to return to us. Patty collapsed to the hard floor and wept loudly. Our loud wails prevented us from hearing the door open, as our father returned.

"Cara?" he bellowed. "Where's everybody?"

Patty and I exited the bedroom and entered the kitchen. We stood, pale and exhausted. Our clothes were stained with our mother's blood and fluids. His eyes bulged at the sight of us, but he didn't speak a word.

"You're not worthy to say her name," Patty stated through clenched teeth. She pointed an accusing finger at him. "You never deserved her. You're a worthless husband and I hope you rot in Hell for killin' her."

"What'a ya talkin' 'bout?" he staggered past us and entered the bedroom. The revolting odor of alcohol was still on his breath. Patty and I followed.

"Cara!" he roared.

He stumbled onto the bed and grabbed our mother's shoulders. He shook them as he called out her name. Fear paralyzed him and he came to the realization that Momma was really gone. Patty and I cried openly now as we witnessed the grief grip him. He called out her name repeatedly. Tears fell from his eyes. He gathered our mother into his arms and screamed. "Oh, Cara! Oh my God, Cara. What have I done? Oh God. Oh God!"

I raced toward him and beat at his back. "You did this. You could've saved her. I begged you to stay, but you left us. I hate you! I hate you!"

Patty grabbed my shoulders and tore me from my father. She held me in her arms and we both cried. We cried for our mother, whose eyes would never again see the beautiful baby she gave her life for. We cried for the baby who would never have a recollection of the wonderful mother we had. We cried for ourselves, for our mother truly was the center of our lives. We even cried for our father, because only a woman as amazing and as extraordinary as her could love a man like him.

We buried our mother in the local cemetery on a cloudy, overcast day. Patty held our little Sabrina as the tears spilled from her eyes. The pastor's words touched our hearts as he described the wonderful soul of our mother. I glared across Patty at my father, who stood at the head of the cheap casket that held my mother's dead body. His face was set like flint. I asked God to forgive me, because I hated him. I hated him with every fiber of my being.

A breeze rustled the grass and trees around us. I closed my sore eyes and pictured Momma floating up into the sky to be with her Savior.

Goodbye, Momma. Goodbye.

CHAPTER 18

Changing Tides

The past remained on Laura's mind the next few days, as they faced the reality of Marlene's condition. Everyone was devastated and frightened for her. And though she seemed to take the news with valor, the fear was evident in her eyes. She listened attentively to the next steps without flinching. It amazed Laura and Tammy, both, how strong Marlene was enduring. Even John, who put on a strong performance for her, couldn't uphold his courage for long. At one point, he broke down and cried. Marlene even insisted he go home with Tammy and Laura every evening. He absolutely refused to leave her side and the girls understood his need to stay with her.

After getting a second opinion, it was affirmed. Marlene was diagnosed with Large Cell Carcinoma, a cancer commonly developing in masses, as hers did. The doctor confirmed that surgery to remove the mass was required. Two days after the diagnosis, the wedge resection was performed on Marlene and the mass, along with over one-third of her left lung, was removed successfully. The oncologist, who assisted in the surgery, was confident that they eliminated ninety-five percent of the cancerous cells.

The CAT scan and other numerous tests confirmed that the cancer was at Stage II, meaning it had invaded neighboring lymph nodes. It was indisputable, chemotherapy and other methods would be necessary to keep the carcinogenic cells from maturing.

When the questions arose as to how and why Marlene's lungs developed the malignancy, the answers weren't definite. Though she didn't smoke cigarettes, asbestos and radon were known to be the leading causes of Non-Small Cell Lung Cancer. Immediately, John had the insulation in the new house tested and was relieved to find it asbestos free. Now, the conclusion was simple, to fight the disease with every fiber of her being.

Meanwhile, during Marlene's stay at the hospital, both Laura and Tammy took turns visiting with her and bringing her home-cooked meals. She was clearly touched at how the girls were taking care of both her and John.

Paul kept his promise and made it a point to visit with Marlene and the Knights on a daily basis. He kept them up to date with test results and helped by explaining things in layman's terms.

Laura was touched by his dedication. Tammy seemed to fall over herself at the mere sight of him. It was evident that he made a few additional visits to see Laura often and for a change, Laura didn't seem to mind. Neither did Tammy.

A week after the surgery, Marlene was sent home. They advised her that she was to begin the following week with chemotherapy. Once she was settled in at home, things seemed to resume back to normal. The day Marlene went in for her first therapy, the girls drove one vehicle and left the other for Marlene. Chemo battered her completely. She was more than nauseated, Marlene was entirely drained and weakened. This resulted in them taking turns driving her to and from her therapy.

One morning, a few weeks into therapy, Laura and Tammy dressed for school. They heard a scream coming from Marlene's bedroom. The two ran in, frantic.

"Mom?"

Marlene sat in the middle of her bed, tears coursed her cheeks. "Mom, what is it?" Laura questioned. Marlene pointed to her pillow, unable to speak. Upon her pillow was a large patch of hair.

Laura swallowed the lump that rose in her throat. She kneeled before Marlene in the bed and hugged her. Marlene wailed loudly. "I'm losing it—all of it!"

Tammy sat next to her and embraced her too. "It's okay," she soothed. "Think about it, Mom. It's only hair. This is not permanent. You're going to beat this. You'll go into remission and your hair will grow back."

"Don't worry, Mom," Laura added. "You can wear cute hats or a wig until your own hair grows back." She wiped a tear from Marlene's cheek. "I can't even try to imagine how scared you are. But you have to continue to stay strong. You've been doing so well. Don't let *this* get you down. It's only temporary."

Marlene smiled through her tears and she embraced the girls and thanked them. "You both were sent to me for many reasons and I believe this is one of them. God knew what was coming and He sent you just in time. I'm so blessed to have you." She paused a moment and added. "Laura, did you really say it? Do you really see me as your mother?"

Laura burst into tears. "I always have. I'm so sorry it took so long to say it, but you're a mother to me in every sense of the word . . . and I love you!"

"Yes, Mom . . . we love you," Tammy added.

"*Oh, thank you, Jesus,*" Marlene cried, turning to the Heavens. "I love you both, too! So much!" The three women pressed closely together. Laura never felt more loved or needed.

* * *

Thankfully, the following weeks got easier. Marlene's hair didn't completely fall out throughout the duration of the chemotherapy. Everyone was thankful for that. Though she did have it cut very short to keep the loss from looking so evident.

Everyone did his or her best to pitch in. Laura continued to work part-time at the law office after school. From there she'd rush home to begin dinner with whoever made it home first, be it John or Tammy. One day in particular, she sat in front of her employer's desk and took shorthand as he recited a letter aloud. Mr. Jasper Stone paced his office as he rattled off the last words of the letter to her. He stopped and leaned his thin figure against his desk for a moment.

Running his fingers through his thinning gray hair he asked, "Laura, I have a question for you. Do you think you'd want to stay on with me after you graduate?"

"Absolutely, Mr. Stone."

"Will you be taking a break this summer before you begin college and continue here part-time? Or would you go full-time throughout the summer months?"

"Full-time. Definitely."

"Great. That tells me your initiative. In a couple months, I'd like you to come with me to Alabama to take on an appointed case for one of my relatives. I've petitioned with the court and they will allow me to represent them without issues. It wouldn't be for more than a few days—four tops. But I'd want you there. Do you think you'd like to come? I'd make it worth your while financially and it'll be educational for you as well. Of course, I'd finance your trip and the stay."

"Mr. Stone, for now I'll tell you, yes. I'd love to, but I don't know where things will be at home. I'd want to make sure my mom is okay, first."

"Understood." He patted her shoulder and pulled out the file on the case he was discussing.

As Laura absorbed the information and began to get a feel for the lawsuit, the telephone disrupted their meeting. Laura ran out of Mr. Stone's office and into hers. She answered, surprised to hear Paul on the line. It had been nearly four weeks since she'd seen or heard from him.

"How are you?" his voice sang.

"I'm good, and you?"

"I miss you. I haven't talked to or seen you in a while. Is Marlene doing well?"

"Yes, thank you. She has two more weeks of chemo and hopefully the cancer will go into remission."

"Great. I hope so." Paul paused a moment and continued. "I feel a bit awkward, because I don't want to come across as bold. But I'm sure I've made it obvious that I'd like to see you outside of hospital visits." They both chuckled and Paul continued. "I wanted to give you space because I know you've been hurting, but honestly, I can't get you off my mind. I guess I'm wondering what you think because I can't tell. I get mixed vibes from you and before I make a jerk of myself . . ."

Laura giggled, "Paul, stop. I'm glad you've given me space, I'll be honest, because Lord knows I needed it. But I also know that you're an amazing person. It's just that, as you know, I've been hurt and . . ."

"All I want is to take you out to dinner. Give me a chance to be your friend, first."

"First?"

Now Paul laughed, "Well, we'll let things happen as they will. Can I take you out to dinner tonight?"

Laura held her breath. "Sure."

"Seven-thirty, okay?"

"Sure."

"You going to give me directions?"

Laura laughed, "Sure." She exhaled and lifted a trembling hand to the chain around her neck. She rattled off the crossroads to her home. After hanging up, she closed her eyes briefly and sighed. Once again, she realized the need to move on. She wasn't sure how easy that was going to be.

After finishing at the office, she rushed home and found that both Tammy and John had begun dinner. Marlene lay on the couch, resting. Laura gracefully entered the family room and knelt before her adoptive mother. Marlene caressed Laura's cheek, as Laura bent to greet her.

"How'd it go today?" Laura asked.

"Same as always," Marlene weakly remarked.

"Do you need anything? Can I get you something to drink or a pillow for your back?"

"Stop fussing over me. I'm fine. Why don't you go change and get ready for dinner. Smells good. I wonder what those two are cooking up in there."

"I don't know. But I don't think I'll be home for dinner tonight. Unless, of course, you need me."

Marlene's dark eyes instantly lit up. "Really, why not?"

"Paul called me . . . again. He wants to take me out to dinner. I can cancel, if you want me to."

"Why would I want you to cancel? John and Tammy are here. You go ahead and have fun. He seems like a great guy."

"I know, but . . ."

"It's just a dinner. No buts!" Marlene struggled to sit up. Her frail body looked lost in the baggy sweat suit. "Laura, you've been through so much. When are you going to start letting yourself live a normal life? Let go of the past and look toward your future."

"With Paul?"

"With whomever your heart desires. Date. Live. Love."

"I know you're right." Laura leaned closer to Marlene and whispered, "I'm so scared."

"Hey, I don't blame you there. But you're smarter and wiser. You know what characteristics to look for. If something doesn't sit right in your heart, confront it and ask questions." Marlene lovingly touched Laura's hair as she spoke. "It's time you started to really live." Laura bowed her head and fiddled with her fingers. "What advice would your mother have given you?"

"The same advice you're giving me."

"Then listen to your mothers."

"Thanks Mom, you're the best!" After a long hug and a kiss, Laura entered the kitchen.

John and Tammy were laughing as they argued over what seasoning tastes better on a steak. "Hi guys," Laura called.

John kissed her on the top of her head as he passed her with a dish in his hands. "Just in time for dinner."

"Oh, I'm sorry. I should've called to tell you not to set a plate for me. I wasn't sure if I was going to go or not."

"Go where?" Tammy questioned.

Laura held a smile, knowing the reaction she'd get from Tammy when she'd announce her date with Paul. "I have a date."

"With who?" Tammy's eyes bulged.

"With Paul."

A piercing scream shot through the air as Tammy danced across the kitchen floor, holding Laura's hands. "Ha-ha! I knew it. I knew he wouldn't stop until you said yes."

"Tammy, it's only dinner."

"Whatever! That hunk is taking you out!" she cheered.

*   *   *

Laura paced her bedroom floor, nervously. She had changed out of her work clothes and slipped on a fitted black skirt and a fashionable pink silk top, with cap short sleeves and a sweetheart neckline. She tied her hair back, displaying a silver set of hoop earrings with a silver necklace to match. She had removed her chain with Tony's ring, but not having the heart to take it off completely, she placed it in her handbag. At last, she retouched her makeup and added a sprinkle of perfume to her neck. Disrupting her thoughts as she paced, Tammy knocked.

"It's open."

Tammy entered and looked at Laura. "Wow, you look great. What're you doing up here?"

"Wearing a hole in the carpet."

Tammy laughed, "Don't be nervous. You'll be fine. Have fun and enjoy yourself. If I were in your shoes . . . well, if I were in your shoes . . ."

"You'd have passed out by now!"

"You're right!" They embraced and Tammy led her down the staircase. "Come on, Mom and Dad want to see you."

Before reaching the bottom, the doorbell rang and John dashed for the door. He greeted Paul and ushered him into the doorway. Paul glanced up. His eyes met Laura's. Her stomach quivered a moment. He looked more handsome than she'd ever seen him. His sandy blond hair was neatly brushed to the side. His face looked smooth with a fresh shave. The light scent of his cologne filled the air. Then he smiled and all her fears seemed to perish.

They greeted one another with a friendly peck on the cheek. Tammy's smile was from ear to ear, as they all entered the family room where Marlene sat. Paul greeted Marlene and asked her how she was. They spoke for a few moments. Laura stole a few glances at Tammy, who was giddy with happiness. Laura's heart felt warm at the excitement Tammy displayed for her. She loved her sister so much.

Paul mentioned the time of their reservations and Laura caught the hint. She excused herself, as she ran back up the stairs to get her handbag and jacket. She stood before the mirror in her bedroom one last time and adjusted a loose strand of hair. She took a deep breath, exhaled and after gathering her things, she descended the stairway.

Waving goodbye, Laura and Paul exited the house and left for their date.

*   *   *

Paul was a complete gentleman. As they left, he escorted her out of the door, holding her elbow the entire way to the car. He even opened the car door of his green 1972 Ford Mustang and helped her in. Laura was impressed at his gentle manners.

In the vehicle and at last alone, Laura's nerves began to wear. Paul tried keeping the conversation light, asking a few questions here and there. Laura tried not to appear apprehensive.

"You've one heck of a father, in John," he added.

"Oh no. Did he say something to you?"

"As he should. He's your dad. He's looking out for his girl."

"What did he say?"

"He gave me a serious look and said, 'You know what she's been through. Please, let's not add to her pain'." Paul mimicked John's deep voice.

Laura couldn't help but laugh. "I'm sorry. But isn't he wonderful?"

"That's what I said, didn't I?"

"He's the best! And so darn funny. No matter how miserable my day may be, one minute with him and he has me in stitches."

John's humor smoothed things over without the necessity of his presence. By the time they arrived at the restaurant, Laura felt more at ease and comfortable with Paul. The restaurant was elegantly decorated, yet cozy. In the far-left corner, a series of windows overlooked a beautiful golf course. The waitress guided them to a table there. They ordered dinner and sat waiting patiently.

Laura looked at Paul from across the table, noticing how his strong jawbone added character to his appearance. When he smiled, the dimple in his right cheek didn't hurt either. He had full lips that looked soft. His eyes were a light blue and his lashes thick. She glanced down at his hands. His nails were neatly manicured, his fingers long. Her eyes traveled upward, as she ranked the size of his forearm underneath his white dress shirt.

"Well?"

Laura nearly jumped at his question. She smiled, "Well, what?"

"Have I passed?"

Dumbfounded, she asked, "Passed what?"

"Inspection?" he asked with a mocking smile on his lips.

Laura blushed, turning a deep shade of red. She hadn't realized she was openly staring at him. She covered her face with her hands, trying to hide her smile. "I'm sorry," she managed.

"Well? Did I?" he pestered.

"Of course you did. You're beautiful!" Laura couldn't believe the words had escaped her lips.

"I can say the exact same for you. In fact, if I haven't said it already, you'll have to forgive me. But you look gorgeous tonight."

Laura blushed even deeper. "How many shades of red are you going to make me turn?"

"As many as it takes to make you understand how beautiful you are." Paul reached across the table and gently picked up her hand. "Laura, thanks for coming out to dinner with me. I've been looking forward to a night out with you, from the minute I laid eyes on you in the hospital."

Laura was surprised, "I can't see why. I was so sick, not to mention tattered. I looked awful."

"Nope." Paul smiled brazenly.

"So tell me, Mr. Persistent—tell me about yourself. You know so much already about me. Let's hear about you."

"Well, as you know, I grew up in Detroit. I'm the youngest of three. Growing up, my mom was a homemaker. My father was a pharmacist, now retired. I have two older sisters, Donna and Peggy. They're both married and have kids. My family and I, although apart, are still very close. I wouldn't be here if it hadn't been for them. They encouraged me to get my medical degree and to do my internship here—even if that meant us being separated."

Laura tried to imagine moving into a city without family or loved ones. She didn't think she could bear the separation. "That has to be hard, being away from the ones you love."

"Some days. But then I just pick up the phone and call. The other thing that made it easier to leave, was Samantha's death. Too many painful memories there and the change of scenery here made the transition a little easier."

"I don't mean to be nosey and if it's too hard to talk about it, I totally can relate, but how long ago did the accident happen?"

"It was two years ago in January. Michigan is known for its horrendous winters, much like New York. It was one of those ice storms that you see in the movies. Everything was covered in glassy ice. I warned her not to go out that day. She promised to stay home. But she'd received a call that her father was involved in a minor fender-bender and needed a ride home. She headed out to help him, but never returned. Her father waited and waited at the police station. They told him there that she'd lost control of the car. It veered into oncoming traffic."

Laura shook her head in sadness. "How horrible. Her family was devastated, I'm sure."

"Her father couldn't forgive himself. I don't know if he ever will."

Their conversation deviated into other directions and that evening Laura was able to see a side of Paul she knew she could easily begin to like. After dinner, they took a drive around town until they reached the Knight's driveway.

"I had a wonderful time, Paul. Thanks for being persistent. I'm glad we went out."

He smiled, his dimple deepening. "Me too. I enjoy your company. Are we going to do this again?"

"Absolutely." Laura leaned over the console between them and kissed his cheek. As she pulled away, Paul gently caught her forearm.

His face was inches from hers. His breath was warm and sweet as he whispered. "I could get used to seeing your face daily."

Laura blushed. He gave her a peck on the tip of her nose. "Goodbye."

"Goodbye." She closed the car door and walked up the porch stairs. She waved one last time before entering the comfort of her home.

It seemed as though everyone had retired for the night. Laura removed her shoes and tiptoed up the stairway. The second floor was quiet. Her hand rested on her bedroom doorknob when John exited his bedroom. "Hey, you're home okay?" he whispered.

"Yeah, thanks."

"Did you have a good time?"

"Yes, I did. He's nice. I just . . ."

"Say, no more." John embraced her and kissed her head. "One day at a time, Laura."

"I know. It's just hard."

"I know. Say your prayers and God will help. Your mom wanted to wait up for you, but she's just too exhausted. She told me to tell you that she's proud of you. I second that notion."

"Thanks, Dad."

"Goodnight."

"Goodnight." Laura entered her bedroom, turning on the lamp on her nightstand. Tammy's sleeping figure on her bed startled her. "Tam? Tammy, wake up. You scared me to death."

Tammy sheepishly smiled. "Sorry. I tried to wait up, but I guess I failed. Fill me in." She sat up in the bed. Her sleepiness suddenly vanished.

"Tammy, you were right. He's really nice and a gentleman. We talked all night. He told me all about himself, his family. He even told me about his fiancée."

Tammy's eyes enlarged. "Oh, the one that died."

Laura nodded. "What else can I tell you? He said he wants to see me again. I said yes. I just . . ."

Tammy frowned. "Don't even say it, Laura."

"I know . . . I know. Forget Tony."

"I don't understand you sometimes. You've the opportunity to get to know someone really great. Don't take it for granted. Some of us would kill for that chance." She paused a moment. When Laura didn't respond, she added, "I'll give you your bed back and get outta here. See you in the morning." With that, Tammy exited the room.

Laura removed her clothes and put on her pajamas. She turned the light off and climbed under the covers of her bed. She thought of Paul. He was charming and handsome. She thought of Tony. Her heart raced. *When would the time come that her insides wouldn't jump at the thought of Tony?*

*   *   *

Tammy crawled into her bed, fighting hard to keep the sob in her throat from escaping. She smothered her face into her pillow and let out the hurt she'd been bottling up. She was happy for Laura. She sincerely was. Laura deserved happiness. She'd been through too much. But it pained her that Laura couldn't appreciate a chance with a man like Paul. *Why couldn't he have liked her instead?*

It was inevitable. Paul was obviously interested in Laura. *And why shouldn't he be?* Laura was beautiful. She took better care of herself. She knew how to apply makeup and do her hair. When Tammy would attempt to apply makeup, she looked like a raccoon. Ultimately, Laura dressed better and Tammy didn't have the courage to wear clothing that made her look more appealing. Tammy didn't feel comfortable getting that kind of attention.

Until now—until Paul Roberts came into the picture. All at once, Tammy wanted to grab hold of *someone's* attention. She wanted to capture *someone's* eye. Only now, it was too late. Even if by some miracle Paul was to look her way . . . it was too late. Laura liked him and it looked as though any chance Tammy may have had with him was gone, forever.

Tammy cried herself near sleep.

CHAPTER 19

New Love

Summer 1978

T he last days of Tammy and Laura's graduating year arrived. Between going to school and juggling their jobs, time was fleeting fast. Thankfully, Marlene's cancer went into remission. For the time being, it appeared to diminish. That meant no more chemotherapy or radiation and that was a relief for all. It was simply mandatory for Marlene to take oral medication daily. In comparison to the dreaded intravenous therapy, Marlene had no problem with swallowing the pills for a while.

Meanwhile, Paul Roberts continued to play a part in Laura's life. After their first date, he called her on a regular basis. Unfortunately, his work schedule required almost all of his time and they seldom saw one another. Laura was fine with this. She wanted to get to know him at a slow pace. She enjoyed his company, but Laura still longed for something that could never be. Her heart still ached for the past and she couldn't bring herself to part with Tony's memory or his ring.

At times, she tried explaining her feelings to Tammy. Tammy listened intently, but didn't understand her love for a man who had hurt her. Laura tried describing her relationship with Tony before that last horrible night. Still, Tammy sympathized, but could not fathom.

"Laura, I believe what you had *was* real. But he's gone. You need to move on!" She'd insist.

Laura knew she was right. She promised herself that she'd try to bury those feelings. She'd picked up the pieces of her life in tougher situations than this. She reminded herself that she could do it again.

*   *   *

At last, graduation day arrived. Laura had talked to Paul earlier who insisted on coming to commencements. It was a warm day. Laura dressed in a light blue airy dress, which complemented her figure. She let her hair down, in long ringlets. After adding gloss to her lips, rouge to her cheeks, and mascara to her lashes, she completed the look with a light touch of blue to her eyes. Finally, she slipped on the graduation gown and zipped it up. She placed the hat on her head and descended the staircase.

John and Marlene, who sat in the living room waiting, gasped at the sight of Laura. "Here's one of my girls!" John began humming the 'Pomp and Circumstance' march, making Laura giggle.

"Oh, Dad!"

He mimicked an announcer's voice. "Graduating with honors, Miss Laura—Ann—Knight!" Laura kissed his cheek and Marlene's.

"Tammy," he shouted. "Hurry up! You don't want to be late for your graduation, do you?"

"Coming," she hollered, as she skipped down the stairway into the living room.

"Oh, you both look so beautiful." Marlene clapped her hands together in happiness. "I'm so proud of you." She embraced them both.

Tammy and Laura beamed with happiness and pride. "Paul will be here any minute." Laura explained.

They sat back on the couch and waited. Everyone was excited and happy. Laura studied her family. Marlene's color had returned and she looked radiant in a rose-colored cotton dress. She wore a summer hat to match. Her hair was still short, but had started to grow in, complementing her small face. She began jabbering about the party she planned to throw that weekend.

John looked lovingly upon her as she spoke. His white polo shirt and matching brown slacks made his golfing tan glow. His smiling eyes made him all the more handsome. He had trimmed his beard, leaving only a shadow, making him look younger than his actual age.

Tammy had dressed in a yellow summer dress, two sizes too big. She tied her hair back and had applied lip-gloss. She looked refreshing, yet her beauty was still hiding behind large framed glasses and bushy eyebrows. Laura eyed her sister. Tammy was a beautiful girl. She just needed some help with her hair, makeup, and wardrobe. Laura made a mental note on what to do. She decided she was going to help her the first chance she had.

At last, the doorbell rang. Laura raced to the door to let Paul in. He appeared frazzled as he kissed her hello and greeted the rest of the family.

"Congratulations to you, too, Tammy," he sang as he gently hugged her. She backed away, seeming almost stunned at the appeal of affection.

John patted Paul's shoulder. "Everything okay, Doc? You look upset," he questioned.

"I'm fine, thank you. I was concerned that I was going to make everyone late, is all."

"No worries. As long as you're all right."

"I'm okay. Ready to go whenever you are." They piled into John's new vehicle and drove away. Paul sat between the two graduates in the backseat. Laura was genuinely happy to have him there. He looked handsome in his blue dress shirt and jeans. Although John was right, Paul did seem distracted and distant, at first. By the time they arrived at the school's gymnasium, he appeared himself again.

*   *   *

In the car, Tammy held a gasp as Paul's leg brushed up against hers. She looked out the window and tried desperately to remind herself that he was off limits. The scent of his cologne wasn't helping. She stole a glance at him and grimaced. *He was so unbelievably handsome.* As John turned the vehicle sharply, she felt his body pressing up against hers. She nearly jumped from her seat. Touching him was spine-tingling.

"Sorry Tam," he whispered. "I guess we better brace ourselves if we're going to adapt to John's driving."

Everyone in the backseat giggled.

Tammy was beside herself with happiness, the way he was joking with her. She just kept reminding herself that the feelings were *not* mutual. She closed her eyes a brief moment and asked God to her help her find a man, *just like* Paul Roberts.

*   *   *

When they arrived, John parked the vehicle and the group walked into the school together. Laura and Tammy waved goodbye as they joined their friends and teachers before the ceremony. Marlene, John, and Paul met up with Uncle Joe and his family and found a seat in the bleachers of the school gymnasium.

Laura felt herself in a dream, as she walked single file with her schoolmates into the enormous gym. The 'Pomp and Circumstance' march played in the background and the huge crowd cheered, while the graduates found their seats.

While speeches were being given, Laura's mind began to wander. She thought of her mom, Cara, and how she wished she could've been there. Her memory flashed back and she thought of Patty and Sabrina. It was unfair that they never got to experience this rewarding day. Yet, had they continued their lives in the cabin as they did, Laura wondered if she'd have ever reached her senior year.

Patty should have been able to finish school. She had gotten so cheated out of life and Laura felt sick at the thought of her big sister and the short hard life that she had lived. Laura truly missed her. She suddenly fought tears.

Then she thought of her baby sister. *Would Sabrina have made it to graduation?* She tried to picture her little face and was terrified that the memories of her precious little one were fading. Laura closed her eyes and envisioned the round little face with the curly brown hair that framed it. Her heart suddenly hurt and she wished for just a moment to hold her baby sister in her arms again. She could feel the memories start to toil with her emotions.

Laura tried to focus on the schoolmate who stood behind the podium and spoke of their awaiting future. She wondered what would become of her life. *Would her relationship with Paul flourish? Was a career in criminal justice what she really wanted?* She knew she had it in her. Tony had always said she was smart.

Pain twitched in her heart just to think of him. *Oh, Tony.* She felt tears fill up in her eyes. Laura didn't want to feel this—*not here, not now*. Yet, the tears spilled down her cheeks, without effort.

Tammy noticed and elbowed her. "What's wrong?" she mouthed.

Laura shook her head and smiled, whispering, "I can't believe we're graduating."

Tammy returned the smile. "I know. I'm proud of us," she whispered.

At last, they began filing toward the stage. Principal Nugenbower called on students to greet him and receive their diplomas. Upon calling out Laura and Tammy's names, a huge blow horn was sounded and the two heard John, Paul, Uncle Joe, and the boys, shouting in the bleachers. The girls blushed, as they shook their principal's hand and walked off the stage.

The rest of the ceremony was short. Before long, Laura and Tammy rushed into the school's main hall to meet with the family. Laura spotted the trio along with Uncle Joe, Aunt Bernadette, and the boys. She grabbed Tammy's hand and they ran past friends and schoolmates to join them.

John and Marlene's arms were outstretched and they immediately embraced them. Marlene lavished Laura's face with kisses, then Tammy's.

Moments later, Laura found herself in John's arms. He squeezed her until her insides ached. Meanwhile, Paul congratulated Tammy by setting a big kiss on her cheek and hugging her. Then Paul reached for Laura and spouted how proud he was to see her receive her diploma. He lifted her up and spun her around. He kissed her cheek, as well. Laura returned the hug. Her insides felt warm and happy. She felt safe. She felt loved. Tears began to dwindle downward.

"Now, don't start the water works again," John warned. His eyes were moist as well. He pointed to Marlene who already was gently blowing her nose into a tissue. Everyone laughed. Tammy and Laura greeted and embraced the rest of them, receiving kisses and congratulations. Soon, Uncle Joe and his family departed, promising to spend time with them at the party, that weekend.

Afterward, John took the five of them out to dinner. They enjoyed the evening together at the Knights' home, afterward. Paul stayed the whole while, but eventually stood from the sofa to go. He said goodbye, thanking John for treating him to dinner. Laura walked him out the front door.

"Thank you so much for making this day so special," she spoke softly.

"I had a great time. Thank you for having me."

Laura stood near Paul's vehicle in the moonlight, staring out onto the front lawn. Her hands were clasped behind her back. Paul stood facing her, leaning his bottom on the hood of his car. He reached forward and gently placed his hands on her waist, drawing her closer to him.

Paul looked into her eyes. "I don't want to go. I don't want this night to end."

Laura sighed, "Neither do I."

He leaned forward and for the first time, placed a gentle kiss on her lips. The kiss was slow and warm. Their lips parted and she looked into his eyes. He looked at her as intently. They kissed again, this time the kiss strengthened. Laura's arms found their way around his neck. He pulled her closer until their bodies touched. A surge of energy seemed to pass through them. Laura inhaled deeply, trying to focus. Her head felt hazy.

"Can I call you tomorrow?" Paul asked.

"I'd like that."

He embraced her one last time and entered his car. Laura watched as the vehicle disappeared into the night. She lazily walked back into the house. Up in her room, she sat at her vanity and looked at her reflection. Underneath the neckline of her dress, she withdrew the necklace with Tony's ring. Unlinking it, she removed the ring, leaving only the charm. She stared into the white stone. Bringing the ring to her lips, she kissed it and stored it away in the drawer of her nightstand. Laura said goodbye to her first love.

*   *   *

The following morning, both Tammy and Laura had an appointment to tour the University of Albany. They showered, dressed, and quickly gobbled breakfast before whirling out the door. The original college plan was to stay at home, rather than live on campus, since the drive was fairly close. But after timing the actual drive, Laura and Tammy agreed that the twenty-five minute drive during rush hour would eventually become wearisome.

"I've got an idea," Laura stated, as Tammy drove around the campus.

"Oh no."

"Oh yes, and it's brilliant."

"Okay, let's hear it."

"Maybe dad will let us stay in one of his rentals near campus. We'll be closer to school. Yet, we're a hop, skip, and a jump from home. We can still see mom and dad daily, if we want."

"Gosh, Laura, that's perfect. We need to see if dad has a rental nearby. We will pay our rent, because we still work. Yet, you know he'll cut us a break. This is great. We'll have our own place and still be close to home. Let's go home and talk it over with them."

"Hold on, Tam. Before we leave for home, I have a surprise for you today. We're going to make a few stops."

"Where?"

"Follow my directions." Laura called out directions as Tammy drove. Before long, they pulled into the parking lot of a beauty salon. "Remember, a few months ago when I promised you I'd help you with a new look. Well, after mom got sick, things fell to the wayside. Today, I scheduled an appointment for you to get your hair trimmed and styled. I also scheduled a facial and makeover. Today is your day to be spoiled, by me, because you've been the best friend and the best sister ever."

"You're kidding me, right? Oh, Laura, thank you." The girls hugged and quickly exited the car.

Shortly after entering the salon, a beautician called Tammy's name and directed her to a chair. Laura followed, hoping to give Tammy some encouragement.

"Okay," the beautician began. "What do we want to do here?"

"Don't take too much off," Tammy cried.

"Don't listen to her," Laura interrupted. "I'm not saying go short, but I think she needs to cut off the splitting ends and maybe a few layers to give her hair a lift."

She agreed after examining Tammy's hair more closely. First, they rewashed and treated Tammy's hair with a special conditioner. Then, the beautician began sectioning off the hair and started to cut. Slowly, Tammy's hair began to take shape. When she took the blow dryer to it, she formed it into a beautiful, contemporary look. Tammy appeared a new person.

The beautician then led them into a different room where another woman sat Tammy down and discussed waxing her eyebrows. They decided on a style and the woman waxed and cleaned up Tammy's brows.

Finally, another woman approached them. She was the makeup artist. She discussed skin tones and colors with Tammy and Laura. First, she applied a facial mask to Tammy. Once it dried, she removed the mask, and applied lotion. Carefully, the professional began to show Tammy how to apply eyeliner, rouge, and lipstick. When, at last, they were through, Laura didn't recognize Tammy. She was ravishing.

Tammy stood before the mirror gazing at her reflection. Tears of thanksgiving brewed in her eyes. "Oh no," cried the artist. "No tears!"

Laura tipped the artist and beautician, paid at the front desk, and the girls entered Tammy's vehicle. Tammy was glowing with happiness and joy. "I can't wait to show mom and dad."

"Oh no. We're not done yet."

"Laura, you've already done enough. What more did you have in mind?"

"We're going to the mall . . . to get *you* a new wardrobe."

Tammy's eyes lit up and they cruised out of the salon parking lot, into the way of traffic. Tammy eased the car down the main road, past their home, and headed toward the mall.

At the mall, Laura directed Tammy into her favorite clothing store. Laura piled outfit upon outfit into their cart. Tammy was stunned at the way Laura spotted the perfect ensembles.

"Laura, here's a size eight in this one."

"You are not a size eight. Why do you insist on wearing clothes two sizes too big? You're a size six, not an eight."

"Are you sure?"

"Just be quiet and follow me into the dressing room."

They entered the dressing room. One by one, Tammy tried the outfits on. She modeled the clothes for Laura who either agreed or disagreed. At last, Tammy had a beautiful selection of new clothing that complimented her figure.

"Okay, you're not paying for these clothes, Laura."

"No, I'm not. But mom and dad are. I told them where we were going today and mom insisted she pay for everything. That means, out with those old frumpy clothes and in with the new."

Tammy was speechless, while they walked toward the registers to pay. In the car, on the drive home, Tammy thanked Laura for her help.

"Tammy, all this time I didn't want to offend you. I wanted to help you, because I could see that underneath those baggy clothes and behind those bushy eyebrows, there hid a beautiful girl. I'm so glad you finally got contacts, because the glasses hide your beautiful features, too. You need to start wearing them daily. Throw out those old glasses. You don't need them anymore."

"I know. I'm not used to the contacts yet."

"In order to get used to them, you must wear them!"

"I know, you're right. I'll try."

"I have to ask you, why do you feel so uncomfortable with your body? It's not like you're overweight."

"I don't know. I'm too shy. I'm always afraid that guys will see past the act and know that I'm just a frump. I feel like I'd be laughed at."

"Are you crazy? You're beautiful, through and through."

Tammy smiled and guided the vehicle toward home.

"Hey, let's stop by the hospital and show Paul your new look," Laura suggested.

"Oh no. I don't want to," Tammy stated matter-of-factly.

"Why? Come on, Tam. You're not still nervous around him, are you?"

"Darn tootin'. Boyfriend or not, he's still a massive babe."

Laura laughed, but on a more serious note asked, "Do you consider him my boyfriend?"

"Laura, he's crazy about you. He spent all day with our family yesterday. Of course, I'd consider him your boyfriend. Don't you?"

Laura looked out the window and confessed to Tammy that he had kissed her for the first time. She also confessed that she took off Tony's ring and stored it away.

"Well, it's about time."

"That I took off the ring or kissed Paul?"

"Both! I don't think I would've held out as long as you."

Laura and Tammy both laughed. It was undeniable that Tammy still crushed over Paul.

* * *

Tammy's nerves itched. She wasn't sure if seeing Paul was a good idea. *How long could she conceal her feelings for him? Were they even feelings, or in fact, just a crush?* She drove the vehicle into the hospital parking lot. The two girls walked into the hospital and across the halls, toward Emergency. Tammy nervously glanced around the busy hallways. She spotted Paul, reading a chart near the main desk. At that moment, he glanced up. His eyes fell first upon Tammy, then Laura. His face immediately smiled.

"What a nice surprise." His eyes never left Tammy's, as he approached. "Tammy, is that you?"

"Doesn't she look great?" Laura exclaimed happily. "What do you think?"

He looked deeply into her eyes. "I didn't even recognize you. You look so different. You're even more beautiful." He smiled and kissed the two girls hello.

Tammy felt the blood rush to her face. Her hands trembled as she fiddled with the purse in her hands. "Thanks to Laura," she managed. "I couldn't have done this without her."

Laura was jumping with excitement. "Oh, Paul, we had so much fun. First, we got her haircut, then a facial and makeover. Finally, I took her to the mall and we got the greatest bargains on new clothes for her." Laura smiled at Tammy.

Paul continued to admire Tammy's new look. "All I can say is—wow!"

Tammy fidgeted under his piercing eye. She cleared her throat and scrambled for a distraction. "If you're busy and have patients to see, we don't want to keep you, Paul." Tammy interrupted. "Go on ahead."

Paul smiled and shook his head in no. "As a matter of fact, I was going to run up to the cafeteria and grab some lunch, while things were slow. Would you both join me?"

"No . . ." Tammy shyly declined.

"Sure we will, Tammy. I don't know about you, but I'm starved." Laura rubbed her belly.

"Come on, let's go." Paul looped both Tammy and Laura's hands through his arms and guided them toward the cafeteria. Tammy's heart raced. He was being attentive of her, more so than normal. She slid her hand down and put more space between them, although it pained her to do so.

In the cafeteria, they purchased their lunches and found a booth to sit in. Paul sat next to Laura, across from Tammy. He joked and teased, flirting with both girls. Tammy wouldn't let her eyes lock with his. She wondered why he kept staring. Had it been in another place and time, Tammy would've been ecstatic. But it wasn't and he was dating Laura, not her.

After they finished with lunch, they chatted a while longer. Paul was suddenly paged and reluctantly had to go. He leaned forward and pecked Laura's lips briefly.

"Are we still on for breakfast, Friday morning? You said you make the best hot cakes."

"Yes, we're on."

He scooted out of the booth and reached over to kiss Tammy. His lips brushed the corner of her mouth and she nearly jumped at the sensation. Laura was digging through her purse for change and didn't notice. She glanced at Paul, who didn't seem to notice either. He waved and left.

"Ready to go?" Laura disrupted her thoughts.

"Sure."

Most of the ride home was quiet. At last, Laura broke the silence. "Tammy, you were right. Paul is wonderful."

"Yes, he is." Tammy glared forward as she drove. She tried not to let the tear in the corner of her eye trickle downward. She was angry with herself. He wasn't flirting with her, she decided. He was being friendly. He wasn't looking at her the way she wished he had. It was only in her imagination. That was another reason she was upset. *What kind of a sister was she? How could she let herself even think about her sister's boyfriend?* She promised herself that she'd deny any feelings she had for Paul.

CHAPTER 20

The Kiss

Both Marlene and John were astounded at the change in Tammy's appearance. They couldn't compliment her enough.

"So, tell us. How'd it go at the university?" John ultimately asked.

"Actually," Laura began, "It went well and that's precisely what we wanted to talk to you about. Tammy and I timed it. There's about a twenty-five-minute drive from here during traffic hours."

"Are you saying it's too far?" Marlene now asked.

"That will depend." Tammy added.

"On what?"

"On Dad."

"Your father? Why your father?"

Laura interrupted, "Mom, Dad, the last thing we want to do is make you feel as though we're not happy here. That's the furthest thing from the truth. In fact, our reason for going to SUNY is so that we will be close to you. But the drive to campus daily is long. We were wondering if it was possible to rent one of Dad's rentals off campus."

John and Marlene glanced at one another. John questioned, "You both want to move into one of my rentals?"

They nodded.

"Dad," Tammy added. "We figured we'd have our cake and eat it, too. We'd be near school. Yet, close enough to see you on a daily basis. But, if of course you don't want us to move out, that's fine, too. We'll make the drive to school the same. We thought this might be . . . educational."

"Well, it's not that I don't want you to learn the experience of being on your own. Obviously, we'd rather you stay home. But, it does make some economic sense. You wouldn't be wasting gas going to and from. I'd make some money from my new renters," they all giggled, "And you'd both learn to be more independent and even more responsible than you already are. Marlene, what do you think?"

Marlene tried not to show her disappointment. "I've got to be honest. I hate to see you both go. But, I'll agree only on two conditions," she stated.

"You name it, Mom, whatever it is." Laura answered.

"Weekends you both eat here and on all holidays you come home to sleep and spend time with us. I want to hear from you both on a regular basis. Don't forget about us."

"Never!"

"Never!" Tammy and Laura embraced Marlene. Laura excitedly added, "You'll hear from us so much, you won't even notice we're gone."

"I better!"

"Okay then," interrupted John. "Here is my list of rentals, currently vacant." He retracted a typewritten list of rental addresses from his brief-case. They looked over the homes and apartments and tentatively picked a completely furnished apartment, closest to the university. John promised to keep the rental vacant for them so that in the next month they could begin moving in. The girls beamed with excitement and happiness.

"I do, however, expect your monthly lease payment of $300 in my mailbox on the first of every month." John stated.

"John, we don't want their money." Marlene whispered.

"Yes, we do. I want them to learn what it truly means to be out on their own. That means, paying the rent, gas, and telephone bills." He lowered his voice adding, "They don't need to know that I'll take that money and apply it toward money market investments for them." John pretended to let that bit of information slip.

"Oh, Dad, you're the best!"

*   *   *

In the next couple of days, Laura and Tammy excitedly prepared a list of things they needed for their new home. Friday morning, Laura rose early and left with Marlene to go shopping for linens, comforters, and other necessities. Tammy had the day off and chose to sleep in.

Around nine o'clock she woke, took a shower, and dressed. She slipped into a pair of her new form-fitting jean shorts and a black tank top. On her vanity table, she practiced applying her makeup as the artist had shown her. She styled her hair the way the beautician had styled it. Looking at her reflection, she smiled and was happy that she was able to maintain the new look.

Startling her, the doorbell rang. Tammy skipped down the staircase and answered the door. She was surprised to find Paul behind the door, dressed just as casually. Tammy remembered his date with Laura and gasped realizing that Laura had forgotten.

"Tammy, good morning!" Paul looked at her and smiled. "I still can't get over your new look."

"Hi Paul, come on in. Thanks, I'm happy I'm able to keep it up."

"You're doing a great job. You look like you just left the salon!" he stated as he entered into the foyer. "I don't smell any pancakes. Is the cook still sleeping?"

Tammy closed the door feeling sick for Laura. "Oh, Paul, I'm so sorry. She must have let it slip her mind. She left with our mother to go shopping. Did she tell you about our apartment?"

Paul looked confused. Tammy led him farther into the kitchen and offered him a seat at the nook table. She explained Laura's idea to move into the apartment. He listened, as Tammy explained the situation.

"Man, I guess our date was just not that important," he pouted.

"Oh, she's going to feel so bad. I'm sorry." Tammy wrung her fingers nervously.

Paul sighed and relaxed his shoulders. "Well, don't worry about it. It's no big deal." He glanced around the nook until his eyes met hers. "So, what're you doing today?" he asked.

Tammy uneasily shifted from one foot to another. "Uh, I planned on staying home and relaxing on a rare day off. I could've gone shopping with them, but I was so tired. I just wanted to sleep in."

"Can't say I blame you there," he responded. An awkward silence filled the room. Paul's eyes searched Tammy's. "All dolled up with no place to go?"

"I didn't have anything else planned." She looked down at her fidgeting hands.

"If I didn't have to get to the hospital soon, I'd take *you* out to breakfast."

Tammy laughed with uncertainty. "That's not necessary, thank you! But, where are my manners? Why don't I make you something really quick? I haven't had any breakfast yet and was going to whip something together. Will you stay?"

Her heart raced. His eyes penetrated hers. Was it her imagination, or was he looking at her the way he had looked at Laura before?

"I'd love to."

"Great! What'll it be?"

"Whatever's easiest."

Tammy nodded and headed behind the counter to prepare something to eat. Her heart still raced. Her hands shook. But Paul kept the conversation light, asking her about Marlene and John, helping her to feel at ease. Soon, Paul was asking about her life. She explained how she became orphaned, which eventually led to how she met Laura. Paul laughed at some of the crazy times she shared with her and the girls from their foster home.

Paul listened intently, giving her his utmost attention. Soon, she served him hotcakes, breakfast sausages, and a cup of coffee. They sat in the little nook and ate breakfast together.

"I must admit, Tam, you make a mean pancake! Thanks for breakfast," he exclaimed before sipping from his coffee mug.

"You're so welcome. It was my pleasure," she smiled.

He gave her a dimpled smile in return and she nearly swooned.

"I must tell you, Tam, you look great. You were always cute. But now you look . . . all grown up."

Tammy blushed again, not accustomed to this attentiveness. She reached for the pancake dish to serve him seconds. Their hands collided as he also reached forward for the dish. They both laughed and Paul grasped her trembling hand.

"Whoa! Sorry!" he quickly apologized.

"I was getting you a couple more," Tammy admitted. She glanced down at his hand over hers. She trembled at his touch.

"And I was getting you some."

The garage door suddenly opened and Tammy quickly moved her hand out from under Paul's. Marlene and Laura returned, entering into the nook.

Laura dashed into the kitchen with immediate remorse. She greeted Paul with a kiss, apologizing for forgetting their date.

"Don't worry about it. I understand. You've got a lot on your mind and I'm not top priority," he teased with a frown.

"Oh, I feel terrible. I'm so sorry."

"Don't worry. Your sister took good care of me. Miss Sleepy-Head woke up in time to make me breakfast instead."

Tammy blushed. "I had to eat, anyway. It didn't make any sense to send him to work with an empty stomach."

Laura smiled, while standing behind her sister's chair. "That's what having a great sister is all about." She kissed Tammy's cheek and sat to help herself to a pancake. Marlene, who'd trailed in behind Laura, said good morning to Tammy and Paul and poured herself a cup of coffee. The four sat at the nook table and chatted about the apartment move. Paul sat and listened, until he ultimately rose to leave.

"Well, I hate to go. But, duty calls." He reached for Tammy and kissed her cheek. "Thanks for the cakes and for the company. They were great." He kissed Laura and Marlene and was off.

* * *

Laura sat at the table and watched as Tammy's eyes followed Paul all the way out the door. Her stomach suddenly ached. *Did she sense something different in Paul?* He *was* quieter than normal—almost distant. Perhaps he was angry that she'd forgotten about him. She prayed that wasn't the case.

Marlene rose from the table and busied herself with some of the dishes. Tammy and Laura helped clear the table. When they were through, Laura called Tammy into the living room to show her the items they had purchased for the apartment. Tammy seemed excited and happy. Laura wondered if it was because of the new apartment or Paul.

* * *

Paul pulled out of the driveway and guided his vehicle toward the hospital. He felt angry and tried examining his emotions. *Was he angry that Laura was careless and forgot about their date?* It certainly bothered him that she could overlook a date they had been talking about for days. *Did he mean so little to her, or was it truly a lapse in her memory?*

Maybe he was angry with himself for starting to look at Tammy with a different eye. *What was he thinking?* As beautiful as Tammy now looked, Laura was still far more refined. But looks didn't matter to Paul. It was finally beginning to sink in that there was a part of Laura's heart he could never fill. That part kept him at arm's length, never allowing him to get closer. He cared about her. He even thought that he might be falling for her. But he was coming to the realization that he'd never have Laura's heart, completely. That bothered him.

Even if things couldn't work out with Laura, he certainly would never consider dating Tammy. That would go against every honorable man's rules.

Yet, something about Tammy lately jerked his heart around. She was more open and definitely easier to talk to. Laura had too many walls. He understood why she did and he wanted to be patient with her. But it was becoming difficult. He examined his feelings further. *Was Laura worth it?* He decided that she *was* worth the wait. Any other feelings he thought he was feeling for Tammy, were just those—feelings. *Feelings he needed to bury.*

* * *

Tammy felt a slight bit of tension as Laura showed her their new purchases. She hated that feeling and wanted to confront Laura immediately. "I hope you don't mind that I made Paul breakfast. I felt like a jerk letting him go, when I still hadn't had breakfast myself."

"No. You did the right thing. Paul's a friend to everyone in this household. I wouldn't have expected you to do any different."

"Really? Because I don't want you to think anything. I always joke about his good looks and *still* think he's gorgeous," she laughed. "But I'd never come between you."

"I know that, Tam. I meant what I said earlier, about you being the best sister. I love you more than anything. I trust you with my life." Laura's eyes filled.

Tammy's eyes filled, too. "Same here!"

* * *

The next day, the Knights prepared a huge party for the girls' graduation. They catered in all sorts of delectable foods and had a decorating crew come in to dazzle the home.

The evening started off with a bang. One of John's friend's sons came to DJ, keeping friends and family moving to the beat. Upon arriving, Paul came up behind Laura and grabbed her waist, shouting above the music that the party was a smash. Friends from school filled every corner of the foyer, living room, and dining room areas. They were eating, socializing, and some even danced. The adults gathered in the nook as they supervised the celebration from afar.

Laura glanced around and noticed that Tammy was still nowhere in sight. She walked through the first floor, checking every room. Laura slipped up the staircase and rapped on her bedroom door. She found Tammy sitting on her bed, staring at her reflection.

"What're you doing?" Laura asked. "Come on down. Everyone is waiting for you." Tammy didn't respond. "What's the matter? You look awesome. I've never seen you look more beautiful." Tammy wore a mini-jean skirt and tie-dye halter-top. Her hair was beautifully done and her makeup looked professional.

"What if everyone sees right through me? They haven't seen me since my makeover."

"Is that it? Who cares what they think? What counts, is how you feel. Do you like what you see?"

"Yes. I love it. But that doesn't mean I'm comfortable with it."

Laura sat next to Tammy on the bed. "Would it help if I told you that I don't feel comfortable with high heels and this dress? Don't you think I'd rather be prancing around in sweats or jeans? But better to be a little bit uncomfortable, than not feel good about yourself. Your self-esteem needs to be built up. Come on down and show everyone what you're made of."

Tammy reluctantly followed Laura down the stairs. The crowd cheered upon seeing the two graduates. Someone whistled, then another. Suddenly, the crowd was applauding at the new Tammy. She beamed with happiness as she greeted her high school friends. Laura joined Paul on the couch.

"So, you found her."

"She was hiding in her room, worried that everyone would notice her insecurities. I told her she looked great. Doesn't she?"

"She looks . . . like a totally different person."

*   *   *

Tammy was glad she'd listened to Laura. Her friends and the family made her feel wonderful. The guys from school all gathered around her, flirting and making her laugh with their comments. At last, she made her way passed the foyer and into the living room. Her eyes clashed with Paul's. She smiled at him and came to greet him.

"Hi Paul."

He stood from the couch and kissed her cheek. He whispered loud enough for only her to hear that she look magnificent. She smiled back at him in thanks.

The rest of the evening was a hit. Everyone danced, including Paul. He even took a hold of Tammy's hand at one point and spun her around to the disco beat. She felt high with happiness, until the DJ changed the beat and slowed it down. Tammy tried to concentrate on her friends, but couldn't help but eye Paul and Laura. Her emotions reeled as she watched them dancing together to a love song. A friend from school asked her to dance. She accepted, but her heart felt raw. When the song ended, she excused herself and slipped out the back patio doors to get a breath of fresh air.

The night was quiet, despite the party, and the air was crisp, but it felt good against her warm flesh. Gazing up at the stars, she let out a long sigh.

"Why the long face?"

Startled, Tammy spun around to find Paul standing behind her. The half-moon silhouetted his face and she could see the lazy look in his eye, as his body stood between her and the sliding glass door.

"Who, me? No long faces here," she exclaimed.

"Could've fooled me." His smile faded and concern replaced his gaze. He strode toward her, but stopped a few feet before her. He reached forward and grasped her hand. Holding it, he continued, "One minute ago you looked as radiant at the sun. The next minute you looked sad enough to cry. What's going on?"

Tammy was suddenly angry, pulling her hand away. "Why do you care? Shouldn't you be in there with Laura?" She turned around and gave him her back.

"She's in the bathroom. I saw you sneak out. I care because you're a good person and I can tell you looked upset." He touched her shoulder.

"I'm not upset," Tammy whispered, still turned away. "Just . . . overwhelmed," she admitted with a sigh.

Paul also sighed heavily. "Overwhelmed? By what?"

Tammy spun around to face him. "I don't know. I don't know what to feel."

He looked down at his hands. "Neither do I."

"Well, whatever it is, it stops right here." She moved to stalk past him, but not before he caught hold of her arm. His face was inches from hers. He lowered his head and planted a kiss on her lips. Tammy was startled and immediately pulled her head back. Her breath came heavy as she struggled to free her arm.

"Don't," she pleaded. "Please, don't ever do that again." She ran past him and entered the house.

Tammy tried to compose herself. Her mind was reeling. Laura had exited the bathroom and was now mingling amongst some friends. Tammy entered the bathroom and locked the door. She gazed at her reflection. Smacking the counter top, she cursed herself. Maybe it was best if she'd never changed her appearance. Then Paul would never have shown interest and her feelings for him wouldn't grow deeper knowing they might be returned. Tammy gathered tissue paper into her hand and dabbed the tears that formed in her eyes. She'd not let on what happened. In fact, she'd now make it a point to make herself scarce when Paul Roberts was around.

And how dare he come over as Laura's boyfriend and sneak her a kiss when Laura wasn't looking? At one point, Tammy wondered whether to warn Laura of his lack of faithfulness. *But how would she tell Laura that he was unfaithful?* Laura might think that it was *her* doing. She knew of her crush on him.

A knock on the door startled her. "Just a minute," she called out. She blew her nose and wiped her tears, trying to sooth her face. Tammy opened the bathroom door. It was Paul. His eyes were filled with remorse.

"I'm sorry. I should've never done that," he whispered. "You forgive me?"

"Don't let it happen again." She stalked past him, putting a smile back on her face for her guests.

At last, the night came to an end. Laura and Tammy both said goodbye to their family and friends as they departed. Everyone filed out but Paul, who stayed a while to help with the clean-up.

Laura and Paul flirted and teased, while tearing down the streamers and other decorations. Marlene and John worked on the food in the kitchen. Tammy quietly collected glasses and soda cans from end tables and the entertainment center.

"I'm so out of the scene. I feel like an old fart." She overheard Paul cry.

Laura burst into laughter. Tammy couldn't help smiling. "You're not old. You're just wise beyond your years," she teased as she stood on a chair to reach a streamer. Tammy watched on, as Laura suddenly lost her footing and landed in Paul's arms.

"Easy there, killer. You trying to hang yourself?" Laura giggled beyond control. She was obviously drunk with happiness. Tammy sighed. She finished helping, then called out, bidding all a good evening.

She walked up the staircase glancing down one last time. Paul held a chair for Laura, but his eyes followed her. They looked despondent as she walked up the stairs. Tammy wouldn't let herself care. She entered her room, closing her door. Slipping out of her clothes and into her comfortable pajamas, she fell on her bed and wept.

This was all wrong. How could she be falling in love with someone she couldn't have? She thought of the kiss and her lips seemed to sizzle. Somehow, she needed to make herself forget him. *The question was—how?*

*   *   *

Laura walked Paul to the door. He had said his goodbyes to the Knights and encouraged her to walk him out. They held hands as they slowly strolled out into the warm spring night.

"Did you have a good time, despite the fact that you feel old?"

"Any time I spend with you is good." He flashed her his dimples.

"You looked a little sad for a moment. Is everything okay?"

"Yeah, I just missed you."

Laura giggled. "You're sweet."

"You are. Come here." He gathered her into his arms and kissed her more passionately than he ever had. Laura felt her heart stir for the first time in months. Paul remarked, "This dress is out of this world. You're absolutely gorgeous. I'm the luckiest guy on the planet." They kissed again and then said goodbye. Laura entered the house. She waved one last time and turned off the coach lights.

*   *   *

Paul pulled the car away. Angrily, he hit the steering wheel with the palms of his hands. He cursed aloud. *"Why did I do that? How could I kiss her?"* He couldn't stop thinking about Tammy. He drove home in haste, only to lie in bed and think of her more. Her lips were warm on his. Even if she tore herself away before he could truly feel it.

He cursed himself, again, for not being able to take the kiss off his mind. He tried to concentrate on his kiss with Laura, but it was dead in comparison. Tammy's kiss brought him back to life. He knew she felt the same. That's why she pulled away so quickly. *That kiss was undeniably real.*

"What have I done?" he asked himself. He realized that kissing her was not the wisest decision. Now, he surely could not forget her. Not when that kiss left him wanting her more.

CHAPTER 21

Unbridled Passions

Startled by her alarm clock, Laura smacked it to stop the buzzing. She groaned as it tumbled onto the floor. Rising from her bed, she picked up the clock and placed it back on her nightstand. It was seven o'clock on a Saturday morning and she grumbled, wishing she could've slept in. But upon recalling her reason for such an early rising, she smiled. After a month of shopping and preparing, Tammy and Laura were moving into the apartment.

Laura shuffled out of her room, through the hall, and into Tammy's bedroom. "Tam, wake up. Come on. Today's the day."

Tammy rolled over, stuffing her head under her pillow. "Oh man," she muffled, "Five more minutes."

"Okay, but I'm going to take a quick shower and you better be up and dressed by the time I get out."

Tammy moaned and pulled the covers up over her head. Laura shook her head with a smile and walked out. Before long, the girls gathered their cleaning utensils and left for the apartment. With the key in hand, Laura excitedly opened the door to their new home. They had seen the apartment a few times, but before moving anything into it, they wanted to clean and prepare it.

The apartment was cozy. The little kitchen area was left of the door. Its cabinets curved in a U shape, leaving one side open for two barstools. The dining area was small. It had a round little table and four matching chairs, sitting near a large window that gave the view of the parking lot. To the right of the kitchen, was the living room area, complete with a rust colored sofa and chair. The end tables were oak, matching the rest of the trim and woodwork in the apartment. A fairly large TV sat perched on a wooden frame. To the left and right of the television, were the bedrooms. Each room had a twin-sized bed, dresser, nightstand, and a full-sized closet. In the far-left corner of the living room, behind the kitchen, was the bathroom.

They opened the shutters and windows to let sunlight and fresh air in.

"Okay, Tammy. Where do you want to start?"

"I'll hit the kitchen and bathroom."

"Sounds good. I'll start in the bedrooms. I guess Dad said that it's been freshly painted."

"Good. That's one less thing to do."

The girls talked in the midst of cleaning. The conversation naturally led to Paul. "He said he might swing by to check the place out," Laura stated.

"Oh?"

"He asked about you the other day. He said that he feels as though he must have the plague. Every time he comes over, you're never around. He thinks you're avoiding him." Laura bluntly stated.

"Why would I be avoiding him? You know I love . . . to see Paul. I've been tired lately. When I get home from work, I want to go to my room and sleep."

"I told him exactly that."

"How are things going with the two of you?" Tammy asked as she scrubbed down the kitchen counter.

"Tammy, you know Paul is wonderful. He's charming, funny, ambitious. He's everything a girl could want." Laura stopped a moment, fiddling with the rag in her hands.

"But . . ."

"There shouldn't be any 'buts'. But there are."

Tammy stopped wiping and leaned on the counter, folding her arms in front of her. "Talk to me."

Laura wiped her brow with her forearm and played more with the rag. "I don't know. I'm starting to feel things for Paul that I'm afraid to feel. I wonder—will I ever love him the way I loved Tony? I don't know and it's not fair to Paul. He deserves someone who will love him with her whole heart. Sometimes, I wonder if mine will ever heal. Dr. Janice says that I'm not letting my guard down. I know she's right, but I can't help it. In the meantime, I don't want to let him go, because I know I've got something good. A man like Paul *is* hard to find. Even *I* know that."

"Does he know you feel this way?" Tammy asked.

"No. I don't want to hurt his feelings."

"Do you love him?"

"I think I do. I care for him a great deal."

"Has he told you he loves you?"

"Not yet. We've only been dating for six months. Maybe he can sense my fears."

"You should talk to him. He needs to know how you feel and you need to know how he feels." Tammy matter-of-factly stated.

Laura thought about it a moment. Tammy was right. *Why hadn't she opened up to him about it?* "You're right, Tammy. First chance I get, I'll have a talk with him."

"Good girl. Now, let's get back to work."

Tammy and Laura continued to clean. After a while, Laura asked Tammy if she was getting hungry.

"I'm getting there," Tammy stated.

"Me too. How about I run to the bakery down the street and get us some muffins?" Tammy nodded in agreement. "I'll be back in a jiffy." Laura waved as she exited the apartment.

*   *   *

The door closed and Tammy stopped cleaning for a moment. She stared at the door, recalling her conversation with Laura. *So, Paul was inquiring about her.* Laura was right. She had been avoiding him. She didn't want to be caught in the same building as him. Tammy was fearful her true feelings would be exposed and that absolutely could not happen.

She tried concentrating on her cleaning again. Minutes later, a rap at the door interrupted her. "Oh! We're never going to finish at this rate." Putting her rag down, she walked to the door. "Forget something?" she questioned after opening it.

"Nothing," Paul teased.

"Oh, hi Paul. I'm sorry, I thought you were Laura."

"She's not here?" He looked around.

"She ran out to grab us a bite."

"May I come in?"

"Sure." Butterflies fluttered in Tammy's stomach, as she backed away from the door to let him enter. Paul sauntered in, looking the place over.

"It's nice in here. Roomy for both of you."

"Yeah, we really like it. Go ahead and take a look around. I'm going to finish wiping down this kitchen."

Tammy stole a few glances at Paul, while he walked through the apartment. He glanced in each bedroom and then the bath. Finally, he strolled into the little kitchen and planted himself in a chair, watching Tammy as she cleaned.

"I haven't seen you around lately. Have you been busy?"

"Yeah, busy."

"How's work?"

"It's fine."

Unexpectedly, Paul stood from the chair and walked toward her. Cornering her, he began, "Tammy, look, I'm really sorry about what happened last month at the party. I shouldn't . . ."

Tammy interrupted him, "Let's forget it, Paul. There's nothing more to talk about."

"I want you to know that I would've never done that unless I really felt something for you."

"What're you saying?"

"Let's just say that I don't go around kissing just *any* woman. I respect you. Yet, I couldn't help myself. I really care about Laura. She's great. But I can't keep denying that I have feelings for you, too."

Tammy was flabbergasted. Her head reeled at the thought of the disaster this could become. "Paul, don't say that. We barely know one another. Whatever it is we feel, we cannot acknowledge it."

He stepped closer to her. "So you *do* return my feelings?"

"No. I mean . . . even if I did, I'll deny it until the day I die!" Paul looked hurt. He shook his head, seeming unable to accept her words. "You can't do this to Laura, Paul. It's not fair. If you don't care for her in *that* way, you have to let her go. She's already been hurt enough. And if you *do* let her go, keep in mind that there would be no chance for us. It wouldn't be right."

Paul groaned and ran his hands over his face and through his hair. He cussed aloud and slammed his fists on the counter top, impulsively. Tammy jumped. "How'd I get myself into this mess?" he muttered.

Tammy had never seen Paul so frustrated. Suddenly, he seized her and held her. His mouth met hers in a strong, passionate kiss. Tammy struggled to free herself, at first. But Paul wouldn't let her go. She found her arms encircling his neck and felt herself drain. The kiss continued, hot, searing, longing. She had longed to hold him in her arms for months.

Trembling, they parted. She could not believe her reaction to his touch. She backed away, her body swaying. Paul's eyes searched hers. Neither one could speak.

* * *

The door opened and Laura entered. "Here's breakfast . . ." She stopped in mid-sentence, surprised to see Paul standing so closely to

Tammy. "Hi Paul, I didn't notice your car out front. Have you been here long?"

Paul quickly turned toward her, welcoming her with a hug. "No, I just got here."

Tammy angrily clenched her rag and continued cleaning. "Tammy, come have a muffin," Laura called.

"I'm almost through here. Go ahead and eat. I'll join you in a minute."

Paul stayed a while longer, nibbling on a muffin with Laura, as Tammy continued to work. The tension in the apartment was obvious, but Laura could not sense why. Paul arose and stated that he needed to go. Laura walked him to the door. He waved goodbye to Tammy, who barely turned around to acknowledge him. Laura walked into the hallway, closing the door behind her.

"Is everything okay with you two?" Laura asked.

"I hope so. I'm kind of worried about her."

"Why would you be worried about Tammy?"

"Remember a few days ago, when I asked you about her?" Laura nodded yes. "Well, I'm no psychiatrist, but it appears to me that Tammy shows some symptoms of depression. When you walked in, I was asking her a few questions about how she's been feeling and I don't think she liked it."

"Now that you mention it, she does seem down lately. She comes home from work, hardly eats, and goes right to sleep. Why didn't I see that before?"

"We may be wrong. I wanted to be sure."

"Thank you for making me aware of it. I'll keep an extra eye open from now on." Paul lightly kissed her lips and was off.

Laura reentered the apartment and found Tammy munching on a muffin. She didn't want to press her further about her recent behavior and went right back to cleaning.

Within the next few hours, the girls completed their work and sat on the sofa to rest. John called, inviting them home to an early dinner. They drove back home in silence.

With John and Marlene's help, by nightfall, they managed to move in some of their clothes, bedding, and bathroom needs. Marlene and John surprised them with numerous bags of groceries. John carried mostly everything in, while Marlene, Laura, and Tammy organized closets and cabinets. At the end of the night, John and Marlene were hesitant to leave their girls.

Marlene's eye formed a tear as she embraced Tammy, kissing her goodnight. "Don't cry, Mom. I feel bad for leaving you now."

"I'm sorry. I shouldn't be this way. I'm happy for you. This place looks great. I just hate to go home to an empty house, especially after having you two around." Both Laura and Tammy embraced her. John kissed them goodnight and made them promise to lock the doors and windows as soon as he left.

Laura and Tammy fell exhausted in their beds. At last, it was done. They moved in and were now on their own.

* * *

The following week, Tammy sat at her desk at the insurance agency. She completed an automobile insurance application for a new customer. The office was quiet that day, and Tammy welcomed the silence. A figure walked past the outside window and entered the building. She sighed, expecting it to be yet another customer demanding service.

The man that walked into her office was tall and broad. He wore jeans and a dark blue T-shirt that exposed his burly arms and shoulders. His dark curly hair was brushed back, giving him a clean-cut look. His dark eyes were surrounded in rich black lashes. Tammy was intrigued by his rugged good looks.

"Hi, may I help you?"

He stood by the door, apprehensive at first, and asked in a deep voice if she was Tammy.

"I'm Tammy. What can I do for you?"

"A friend referred me to you. I'm interested in auto insurance. Could you quote me a price?"

"Absolutely." After collecting his name, address, and other information, Tammy came to find that Alfonso Rengali was a single, 23-year-old, who owned his own business, and drove a Chevy Corvette. Tammy was impressed and tried her best to make him aware of that. He laughed at how she teased him about his mysterious business.

"It's nothing big, really. I own a transporting company, actually," he admitted. "My company ships imported foods to store owners and restaurants all over New York. Most of the foods come from Italy, Greece, and France."

"No kidding." She inquired further, asking how he got into the business, trying to keep the conversation in motion. Alfonso seemed sweet. He joked and flirted with her in return. Soon, he began asking her questions, and before long, they became engaged in conversation about one another.

Tammy hadn't noticed anyone walked past the window, yet heard the door to the building open. Still, no one emerged. Her conversation with

Alfonso carried on a few minutes longer. Finally, she excused herself to
peer around the corner. Paul stood in the foyer of the small building, surprised to see Tammy appear.

"Paul," she whispered, "What're you doing here?"

"We need to talk."

"Well, don't just stand there, come in. I'm with someone right now, but
I shouldn't be long. Have a seat." Tammy sat back down at her desk and
continued to write up the quote for Alfonso. After explaining the insurance
quote to him, he thanked her for her time.

"It was nice chatting with you, Tammy. I'll think the price over and get
back with you." He extended his hand, shaking Tammy's gently. He stood
and walked toward the door. He nodded at Paul, who was glaring at him
from across the room. Paul nodded back, waited for his exit, and then rose
to sit closer to Tammy.

"What are you doing here, Paul? Why are you making this so hard?"
Tammy angrily lashed.

"Who was that?" he asked, with a hint of jealousy.

"A nice customer."

"He seemed really friendly for a customer, telling you about his personal business."

"You had no right to come in and eavesdrop on me. Why are you here,
anyway?" She looked into his frazzled face. He still made her heart jerk.

"I told you, Tammy. We need to talk."

Tammy sighed. "There's nothing to say, Paul."

"You call Saturday morning nothing? You kissed me back. I know you
care about me."

Tammy softened. "Paul, there's no denying that. But I told you, it
could never happen." Upon remembering his words with Laura in the hallway, her anger boiled and she added, "Besides, why would you want to be
with someone *so depressed*?" Paul appeared shocked. "That's right! I overheard the excuse you gave Laura that day. Those walls are like paper."

"What did you expect me to say? Tell her the truth? Tell her I'm in love
with her sister?"

Tammy caught her breath, stunned. Her voice trembled as she spoke.
"Let's get one thing straight, okay? You're not in love with me. You may
think you are. But you're not. From now on, when you see me, be civil, but
don't seek me out. Don't bump into me. Don't bother me. I don't want to
see you outside of family functions. If you don't love my sister, then let her
go, because she cares a great deal for you." She inhaled deeply and added.

"Please go, Paul. This is so hard." Tammy thought she heard the front door open again, but her attention was diverted back to Paul.

Paul's eyes welled with unshed tears. "Okay, I'll go. I'm going to give my relationship with Laura my all. You mark my words—it's love I feel. You can run and you can try to hide from what you feel, but it'll always be right there." He pointed to her heart. Leaning over the desk, he kissed her lips one last time. He turned on his heel and left the building.

Tammy crumbled apart at her desk. The sobs escaped her throat with no restraint. She felt as though she couldn't take much more. Trying to gather herself, she blotted her tears with a tissue, and closed down the office. It was time to go home.

* * *

Despite a long day at work, Laura arrived home refreshed and happy. Paul had called her at work and invited her out to dinner. She looked forward to an evening with him, anxious to talk to him. She changed out of her business suit and slipped into a baby blue, silk tank-top dress. After refreshing her makeup and hair, she sat waiting on the sofa and turned on the TV.

Moments later, Tammy strolled in. She looked sad and distraught. "Hi, Tammy. How was work?" Laura lowered the volume on the TV.

"Fine." Laura could tell she was forcing a smile. "How about you?"

"Good."

"You look nice. Are you going somewhere?"

"Paul called and asked me out to dinner. He said to dress up for a special night out."

Tammy looked away, then mumbled, "It's about time."

"Why do you say that?"

"Well, you're both always so busy with work and what not. You rarely go out. I'm glad to see you're both making an effort to spend time together." Tammy sat next to her on the couch.

"You're right, Tam. I'm really excited about tonight. I think I'll have that talk with him. It's high time I close the door to the past and open the window to the future—one with Paul."

Tammy gave her a wry smile. "All I want for you is happiness, Laura. You certainly deserve it."

"Thanks. So do you. I wish 'Mr. Right' would come your way."

"Maybe he has."

"What?"

Tammy told Laura about Alfonso Rengali. She described his handsome appearance and his sweet personality. Laura was thrilled for her and hoped this mystery man would come back and visit her soon.

Tammy got up from the couch and entered her bedroom. They conversed further, as she changed out of her work clothes and into shorts and a top. Meanwhile, Laura was becoming antsy. She glanced at the clock above the kitchen table and fretted. Paul said he'd be over by five-thirty. It was nearing six-thirty and still there was no sign of him. She called his apartment, but didn't get an answer. Her eyes grazed the TV screen. A local news reporter was live at the scene of a car accident located two miles from the neighborhood near Paul's home.

She raced to the TV and increased the volume. " . . . It's remarkable the driver is alive, despite the serious injuries. Luckily for him, he was wearing his safety harness. As you can see behind me, this model '72 Ford Mustang is in devastating condition here on Maple Avenue. Please seek an alternate route. Reporting live with traffic . . ."

Laura's legs weakened. She recognized the green Mustang instantly. Taking the phone in her hand, she dialed the hospital's number, shouting to Tammy what she feared.

*　　*　　*

Tammy dashed from her room, too late to see the scene on the TV. Her heart pumped the blood in her body so hard and fast, it obstructed her ears from hearing the conversation Laura was having. Tammy watched as Laura slowly hung up the phone. Her face was pale and tears already slipped down her face.

"Paul was in that accident."

CHAPTER 22

The Doctor's Ball

Laura and Tammy sped to the hospital. At the front desk, they found that Paul had been admitted and they rushed to his room. Laura entered with Tammy behind her. Paul's eyes were closed. A bandage covered part of his head. On his brow, he had a bruise and his knee was bandaged as well. A nurse took his blood pressure and monitored his vitals. Paul's eyes opened to the clicking of Laura and Tammy's heels. He smiled weakly.

"Are you okay?" Laura whispered.

"I'm fine. Just a few bruises."

The nurse confirmed that he'd be okay, but stressed that the bump on his head was serious and that he needed to stay overnight for observation.

"Told you." Paul stated.

"Just double checking." Laura stroked his cheek with her hand and kissed him. "You scared the daylights out of us."

"*Us?*" Paul peered around Laura. Tammy stood behind her apprehensively. She moved forward and touched his wrapped knee.

"Hi, we're glad you're all right," she managed. "Tell us what happened."

"I don't know, girls. It was weird. I know I needed to get the brakes on my car checked, because they were previously making noises. But I never would've imagined that they'd have given out on me like that. I pulled out of the parking lot of my apartment and started for your place. I did notice that I had to pump the brakes to get the car to slow down at the first stop sign exiting my apartment complex, but I was going slow. As I pulled forward and increased speed, the first light I came to was green. I picked up more speed and passed the intersection. All of a sudden, the car in front of me started to stop. I pressed my brake, but nothing happened. I pumped it and quickly veered the vehicle to the right to avoid a collision. My car wouldn't slow down. It was going too fast. I lost control. The car jerked to the right and I knew I was heading for the ditch. I jerked the wheel left and the car rolled over, into the ditch, landing upside down."

Laura sighed in relief. "I'm glad you weren't hurt more seriously."

"It looks like you have a guardian angel to thank," Tammy added.

"You're right. I could've been killed."

Laura saw the seriousness in his eyes and couldn't help the tears from welling up in her own. She couldn't bear the thought of losing him. Perhaps this was meant to be an eye opener. She leaned over, kissed his cheek again, and hugged him.

*   *   *

As Laura hugged Paul, Tammy watched on. Paul's eyes met hers. They looked empty and sad. He closed his eyes again as if to shut her out. Tammy's heart ached.

*   *   *

Paul hated what he was feeling. Before him stood two of the most wonderful women he'd ever meet and he was torn between the two of them. But now Paul knew what he needed to do. The message was loud and clear. He'd avoid Tammy at all cost. Even if it meant his heart would break in the process.

*   *   *

Paul was released from the hospital the next morning. He used a crutch to ease the pressure on his battered knee. Within a week, he was on his feet and back to work. Laura tried spending more time with him, no longer wanting to take him for granted. She felt herself growing closer to him every day.

One Saturday evening in August, they sat on the couch at the apartment. Tammy was out. Laura snuggled closer to Paul, as they watched the TV before them.

He wrapped his arms around her and held her close. "What're you doing two weeks from today?"

"Nothing that I know of. Why?"

"The hospital is having their annual Doctor's Ball and I was wondering if you'd like to join me."

"I didn't know they threw an annual ball."

"We sure do. It's a formal charity ball to help raise money for the Leukemia foundation. We auction off local artists' work to the highest bidder.

200

The money goes to a great cause and I'll get to spend a romantic evening with my best girl."

"That sounds great. I'd love to go," she exclaimed. Gazing at his smooth face, her hand gently grazed the bruise on his forehand. "Does it still hurt?"

"It's fine," he whispered calmly. "Stop fussing over me. Not that I mind. I adore the way you've been doting on me. I feel so close to you."

Laura's hand continued to caress him. "Well, after the accident, you can count on me never taking you for granted again."

Paul sighed heavily. "You weren't taking me for granted. You were scared. I don't blame you. I'm happy that I've been able to gain your trust. I love you, Laura."

Laura sat up, still gazing into his eyes. "Paul, I . . ."

He placed a finger on her lips. "Don't say it until you feel it. I won't be offended if you need more time. I want you to be truthful to yourself first."

She shook her head. "That's just it, Paul. I know I love you. The accident proved it. The fear I felt in my heart over possibly losing you horrified me. I don't want to be without you."

Paul cupped her face in his warm hands. Leaning forward he gave her a kiss.

* * *

After spending the evening with her parents, Tammy drove home in the quiet of the night. The radio softly played a love song and she felt her eyes beginning to tear. As it always would, her mind recollected the kiss at the apartment with Paul. It was pointless to continue to think about him, yet she couldn't help it. She finally understood why Laura struggled to move on after Tony. The thought of the touch of his hands, pierced a dagger into her heart. *Would she . . . could she ever forget?* Tammy wiped her face dry with her hand.

How she wished she had someone to confide in. If only she could go to Marlene or even John about this. But she couldn't. *What would they think of her?* She could barely stand to look at herself in the mirror, knowing that she had betrayed Laura with a few stolen kisses. Tammy thought of Jesus. Laura always said that you could talk to Jesus as you would your best friend.

As Tammy drove the vehicle homeward, she talked to God. Through her prayers, she asked Him to make it possible to either forget Paul or find a way to be with the man that she loved, without hurting Laura. She asked Him to forgive her selfishness. Never in her wildest dreams, did she believe that she could capture his heart the way he'd captured hers.

Tammy maneuvered the vehicle into her parking spot in front of the apartment building and noticed Paul's vehicle. She glanced at the clock. It was ten-thirty and though she didn't have to work the next day, she was tired. Trying to avoid a confrontation with Paul, she backed the vehicle up and decided to go to the 24-hour supermarket down the street.

In the market, she gathered a few items and placed them in her cart. Remembering that they were low on milk as well, Tammy strolled down the dairy aisle. Reaching for the milk, she searched the gallon for an expiration date, while backing toward her cart. She felt herself plunge into another body. Immediately, she apologized for her clumsiness. The large man gripped her arms to steady her. Tammy looked up to find herself in Alfonso Rengali's arms.

"So, we meet again," his husky voice stated.

"Oh my gosh, Alfonso. I'm sorry. I didn't see you behind me."

"No apology needed. It was my pleasure," he teased. Tammy blushed. "What're you doing here so late? Don't you know that weirdos always prowl around in grocery stores this time of night? You know, like me." He laughed at his own joke. Tammy giggled.

"You're far from weird. I needed to get out and we were low on milk, so . . . here I am."

"We?"

"I live with my sister in an apartment, near the university. We moved in a few weeks ago."

"Nice." They stood in the aisle way. Alfonso seemed to search her eyes. "Were you all done with your shopping?"

Tammy nodded.

"Why don't we check out and I'll walk you to your car. I'll feel better knowing you're not headed out into the parking lot alone. Next time you decide to venture out this late, you take someone with you," he ordered.

"Yes, Dad."

"So sue me for caring," he stated.

Tammy loved his accent. *Was he from the City, or possibly a Californian?* She'd have to ask. Meanwhile, she thanked him and they ambled back down the aisle toward the cashiers. In the parking lot, he helped her with her groceries. Again, Tammy thanked him for being a gentleman.

"Tammy, I'm happy you bumped into me," he teased. He cleared his voice, and then continued. "Can I call you sometime? Maybe we can get together for a dinner, possibly dancing?"

Tammy smiled, "I'd love that. You know where I work. Give me a call." She waved before getting in her car, and then headed home.

Back at the apartment, she parked the car. Scanning the parking lot, she blasted upon seeing Paul's vehicle still there. Nevertheless, she gathered her purse and groceries. Tammy slowly ascended the stairway toward her apartment. One of the grocery bags was suddenly seized from her arms. Paul stood before her, holding it.

"Looks like you could use a little help."

Tammy was surprised to see him. "Thanks," she mumbled. She gazed at him. He easily shifted the heavy grocery bag into his left arm. He looked handsome in a white T-shirt and black jeans. His sandy hair wasn't in the perfect order he usually kept it, nevertheless it looked soft enough to touch. Tammy had to look the other way.

As they walked toward the apartment together, Paul asked if she had just purchased the groceries. "Yes, I came home and saw that you were still here. I figured I'd give you two some more time alone."

Paul stopped and turned toward her, sighing in frustration. He kept his voice just above a whisper for fear that Laura might hear. "You don't have to completely avoid me, Tammy."

Her eyes bulged. "Oh, yes, I do. Until we can put our feelings aside, it has to be this way," she whispered.

He looked at her longingly. His hand touched her cheek, but Tammy pulled it away. Paul looked hurt. She watched him place the bags outside the door of the apartment. His eyes held hers for a long moment. "Goodnight," he whispered, kissing her cheek and then descending the stairway.

A lump formed in Tammy's throat. No matter how much time went by without seeing him, it still didn't change how she felt about him.

*   *   *

Two weeks later, Laura fussed over her makeup and hair, as she prepared herself for the ball. Tammy helped her shop for a dress, after Paul's invitation. Laura stood before the bathroom mirror and glared at her reflection. She felt like a princess. The silver strapless gown tapered down her torso, then ballooned at her hips. The beautician at the salon styled Laura's hair in an up-do, leaving ringlets of golden-brown to cascade around her face. Tammy looked at her sister and whistled.

"Paul is going to die when he sees you. You look awesome."

"Thanks."

It wasn't long before Paul arrived. A rap at the door sounded and Tammy ran to answer it.

*   *   *

Tammy opened the door and set her eyes on the most beautiful man she'd ever seen. Her stomach tightened at the sight of him. She tried not to unveil her adoration for him, but quickly stumbled upon opening her mouth.

"Paul, come in. You look incredible!"

"Thank you." His eyes held hers as he entered. A hint of sadness was still in them. "Is Laura ready?"

"She sure is."

Laura emerged from the bathroom door. Paul's eyes protruded. "Holy Mother of God! You look absolutely, positively, beautiful." Laura gracefully sauntered across the room to greet him. He kissed her cheek and embraced her. Tammy tried busying herself, preparing her dinner. From her peripheral view, she saw Paul spinning Laura around to get a good look. Then, as Laura collected her purse and shawl, Paul asked Tammy what her plans were for the evening.

"I'm making myself dinner and I'm going to sit in front of the TV and vegetate."

"Well, enjoy your meal."

"Have a good time," she called back.

The door shut and she was finally alone. She closed her eyes a brief moment and sighed. Tammy promised herself that she'd no longer shed a tear over the situation again.

*   *   *

The ball was in full swing when Paul and Laura arrived. A man dressed in a tuxedo stood at the door announcing each invitee by name.

"Mr. Paul Evan Roberts, accompanied by Miss Laura Ann Knight." Paul nodded at his fellow co-workers and friends, while he led Laura into the hall. Laura whispered to him that she didn't believe the ball to be as formal as it was.

"Oh, you haven't seen nothing yet," he claimed. Laura gave him a questioning look. "Shh. It's a surprise," he whispered.

He walked with his back straight and proper, until he showed her to their table. Laura giggled at his silly behavior. Soon he relaxed and began introducing her to his great multitude of co-workers.

Laura truly felt special and admired. Most of Paul's friends, whom she hadn't yet met, were delighted to finally meet the girl he spoke so fondly of.

After their arrival, it wasn't long before dinner was served. Soon, a glorious sweet table followed. Paul brought Laura a few cocktails from the bar. He sat next to her, staring out onto the dance floor. Laura noticed that he had already downed three drinks and was working a fourth. At last, a slow song was playing and Paul and Laura moved onto the dance floor. The love ballad nearly brought tears to Laura's eyes. She looked into Paul's face, trying to read him. It was evident that since dinner, something in his demeanor had changed. He was nervous and that worried her.

In the midst of the song, Paul clutched Laura's hand and led her off the dance floor and out of the hall. Leaving from the rear exit, he guided her out onto the banquet hall's patio.

"Paul, is everything all right?" Now, she was truly concerned.

"Never better," he replied. "Laura, I need to talk to you and it's way too loud and crowded in there."

"Paul, you're scaring me. What is it?"

They sat on a concrete bench, overlooking the beautifully decorated landscape. "Laura, I love you. You're the most beautiful person I know. I know we've only been together for seven months. But it wasn't long before I realized that you were the girl for me. I want to spend my life with you. I want to marry you."

Laura was shocked. She certainly wasn't anticipating a proposal. When she opened her mouth to speak, he stopped her. "We don't have to get married right away. We can have a long engagement. A two or even three-year engagement is fine with me. I just want to give you this ring, as a token of my love, as a sign of our commitment . . ." he struggled to remove the ring from his pocket, ". . . and as a reminder to the world that you're mine." He pinched the ring between his fingers.

Laura didn't know how to answer. In her mind, she quickly mulled over her feelings. She knew that she was falling for him. She really did care for him. Although the love she felt for him wasn't the same kind of love she shared with Tony, it was still love. Paul was a good person. A long engagement made sense. They were already committed. This would make it official.

"Yes, Paul. Yes, I'll marry you." Paul kissed and hugged her before sliding the diamond ring on her finger. She gazed at the clear, white stone. It was beautiful.

They reentered the hall and announced their engagement to Paul's friends. Everyone was happy and congratulated them.

Something still bothered Laura in Paul's behavior that evening. It was out of character for him to down one drink after the other.

*   *   *

Laura was irritated with Paul by the end of the night. He was drunk and couldn't drive Laura home. Laura took hold of his keys. He clumsily walked her to the used '75 Ford Mustang he'd newly purchased. She didn't want to stay at his apartment, so she drove them home to hers. He fell asleep on the ride home.

Laura struggled to help Paul up the stairway. She fumbled for the right key and opened the door. The TV was still on, but Tammy had fallen asleep on the couch. Paul mumbled aloud that he was sorry for his behavior. Laura shushed him. After turning the TV off, she nudged Tammy awake.

"Tammy, do you mind? Paul is totally wasted. I was hoping he could sleep it off on our couch for the night." Tammy peeked through her sleepy eyes, as she rolled off the couch.

"Sure. I'll go to bed. Goodnight. Oh, hey," she asked as she entered her room. "How was the ball?"

"Nice," Laura stated.

"Well, aren't you gonna to share the good newzzz," Paul slurred.

"Good news?" Tammy asked.

"Yeah, me and Laura are gettin' married. See the nice ring I buyed her." Paul garbled, struggling to maintain his balance.

Laura, now clearly irritated, rolled her eyes. "You mean, bought."

"Whatever," he waved his hand at her. "Go on, show her."

Tammy held Laura's hand in hers. Tears filled her eyes and she embraced her sister. "I'm happy for you both. Congratulations."

Laura helped Paul onto the couch. She loosened his bow tie and removed his shoes and jacket. He lay down and was passed out in nearly seconds.

"He definitely partied too hard," Tammy added.

"I don't like it. It's not like him to drink. Why now? Why tonight?" Laura kissed his cheek, waved goodnight to Tammy and got ready for bed.

*   *   *

Tammy quietly closed the door behind her. A lump formed in her throat, building tears in her eyes. She crawled into bed and tried not let Laura hear her sobs. It was official. Paul took the ultimate step in ending whatever it was they had. In one sense, Tammy was relieved. Now she'd truly be forced to move on.

*   *   *

Shortly after everyone fell asleep, Paul awoke with an unmerciful stomachache. He looked around feeling disoriented. *Where was he?* It was dark and though the moon was bright, he couldn't conclude his whereabouts. He felt his way around the couch and realized he was at the girls' apartment. Finding the bathroom, he vomited the poison from his system, feeling relieved. He washed his hands and face and reentered the family room.

It suddenly struck him what had happened. He remembered drinking too much. He remembered Laura driving his new car home. It pained him to remember that they told Tammy about the engagement. *Dare he go into her room and talk to her?* He summoned up his courage and quietly opened Tammy's bedroom door. Paul tiptoed to her bed and kneeled before it.

Before he could wake her, Tammy surprised him. "What're you doing in here?" she whispered.

"Tammy, forgive me for acting like such a jerk. It was the booze."

"Paul, go away." She rolled over and gave him her back.

"I'm sorry, Tammy. I'm so sorry," he cried. The tears slid down his face. "I wish I could change things for us, but I can't. Please, forgive me."

Tammy turned back around. Whispering, she said, "Paul, I forgive you. You did the right thing. Laura will make a beautiful bride and a wonderful wife. Forget about us. I have. Now get out before Laura finds you in here."

"I'm sorry." Paul wept and exited her room to go back to the couch.

Before Tammy would wake up the next day, he vowed to be gone. He couldn't stand to face her again.

*   *   *

Laura stared at the ceiling of her bedroom, unable to sleep. Thoughts of Tony and Paul were clouding her mind. It was undeniable that she was disappointed in Paul's proposal. She recollected her engagement to Tony and nothing could ever compare to that wonderful day. It seemed as though it was just yesterday, when he had slipped the ring on her finger . . .

CHAPTER 23

Tony's Proposal

August 1976

It was a beautiful summer morning. The grass was still wet with morning dew. The birds' chirping filled the air. The flowers were still in full bloom. In the sky, the sun shone upon the earth, filling all things with its light and warmth.

It was a Friday, the day I normally set aside for cleaning and laundry and though it was only morning, my body perspired from the exhaustive heat. I worked hard, wanting Tony to come home to a clean house. After dusting, washing, mopping, and scrubbing, I felt tired, but continued working my own list of chores. Before preparing our dinner, I showered, hoping to feel some relief from the heat. Dressing as light as possible, in a loose tank top and shorts, I descended the stairs to begin dinner. By the time Tony strolled in, it was nearly done. I was fussing over a salad, when I heard the front door open and Tony whistle.

"In the kitchen," I hollered.

Tony lazily strolled in. Even after a busy day's work, he looked radiant with his bronze summer tan. His eyes glimmered as they met mine. He smiled. My face lit up at the sight of him. I noticed he had one arm hiding behind his torso.

"What ya got there?"

He pulled forth his arm and displayed a beautiful array of wild flowers. Without a word, he gathered me into his hold and fully kissed me. I was astounded at his parade of tenderness. Not because he never bestowed it, but because something in the way he kissed me told me he was up to something. I thanked him for the flowers, and put them in a vase. Centering them on the table, we said our thanks to God and ate dinner.

Long after our meal, we both lay in bed, trying to sleep. Even in my thin silk pajama shorts and tank, the heat was unbearable. The blankets and sheets rested at the foot of our bed. It was too hot even for snuggling.

"Tony? You awake?"

"As ever."

"What're you thinking about?"

"How hot it is up here. You?"

"Same. I feel like I can't breathe. It's got to be 120 degrees up here."

"You're right." Suddenly he got up. I saw the moonlight shine on his broad bare shoulders. Before I had a chance to ask, he whisked me to my feet.

"Here, hold this." Tony handed me our pillows and a blanket. Then taking two sleeping bags from the spare, he led me down the stairs and out the back door.

My feet brushed through the prickly grass and he guided me toward the large oak. He opened up the sleeping bags and neatly placed them on the grass. Taking the pillows from my arms, he laid them to one side. Finally, he made himself comfortable on it and used the blanket as a cover.

A smile played on his lips. "Aren't you coming to bed?" He patted the pillow next to him.

"We're going to sleep out here?" I asked skeptically.

"Why not?"

I put my hands on my hips. "Okay, here are a few choice reasons: Mosquitoes, bugs, bats, snakes, and wild animals. Need I say more?"

Tony propped himself up on one arm. "Okay," he sighed. "Don't worry about the mosquitoes and bugs because the bats will eat them. Don't worry about the bats, because the snakes will eat them. And you certainly don't need to worry about the snakes, because . . ."

"Okay, stop right there, because I don't know any wild animals that eat snakes."

"Well, I do."

"Yeah, right. Like what?"

"Chickens! Bawk!" he taunted. Tony seized my leg and wrestled me to the ground. "Get over here, you big chicken." I giggled in delight, while he tickled my sides and kissed my neck and face.

"Okay, okay. So, I'm a chicken. But all those things creep me out."

We relaxed together. "Do you think I'd ever let anything hurt you? We can cover ourselves with the blanket to keep the mosquitoes away. As for the bugs, well . . . just hope they don't crawl into your ear and eat your brain."

"Oh, you're terrible. Now, I'm going to be thinking about that all night," I shivered.

Tony roared with laughter, "Go to sleep, little girl." He kissed my lips and held me close. The night air was definitely cooler than the second floor of the house and we were finally able to rest.

I suddenly propped myself up on my side and looked at his silvery-blue face. His eyes were already closed and a smile rested on his lips. "This is so romantic," I whispered.

"I thought you were tired," he jested.

"Now that we're out here, I'm wide awake."

Tony opened his eyes and gazed into mine. "What's on your mind?"

"You'd never believe it if I told you."

"Try me," he urged. Suddenly his eyes didn't look as sleepy and his interest seemed perked.

I let out a long sigh, while my hand twirled his thick hair. "I've had my mom's family on my mind. I'd like to find them, someday."

"Maybe one day you can."

"Yeah, well, the only thing that's stopping me is the way Momma talked about them. They wanted nothing to do with her. Maybe it's better I leave well enough alone. If they rejected my mother, they'll surely reject Matthew Duke Marc's evil spawn."

Tony sat up and helped me to meet his gaze. His forehead wrinkled, his eyebrows knit together, and he whispered, "I don't want to hear you talk like that. You're the furthest thing from evil. I've never met a more loving, selfless person. They should feel honored to have you as a part of their family. Your mother did a wonderful job raising you."

I ran my hand through his hair and touched his face. His ruffled eyebrows relaxed at my touch. "Thank you," I said.

"Well, it's true. Don't make me have to correct you about that again. No matter what your father may have done, you're nothing like him. You've only acquired good qualities. Probably from your mom."

I nodded in agreement. My mother suffered through years of abuse and still managed to instill Patty and me with wholesome qualities. "You're right, again. Momma was the best. I thank God I was blessed to have her as long as I did." My hands rubbed his chest a moment, then we both laid back down. I closed my eyes and tried to picture Momma's heavenly face. It had been so long, I could barely remember her. I felt my stomach tighten and my throat constrict. Talking about her made me realize how much I missed her.

As if reading my mind, Tony held me tighter. I reached up and brought my lips to his. He kissed me, long and slowly. I closed my eyes, savoring his touch, his feel. "I love you," I whispered.

"I love you," he whispered in return.

I rested my head on his chest. A tear slipped down and landed on it. He caressed my head and shoulders, while my silent tears rained on his heart. He didn't speak, he just held me. Understanding. Knowing. Feeling every one of my emotions. Words weren't necessary.

Keeping my eyes closed, I victoriously fell into a peaceful sleep.

Somehow, by dawn, I found myself back in our bed. Tony's head rested on my belly. He had been gazing at me as I slept. I rubbed my eyes and questioningly looked at him.

"What?" I whispered.

"Did you sleep?"

I nodded and asked, "How'd we end up back here?"

"Early this morning it got chilly. So, I picked you up and carried you to bed. You're getting heavy," he teased.

"Well, who told you to carry me all the way up the stairs?"

"I wanted to. Anyway, I'm joking. You're as light as a feather and I didn't want to disrupt your dreams. They sounded so . . . interesting. You kept repeating my name."

I giggled at his comment. "I was not."

"Oh, yes you were. You were calling me. '*Tony. Oh, Tony*'," he imitated in a girly voice.

"Stop it." I lightly pulled on his ear.

"Hey, I'm not lying, nor am I complaining. Better my name, than any-body else's."

The blood rose to my cheeks. I couldn't believe I was that transparent. It was true, I had dreamt of him. I felt embarrassed as he tenaciously stared at me.

"You're so beautiful when you blush. Are you okay today?"

I nodded my head. "Sure, why wouldn't I be?"

Tony gently traced my face with his fingers. "Oh, because it always worries me when you cry. I hate to see you hurting."

I took his hand in mine and kissed it. We had become like one soul. My hurts were his and his mine. His happiness was mine and mine his. We completed one another.

"Come on, let's get up. I'm taking you somewhere special today. Put on your swimsuit. We're going swimming." Tony jumped from the bed and made haste. He dressed and prepared himself for our special day.

"Why? Where are we going?" Tony didn't answer, he continued on his way. I was being lazy and snuggled into my pillow. Tony peered back into the room and hollered at me to rise and shine. I mumbled back that I was coming and reluctantly rose to remove my pajamas.

I slipped my clothes on over my swimsuit, made the bed, and briskly washed my face, brushed my teeth, and tied up my hair. I slipped down the staircase and found Tony in the kitchen, preparing a basket of goods to eat.

"A picnic? All right!" I shouted. Delighted, I helped Tony fill the basket with fruit and sandwiches.

As we worked, Tony explained. "I found the perfect picnicking area, yesterday. I was on my way home, walking up Crabtree to our house. I noticed the flowers first and walked off the road into the woods to cut them. Just passed the deepest of trees, I found this patch of clear land, leading to a small lake. The water was so clean, I knew at that moment, I had to bring you there."

"I'm so excited. I can't wait to get there." I glanced at our basket. Seeing that we'd packed nearly everything he had prepared, I asked, "Let's go?"

"Let's go!" Tony lifted the basket with ease. After slipping on my sandals, I followed him through the door.

We walked hand in hand, down the dirt trail. The sun was already blistering hot. Luckily, the trees gave us plenty of shade for our stroll. Tony whistled merrily and we swung our entwined hands like children. I laughed at his enthusiasm. Sometime, he behaved more like a kid than a grown man. I wouldn't have changed that characteristic in him for all the money in the world. That was my Tony.

A half a mile down, he brought me through a thicket of trees and onto the open land. Wild flowers bloomed around the small beach area. He laid out the blanket and placed the basket under a shady tree. I sat to remove my sandals and watched as Tony peeled off his T-shirt. Gazing back at me, he threw it on the basket. His shoulders and arms were toned and strong. His skin gleamed a golden brown tone on account of hours working in our yard. Even his hair held blond highlights from overexposure of the sun's permeating rays. He looked like a model, strong and beautiful in every way. My heart ached just to gaze upon him.

"Stop staring and take your clothes off, woman. Let's get this party started." I blushed and then stood to quickly remove my clothes. Standing in my bathing suit, Tony now stared longingly at me. "I better head for the cold water," he warned. I giggled again. He grabbed my hand and we ran down a small hill, toward the lake. The opening at the small beach area allowed the scorching sun to fully hit our bare skin. Even the sand was unbearable to walk on. We ran across it in large strides. Reaching the water, I extended my toe, only to quickly retrieve it.

"It's freezing," I cried.

"Is it really? Good." Suddenly, I felt his strong arms underneath me. Before I had a chance to retaliate, he threw me into the nippy lake. Like a bolt of lightning, I jolted from the waters. I brushed my hair from my eyes and angrily glared at Tony.

"I'll get you for this!"

"Just try," he challenged.

"Oh!" I stamped furiously out of the water. Tony held out his hand to help. With all the strength I could muster, I fought to drag him into the water, but failed. He laughed—his feet firmly rooted to the ground. Then ruthlessly, he let my hand go, and again I slipped into the frigid water. I could hear his snickering as water submerged around me.

Frustrated and enraged, I plotted my revenge. Tony held out his arms. "Come here. I'm sorry," he chuckled. I walked toward him with a pout. We hugged briefly and a tiny wave splashed our feet. "Oh, you're cold."

"No kidding." Before we parted, I wrapped a foot around his shin and pulled my foot back. Tony lost his poise and plunged into the water. In an instant, he stood and ran out of the water after me.

I raced up the small hill as fast as my legs would allow. My strength was no match for his and he caught up to me, tackling me onto the bristly grass. We both laughed with hysteria, panting for air. We rolled on the grass holding one another, until Tony pinned my hands above my head.

"You sneak!" he accused. "I didn't see it coming. I didn't think you'd have the strength to get me into that water," he heaved.

"You deserved it! I have more water up my nose than there is in the lake."

"Is that what's filling your head," he teased. We laughed together. Letting go of my hands, Tony slowly lowered his head to meet my lips. My arms rested on his neck and shoulders. Our kiss was sweet, yet demanding. When our lips separated, we were both breathing ruggedly. His eyes were burning with passion. "Laura, we better stop while we can."

"You're right." After a long pause, he kissed me again. Tony's body remained glued to mine. We could not tear our eyes off one another.

"The problem is my body won't listen to my brain," he jeered.

"Then maybe we should listen to your body, instead of your brain."

"That could be dangerous," Tony warned. "My body has a mind of its own, you know."

"Oh, you're terrible!" Tony rolled over in laughter. I slapped his arm and rose to my feet. He slapped my rear in return, while I walked away. His cackling continued to trail behind me.

We laid our towels on the sand and dried off in the sun, before eating our lunch. The rest of the afternoon, we lounged on the beach, discussing our future together. We talked of how many children we'd have and what their names would be. We even discussed the possibility of finding my mother's family and reuniting with them.

Before the sun began to set, Tony and I gazed into the brilliant sky. Suddenly disrupting the quiet, Tony disappeared to return with his hand hiding behind his torso, once again.

"More surprises?" I asked excitedly.

"Well, no sense in talking about a future if we're never going to make it absolute." He knelt on the sand before me. I sat up, unsure. Exposing a red velvet jewelry box, Tony's eyes met mine. He opened the case, displaying a remarkable solitaire diamond ring. I gasped and the tears quickly filled my eyes. I felt paralyzed by the moment's happenings.

"Laura," he began, "You're my life. I've loved you from the moment I laid eyes on you. I knew immediately I wanted you to be a part of my life. But even then I couldn't fathom this strong a bond would form between us. When I'm at work, I can't wait to come home to you. No matter how rotten my day, your smile makes all the bad go away. I can't imagine life without you. I want nothing more than for you to be my wife, the mother of my children, and my lifelong companion. Laura, will you marry me?"

I was openly crying by the time that he asked the final question. I shouted a 'yes' and threw myself into his arms. We both cried as we embraced. Tony pulled me back and took the ring out of the box. Taking my trembling hand, he placed the diamond on my ring finger. I gasped at my hand, unable to stop my tears.

"Do you like it?"

"Tony, of course! It's beautiful." I sobbed. "It must have cost you a fortune."

"Well, I've been saving for it, for a while. When I finally bought it, I couldn't wait to give it to you. But I promised myself to wait for the perfect timing. I'm glad I did, because this day has been incredible."

"Not just for you, Tony." We embraced again.

Before it got too dark, we gathered our belongings to head for home. The walk home was surprisingly quiet. Tony and I held hands, occasionally looking into each other's eyes. He'd smile, then I'd smile and our eyes would fill up with tears of joy. I don't remember a more wonderful day.

Upon arriving, we put our belongings away, showered, and prepared for bed. Despite the heat, we held each other closely in our bed.

Tony's hands caressed my arms and back. "I can't wait to marry you, so we can make love," he whispered into my ear.

A shiver ran down my spine. My heart throbbed at the simple thought of it. Making love to Tony seemed all I thought about lately, regardless of the many reasons why we shouldn't. I'd turn 17 in a month and was still too young, even if I was in love. *Could I wait until we were married?* I believed I had to. It suddenly occurred to me that I'd rest better knowing that we had a date set. I voiced my thoughts. "Should we set a date?"

"Looks like I'm not the only anxious one," he teased.

I propped up on my elbow and looked at him. "I won't deny that I want to make love to you, Tony. We're too young to get married now, yet who can wait another two or three years, until I'm a decent age?"

Tony's eyes brightened and he let out a rumbling chuckle. "Who says you have to be over 20 to get married, Laura? As long as you're 18, you can get married by any church or justice of the peace. I can't wait another three years, either. Not unless I have to," he chuckled again.

"Then let's get married soon," I begged.

"That's fine with me. Laura, as much as I want you, I'll wait however long it takes. God wants us to wait until we're married. We have to, because once we make love, we're bound together for the rest of our lives. The Bible even says so."

"I know. I read the same verse myself. I want to do what's right. But, it's so hard. Uncle Frank was right to warn us, when he found out about our feelings. We sleep in this bed together, *every single night*, when we should each be in our own beds. Lord knows the temptation is *always* there. I believe that if we set a date, I could rest my goals on that date and maybe it would help us to hold off."

"Do you want me to sleep in my own bed from now on?"

"Truthfully? No. I want you next to me, now and always."

Tony sighed with relief. "Okay, good. I hate not sleeping next to you. I'll tell you what. At the beginning of the New Year, we'll set a date. I can ask my uncle for a raise, we'll save money and next year, after you turn 18, we'll get married." I saw his warm smile in the dark. "In the meantime," he added, "Maybe we should be more discreet and not let things get too hot and heavy between us."

"You're right. That mean . . . you put on pajama shorts and a shirt to bed. Otherwise, how can I resist you?"

"How can I resist *you?* I've got to buy you clothes of steel so I can't feel your warm skin on mine." We giggled in unison. "Being near you is enough to drive me crazy for you. It's not going to be easy, Laura. We'll try to keeping 'making out' to a minimum and we'll be able to hold off another year."

I agreed. Once again, Tony's counsel was wise. We'd need to resist one another for a while longer. "I pray next year flies by," I said above a whisper.

"Me too." I leaned forward and kissed my fiancé. His arms pulled me closer, until I fell into them.

Our engagement day *was* a dream. No man, time, or space would ever change that.

CHAPTER 24

Unintended Betrayal

Thunder rolled across the sky, waking Laura from a restless slumber. She opened her eyes and looked at her clock. Despite the time, darkness still lurked nearby. It was eight-fifteen and the dreary weather foreshadowed the gloom in Laura's heart. She recalled the previous night and moaned. She had seen what alcohol could do to someone. She certainly didn't want to see it happen again.

Up until the proposal, Laura was happy with the events of the evening. Then it seemed as though Paul was trying to drown himself in his drink. *Was he not happy about marrying her? If so, then why would he ask? Was there something more to him then he let on?* Laura panicked. *Did she really know him that well?* She'd talk to her parents about it and get their perspective.

Rising from her bed, Laura strolled into the living room to find Paul still sleeping on the couch. She looked down at his face, already dark with after-five shadow. For a split moment, he seemed almost peaceful. Suddenly, his head rolled back and forth. Laura moved closer, extending a hand to wake him. Just before her hand touched his, he spoke.

"Tammy," he mumbled in his sleep.

Laura withdrew her hand and stood rooted to the ground.

"Tammy, I'm sorry," he grumbled and rolled over. "So sorry."

Laura began feeling unsettled. *Why was he apologizing to Tammy? Was there something going on between them?* Laura backed away and crept toward Tammy's bedroom. Peeking in, she found her sleeping soundly. Paul appeared to fall back into a deep sleep. Laura was disturbed by the occurrence, but continued on with her morning. After plugging in the coffee maker, she showered and then dressed. Throwing on a pair of shorts and T-shirt, she exited the bathroom a half-hour later to find Tammy sitting at the kitchen table staring blankly at the wall. She sipped on a cup of coffee, still in her wrinkled pajamas.

"Morning," Tammy whispered.

"Hi." Laura poured herself a cup and sat next to Tammy. Tammy's eye grazed over the diamond on Laura's finger. "It's really beautiful."

"Thanks." Laura couldn't help not showing enthusiasm.

"Hey, what's wrong?" Tammy looked at her through concerned eyes. "Are you upset?"

Laura pointed to Paul. "Yes," she whispered.

"Why?"

Laura sighed, trying hard to keep from falling into pieces. Already a lump was forming in her throat and she was angry with herself for immediately giving in to the need to cry. "I'm getting a bad vibe. Paul wasn't himself last night. It wasn't just pre-engagement jitters. I felt as though he was trying to drown his sorrows."

Tammy took a hold of Laura's hand. "Laura, he wouldn't have asked you to marry him if he didn't love you." She turned her eyes away and whispered, "Maybe it had something to do with his first fiancée."

"I don't know." Laura looked at Tammy, debating whether to tell her her deepest fear. Tammy was her closest friend and she wanted to be truthful to her. "I walked into the living room this morning . . ." Laura paused.

"And . . ." Tammy encouraged.

"And Paul was talking in his sleep."

Tammy's face turned ashen. She let go of Laura's hand to sip her coffee. Swallowing hard, she asked, "What did he say?"

"He was calling *your* name. He was saying he was sorry. Why?"

Tammy held her gaze downward and suddenly began fiddling with the handle of the coffee mug. "The other day, he really insulted me. He suggested that I might be depressed. He was insisting I see a doctor. I told him off. Maybe he was dreaming about that."

Laura skeptically gazed at her sister. "Maybe? He did tell me that he confronted you and that he felt bad about it."

Tammy's eyes met hers. "You see, that's all it is."

*   *   *

Paul groaned as he slowly sat up on the couch. "Oh man," he whispered. "Is that coffee I smell? Cause I'm going to need about a gallon to get me up and going today." He looked over the couch and eyed the two girls whispering in the corner of the kitchen. He rolled off the couch and looked down at his wrinkled tuxedo. He steadied himself with a hand on the end table. "Whoa! What kind of a concoction was I drinking last night?"

"It's called, 'everything under the bar'." Laura sarcastically answered.

"Oh man, I'm sorry, Laura. I must've made a fool of myself." He joined them at the table. Laura rose to pour coffee into a mug for him.

"No, not really. But, I'd like to know why you would choose our engagement night to get drunk," she frankly stated.

Paul looked at Tammy and then stared into the mug Laura handed him. "If you give me a chance, I'll explain later when we're alone. In the meantime, I'd like to go home, take a shower, and go tell your parents about our engagement."

Laura agreed, and after gulping down his coffee, they left to head back to Paul's, where he showered and dressed. He took Laura to a pancake house for breakfast. There, they talked openly about the night prior.

"Paul, honestly? I'm upset. We've been out dozens of times where you could've gotten trashed and didn't. Of all nights to get bombed. It's not like you. You're always so responsible. Unless you were drinking to force yourself into asking me to marry you. If that's the case, we can call this all off, before it even begins."

"Oh my gosh, Laura. That's not true. To be honest, a small piece of me felt as though I was betraying . . . Samantha. I know she's been gone for over two years, but still, getting engaged to you triggered some memories of my engagement to her. Of all people, I'm sure you understand."

"I do. Maybe it's still too soon. I want to be sure we're not rushing into this. I know we agreed upon a long engagement and I like that. It'll give us plenty of time to get to know one another and prepare for a future together. Please don't be upset if I ask you this question, but are you positively certain that I'm the one you want?"

Paul nearly choked on a mouthful of buttery pancakes. He coughed, swallowed, and wiped his mouth with a napkin. "What's that supposed to mean?"

"Paul, it may appear as though I'm blind, but I'm not. I can feel the tension between you and Tammy every time you're in the same room. I don't know what to make of it, but it's obvious."

Paul stuttered, unsure of what to say at first. "I-I-I told you, already. Tammy is upset because I confronted her about her depression. Nothing more, nothing less."

"Then why were you calling out to her this morning in your sleep?"

Paul was stunned. He put the fork full of food down and slowly came to an answer. "I have no idea what you're talking about," he lied.

Laura sought his eyes for the truth. "You were apologizing to her. I'd like to know why."

"Laura, I have no idea. I gotta be honest with you, it's been bothering me that she's angry with me."

"But she's not. Tammy knows you love and care about her."

"Good, I don't want her to think I'm a jerk."

"Far from it. Tammy has always adored you."

"I care for her, too. Will you forgive my behavior last night?" He reached across the table for her hand.

"Of course, I do." Laura let out a long sigh.

"Good. Let's start fresh for today. Good morning, Laura."

"Good morning, Paul." He leaned over the table and kissed her briefly on the lips. Laura sighed again.

She seemed satisfied with the answers Paul gave. They finished their breakfast and drove to the Knights. John and Marlene were delighted to see the two arrive. Tammy was already there having breakfast with them.

* * *

"So, what brings everyone by this morning?" John asked.

"Mom and Dad, Paul and I have some good news to share with you. Last night at the Doctor's Ball, Paul asked me to marry him and I accepted."

John and Marlene looked at one another. John's mouth fell open. Neither husband nor wife knew what to say. In fact, they both appeared doubtful.

Before they could voice their opinion, Paul interrupted. "I know that you're thinking it's too soon. But we plan on a long engagement so that I can finish my internship and get established as a doctor and so Laura can get her degree. I gave her that ring as a sign of my love and commitment to her. Mr. and Mrs. Knight, we won't be happy until we have both your blessings."

"I must admit," John affirmed, "I'm shocked. I wouldn't have minded if you would have at least come to me first, Paul. May I ask why the rush?"

Before they could answer, Marlene stepped in. "Truthfully," she began, "I'm a bit concerned. Not because I don't think you're a wonderful person Paul, but because I feel that Laura is too young and not ready yet emotionally. I'm glad to hear the engagement will be long, because Laura, honey, I want you to finish school. But more importantly, I want you to heal."

"Mom, I'm getting better every day. As for school, I do plan to finish. Paul wants to finish his internship and he still has two more years to go. Meanwhile, I can get my associate's. Once we get married, we'll wait a few years while I go for my bachelor's and then we can start the family we've always wanted."

"I don't know what to say. The plan sounds good. You need time to get to know each other better. Go slow and take your time. John?" Marlene looked to her husband.

"I agree. I just have to ask—couldn't you have just made it a promise ring? This seems a bit rushed."

"But I know I'm going to marry her," Paul insisted.

John nodded. "Committing to one another is awesome. I mean, I'm happy for you both. I couldn't ask for a finer man for our Laura. As long as you promise to take care and love my girl, you have my blessing."

They looked at Marlene for her blessing. She smiled, though still doubtful. "As long as you're both happy. It does sounds like a great plan. Congratulations, to you both," Marlene blessed the engagement. They exchanged hugs, congratulations, and kisses. Laura felt relieved.

*   *   *

The next few weeks were hectic for both Laura and Tammy with the start of school, amongst other things. Laura was busy at work, as the big case in Alabama was quickly approaching in the next week, before her college courses began.

She worked out the details of the trip with Mr. Stone. They'd leave the following week on Monday night, and be back by Friday evening. She was excited to actually be in the courtroom with her boss. She rarely had a chance to see him in action, since she ran his office for him most of the time. Laura was actually happy to concentrate on her career, for a change.

Within that same time, Tammy's job was keeping her busy, as well. After literally bumping into Alfonso at the grocery store, he kept his word and called her at the office. He decided on Tammy's agency for the auto insurance he was inquiring about. Within that first week, Tammy saw Alfonso three times—the day he came in to purchase the insurance, two days later he took her out to lunch, and that Friday night, three days prior to Laura's leaving.

That evening, Laura invited Paul over for a home-cooked dinner. Paul accepted and during his dinner break, he hustled off to the apartment to meet her. As they sat down to an early dinner, Tammy rushed in from work, waving her hellos.

"How about some dinner?" invited Laura.

"Sorry, I can't," she shouted from her room. She tumbled through her drawers for something to wear.

"Why not? What's your rush?"

Tammy peered momentarily out of her bedroom door. "I've got a date."

"With who?" Paul suddenly asked. "Anyone we know?" He tried to play down his curiosity.

"I've mentioned him to Laura before," she called back from in her room. She closed her door to change. After a few moments, she reopened it to run into the bathroom. "Remember Alfonso?"

"Sure, the guy who wanted insurance from your agency and then bumped into you at the market?"

"Correction, I bumped into him."

Laura burst into laughter and explained the story to Paul. "Well, that's great. I hope you have a good time," Laura called back.

Tammy exited the bathroom. She looked beautiful in a black sleeveless dress, with her hair contemporarily styled and her makeup refreshed. Slipping on her black pumps, she entered the kitchen and looked curiously at the dinner Laura made. "Looks like you outdid yourself again, Laura. Dinner looks and smells great."

"Thanks."

As Laura and Paul cleared the table, Tammy waited for Alfonso to arrive. Soon, Paul mentioned that he must head back to the hospital, but seemed to delay his departure a while longer. Laura guessed that he was as curious to meet Alfonso as she was.

Exactly on time, Alfonso knocked on the door at six-thirty. Tammy smoothed her dress with her palms and took a deep breath. She answered the door, greeting Alfonso with a hug. His large frame entered the apartment. Next to Tammy, he was a giant—towering her in height. He had thick shoulders that looked round and hard.

Tammy quickly introduced Alfonso to Paul and Laura. Paul firmly shook his hand. Alfonso's eyes traveled to Laura and his smile brightened.

"It's a pleasure to meet you," Laura smiled.

"The pleasure is all mine." He shook her hand, surprisingly gentle for his large demeanor.

"Well, we better hurry if we're going to make that reservation, Alfonso."

"After you, milady." He waved goodbye to Paul and Laura. Tammy winked at Laura on her way out. A smile played on her lips. Laura couldn't help but giggle at her silly little sister.

*   *   *

Laura prepared her overnight bags and placed them near the door. It was Monday afternoon, and the flight departed that evening at 9 p.m. She looked the apartment over once more. Making her way down the staircase, she juggled the bags and her purse to meet her father in the parking lot. Now her plan was to go home with John for a quick dinner, and then have him drive her to the airport.

She had seen Paul the previous night and they said goodbye. Tammy promised to meet Laura after work, at their parents' home. After, she planned to whisk off to meet Alfonso for coffee at a nearby shop.

Shortly after they arrived at the Knight home, Tammy arrived as well. They had dinner and by seven o'clock, John announced that they had better leave. Laura hugged Marlene, asking for a prayer for a safe trip.

"Don't you worry. A hedge of angels is guarding that plane tonight."

"Thanks, Mom. I love you."

Laura embraced Tammy. This was the first time in nearly two years that they'd be apart. "Take good care while I'm gone. I love you, little sis."

Tammy returned the kiss and hug. "I love you, too."

Laura waved to Tammy and Marlene from the car window, as John drove away. She would miss them.

*   *   *

Two days into Laura's business trip, Tammy sat on the couch waiting for Alfonso to show up. He had stood her up Monday night at the coffee shop. The following day, he called apologizing that he couldn't make it. He promised to make it up to her with dinner and a movie. She dressed casually in jeans and a sheer blouse with a tank top to match underneath. Tammy began growing agitated after glancing at the clock again. Seven-thirty and he was over forty-five minutes late. She was about to call it a 'night'.

At last, there was a rap at the door. Tammy stomped toward the door in aggravation. She was shocked to find Paul. He wore a silly hat and a pair of sunglasses.

"Please, hurry. Let me in." He looked back down the stairway before entering and closing the door behind him. Before taking off his sunglasses and hat, he ran to the living room and kitchen windows and pulled the shades down.

"What's going on, Paul. Why are you dressed like that?" Upon entering, Tammy noticed that he wore a strange jacket and oversized jeans.

"Listen. It's important that what I say to you stay between us. Are we alone?" He breezed through the bedrooms and the bath, quickly closing each door.

"Of course we're alone. Who else would you expect?"

"Just making sure." Finally, turning his attention toward her, Paul tore off the hat and glasses and pulled Tammy into his embrace. He abruptly kissed her, stunning Tammy, who didn't have the time to resist. He placed his hands on Tammy's shoulders. "Tammy, we're in serious danger."

"Have you been drinking, again?"

"I've never been more serious in all my life. Are you still seeing that goon?"

"His name is Alfonso and he's not a goon. In fact, I'm expecting him any minute." Tammy pulled away.

"No! You are not to see him, Tammy."

"Paul, you've no right barging in here demanding who I can or cannot see. It's none of your . . ."

Paul placed a soft hand over her mouth. "Shh. Listen, you don't understand. If and when he gets here, you must tell him that you cannot go tonight."

"Let go of me," she commanded. Paul withdrew his hold. "I can't do that. What am I going to tell him?"

He stalked to the kitchen window and peered through the shutters. "I don't know, but you better think of something fast. He just pulled up." After picking up his hat and glasses, he ran into Laura's bedroom, raising his hand to his lips. "Trust me. I'll explain after he leaves." He closed the door.

Tammy tried not to appear frazzled. Alfonso knocked on the door a few moments later and she let him in. "Sorry I'm so late," he apologized. "But, I got caught up at work. You look nice. Are you ready to go?"

"Alfonso, I'm going to have to cancel for tonight. I tried calling you, but you'd already gone. I've the worst migraine and I know I'll be terrible company. I think I'll take the medication my doctor prescribed and go to bed."

"Oh, I'm sorry. No problem, we'll make it another night." He kissed her cheek and left.

Paul opened Laura's bedroom door slowly. He tiptoed to the window and waited until Alfonso's vehicle disappeared. Turning around, he nearly stumbled over Tammy, who lurked through the window besides him. She glared at him angrily.

"If I didn't trust you so much, I would've never done that. You better have a good explanation for all this."

"Tammy, I don't want to tell you too much. I fear you're already in danger as it is. All I'll tell you, is that someone is *really* looking out for your sister."

"What do you mean?" She gazed at him with questioning eyes.

"I mean, they're threatening your life and mine. That's why I had the accident, that's why I asked Laura to marry me, and that's why I've been trying my hardest to make my relationship with her work. I hate lying to her. She doesn't deserve this. Yet, I don't have a choice."

"What? I'm so confused. Who'd threaten you? She has no living relatives. Tony is dead. Who'd care enough to endanger you, if you don't follow through with your relationship?"

"Tammy, I have absolutely no clue. All I know is that I've done some investigating of my own, since Laura left town. Something about Alfonso didn't sit right with me and it wasn't just because you've been dating him. Although, I must admit, I hated thinking that someone else could be touching you or kissing you."

Paul ran a hand across her cheek. Tammy closed her eyes at his touch. He guided her to the couch where they sat. He continued to explain in whispers. "Tammy, Alfonso looked familiar to me, but I couldn't pinpoint from where. Then I remembered that I had worked on a few gashes to his head at the hospital. After we stitched his cuts, I remembered the cops coming in to arrest him. I knew he wasn't to be trusted. Anyway, Monday night, when Alfonso didn't show up for your coffee date, it *was* because he got tied up at work. But not the kind of work you're thinking he does.

"I followed him and found him going into a warehouse with two other thugs. Only one came out with him. The other was missing. After they left, I couldn't stand the suspense. I made my way in and found the third guy. Let's just say, he had an extra hole in his head."

Tammy gasped. "You should've never gone in there, Paul. You've put yourself in serious danger. That explains the sunglasses, hat, and funky clothes. Oh, Paul. What's happening?"

"I'll tell you what's happening, you're not to leave this apartment for any reason. I'll stay here with you until I get my finances in order. Right now, my car is parked at the hospital. I borrowed a friend's vehicle to come here, to throw them off. Friday morning, we're leaving. No goodbyes, no explanations. Let everyone think we've eloped. As much as it'll hurt Laura, I'm sure she'd rather have us together, than have us 'swimming with the fishes'. One day, when this whole thing blows over, maybe we can explain and she'll understand."

"I can't believe this is happening. Now, get to the part about us. How do they know?"

"Tammy, the Mob has eyes and ears everywhere."

"THE MOB!"

"Shh! Well, who do you think we're dealing with? This is big-time. They want to make sure Laura Ann Marcs/Knight is living a happy life. And since they think she's in love with me, I need to deliver."

Tammy shook her head in disbelief. She could not fathom leaving Laura, John, and Marlene, especially without an explanation. She sat back, frustrated to tears. Paul placed a gentle hand on her shoulder.

"This is my fault," he accused.

"How's this your fault?" she sniveled.

"I should've never pursued you, never should've kissed you. Our friend, Mr. Rengali, heard everything that day I came to see you in the office. They told me this afterward. They've been watching us. Tammy, the pieces don't all fit the puzzle, yet. But, he's connected to the visits I've been getting. His job was probably to help woo you away from me. Well, I'm not taking any chances on something happening to you. We need to be careful on Friday."

"So, what's the plan?"

Paul explained that he was having his money liquidated and wired to him. But because he was relying on his parents to help liquidate his accounts, they needed time. By Friday, all the monies would be wired into his bank account in Albany. They'd leave together in disguise, go to the bank to clear the account, get his vehicle back from his friend, trade it in for another at the dealership, and vacate the state permanently. Paul stated that he had a friend in Florida who'd help to get them false identities and they'd live there, for the time being.

The plan made sense. Tammy prayed it would work.

CHAPTER 25

A Deadly Resolution

That evening, Tammy sat on the couch, deep in thought. Her mind was racing and she couldn't control her distraught emotions. Paul stood behind the kitchen counter and made sandwiches for them. Placing them on a plate, he walked into the living room and urged Tammy to eat.

"You're not helping, Tammy. You've got to pull yourself together."

"I'm sorry, Paul. But I have a bad feeling about this. I'm scared, yet I understand that we've no choice. I just don't want to desert everyone. What'll they think of us? Please, if I could talk to my parents and tell them . . ."

"Then you put them in danger, too. If you want to, you can call them tomorrow, but not Friday. They need to think that everything is okay for the next day or two. You cannot let anything slip. The phones may be tapped."

"Oh! I'm so frustrated."

Paul begged Tammy to eat. Together, they nibbled on the sandwiches in silence. That night, Paul suggested she go to bed in her room and he'd stand guard in the living room. He searched the oversized jacket and withdrew a handgun.

"Paul, where did you get that?"

"It doesn't matter."

"Do you even know how to use it?"

"Nope, but I'm sure I'll learn quickly if someone tries to hurt you. Go to bed, you're exhausted."

"Can I stay here with you?"

Paul placed the gun on the end table and opened up his arms. Tammy sat next to him and allowed his arms to enfold her. Her pulse throbbed, firing her desire. For the first time, she allowed her love to break through the walls she'd harbored for months. They held one another's gaze. Paul touched her lips and brought her head to his.

Their kiss was filled with every emotion. Love, fear, passion, and guilt. He lifted her into his lap. Her legs hung over his as he kissed her fiercely. Tammy's hands held his head, while he brought her near heights she only dreamed of. After months of denying their love, they succumbed to what burned within. His lips met hers, again. With her hands on his face, she tore her lips away. Paul's hair was rumpled and his face was red with fire. "I love you," she whispered.

"Not as much as I love you," he breathed. It made no sense denying it anymore. Their love would soon be evident to all.

*   *   *

On Friday evening, two days later, Laura sat in a window seat of the plane that flew her back into the city of Albany. Mr. Stone and his wife, Josephine, sat two rows behind her. Laura was amazed at how the city of Albany looked lit up from the sky. The 'safety belt' indicator flashed and the captain announced their arrival. Laura was now anxious to get home and see everyone. She whispered a prayer, as the landing gear came to touch the runway. Thanking Jesus, she waited for the plane to stop before unbuckling her safety belt. At last, they had arrived. Now, she'd have Mr. Stone drop her off at her parents' home where she'd spend a few hours with everyone and then retire to her apartment.

She couldn't wait to tell everyone about the hearing and how successful Mr. Stone was in winning the case. She also couldn't wait to give everyone the gifts she purchased while she was away. On the trip, after court was adjourned, Laura would join Jasper and Josephine for dinner. After, they'd normally retire to their suites, but Laura would walk the streets of the small town and hit little shopping strips. There, she purchased a few little trinkets as a remembrance of her first business trip.

The ride home was quiet. Mr. Stone drove his vehicle at a sluggish pace, making Laura all the antsier. It seemed forever before they pulled into the driveway at the Knight home. She noticed the lights were out and it appeared as though nobody was home. Laura asked Mr. Stone to wait a moment. She skipped up the porch steps and rang the doorbell. When no one answered, she used her house key. Calling out in the darkness, her voice seemed to echo. Perhaps they were at the apartment. But, she swore they said they'd wait for her here. An ill feeling swept over her and she quickly locked the door and ran back to the vehicle.

"Mr. Stone, no one's home. Would you mind driving me to my apartment? I know it's out of the way for you. But I don't have a ride."

"No problem, come in."

Laura's heart sped in her chest. At last, they arrived. She thanked her boss profusely for the extra miles. Mr. Stone helped her with her bags. Laura waved goodbye and walked up the stairway with her things. The apartment complex was quiet. Laura didn't like the looks of things.

She fumbled for the key and inserted it into the lock. Finding the apartment also deserted, Laura panicked. After bringing in her bags, she raced to the phone. She dialed Paul's home phone, but nobody answered.

What on Earth was going on? Where was everyone? Uncle Joe and Aunt Bernadette suddenly came to mind. She flipped through her phone book to find their number. Her fingers dialed and she waited for an answer. Even they gave no reply. Laura took off her jacket and shoes. She scanned the apartment for a note or a clue as to where they might be.

On the coffee table, next to the lamp, were Paul's shades. Laura tried to recall if they were there from before. She couldn't remember. As she started to unpack her belongings, the telephone rang. Laura nearly tripped over herself to get to it.

"Hello?"

She heard a voice, but it was barely audible.

"Hello?" she repeated again.

"Laura."

"Paul, is that you?"

"Yes." A long pause troubled her more.

"Paul, what is it? You're scaring me. Where are you? Why are you crying?"

"Come to the hospital. Hurry!"

"Why Paul? Paul?" The line went dead. Laura reached for her purse and keys and ran out the door.

*   *   *

The hospital emergency room was all but empty. Laura saw no sign of her family. One of the women behind the emergency room sign-in desk recognized Laura and quickly guided her through the never-ending corridors. They took the elevator up two flights and routed through more hallways.

From afar, she thought she heard a woman sobbing. Laura's heart froze. She recognized the voice. As Laura turned the final corner, her eyes came to rest on her parents. Uncle Joe, Aunt Bernadette, and the boys sat on a bench nearby. John was holding Marlene in his arms. She was hysterical. All their faces were moist with tears. Laura's legs weakened.

"Mom, Dad, what is it? What happened?" Marlene parted from John and fled into Laura's arms. Looking over her mother's shoulder, her eyes questioned John's. He shook his head and covered his mouth with his hand, trying to compose himself enough to speak. "Mom, please," she pleaded. "Where's Tammy? What has happened?"

Marlene cried out Tammy's name. " . . . An accident. A terrible car accident." John took hold of Marlene. He helped her onto a chair and told Laura to sit down. Laura's legs trembled.

His hand touched her hair and he began explaining. "Laura, honey, there's been an accident. Tammy's seriously injured. They don't believe she's going to make it. Her heart has already failed her two times. She's . . . she's brain dead." A lump formed in Laura's throat. When John saw the horror in her eyes, he wept, trying to continue. "They don't think she'll make it through the night," he finally managed.

Marlene let out a howl and fell into Laura's hold again. Laura's head reeled. *This couldn't be happening. Not to our Tammy, not to my Tammy.* Laura swallowed hard and asked to see her. John pointed to the door and took Laura's place holding Marlene.

Laura made her way to the door on wobbling legs. Pushing it open, she found Paul leaning on the bed where Tammy rested. His eyes were red and exhausted. Laura focused on Tammy and nearly doubled over in pain. She was unrecognizable. Her head was swollen and her face disfigured. Laura sobbed loudly, unable to take in the horrid reality.

She staggered to Tammy's side, taking hold of her limp hand. "Tammy?"

Paul shook his head. "She can't hear us."

"No, Tammy." Laura wept bitterly, slumping back into a chair. She couldn't control herself enough to talk. She cried as she stared in disbelief at her beautiful little sister. *How cruel was life to make her witness the suffering and death of so many of the people she loved!*

Laura felt that same retched pain sear a scar deep into her soul. This couldn't be happening again. She couldn't be losing another sister. She sat a while, until she felt strong enough to move closer to Tammy's listless body. Summoning her courage, she leaned forward on the bed and touched Tammy's hand. Laura swallowed, trying to moisten her parched lips.

She whispered near Tammy's ear, "They say you can't hear me. But I don't believe them. I know your spirit is still with us." Laura licked her lips again. She ran a gentle hand over Tammy's bandaged head. "Give me a sign, Tammy. Squeeze my hand. Please, we've been through so much. We've so much more to do."

Laura sniffed back her tears. John and Marlene entered the room. John placed a hand on Paul's shoulder that shook with every tear. Marlene came to Laura and placed her hand over Laura and Tammy's.

"Tammy," Laura continued, smiling through her tears. "Remember how much fun we had at the Belfords? How many laughs we had with Ang and Barb? Let's do it again. Don't let go. Tammy," she urged, "You're supposed to be my maid-of-honor and Godmother to my first baby someday. Then you'll need me to do the same for you. Let's grow old together and we'll be like those old ladies we see walking at the mall. Remember, the ones with the fancy sneakers? That'll be us 50 years from now."

Tammy didn't respond. Laura raised her wet eyes to Paul, then to John and Marlene. She felt a sudden anger. Under clenched teeth, she angrily grumbled, "How? How'd this happen?" No one answered. "It wasn't in her car, because I saw it parked outside the hospital."

"No, it was a friend of mine's vehicle," Paul whispered.

Laura looked questioningly at everyone. "What? Why would she be driving *your friend's* car?"

Paul replied without tearing his gaze from Tammy's battered face. "Laura, I promise to tell you everything, but not here, not right now. Please, we don't know how much time we have left with her."

Laura looked back at Tammy and could not accept what she saw. She sat back down and let her face fall into her hands. Marlene kissed Laura's head and stepped closer to Tammy. She kissed Tammy's forehead lovingly.

"Tam, I love you . . ." Marlene's voice cracked, but continued, "I just want you to know that you're a wonderful daughter. The day you entered our lives, our lives truly began." She broke down into hysterical sobs and this time Paul tried to gently guide her back into the corridor.

"NO! I need to say goodbye." She angrily snatched her hand away from Paul's grasp and slumped down near Tammy's body. "Tammy, don't leave us! Dear God," she cried. "Don't take her!" Laura helped Marlene back to her feet, embracing her as the women cried inconsolably. Paul again offered his hand to guide her from the room and Marlene accepted. The door closed, leaving Laura alone with Tammy and John.

John stepped forward and leaned an elbow on Tammy's pillow. He caressed her cheek. "Hey you . . ." his voice shattered. "If . . . If you see Jesus, if He calls on you . . . you run. Go to Him. He'll ease your pain. He'll heal your hurts. I don't want you to go. In fact, I'd give my life for yours. But it's His will, not mine. I love you, Tams." John kissed her cheek, his face red with emotion. The tears slid lazily down his cheeks and he exited the room.

Laura finally sat alone with Tammy. She scooted the chair closer to the bed and held her hand, once again. "Tammy, you heard Dad. It's God's will. But I say . . . if you see Jesus, ask Him for another chance. Ask Him if He'll allow you to be His miracle. Ask Jesus to heal you and make you whole again. You never know, unless you ask."

Laura's tears fell freely now. "Tammy, if Jesus says no and you have to go, please . . . know that I'll never forget you. Know that I love you and that I look forward to the day when I'll see you again. We'll be together, forever." Laura had to pause to collect herself. "Tammy, do me a favor. If you go with Jesus, when you see my momma, my sisters and Tony, tell them I love them and miss them. Tell Jesus that I said thank you for you—even if it was for a short while. I love you so much, Tam." Laura sobbed with abandonment.

Paul entered the room, holding back his own tears. He hugged Laura and rubbed her shoulders. Laura's hand still held Tammy's. Paul placed his hand on theirs. Unexpectedly, Laura felt her fingers being squeezed. Tammy's hand suddenly twitched. Laura looked at Paul to see if he'd felt it. He smiled at Laura, but upon looking at the screen that monitored Tammy's vitals, his grin quickly faded. There was a sudden increase in her heart rate. Paul buzzed the nurse's station and summoned the doctors to come at once. John and Marlene raced in after them. Tammy's heartbeat accelerated abnormally.

Suddenly, the monitor flatlined.

Paul thrust everyone out of the way. "No, Tammy. NO!" With the help of the nurse, he cleared her chest and tried to revive her heart. "Stay with me, babe. Don't let go, not yet." Paul tried continually to recharge Tammy's heart, though it was to no avail. Other doctors and nurses came in to help, but they realized soon that it was too late. One doctor finally had to pry Paul away from Tammy's body.

"Let me work on her more," Paul argued. "Maybe, we can bring her back. Let me go. I can help her. We can get her heart started again."

"Paul, she's gone. It's been over twenty minutes. We've tried all we could," the doctor coerced.

"No, we can't give up," Paul insisted, in a defeated voice.

Laura gathered Paul and led him into the corridor where John, Marlene, Uncle Joe, and his family mourned. The group embraced, while a river of tears was shed. Laura held her mother's hands and told her that Tammy had responded to her just before dying. Marlene faintly smiled and whispered that she knew that Tammy was with Jesus.

Confirming the obvious, the doctors announced Tammy's death. They all had a few minutes alone with her, before Tammy was wheeled away to the morgue. The doctors encouraged the Knights to go home, but not before confirming the name of the funeral home in which she was to be brought.

They sluggishly walked the halls of the hospital, back to the parking lot. Joe and Bernadette paid their respects one last time and left for home. Too distraught to drive, John convinced Laura to leave her vehicle and come home with them. Paul drove along with them.

Halfway home, Laura finally spoke, "Why did this happen to my sister?"

"Paul, it's time to come clean. What happened today?" John asked insistently, glaring at him through the rearview mirror.

Paul sighed deeply. He ran his hands over his face and seemed to try to compile his thoughts. "Hasn't Tammy been seeing that new guy, Alfonso? Well, he looked familiar to me. I couldn't recall from where. I did research and found that he was a patient of mine, from emergency. I finally remembered that he came in for stitches to a few gashes on his head. Shortly after I stitched him, the cops came in and arrested him, for reasons unknown to me. After remembering those details, I knew he wasn't good news. I remember Tammy saying that he was private about his line of work and . . ."

Laura interrupted him. "I don't remember Tammy saying anything about that in front of you."

"Maybe she didn't. Did you? Anyway, does it matter? I followed him Monday night. I witnessed something that I'd rather not repeat, as not to endanger any of you. After further investigating, I concluded that Tammy was in danger. Anyway, I called Tammy at work on Thursday and she'd called in sick. I was concerned and went to the apartment Friday to see if she was okay."

"That's right," Marlene interrupted. "Because she called me Thursday morning, said she didn't feel good and not to expect her for dinner. I wanted to go to her, but she insisted I stay home, in case she was contagious. What happened from there?"

"I drove to the apartment in a friend of mine's vehicle, because I'd been promising him a spin in my new Mustang for days. Therefore, we swapped cars. Tammy was already feeling better and was getting dressed to go out with that goon. I panicked and demanded she cancel. I sat her down and explained why. I made her promise never to see him. She acted on that promise. I warned her not to leave the apartment until I returned. I wanted to go back to the hospital, get my car, and bring Tammy to safety. I figured I'd bring her to your place or even to mine, until we were able to secure her safety.

"To throw Alfonso off, *I* took Tammy's car. As I pulled away from the apartment building, she must have noticed Alfonso following me out of the complex. As I drove down the road, I noticed that I was being followed. I also noticed Tammy driving behind me, in my friend's vehicle. She was speeding to keep up with us." Paul paused, too choked up to continue.

Meanwhile, John pulled into the driveway and the family begrudgingly walked into the home, where too many memories of Tammy lingered. Laura made some coffee and they sat in the living room to hear the rest of Paul's story.

When, at last, they sipped the warm coffee, he continued. Large drops of tears rolled down his face. "I could see both cars in my rear-view mirror. Traffic began to slow. I watched in terror, as the vehicle Tammy drove continued at neck-breaking speed. The car swerved from side to side. She wasn't slowing down. She tried to avoid hitting the vehicle in front of her, but her car wouldn't stop. She clipped the car anyway and it bounced her into oncoming traffic. Three other vehicles hit her car, the car that *I* was supposed to be driving, the car whose brakes were meddled with to finish *me* off. Tammy died . . . in *my* place." Paul's face fell into his hands as he wept.

Laura wiped her tears with a tissue and offered one to him. He dried his reddened face. "I'm so sorry. They outsmarted me. They were going to kill me for what I'd witnessed. Instead they killed Tammy."

John stood in the living room, leaning up against the entertainment center. He wiped his face, while seeming to digest Paul's explanation. "Paul, if what you're saying is true, then you're still in danger. And it's possible that you've now endangered us, as well. We need to tell this to the police so they can find these thugs. You're an open target. Not only you, but all of us."

"NO! We cannot go to the police. I'm willing to walk out of your lives forever rather than put you in danger. I know I'm not thinking straight right now. You'll have to forgive me. But I'll go and free you all from any further jeopardy."

"What? You can't go," Laura cried. "You'd walk away from me that easily?"

"It's not like that. I'm sorry, Laura, but I won't risk your life, too! For now, until I can figure out what else to do, I'll run."

"Paul, put yourself in police protection. The law will protect you," John urged. "You can't run forever. You've too much to lose. Your life, your career, the woman you love."

"Yes," Marlene agreed. "Let's call Massimo and see if he can help get you out of town, under his protection. Once the police investigate, it's possible the people behind this will be put behind bars."

234

Paul seemed to age all in one night. His hair was a mess and his eyes looked tired and old. He held his hands together, bringing his fingers to a point as he spoke. "Mrs. Knight, I wish it was that simple. We're talking Mafia here. They never get caught."

John took a step closer to Paul and stated, "That's not true. That's what they want people to think. If no one comes forward against them, they'll keep getting away with their crimes. From a father to a son, Paul, get help. Go into protective custody tonight, before it's too late." John paused a moment, while Laura took the phone into her hands to call Massimo. As Laura waited for a response, John asked the ultimate question. "I have one last question for you tonight."

Paul looked up at John. "Yes?"

"Why would Alfonso be a threat to my girl? Tell me the truth."

The question stumped Paul. He shook his head slowly. "I don't know. But I do know that he was trouble. Tammy needed to be warned."

John skeptically looked at Paul. "I don't know, Paul. But I'm glad the police will be involved now. Because there are too many unanswered questions."

*   *   *

It wasn't long after Laura's conversation with Massimo that a crew of police vehicles pulled into the driveway. It seemed as though the horrid night would never end. Paul retold the story in detail. The police promised him protection. He stood in the foyer facing Laura. She hugged him.

"I want to be here for you. I want to stand beside you at her funeral, but now I won't be able to," Paul cried.

"I know your heart is with me. Thank you for trying to help my sister. Don't blame yourself. You never intended this to happen. For now, be safe. I'll pray that God protects you. God's speed," she whispered. They embraced again.

*   *   *

Paul's tears spilled, as he walked down the porch stairway with three police officers on guard. He looked at the house, while the vehicle pulled away with him in it.

Dear God, forgive me that I didn't tell her the truth. I can't hurt her anymore. Not now that Tammy is gone. It wouldn't make sense to add salt to the wounds of her already bleeding heart.

*   *   *

That night, Laura stayed at home with her parents. John called the Apolone family with the tragic news. After making a few necessary calls, the three agreed to put an end to the horrid day and head for bed. Laura crawled under the soft sheets of her familiar bed. Her head reeled with thoughts of what had happened. It was inevitable that she cried herself to sleep.

CHAPTER 26

Without Tammy

Tammy's wake was held two days later. Because her beautiful face was far beyond recognition, they kept a closed casket. Flowers filled the room. Laura felt as though she was viewing the scene from afar. As people circulated in and out of the funeral home, giving their condolences, Laura sat in a daze. She felt numb and spiritless.

Before the funeral, Laura called and informed Mrs. Belford of the horrible news. Mrs. Belford was able to give Laura the names and numbers of the whereabouts of Angela and Barb. Laura placed the calls and told her friends of their catastrophic loss. Both Angela and Barb promised to be there.

At the wake, Laura appeared in control. It was upon seeing her dearest friends arrive, that all restraint was gone. The girls were in hysterics over the death of their friend.

The morning of the burial, John, Uncle Joe, Marco Apolone, and Uncle Joe's boys Michael and Peter, carried Tammy's coffin from the hearse to the gravesite. Flowers blossomed around the burial site. Despite the gloom, the sun shone brightly in the sky. Laura thought how it would've been a perfect day in Tammy's eyes, as she stared expressionlessly at the coffin. A soft summer breeze warmed her.

With one hand, Laura held tightly the charm around her neck that Aunt Bernadette had purchased for the two of them. Her other arm was linked with John's, while Father Bill voiced a beautifully moving homily.

"It's times like these that in our flesh we might ask God—why? Why does He allow tragedies to happen? And it is then, that in our faith, we must understand that God knows the ultimate plan. Is it to bring the soul of a loved one closer to God, in the midst of their grief? Or is it to bring judgment upon those who could commit such a heinous crime so that they too might come to know Jesus and repent? We don't know. But we do know that the Bible tells us that, "all things work together for the good of those that love Him". That's why we must trust our God with all things. We may not like what we're going through. In fact, we may hate it. But, the only way to carry our cross is to ask Jesus for help. For if we turn away from God in the midst of our pain, then we've gained nothing. But should we turn to God in our darkest hour, we've gained our salvation, healing, and best of all . . . an everlasting love."

Laura thought of the priest's words. She wanted to believe them. But the loss of Tammy had hardened her heart. Laura felt an anger toward God that she couldn't explain. *Wasn't losing her mother, at the age of ten, tragic enough? Then, losing the rest of her family four years later. Wasn't that enough tragedy to last anyone a lifetime? No, the love of her life was also ripped away to leave, yet, another hole in her heart.* Tammy's death was more than Laura felt she could bear. *And now what would become of Paul? Would she have to give him up to save his life?* Laura cried.

She whispered a small prayer for forgiveness. She understood that she shouldn't be angry with God. *For who was she to raise her tiny fist to God Almighty? And isn't that what the devil wanted, for her to hate God and turn away from Him?*

The coffin was lowered into the grave. Marlene and John tossed a red rose onto it. Laura also sent her rose to its certainty.

The group of family and friends departed. John, Marlene, and Laura went home.

The following days were all the more hollow for Laura. She continued to stay at home, promising to move back home indefinitely. Suddenly, making a daily trip to the University of Albany didn't seem so inconvenient. Meanwhile, Mr. Stone gave her the week off to be with her family. Between classes and in her spare evenings, Laura began packing up the apartment.

A few days later, she sat on the floor of Tammy's bedroom and boxed up her things. In the drawer of her nightstand, she found Tammy's Bible. In the Bible, Tammy had stuck a picture of herself and Laura, sitting on the beach in Florida. Laura clutched the photo and sobbed.

"God, why did You take her? I don't understand!" she cried aloud. "What do You want from me? What have I done? I try to be a good Christian. I know that I fail, but I ask Your forgiveness and You promise me grace. So why do You call me to suffer like this?" she sobbed.

Laura was too afflicted to listen for God's reply. The sobs escaped her throat. It was a while before she could calm herself. Rising to get a tissue, the Bible fell open from her lap. Laura's eyes fell upon some of Tammy's handwriting, next to a highlighted paragraph. In red ink, she blotted that this was her favorite passage. Laura recognized the verses as the Beatitudes.

> "Blessed are the poor, for theirs is the kingdom of Heaven.
> ***Blessed are those who mourn, for they shall be comforted.***
> Blessed are the meek, for they shall inherit the earth.
> Blessed are those who hunger, for they shall be filled.
> Blessed are the merciful, for they shall obtain mercy.
> ***Blessed are the pure of heart, for they shall see God.***
> Blessed are the peacemakers, for they shall be called sons of God.
> Blessed are those who are persecuted for my sake, for theirs is the kingdom of Heaven."

Laura reread the second and the fifth Beatitude that Tammy had underlined. She knew the Bible was speaking to her. She knew that Jesus would comfort her and carry her through this. But she still didn't want to feel the pain. Closing the book, Laura placed it in the box with other items. Finally, exhausted and hungry, she lifted the boxes she'd packed and carried them to her car. Going to the comfort of her true home, was sounding better every moment. Locking the apartment door, she left.

The drive home wasn't much better. The sky turned a dark gray and it began to rain. The darkening day resembled Laura's spirits. She thought of Paul and what he must be going through. When she drove the vehicle into the driveway, Laura dashed out the door of the car and into the shelter of the garage.

"Mom, Dad," she called out, upon entering the home.

"In the kitchen," John called.

Laura slid into the nook where John and Marlene both sat at the table. Marlene looked exhausted, as well as John.

"Are you guys okay?"

"The question is—how are you?" Marlene asked.

Laura sighed deeply, "Been better."

"Sit down, honey. We want to talk."

Laura sat and wearily smiled at her adoptive parents. "I'm okay. I just need time."

Marlene leaned forward firmly grasping Laura's hand. She looked thin and frail, but her eyes were set in determination.

"You've had a hard life already. You've lost so many of the people you loved. This morning when you left, we made it clear that we didn't want you to go alone. But because you insisted, we knew you needed time to yourself. From now on, we grieve as a family. You can't do this alone. Let us help you. When we help you, you help us. Because we'll know how you really are and we'll worry less. Does that make sense?"

"Yes, Mom. I'm sorry if the last couple of days I've been so distant. I've been angry with God. But I had my say with Him today and I told Him how I felt. Despite my anger, I know how awesome He really is. He comforted me with his own words, even if I didn't deserve it."

"And . . . did it help to let your frustrations out?" John asked.

"I think so. If there's one thing I've learned from all the therapy, it's not to bottle things up."

"That's right. That's what we're here for, too. You can vent, cry, scream, hit, or just talk," John added. "Of course, go to your mother when you feel the need to hit."

"John!"

"Dad!"

They all laughed. "I'm joking. Besides, didn't someone once say that laughter is the best medicine?"

"Well, if that's true, then I'm sticking with you."

"Just what I wanted to hear." John rose from his seat to hug his daughter. Laura returned his embrace.

"Anyone call for me?" she asked.

"Were you expecting a call?" Marlene questioned in return.

"Not really. But I was hoping to hear from someone about Paul. I think I'll give Massimo a call and see if there's any news."

Laura dialed the number to the Cicero Police Department, for by now she had it memorized. Massimo was unable to come to the telephone and they took Laura's name and number.

Since there was still an hour before dinner, Laura decided to rest on the couch. The sleepless nights were, at length, catching up with her and she felt fatigued.

It wasn't long before she fell into a comfortable sleep. In her slumber, she dreamt that she was back at the abandoned house with Tony. It was the night of their engagement and they laid in bed, trying to fall asleep. Tony ran his hands over her back, sending shivers of excitement down her spine. He whispered that he loved her. In the same sentence, he gave her a warning. *"There's more to the story."*

Laura awoke with a start and those words on her mind. *What did they mean?* She wished she could go back to the dream to ask Tony what he meant. Closing her eyes, she replayed the dream in her mind. The thought of Tony's hands on her, the feeling of security the old house brought . . .

would Laura's subconscious ever let her forget? A part of her prayed it would, another did not. For in light of everything that was happening, Laura wished for those days again. She'd prefer her time with Tony above all.

The telephone rang, disrupting her thoughts. Remembering her expected call, she rose from the couch and dashed into the kitchen. John answered the telephone. He signaled to her that it was Massimo. Laura took hold of the telephone and sat at the table.

"Hi Chief. How's it going?"

"It's going all right. How are you? You'll have to forgive me that I haven't called you sooner. The last couple of days have been treacherous."

"Don't worry, I understand. I'm okay."

"I know it must be difficult for you. You both were so close. Sometimes we have to remember to be thankful for the time we had with lost loved ones."

"You're right. Tammy was a blessing. I just can't understand how this happened. Which brings me to my reason for calling. How's Paul?"

"Laura, he's fine and that's all I can tell you. We have to be extremely careful. We don't want to leak info on his whereabouts. For now, you have to trust us and pray that we can figure this out. Speaking of which, maybe you can help. I have a few questions for you. Some things have been nagging me and perhaps you can clarify them for me."

"I'll certainly try. What is it?"

"Forgive me for my boldness, but it's possible the smallest detail could help to solve this case. Can you tell me what kind of relationship Paul had with Tammy? How would you describe it? Now, I want you to give me explicit detail. Anything that you can remember."

"Why do you need to know?"

"Too many unanswered questions, Laura. I feel there's more to Paul's story than he's letting on."

Laura thought of Tony's words in her dream. She knew that Massimo was right. She even sensed that John felt the same.

"Well," Laura began, "In the beginning, Tammy liked Paul. She was crazy about him. I used to tease her about her crush on him. He'd be playful with her, tease her, and innocently flirt. But he did make it obvious that his interest was in me.

"After things got serious between us, their relationship changed. Suddenly, Tammy avoided him. I felt as though she was angry with him, for reasons I didn't know. As for Paul, he always played the 'big brother' role. He was concerned for her when she showed symptoms of depression. He was also protective of who she dated, obviously."

Laura waited for Massimo's response. "Would you say that there may have been deeper feelings for Paul, on Tammy's part?"

"I don't know. I guess it's possible. She never let on, if she did. If anything, it was the opposite. She always encouraged my relationship with him. Especially, in the beginning."

"How'd she take the news of your engagement to him?"

"Well, now that I think about it, she wasn't as happy for me as she was on my first date with him."

"Can you give me a specific time in which you noticed a change in their friendship?"

Laura didn't like all the questions Massimo was asking, but she trusted him to find out the whole truth, even if she didn't want to hear it. She thought back a moment and remembered the tension in the room the night of their graduation party. "Three months ago. The night of our graduation party, the tension was so thick I could've cut it with a knife."

"Laura, this is really helping me. I have one last question. Did you ever notice any strange behavior on Paul's part? Again, be specific, leave out no details."

"Sure, I do remember three particular incidences. The first one was my graduation day. He arrived over twenty minutes late and he's always on time. He appeared frazzled, nervous. Another time, more recently, I found him at the apartment with Tammy. Tammy and I were there moving in. I left for a moment and came back to find him standing extremely close to her. That's one of the times I noticed Tammy's anger toward him. When he left, I walked him out the door and he told me that he'd confronted her about the symptoms of depression. A few days later, she confirmed his story. Then . . ."

Massimo interrupted, "Were you outside or in the hallway when he told you he'd confronted her?"

"We were right outside the door. But we were whispering."

"Could Tammy have overheard you?"

"I wouldn't think so. But I guess it could be possible."

"Okay, you mentioned one other time . . ."

"Yes, the night of our engagement. Paul has always been a responsible suitor. He never got drunk on any of our dates. Of all nights to get drunk, he chose that one. I was upset. He said he was just nervous."

"Laura, you've been a major help. Thank you for being so honest. Listen, let's try to keep the calls to a minimum. As I said, we need to be careful. We're dealing with professional murderers."

Laura hung up the telephone shortly after and explained to her parents all that Massimo had asked. John and Marlene seemed even more concerned now.

*   *   *

The week seemed to crawl without Tammy or Paul. The move did help to occupy their time. Although, going through Tammy's things was a difficult task. For the time being, they placed all her things back in her room and left them there to sort through at an easier time.

The following Monday morning, her day off school, Laura dressed for work. She had been off since the night they arrived from Alabama and it was time to get back into the groove. Laura dressed in a gray pinstriped skirt and a white buttoned-down shirt. She tied her hair back in a ponytail and added some blush to her ashen face. After applying lipstick and eye makeup, she stepped back and looked at herself. She still looked tired, though the makeup did help to bring her face back to life. Quietly, she slipped out of her room and descended the stairway. After a quick bowl of cereal, she kissed John goodbye, while he sat at the table, drinking his coffee and reading the paper. He whispered to her to have a safe drive and that he loved her. She whispered her love in return and was off.

The highway was busy as usual. Laura guided her vehicle carefully through the miles of traffic. At last, she drove into the parking lot of Mr. Stone's office. Pulling around toward the back entrance, Laura parked the car and opened her door. Reaching across the seat, she lifted her purse and briefcase. A sudden sting in her left arm surprised her. A warm glow came over her and Laura collapsed in her car seat.

CHAPTER 27

The Whole Truth

Somebody mumbled something softly. Laura was unable to make out the words or register the voice. She tried to open her eyes, but it was in vain. They felt heavy and inert. *What had happened?* She tried to remember where she last was. She recalled waking up and getting ready for work. She recalled the drive *to* work. From there, her memory was fuzzy. Although, there was a sense of familiarity of the surroundings, she felt too drowsy. Forcing her eyes open, she caught a haze of the room before her. Somebody sat on the bed and mentioned her waking. A peace came over her. She'd wait for the grogginess to pass. Once again, she gave in to the slumber and drifted off.

*   *   *

A while later, the sun's rays penetrated Laura's eyelids. She lifted her arms and rubbed her eyes. Rolling over, she rested on her side. The bed squeaked and Laura felt a hand on her leg. Breathing in deeply, she took in the familiar scent. Slowly, she opened her eyes.

Panic filled her heart. Laura found herself lying in her bed at the old abandoned house. She turned around in a flash. Her eyes clashed with Tony's.

Tony!

Laura stumbled out of bed and scampered to her unsteady feet.

He stood and spoke with concern in his eyes. His arms extended in an attempt to calm her. "It's okay, don't panic. I won't hurt you."

Laura toppled backward, finding herself cornered against the bedroom wall. Her brain could not grasp the image that her eyes sent.

"No," she panted. "You're dead."

"Please don't be afraid. I won't hurt you."

Laura ran forward and embraced him, before she could stop herself. He was real. It wasn't a dream. He returned her embrace, nuzzling his face into her neck. Suddenly, she pulled away and shook her head in disbelief. She looked at him. It had been nearly two years since she'd seen him. Their last encounter was in the dark. It was now evident that Tony was a grown man. The lines around his eyes revealed his age. He no longer had his baby face. The white tank and fitted blue jeans he wore, gave away his thinner build. Still, his muscles were toned and rippled at the movement of his arms. Tony Warren looked matured . . . and tired.

"How can this be?" she finally asked. "They told me the van blew up. They couldn't find a fragment left of you." She paused a moment to think. "Because . . . because you never died," she stated in a heave.

"That's right. My death was staged," Tony confessed.

Her head was spinning, yet she let the anger burn in her voice, "Why? Do you know how much I cried knowing I'd lost you forever?"

Tony appeared touched. "I'm sorry. But that's exactly why you're here. It's time you knew everything."

Laura's attention diverted to another figure standing near the door. "Uncle Frank!"

"Hey, it's okay. You're safe." He made his way to her, pulling her into a hug. Seeing him reminded her how very much she missed him, as well. He smiled and gently guided her back to the bed, where they both sat. "Laura, I'd never put you in danger. Listen to Tony, he's telling the truth. I'm here to make sure that you're safe. There's much going on and you must give Tony this chance to explain. Do you trust me?"

Laura couldn't respond. She stared at Tony, still in shock. Her hands trembled in Uncle Frank's. He repeated the question. *Of course, she trusted him. It was Tony she couldn't trust.* Coming to her senses, she nodded.

He rubbed her back reassuringly. "Okay, if you trust me, then listen to what I'm saying." Laura finally tore her eyes from Tony's and looked at Uncle Frank. "I need you to listen to Tony. He won't harm you. I promise. But if for any reason we see a change in his personality, I'm right here. I have an injection with a sedative, like the one we were forced to use on you, that'll put him out in an instant."

Laura looked to Tony, who nodded in agreement. She rubbed the arm that was pinched by the needle. Uncle Frank rose from the bed and stood near the closed bedroom door. Somewhat reassured, Laura sat up straighter, using the headboard to lean on.

Finally, she spoke, "All right, I'm giving you five minutes. If I don't like what I'm hearing, I'm out of here."

Tony seemed to relax and chuckled, "Wow, some things never change. Oh God, Laura. I've been waiting for this for too long. I don't even know where to start."

"Start from wherever you feel you need to explain," Laura suggested.

Tony nodded and asked if she was at ease with him sitting at the foot of the bed. She said yes and he made himself more comfortable. His face grew serious and Laura found herself mesmerized by his eyes, as he began to tell the story that would change their lives forever.

"My real name is Antonio Giacalone. Tony Warren is a false identity I picked up over five years ago. I'll get to the reason why later. I *was* born and raised in Syracuse, as I told you. My father's name was Vito Giacalone, my mother's . . . Maria Fontana."

"The same name . . ."

". . . On our bills. Yes. This home was left to my mom, the daughter of Paolo and Lisa Fontana. That obviously explains why the owners never returned and how Uncle Frank was able to 'purchase' it for us. My grandparents only used this house on the occasions when they came here to visit from California. After they passed, they left the house to my mom.

"Almost everything I told you about my family dying was true. Except for the part about how the fire occurred. Laura, my family was also murdered. Back in '66, when I was 12, my dad's construction business was going under. His brothers, his partners, bailed on him before the business started to plummet. They tried to warn him. They tried to get him to file bankruptcy. His stubbornness caused a huge family war and my uncles never spoke to my father again. They went as far as to move away from him, out of Syracuse and away, to White Plains, New York. I haven't seen my father's family since. They even refused to take me in when my family died.

"Dad, in his arrogance, said he didn't need his brothers and bought them out, putting us in even more debt. He tried everything in his power to maintain the business. We maxed out our mortgage and still the money wasn't enough. My mother worked to try and help out. That's when my father made the fatal mistake of going to a big-time mobster named Mario Galante.

"Galante loaned him a quarter of a million dollars, trusting my father could rebuild his business and return the money within two years, with interest, of course. For over a year and a half, my dad struggled to keep his business alive. The Galantes were becoming impatient because they had yet to see any payments. But there were no profits. My dad used Galante's money to pay off his debts and lost the rest of it to equipment and expenses.

"First, it began with a few threats. Another time, we found my father in the parking lot of his shop, nearly beaten to death. He begged them for more time. We tried selling the business to pay off the loan. They were no longer patient with him.

"Somehow, the Galantes found out about the life insurance policy. Since I was the eldest and the first who'd come into the money, they planned the death of my family, with me as the exception."

Laura leaned forward and touched his hand. "Tony, I hate to interrupt, but what does this have to do with what happened to us?"

"I'm getting there. My behavior has everything to do with the death of my family. I know . . . I don't have the right to ask this of you, but please, trust me."

"Okay, go on."

"*They* started the fire. After the fire investigation, I came to find that the house was doused in gasoline and ignited. Every room, but mine. When Vincey and I escaped out of the window, two men grabbed us. One held me, while the other tossed Vincey back into the burning inferno." Tony paused and it appeared he was trying to collect himself. "I'll never forget. The one who picked up my baby brother had a large mole just beneath his left eye. Every time I see a dark complexioned man with a mole, I wonder if it's Vincey's killer."

Something struck a chord in Laura's memory. She recalled a man with a large mole, but was uncertain from where. She stared at Tony, watching him mournfully tell his story. She allowed him to continue.

"Both men held me down to keep me from running into the house. I heard little Vincey screaming until the smoke and the fire consumed him. Laura, I tried to save him. Built as I was, I was only 14 and I wasn't strong enough to fight off those grown men. I listened to my brother scream for his life." Tony struggled not to cave in. "As the fire trucks turned the corner, the men let me go and disappeared. I tried to get to the girls, as I told you I did. The explosion tossed me. I laid there in shock, as the firemen worked to save my family. Obviously, it was too late.

"They brought me to the hospital. I wasn't physically hurt, aside from that burn on my hand, bump on my head, and a little smoke inhalation. But after careful analysis from psychiatrists and psychologists, I was diagnosed with a stress disorder.

"Very recently they named the disorder: Posttraumatic Stress or PTSD. It's common among people who have experienced traumatic incidents. Some of my symptoms of PTSD were frequent flashbacks of the experience and losing touch with where I was and what I was doing. I was jumpy, edgy, always easily startled. The worst symptom for me was the insomnia. Remember the pills I gave you that first night when you couldn't sleep? Well, these were just a few of the things I was dealing with, even long after the fire.

"While I was healing at the hospital, the fire investigation continued. It was true that they suspected me for the murders of my family. I was held, until they discovered my father's dealings with the Mafia. That's when I was released into foster care.

"All the while, I was keeping in touch with Uncle Frank. My aunt was ill and Uncle Frank couldn't come to New York to help me. He was, and still is, the trustee of my father and mother's estate, but he couldn't take on the role of my guardian. I spent nearly four years in foster care. Remember what I told you about foster care?"

Laura nodded, recalling how he deeply expressed his disgust with the care he was given. Tony continued, "Well, I wasn't lying. It was terrible. When I turned 18, I intended to move to California with my aunt and uncle. Just before my 18th birthday, Uncle Frank called me and told me my aunt passed away. I couldn't wait to leave and go to him. The day I left foster care, I was at the airport ready to leave, when the Galante famiglia took me.

"They wanted me to give them the name of the trustee to my parents' estate. You see, my father may have made the fatal mistake of going to the Mafiosos, but he was not daft. He kept this house in my mother's maiden name, so they couldn't claim it as collateral. He also saw to it that the will was sealed by the state so that no one but the trustee would know what went to whom and when.

"When I refused to give them my uncle's name, they beat me. Laura, they threatened to keep me until I inherited the money and then they swore to kill me. Or, they'd spare my life, if I'd give them the name, so they could 'convince' him to hand the money owed over to them.

"Afraid to put my uncle's life in danger, I didn't speak. Laura, they tortured me. They kept me in a nine-by-nine cell without a cot, nor a pillow, to rest my head. Not even a blanket to keep me warm. Just four walls and the most cold-hearted man as my keeper. He was assigned to get the info out of me.

"He'd starve me for days and then tease me with a morsel of bread. Other times, he'd turn on a space heater and leave me there without water or fresh air. Then, he'd do just the opposite, strip me of my clothes, and blow in freezing cold air, until I couldn't stand it anymore.

"Laura, my mind couldn't take it. Suddenly, I began noticing time lapses in my memory. I'd be sitting in one corner in the morning and the next thing I'd know, I'd find myself in another corner and it would be nighttime. The memory of the whole day would be gone. Something was happening to me and I didn't know what it was. The next day, my torturer would tell me how crazy I acted and how he had to beat me to stop me. That explained the cuts and bruises I'd have with no recollection of how I got them. I felt as though I was starting to go crazy . . . and I was.

"One day, about four weeks later, my keeper played with a nail-clipper. He cussed and cursed, telling me that my life would be over shortly. He whipped the little clipper at me, hitting me in the head with it. It far from hurt. He was just venting because of the pressure he was under to get me to talk. Little did he know that his little fit saved my life.

"After he left, I studied the nail-clipper, finding it had a small emery board that came to a sharp point, inserted into the side. I tried to use it to pick the lock, but it didn't work. I studied the walls closely. I crawled over every inch of my prison. On one wall, I noticed the mortar flaked easily. Using the tiny point, I began working away at it. That was the last memory I had of that cell. The next thing I knew, I was standing in the middle of nowhere—somewhere I'd never been before.

"In the dark woods, I saw you running into the night with tears streaking your face. A camping bag was laying at my feet. In a daze, I picked it up and I entered the cabin you'd just left. Laura, I found myself staring into the dead face of my . . . my torturer."

Laura gasped, "NO! Oh my God!" She rose from the bed, holding her stomach as a queasiness seized her, threatening to spill forth her breakfast. She paced the room, trying to walk off the sick feeling and absorb the nightmare of Tony's story. "No, it can't be true! Oh Lord. I don't want to believe it! I know he was rotten to the core, but could he be so evil? I can't believe it!"

"Laura, it's true. It was your father. He worked for Mario Galante as an enforcer."

"This is sick! I can't believe it!" she insisted.

"I don't expect you to believe me, because I kept the truth from you for so long. But I'm not lying. I wish I was. Uncle Frank can vouch for me. I'm telling the truth."

Laura met Uncle Frank's sympathetic gaze. He nodded. "I'm afraid it's the truth," he whispered.

Laura closed her eyes and absorbed their harsh words. She shook her head in denial. Yet, suddenly, it was as though a light came on in her mind. "That explains so much: the mysterious job, the money, the clothes, him sobering up, and him being able to keep a job despite the fact that he was illiterate. You don't need to know how to read in order to torture some-one." Laura sat back down on the bed. She reached for Tony's hands and held them. "I'm so . . . so sorry he did that to you!"

"Shh. Please, don't apologize for something you didn't do and couldn't control. Unfortunately, what he put me through ultimately led to the near destruction of my sanity. I recently came to find out why I was having so many lapses of memory. During my imprisonment by the Galantes, I developed an illness called Multiple Personality Disorder."

"What?"

"Because my mental state was already fragile, the torture I sustained caused my brain to develop a second character. One that could better with-stand the torment and help me escape the pain. You met him. *He's* the one who hurt you. He calls himself . . . Max."

Laura thought for a moment and recalled the scenes of Tony's alternate behavior. The way Tony struggled within himself to regain control, his outburst of anger and rage. She recalled the night after Thanksgiving, almost two years ago, how Tony had cursed an 'Antonio'. His alter ego was talking about Tony. Thinking back, she remembered the night Tony came to find her at the Knight home. He wrestled with his second personality and he couldn't bring himself to hit her.

"How? How does a mind do that? Just splits off like that? I don't understand," she cried.

"It's a protective mechanism. The torture was too much for me to bear, so my mind created a second personality. One that could endure the pain, so I wouldn't have to. I know it sounds crazy. But I'm obviously not the only person that this has happened to. There are documented cases very similar to my own. People living a double lifestyle without even knowing it. It's scary, but it's real. Because I was mentally already dealing with the PTSD, the torture was too much. I broke," Tony whispered.

A lump rose in Laura's throat, burning until her eyes filled up. She felt such an immense wave of compassion for Tony that she burst into tears. "Oh, Tony! I'm so sorry! I'm so incredibly sorry!" Her shoulders shook with sobs.

Tony pulled her into his arms. "Don't cry for me. I'm going to be okay. Just having you here is healing me."

She looked up into his face. "This is the missing piece of the puzzle. I always knew it wasn't you. I knew you could never hurt me."

"My God, Laura, never! I swear I'd rather die than hurt you." Tony's sorrow was visible through his tormented eyes. He cast them downward. "Still, that's exactly what I did," his voice rasped.

"No," Laura clasped his hands. "You were a victim. You never asked for this." Laura looked at Uncle Frank. "Uncle Frank, please tell him," she begged.

Frank stepped closer to the bed and rested his hand over Tony's shoulder. "I *have* told him and I will *continue* to tell him. You both have been through hell. It's time to close this chapter of your lives and find peace and happiness. If you're okay with it, I'll step out and give you both some privacy. I'm gonna head down and make you both something to eat."

Laura nodded, while she rubbed Tony's hands with her own. Frank exited the room and Laura slid closer to Tony. She brushed his cheek with her hand. Tony shivered at her touch. "I never stopped loving you," she whispered. "Tammy used to get so mad at me. I could never explain it. I just never stopped."

Tony fought tears. "I never thought I'd *ever* hear you say those words."

She leaned forward, cupping his face with her hands. She tenderly kissed his tear-filled eyes. Her lips traveled downward and she kissed his prickly cheek. Laura held her breath until finally, she kissed his full lips. They trembled. They embraced.

"Tony, I've missed you so much! When they told me you died, I died inside," she said breathlessly.

"Do you know how much it killed me to know that Max tried to hurt you? I wanted to go to you so many times, but I made myself resist until I could control him. I ached to hold you and tell you that I loved you. Some nights, I felt like a madman without you at my side." He pulled her closer, pressing her chest to his. "Laura, I don't ever want to be without you. I don't think I could bear it."

"Now that I know what I know, nothing will ever come between us. I can't deny my love for you, not for anything or anyone!"

They kissed passionately. Tony's hands traveled over her back, holding and squeezing her. She held on to his strong shoulders. Their lips parted and they searched one another's eyes.

"Laura, there's more. I have to finish telling you everything," he said with a frown. She nodded, as he brushed her hair away from her face and wiped a tear with his thumb. "I can't believe you're here. Sorry, about the injection. I had no other way of getting you here without placing everyone in danger and revealing my own identity."

Laura held his face in her hands. "Tony, everything you're saying makes sense. It fills in all the gaps. I'm glad you did this. Although, I should let my family know that I'm okay. For now, finish telling me everything."

He nodded. "Okay, where was I?"

251

"You said you found my father in the cabin."

"Yes. Oh man! It was terrifying. When I saw him dead and little Sabrina beside him, I panicked. I dropped the camping bag I'd just found and searched it, afraid I'd find a gun, but I didn't. I did find a wallet, and in it was a new driver's license with my photo, but the name Tony Warren. That's when I realized a year had gone by. From the time I'd escaped the Galantes, I'd lost a year, Laura! I was horrified. Looking at the license, I didn't even recognize the address.

"At first, I was so confused. I didn't know what was wrong with me. How could I understand that my brain had developed another character that took over, when the going got tough? I could only put the pieces of the puzzle together, little by little. I came to understand that in some other state of mind, I'd escaped the cell and came to my captor's house.

"I didn't know why I was there. I only knew that he was dead and so were two of his kids. Then, the realization that you were completely alone, hit me like a tidal wave. *I had to help you!* I followed you into the sewer and lied to you about the raids. I made it all up to convince you to let me help you.

"When we left the sewer, I was thankful to find that we were in close proximity to my grandparents' old home. I purposely led us here. Then, when we found the house boarded up, I wasn't sure what was going on. The electricity wasn't running, yet it was stocked with clothes for a girl just your size.

"Later, after I discovered I'd developed Max, I gathered that he'd fooled Uncle Frank. When my flight came into California and I wasn't on it, Uncle Frank left California and came to find me. He held all kinds of searches in vain. Once back here, he decided to re-establish his life in Cicero, his original hometown. When I did reappear, four weeks later, I was Max. Uncle believed it to be me and Max played the part. He told him about the Galante famiglia and how he had escaped. My uncle took Max in. To protect me, Uncle had falsified documents made up, thus Tony Warren was created. The driver's license had Uncle's address.

"After I found you, I went to that address not sure what I would find. There was Uncle Frank, wanting to know where I'd been the past two days. I didn't tell him I had no idea what he was talking about. I just blurted what I'd discovered—you.

"When I told him that I found my torturer's daughter and that my torturer was dead, he panicked too. He was afraid we'd be discovered by the Mob—by the cops. We had to keep you in the house for your safety. He allowed us to live in this house, without turning you over to the authorities, to keep you safe. We didn't know if the Galantes might catch wind that we had the daughter of one of their men. They could come after you. We were afraid for you—for us. Remember when Grillo's store got 'raided'? Well the truth is, the Galante famiglia was still searching for me."

"My only fear, the real horror that I've been carrying with me . . . I'm not certain, but I'm afraid that this second personality . . . I'm afraid that he . . ."

"Don't say it," Laura pleaded, shaking her head in refusal.

"But it's highly likely. In fact, I'm almost certain that it was Max . . . who killed your family."

"No, Tony. No!" Laura's face fell into her hands.

Tony grasped her and made her look at him. "Laura, you've seen Max. You know what he's capable of. Look what he did to you. He hurt you, stalked you, he tried repeatedly to harm you. He *is* capable of killing."

"No, you're wrong, Tony! You always stopped him from harming me. I saw the struggles. I believe you wouldn't have allowed it to happen. You said yourself that you didn't have the murder weapon. In fact, let's think about it. My father came home that day in a rush. He wanted to get us out of town. Maybe someone else was after him. Perhaps this Galante family?"

He shook his head in doubt, "I don't know. I guess it's possible."

"I also remember him saying something about never living in poverty again. Could he have tried stealing from this family and they came after him?"

"Or, did Max beat them to it?"

"Tony, stop. I'm remembering one more thing. Massimo Desanti, the police chief, did send his men to the cabin. There was absolutely no evidence of the murders. He said that the job was done professionally. They searched the graves for the bodies. The bodies went missing. Do you remember having any more lapses in your memory after finding me?"

"Positively not! The next time Max emerged was on that horrible day, after Thanksgiving. Though, I have to tell you, when Uncle Frank and I went to the cabin to bury your family's bodies, they *were* already gone. We were stumped, even afraid for you. We figured someone else *had* to be involved, as well, because it was as if the murders never happened. But to give you peace of mind, we dug up the ground and made three fake graves."

"Their bodies were gone?"

"Gone—vanished. No sign of the murders. The evidence had to have been professionally disposed of."

"Well, who would have cleaned up after your mess, if in fact you killed them? See, I told you. Max didn't do it," Laura insisted.

"I don't know. There is so much I still cannot explain." He touched her chin with his forefinger and gazed lovingly into her eyes. "Laura those three years together with you *were* real. My feelings for you *are* real. That's why the night we almost made love, I could not live with myself. I felt like I was living a lie. All our talks about Jesus and here I couldn't find the courage to tell you the truth. The guilt was killing me. I wanted to come clean, until Max stopped me."

"Why? What caused him to surface?"

"Laura, I've no idea. I don't know what Max is thinking and I don't know what he does. But my guess is that, that night you were asking questions about my father and because I despised him so much for getting my family killed, it must have triggered the anger—the rage. Maybe Max came out to seek revenge on Matt's beloved daughter."

"Beloved? My father could care less about us—about me."

"No, you couldn't be more wrong. I specifically remember him talking about how you had a rare beauty that he loved. He said he didn't like his oldest daughter because she was too much like him. As for Sabrina, she was just a reminder of Cara's death."

Laura exploded in anger, "He really was a monster! Patty was nothing like him and if she had attitude, she had a right to. And poor Sabrina, he couldn't look at her because it reminded him that *he* killed his wife."

Tony held her hands, understanding. "Laura, I'm sorry to have drudged this all up. I hate to see you hurting."

"No, Tony. You're right. It's time I knew the truth." Laura looked into his red-rimmed eyes. "I'm just having trouble understanding one thing. Explain to me again, why I was also in danger."

"Laura, after I returned to my normal state and found you, I was petrified that I'd be caught. I was even more petrified that they'd find that I had Matt's daughter in my possession. For all I knew, they could retaliate for my murdering your father. I had a will made up. You're the beneficiary, if I don't make it to the age of 25. I didn't want anyone to know you were even alive. My plan was for us to get married and move to California, to protect us from danger. What I didn't know was that *I* was the real danger."

Laura's mind was reeling. "I would have gone with you to the ends of the earth," she confessed.

Tony shook his head in regret. "You don't know how mad I am that Max reappeared after all those years. He ruined everything!"

Remembering something that always left her perplexed, she questioned, "Tony, when Max came out that night after Thanksgiving, when did you come to the realization that he had returned?"

"After I was arrested and the chief was questioning me."

"I knew it! Massimo said that you first denied hurting me. That would've been Max. Then he thought you were putting on an act, showing concern for me, but you truly were, because you were you."

"Yes. When I took hold of my personality and realized what I had done, I pled guilty so that I'd remain locked up and Max would no longer be a threat to you. While I was in prison, I studied up on my symptoms. That's how I came to find that I had MPD. I befriended one of the officers at the jail. He had compassion for me, after I explained my situation, and got me the name of your foster parents so I could explain to you the reason I'd hurt you. I called Mrs. Belford pretending to be a distant relative wanting to know your whereabouts. Wanting to help connect you to your relatives, she gave me your new name and address. When I wrote you that letter, I was sincere. I wanted you to know that I never intentionally wanted to harm you."

Laura considered his words. Thinking back to the day she received his letter and then to the night he died, she felt remorse.

"I'm so sorry! I was so unforgiving."

Tony shook his head in disbelief. "Are you kidding me? I don't blame you. I destroyed our life together." Tony looked down, unable to meet her gaze. "When the chief personally told me you wanted nothing to do with me, it hurt so much, that Max returned.

"I don't know what he did that night. I only know that I was coming in and out at the Knights. Afterward, I found myself here. I was confused, frustrated, and angry because I didn't know what Max was up to. A van that I'd never seen before sat on our trail and I knew that it was *his* doing. I had had it. At that point, I decided to put an end to *his* reign. But I couldn't leave until I knew what he had done. I went downstairs. The stains of your blood still covered the steps. I cried at the hurt I'd caused you.

"Just near the last step, I found your ring. I picked it up and placed it in my pocket. But I couldn't leave you without saying goodbye. So I drove back to Albany and snuck into the hospital. When I saw what Max had done to you, I knew leaving was the answer. I planned my death to rid you of me, for good. I left you the ring and after a kiss, I left.

"In the parking lot of the hospital, I took a crowbar to a side window of the van Max stole. I took off in it, deliberately letting security notice me, but not before I planted DNA and other evidence in the van that would confirm my death. The cops set up a roadblock at the closest overpass. I planned to have the van go over the hill just before it. When the van veered downward, I jumped out of the broken window into the dark. I nearly killed myself, but somehow managed to maneuver my body to roll away from the van. A tree stump broke my fall.

"I got to my feet and ran from the vehicle before it exploded. The blast sent me spinning, and I broke my wrist. But I took off on foot, never to return. I knew that since none of the doors were opened, they'd presume my body was still in the van. And so the death of Tony Warren/Giacalone would get the police *and* the Mob off my back.

"The reason I came for you now, is because again you're in serious danger. They found that you're the beneficiary of my will. This past week they confronted Uncle Frank, finding that he's the trustee to my dad's estate. We made the stupid mistake of claiming this house, so we wouldn't lose it.

"When Uncle Frank actually had the deed changed over to his name, he needed to provide my mother's wedding and death certificates, along with him as the trustee to my parents' estate. Because Mario Galante has eyes and ears everywhere, word of the Giacalone's trustee came forward. They found Uncle Frank and promised to break a few bones if he didn't find a way to get their money to them.

"He told them he couldn't have legal access to the money, until the courts decide whom the money goes to. We don't know if they bought it, but we didn't want to take the risk of them coming after you. The only reason you didn't collect the money upon my 'death', is because I put a clause in *my* will, stating that you couldn't collect the money until *your* 25th birthday.

"Meanwhile, I've been keeping a close eye on you. I'm sorry about Tammy's death. I'm sure you have to know that there's more to that story, Laura."

Laura remembered his warning in the dream. "I had a dream of you just this past week. You said those same words to me. The Holy Spirit speaks to me through you, in my dreams. And I'm afraid you're right."

Tony gazed longingly into her eyes. "We'll get to the bottom of everything, I promise. I'm just so sorry you've been through so much. I'm sorry I hurt you. Please, forgive me?"

Laura tilted her head to the side and smiled, letting a tear slip down her eye. "Tony that goes without saying," she reassured. But suddenly a frown fell over her face and she whispered, "I have a question—one horrible fear. What makes you so sure that you can keep control over Max now?"

CHAPTER 28

The Truest of Loves

The fear in Laura's eyes was evident. Tony ached knowing he couldn't give her a certain answer. He caressed her warm hand with his. "Laura, I don't know for sure that I can control Max. But since I've been hiding out this past year, I've learned more about my disorder. I know that with God's help and psychotherapy, I can bury him away forever. Recent studies show that my two personalities can even merge.

"The reason I've been able to suppress him so far, is because I've learned a method where I don't allow myself to get too deep into that emotional sector of my memory. I can tell this story calmly and rationally. So long as I keep cool, I'm in control."

Laura sighed, while concern replaced the fear in her expression. "I trust you'll get professional help."

"First thing."

"Okay, last question. Why didn't you and Uncle Frank just collect the inheritance and pay the Galantes off?"

Tony was expecting this question. "Because the amount borrowed was a quarter of a million. Now, they've doubled the amount and want the full half-a-mill that my father left me."

"So, what? You'd be free. We could work and build a life for ourselves. We don't need that money. Pay off the debt, and rid them from our lives forever."

This time it was Tony who sighed, frustrated with trying to explain the Mafia to her. "Laura, if it was that easy, I would've paid them off long ago and not suffered the torture. The problem is that they'd take the money and we'd still be dead. They won't take the chance of us retaliating. They'd snuff us out like a lit candle."

"So, we run the rest of our lives? Let's give them the money and make them keep their word."

"Laura, we don't have the power of the Mob to make them keep their word. These aren't men of honor and we're too weak to hold them to it."

"Well, what can we do?"

"For now, let's get you something to eat. I smell Uncle Frank's cooking. Maybe he can help us come to some kind of a conclusion." Tony stood and helped Laura get to her feet. Standing so close, Tony could almost feel Laura's heart beating. He lifted her chin again and stared into her eyes. Laura's eyes filled. "I still can't believe you're here," he whispered.

"Is this really happening? Am I here with you?"

Tony lowered his head and kissed her.

*   *   *

Laura wrapped her arms around him and held him. She wanted to preserve that moment, afraid to wake up and find it was all a dream. After the kiss, she opened her eyes and gazed at him. It was real and Tony was holding her. Overcome with emotion, she erupted into more tears. Tony held her closely. Laura finally realized why she could not let him out of her heart. Their love was pure and true.

They headed down the stairway, through the living room, and into the kitchen, where Uncle Frank prepared a small meal. "Everyone okay?" he questioned.

"Never better, Uncle," Tony stated. He hugged Laura, who still wept. She dried her tears, as Tony pulled out a chair and helped her sit down.

"Glad to hear that, Nephew." He placed a hand over Laura's and briefly sat next to her. "Did Tony's explanation make sense?"

"One hundred percent."

"He's been through so much, Laura. One thing I know for sure is that he loves you more than anything."

"I believe you and the feeling is mutual. The only thing I want now is for these people to leave us alone. How do we go about doing that? Can't we give them their money and be done?"

"I don't know," Uncle Frank replied. "But they'll be coming for me soon. When they do, I need to know what to say to them."

"Uncle Frank, cash in Tony's inheritance and pay them off. They've waited long enough to get their money. Pay them and save all our lives," Laura argued.

"Laura, if that's what Tony wants, I'll do it. We need to pray that that's all they want. Neither you, nor I, pose a threat to them. Tony on the other hand . . . let's say, he's better off remaining 'dead'."

"Uncle, you've been discovered as the trustee and they think I'm dead. They'll find that Laura is the beneficiary and will come after her. I'll do whatever it takes to keep you and Laura safe. If there's a chance that they'll be satisfied with that money, then give it to them. I no longer want either of you at risk. I don't want or need that money."

It was settled. Uncle Frank would take the risk, exhaust the total monies out of the estate, and distribute it to the Galante famiglia. Together the three ate, while engaging in intense conversation regarding the Mafia and their dealings. After cleaning up, they continued to sit at the table and converse over a cup of coffee.

Laura looked into the cup, as she stirred it with a spoon. "I've been prolonging this all day, but I need to get in touch with my parents. I know they're worried sick about me. With whom and where do I tell them I am?"

"Well, we should keep Tony's identity out of it, if we can," suggested Uncle Frank.

"For how long do we pretend he doesn't exist?"

Uncle Frank and Tony shared glances. "Tony?" Uncle Frank questioned.

"I want to live the rest of my life with her. I don't want to hide anymore. Maybe, I need to turn myself in."

"Son, that's out of the question. It's suicide. Do you realize you'd be thrown back in jail, hunted by the Mob, and possibly even convicted for the murders of Laura's family?"

"But he's innocent!" protested Laura.

"You and I know that, but can we convince a jury?"

"He has a real disorder. The law will protect him. If my boss represents him, Tony will be exonerated. As for the murders of my father and sisters, it's evident that Max didn't kill them. There's no supporting evidence. Without evidence, they have no case. As for the Galantes, we'll pay them off and promise to keep their name out of it."

Again, the men exchanged glances and smiled at Laura's innocence. "We'll have to consider that. Meanwhile, just tell your parents that you're okay. I'm sure they need to hear from you," Tony suggested. He pointed to a new telephone propped up on the kitchen wall.

"You finally got a telephone?" Laura smiled, remembering that being one of her requests.

"I thought you might like that," Tony returned the smile.

Laura looked at the new number taped to the phone and immediately memorized it. She dialed the number to her parents' home and waited.

In a quavering voice, Marlene answered, "Hello?"

"Mom, it's me."

"Oh, thank God. Laura, are you okay?"

"Yes, Mom. I'm fine. I'm so sorry I couldn't call you sooner. I'm okay. In fact, I couldn't be better. I can't tell you where I am right now. I can only say that I'm safe. Please don't worry about me. Trust me and know that I'm all right."

"But Laura, you never showed up to work this morning. We're all concerned. We even called Massimo."

"Mom, please. Call him back and tell him I'm okay. As soon as I can tell you more, I will. I'll call you soon. Don't worry about me, okay?"

"No, Laura. I *am* worried. When will you be home? "

"I love you, Mom, so much. I'll call you soon. Goodbye." Laura hung up the telephone. She felt sick at having worried them.

Frank rose from the table, glancing at the clock. It was near eight o'clock in the evening and the sun had already begun to set. "I'm exhausted. I'll crash on the couch?" he asked.

Laura looked at Tony who stood behind her. He wrapped his arms around her and whispered to her, "Do you believe in me?"

Laura looked into his eyes and nodded reassuringly. "With all my heart," she breathed in return.

"Uncle Frank, it's up to you. But I don't think it's necessary. There's no way I'm letting Max anywhere near her. If you want to stay, stay. You can take my bed and I'll sleep on the couch," Tony suggested.

"If Laura feels safe, I'll go home and rest in my own bed. Truthfully, I think you two need to be alone, to make up for lost time."

"Well, there's a first!" Tony teased.

"Don't get too used to it! I'm still watching you two," he threatened. Humor was twinkling in his eyes.

Laura laughed. "It's so good to be back. I miss hearing you two bicker."

"It's been Hell without you, Laura," Uncle Frank admitted. "Tony was beside himself with the grief of losing you. For a while there, I didn't know if he was going to pull through okay." Uncle Frank gazed at Tony and nodded. "But he's stronger than he thinks he is and by the grace of God you're back here with us, safe and sound."

"Is it safe for *you* to go, Uncle? Do we need to worry about the Galantes coming for you?" Laura asked.

"Don't worry. If they come for me, I'll be prepared." He hugged and kissed Laura. "I'll check on you as soon as I get home, before I go to bed, and first thing in the morning."

Laura giggled at his over-protectiveness. "Thanks."

Uncle Frank pumped Tony's hand and gave him a brief hug. Tony's smile deepened. He thanked his uncle profusely, as he walked him to the door. Uncle Frank gave Laura one last reassuring smile and left. Tony closed the door and forcefully blew out a breath. He looked worn and tired. Laura stood between the entranceway of the kitchen and the living room, unsure of what would happen next. Then, Tony extended his hand and she quickly took it. He led her to the sofa, where they sat.

"I know today has been a full day. But I wanted to talk to you about one last thing," said Tony.

"What's on your mind?"

"Your future and mine. You're engaged to Paul." He glanced at the ring on Laura's hand.

Laura's heart sank. She had nearly forgotten. Playing with the ring, Laura answered, "I can't marry Paul, now. Tony, I love you. I'll stand by you, until we clear your name and if it's God's will, we'll have the rest of our lives together."

Tony sighed in relief. "Honestly, I don't deserve you. But I'm not going to be stupid and deny myself a chance at happiness with you."

"Well, I feel terrible for Paul. He's a good man and I don't want to hurt him. But I'd be hurting him if I stayed in the relationship without giving him all of my heart."

"Laura, do you believe Paul was faithful?"

"What do you mean?"

"Tammy's accident was meant for Paul."

"I knew that. How did you?"

"I told you. I've been keeping an eye on you, trying to make sure the Galantes stayed away. I've seen things not meant for my eyes. They weren't true to you."

Laura thought about Tony's words for a moment. Someone finally voiced what Laura feared. "Tammy always had a crush on him, but she'd never betray me. Would she?"

"Not intentionally. You'll have to get the truth from Paul."

"What a nightmare this has all been." Laura ran her fingers through her long hair. Changing the subject completely, she asked Tony, "Were you serious about turning yourself in?"

"I'll do whatever you want. So long as we're together, I'll face whatever consequences. I don't want to lose you again." Tony touched Laura's hand with his. He held it and kissed it. Laura felt a warmth burn within. How she had longed to feel his touch again.

A short while later, the telephone rang, startling them. Laura rose and ran to the phone. Uncle Frank had arrived home and was calling to make sure all was well. Laura assured him. He promised to call first thing in the morning. They bid one another goodnight and hung up. Laura made her way back to the couch.

Tony snickered. A smiled played on his lips. "What's so funny?" Laura asked.

"He really loves you."

"I love him, too."

"He was so happy when we got engaged. Do you remember that day?"

"How could I forget? It was magical, even if you did throw me in that freezing cold water."

"Yeah, well, if memory serves me right, you got me back." They laughed together at the memories. Tony's face suddenly grew serious. "Oh, Laura. I'm so sorry. I'm so sorry things happened the way they did. I never meant to hurt you."

"Shh, don't say another word. Just hold me and pretend nothing bad ever happened." Laura snuggled closely in Tony's arms. She rested her head on his chest, as he leaned back on the arm of the couch. Tony gently played with Laura's hair, caressing her face and neck.

After a moment, Laura looked up, still amazed she was lying in his arms. His lips met hers in an ardent kiss. Laura felt her body come alive, as it hadn't since the last night she was with him. Her hands traveled upward and stroked his thick hair.

"Tony."

"Laura," he breathed.

"I've missed you so much. How do I know if and when I'll get the chance to be with you, again?"

"Laura, we have the rest of our lives to be together. I'm counting on God for that," he exclaimed.

Laura tried to hide an unexpected yawn. She rested her head against his chest again.

"Come," Tony urged. "You're tired. Let's go up to our bedroom and lie next to one another. I've missed that more than anything else."

Laura and Tony rose and closed down the house. Hand in hand, they climbed the stairway. Laura found her old pair of silk pajamas and slipped them on. Tony put on his shorts and a tank top and lay down. She sat on the bed next to him. She ran her hands over his chest. Closing her eyes, she felt as though in a dream. Tony pulled her down next to him and held her closely in his arms.

"If this is a dream, I don't ever want to wake up," Laura whispered.

"It's not a dream. This is as real as love gets."

Laura sighed with contentment. They held each other until sleep tickled their eyes.

* * *

Sometime in the middle of the night, Laura felt Tony's hand gently playing with her hair. She opened her eyes and caught his gaze in the darkness. He was propped up on one arm, engrossed in her. Before Laura could speak, his lips lightly brushed hers. She closed her eyes to savor the sweetness.

Was it a dream? Yes, it had to be! And soon she'd wake up and Tony would be dead and Tammy would be gone, too, and the ugly reality of life would still be there. Yet, Tony felt so real. She didn't want the feeling end. Her head felt fuzzy with sleep, yet her body was awake with desire. He kissed her again, only stronger and more urgent. Laura all but melted at his touch and inevitably . . . they succumbed to their desire for one another.

Tears streaked Laura's cheeks from the true passion they experienced. Tony kissed her lips, cheeks, eyes, unable to stop.

"I love you," Laura finally whispered.

"I'd give my life for yours."

"Never."

They curled up in each other's arms and fell back asleep.

* * *

Early the next morning they awoke, clinging to one another on the warm bed. It was as though time stood still—as though the past two years were nonexistent. Holding Tony was beyond any joy Laura ever imagined.

Her eyes met his and he held her gaze. The seriousness in his eyes was evident. Tony wanted her again and she felt her body respond to his.

Though Laura feared that their time together would be short lived, she knew she'd eventually have to come to terms with the poor decisions she was making that very moment. She knew that with every sin was a consequence. Living in the moment, would eventually have a heavy price. She prayed that God would forgive her, for not trusting Him with the short time they possibly had.

* * *

After breakfast, they waited for Uncle Frank to return. It wasn't long after that he called and mentioned that he was on his way. Laura and Tony waited. It was decided that Laura and Uncle Frank would accompany Tony to the police department, where Laura would ask for Massimo. From there, she prayed he could help.

Meanwhile, she called Mr. Stone and explained the entire story. She asked him if he'd represent Tony and meet them at the police department later that afternoon. Jasper Stone was happy to hear that Laura was okay and promised to leave for Cicero immediately. He gave them certain legal advice. Even though, after nearly a year of working with him, Laura knew what their legal rights were.

An hour later, both Tony and Laura grew worried. Uncle Frank had yet to arrive. Tony tried calling his home and then the store, but still no word. Alarmed, Tony put on his shoes.

"Where are you going?"

"Laura, I have to go to him. What if he's hurt?"

"Then let me come."

"No! Absolutely not! You stay here and wait for me. If I don't come back within the hour, go to the chief and have the police come find us."

"No Tony, please don't leave. I can't lose you again."

Tony cupped her face with his hands. "Believe me when I tell you, that I'll do everything in my power to come back to you. Nothing will keep us apart again." He kissed her fervently.

"Be careful. I love you."

"I love you, too." He opened the door and skipped down the porch steps.

Laura stepped out onto the porch, peering into the woods. Suddenly, she cried out, "Oh my God! Uncle Frank!" From behind the string of trees, Uncle Frank staggered toward them. Laura and Tony both raced to meet him and helped him inside.

He was beaten severely. His face was bloodied and bruised, and his hand held a puncture wound to his side. "Uncle, what happened?"

Uncle Frank coughed and sputtered, as he tried to speak. Tony helped him onto the sofa, while Laura quickly ran for towels and bandages.

"They came for me," he sputtered.

"The Galantes?" Laura asked and he nodded.

"I told them I'd give them the full half-a-mill. There is only one problem . . ." he gasped. " . . . They want another quarter million dollars."

"What!" Tony screeched.

"Another quarter million! Why?" Laura asked, as she tended to his bruises and cuts.

"Because, that's what *your* father stole from them just before they killed him," he said, directing his comment to Laura.

"So, I was right. He did steal from them. They found out and came after us. And spared me? It can't be."

Tony held her gaze as he explained, "God protected you. But, because your father's body landed on yours and his blood covered you, they must have assumed you were dead."

Uncle Frank nodded in agreement. Laura lifted his shirt and pressed down on the bleeding wound with the towel. "Uncle Frank, we need to bring you to the hospital. You'll bleed to death if we don't."

Frank lifted Laura's chin until their eyes met. "Do you have any idea where that money can be?"

"I have no clue."

"What do you recall from that day?"

"Oh, it's all a blur."

Tony took over applying pressure on his uncle's wound, while Laura tried concentrating on the happenings of that dreaded day.

Suddenly, she recalled a briefcase. She remembered him taking it out to the old truck, but never seeing it again. "Maybe we should go back there," Laura wondered aloud.

"It's something to consider. For now, let's get to the hospital and fast," Tony suggested. "Uncle, where's your truck?"

"I got here on foot. It's still at the store." His breathing was less labored.

"Well, it'll take too long for me to run and get it. We'll call the ambulance."

"No! No Son, don't bring anyone here. This is your safe house and nobody needs to know about it. I'll be okay. Go get the truck, quickly. Be sure to check it for any tampering."

Tony and Laura exchanged glances and Tony abruptly left in pursuit of the truck. Meanwhile, Laura did what she could to keep the wound from bleeding. Not more than fifteen minutes later, Tony returned. Laura and Tony helped Frank into the vehicle and drove him directly to the local hospital.

Within the hour, Uncle Frank was stitched up and resting in the hospital bed. The x ray results indicated no damage to his vital organs. Laura and Tony were relieved to know that he'd be okay. A short time later, he was released, and they brought him back to the safe house. Laura glanced at the clock and reminded Tony that Mr. Stone would be at the station, shortly.

While Frank rested on the couch, Laura and Tony drove the vehicle into town. Before exiting the truck, Laura clasped Tony's hand. "Whatever happens, remember that I love you and that I'll never give up on you. I'm with you every step of the way."

Tony leaned his head back on the driver's seat. He exhaled loudly, seeming to gather his courage and strength. "Thank you. I can't do this without you. As far as our love is concerned, I'll never give up on it again!" They kissed just before confronting their fate.

CHAPTER 29

Max's Revenge

Laura and Tony stepped out of the vehicle. They reached out to hold hands. The screeching of car tires startled them both. Tony embraced Laura as an assembly of squad cars surrounded them. They stood on the stoop of the Cicero Police Department, while police officers drew their guns.

"Let go of the girl and we'll hold fire," an officer called out.

"Turn her loose and hand yourself in, Tony Warren," another shouted.

"You don't understand," Laura tried to explain. "He *is* turning himself in."

"Don't worry, Miss Knight. We won't allow harm to come to you. Walk away from him, if he'll let you," one of the same officers continued.

"He won't hurt me. He's here willingly. Please put your guns down."

"Let the woman go," they insisted.

"Do as they say, Laura," Tony whispered. "It'll be okay. We'll explain everything the first chance we get."

"Please," Laura pleaded, as they reluctantly descended the stoop together. "Don't hurt him. He's innocent." The police officers charged past her and immediately took Tony to the ground. Laura screamed, as they brutally wrestled his hands behind his back and cuffed him, shoving his face onto the hard concrete.

"Get off of him!" Laura cried.

Another police officer, Laura recalled named Manelli, moved Laura aside.

He shouted at Tony. "Thought you could fool us, didn't you? Played dead so you could get away with what you did. You've the right to remain silent . . ."

"Get off of me!" Tony shouted. "I'm unarmed."

267

"Shut up! You gave up your rights the second you broke the law. Now, get to your feet." The police officer dragged Tony upward. Twisting his arm with brutish force, he suddenly dislocated Tony's shoulder. Tony cried out in pain.

They pressed on his arm, lodging the shoulder back into its socket. Tony screamed out in agony. She witnessed, in horror, as his demeanor instantly changed. His eyes collided with hers. Becoming more enraged, he lashed out against his abusers. Two men struggled to hold him down. Laura helplessly watched, while they ruthlessly hauled him down to 'lock-up'. She stood in the building foyer, trembling.

The entranceway doors opened and Massimo entered with Jasper Stone, closely at his heel. "Laura!" Massimo hugged her.

Laura immediately explained what had just occurred. She demanded to know why the need for such brutish force. Massimo clarified how somebody recognized Tony at the hospital. The police were called and they followed Tony and Laura to the station. Because of his past record, Tony was considered armed and dangerous. Laura was furious, while Massimo apologized.

"Please, let me take you into my office where we can talk in private," he begged. Jasper encouraged her, as well, promising to help.

Massimo guided them into his office and allowed Laura some time to explain. He and Jasper both jotted down information, as she continued to tell them the mystery behind the murders of her family and Tony's. Massimo soon came to the understanding that Tony was a victim as well. The true enemy was the Galante famiglia.

"Do you see why I'm so angry?" Laura cried. "Tony had repressed Max for almost a year. He worked so hard to keep him restrained. Your men provoked him, angered him, and that brought Max out. Now, I pray that Tony is strong enough to overcome Max again."

"I'm sure with therapy and professional help, Tony will be okay. Laura, I can't apologize enough."

"It sounds like my client could easily have a case against this precinct, Chief. I suggest you play your cards right, or you'll find a lawsuit slapped against your force," warned Jasper.

"I promise I'll do whatever I can to help."

Laura pleaded with Massimo to let her see Tony. But because Max was dangerous, Massimo didn't want to take any chances. Laura begged, until he led both her and Jasper down to lock-up. Max sat on the bench, in his cell. He angrily glared at his visitors.

"You," he accused. He stood and pointed a finger at her. "It's your fault Tony is in this mess. I should've never let him trust you. Never again," he shouted.

"Tony? Tony, come back," Laura urged.

"No way! You know, it's so typical for a guy like Tony. A little bit of lovin' and he weakens. Well, not me. I'm stronger and he's never gonna resurface again."

Massimo whispered not to listen to him. Tears filled her eyes. She watched the frame of her lover sulk in the corner of his cell. "I promise. We'll get him the help he needs to overcome this."

Massimo led them back into his office and immediately they began the necessary arrangements to have Tony hospitalized. First, a psychiatrist, specializing in Multiple Personality Disorder, would come to authenticate Tony's condition in order to find him the proper help. From there, he'd be institutionalized and receive urgent attention. Laura wanted to have him taken to a facility near Albany where she could visit with him daily.

Meanwhile, Mr. Stone would arrange all the necessary paperwork to have the charges against Tony put on hold until he could assist in his own defense.

Laura called Uncle Frank and explained what had happened. He was upset and urged Laura to help Tony any way she could. She promised him that she would and before hanging up, stated that she'd be home shortly.

Jasper looked at Laura and frowned. "What do you mean, 'you'll be home soon'? Your home is in Albany. Your family is worried sick about you. Let me take you back where you belong."

"Mr. Stone, I appreciate everything you're doing for us. But until they transfer Tony to the hospital, I need to be here with him. In the meantime, his uncle is wounded and needs help. He has no one but Tony and me. Tony can't help him, so I will."

"I understand," Jasper then stated. He stood and gathered his paperwork together. "I'm going to find a place to stay for the night. I want to be here first thing in the morning when Tony is evaluated and arraigned. I'll see you first thing. Oh," he paused a moment before leaving. "By the way, you know your position will still be there for you, when all is said and done. For now, consider this an extended vacation."

"Mr. Stone, you're the best!" Laura extended her arms and hugged the man. "Thank you. I'll owe you for the rest of my life for this."

"Don't be ridiculous. You're my right hand and have helped me run my business efficiently. I owe *you*." He waved goodbye.

Laura waited a moment, while Massimo finished a conversation with a specialist assigned to Tony's case. He gently cradled the receiver on the base. "Everything is all set," he affirmed.

"Before I go, can I see him again?"

"Laura, I don't advise it."

"Please, Chief," Laura's eyes filled. "I need to see him before I go. I can't stand the thought of him being closed up again. That's what caused his personality to split in the first place."

"I understand. But as Max, he's a threat to you and I won't release him until he's in the custody of the psych ward." Massimo's face softened, when Laura choked up and sobbed before him. "Come on. I'll accompany you to his cell." Handing her a tissue, he led her back to lock-up.

The clicking of Laura's heels on the cold floor stirred a resting Max. He sat up in the bench, as she approached his cell.

"What do you want?"

"I want to talk to Tony."

"Tony is gone, okay? How many times do I have to tell you?"

"He's not gone. He's inside of you and you *will* let me talk to him."

"Hey, nobody tells me what to do. Especially not you!" he spat.

"Why do you hate me so much?" Laura asked.

"You were one more responsibility Tony didn't need."

"Let him be the judge of that."

"Tony's done."

"No, Tony will prevail. He no longer needs you."

Laura trembled as Max made his way toward her. Only the bars that imprisoned him kept him restrained. At first, he glared at her angrily, and then he gazed at her longingly.

"I'll give Tony credit for one thing . . . he sure knows how to pick his women."

"Watch yourself, Warren!" Massimo stood out from behind the shadows and revealed himself.

"Don't give him the satisfaction, Chief. It's not my Tony. This character is merely a sliver of the man Tony really is." Laura dared to step closer to the bars, but Massimo held her back by her shoulders. "Tony, I love you. I know you can hear me. Don't worry . . . everything is going to be okay. We're going to get you help."

Max growled at her as she stepped away from the cell. She wiped the tears from her face and followed Massimo back to his office. Laura called her parents and promised she'd be home soon.

*   *   *

270

The following morning after replacing Uncle Frank's bandage and making him breakfast, Laura scooted out the door and left for the station. The two police officers who escorted her home the night prior, stood watch over the home all night, and now, drove her back to the station. Laura was anxious to get back to Tony. At the police station, she found that the assigned doctor had already examined Tony, with Mr. Stone's okay. It was without a doubt, that Tony was mentally unstable and diagnosed with MPD. After further research, a suitable hospital was found in Albany named the 'Capital District Psychiatric Center'.

Still, the charges against Tony weren't so easily expelled. The prosecutor did file a motion to dismiss the charges. The judge was only in agreement to drop the charges if extreme psychological treatment could restore his mental health. If, and when, Tony was no longer considered a threat to society, the court would cease to hold him accountable for Max's actions.

Laura shared the news in person with Uncle Frank, who was happy that Tony would, at last, receive treatment for his illness. She begged him to come stay with her at the Knight home, where he'd be out of harm's way. He refused to place her and her family in danger. He swore to stay in the safe house, so long as Laura agreed to call him daily regarding Tony's condition. Laura promised, then kissed him goodbye and went back to the police station.

Before Tony was released into the custody of the hospital, Laura went to see him. Max fiddled with the lace of his shoe, before acknowledging his visitor. Laura cleared her throat to get his attention. Max rolled his eyes. "Stop coming here," he ordered.

"Sorry. You better get used to seeing me. I'm not giving up."

"Great," he moaned.

"We found you a good hospital," Laura informed.

"Yeah, thanks to you, I'll be stuck in a nut house."

"Please Max, I'm begging you. Let go. I love Tony and I want him in my life."

"Too bad."

Laura took one last look at Max through the steel bars of his cell. He shook his head in disgust, before pouncing down onto the bench. "Goodbye," she whispered.

She hadn't talked to Jesus in a while. It was high time she started.

*   *   *

After injecting Tony with a high dosage drug, he was placed in a secured ambulance and taken to the facility in Albany. Laura and Massimo followed closely in a squad car. The late summer day was as gloomy as Laura's heart. It rained non-stop from the moment they left Cicero. Throughout the drive, Laura couldn't seem to halt her tears.

Massimo sighed. "You've got to stop this. You'll make yourself sick."

"I'm sorry. I can't help it. One moment, I was back in his arms. The next, he's a complete stranger."

"Laura, forgive me, but you're so young. You've your whole life ahead of you. I know you love him, but Tony is a sick man. You need to move on."

"Chief, if you had a second chance to be with your wife, wouldn't you take it? I see this as a blessing from God. If Tony returns and gets help for his disorder, I want to marry him as we planned."

"And if he doesn't?"

"He will!" she insisted. "He has to. With God, all things are possible, right?"

"Yes, I do believe that. But . . ."

"No buts," Laura insisted.

When they arrived at the facility, Tony was still sedated and carried into his assigned room. The doctors insisted that Laura go home and rest, for it would be a while before the drug would wear. After a tearful good-bye, Laura kissed Tony's resting face and left.

Massimo brought Laura home, where John and Marlene anxiously awaited. She entered the door and rushed into John's waiting arms.

"Laura," he cried.

"Dad!" she held him and he kissed her face and squeezed her. Marlene embraced them both, crying tears of relief. Laura held her mother. "Oh, Mom, I missed you so much. I'm sorry to have worried you. I'm so sorry."

They held each other, and then made their way into the living room. Massimo stayed and helped explain all that had happened. Both John and Marlene were astounded.

"So, what happens to the Galante famiglia? Will they pay for the harm they've caused?" John questioned.

"We're working on that," Massimo stated. "The problem is that our prime witness is mentally ill and unable to testify. With Tony locked away in a hospital, the Galante famiglia will be sure to stay clear of him. Frank Blandino is smart enough to lay low and is also under police protection. As for Laura, I'll be sure two of the Albany Police Department's best men will be guarding her at all times. Your home will be under surveillance until we can put to rest this vendetta. We will re-inspect the area in which her family was murdered, with the hope of finding the money that Laura's father stole. It might help us to link it to them, at last, incriminating them. Either way, we'll be working on finding that concrete evidence."

Marlene stared at a picture of Tammy on the end table and asked, "Do you think this somehow relates to Tammy's accident?"

"I haven't figured that out yet."

"Speaking of which, Chief, we need to talk to Paul and get the truth from him," Laura insisted.

"What's this 'we' stuff? If anyone is going to talk to Paul, it's me."

"Chief, I want to be there. You need to go to his hideout the same. Just take me with you."

"Look, I'll take you if your father and mother agree."

"Laura, as your father, I forbid you to go," John claimed.

"Dad, look, I know you're both scared. I love you for your concern, but I *have* to go. I need to find out why my sister was murdered. Please, don't forbid me. I don't want to go against your wishes . . . but, I will."

"Oh, you're so stubborn!" John shouted. He stood from the sofa and hollered, "I can't stop you from going, because you're almost 19 and you're of age. You better not leave Sam's side. One more disaster in this family and two more people will be joining Tony in that mental institution." John stalked out of the room. Slamming the back sliding door closed.

"I'm sorry, Mom, but I have to do this. I can't stand another minute of these lies. Do you understand?"

Marlene frowned, but shook her head, "Laura, I trust you and Sam will get to the bottom of this nightmare. Mostly, I'm going to have to trust Jesus, to keep you safe and help us find the answers we need to move on."

"Thanks Mom."

*   *   *

The following morning, Massimo told Laura he'd stop by at 10 A.M. Laura showered, dressed, and was ready in time. Massimo picked her up and they drove together a total of 60 miles northeast of Albany to a secluded area. The sun was bright, slightly lifting Laura's spirits. She was looking forward to seeing Paul and finding the truth.

Amidst a stand of timber, a small cabin sat nestled on a patch of grass. Massimo was careful not to have been followed and eased the vehicle up the spiraling gravel driveway. Laura exited the car wearing a police uniform as a disguise. She followed Massimo to the cabin. The police guard on duty exchanged a few words with Massimo and then opened the door for them. Laura removed her cap as soon as the door closed. Paul stood by the front window, but quickly raced toward Laura as soon as he recognized her. He lifted her up into his arms and hugged her.

"Thank God, you're okay," he stammered. "The cops on duty told me what happened to you. Did Tony hurt you?" He put her down and kissed her cheek.

"No Paul, Tony didn't hurt me."

"I'll leave you two alone to talk, but you and I will have a conversation before we leave," Massimo spoke directly to Paul. Paul nodded as he watched Massimo exit through the door. He turned his attention toward Laura and led her to the couch to sit.

Taking her hands in his, he asked, "Tell me what happened?"

Laura briefly explained Tony's story. Paul listened closely, unable to believe the reality of Laura's past.

"This brings me to the reason I'm here. Paul, I'm going to be straight with you. You've been a wonderful part of my life. You helped me move forward, when all I wanted to do was turn back. But there are too many things that stand between our future together. For one—Tony. I can't deny that I'm still in love with him. I thought those feelings died when he died, but they haven't. As much as I care and love you, it . . . it can't compare."

Paul looked away with tears in his eyes. "I'm sorry, Paul, but there's more. The other obstacles that stand in our way . . . are lies. You've not been truthful to me and I know it. I want you to look me in the eye and tell me your true feelings for Tammy. Then, I want you to explain to me what really happened the week I was gone and the day she died."

Paul rose from the couch, walked toward the bay window and stared out of the large opening. "I don't know what you're talking about, Laura. I already told you what happened," he denied.

Laura stood firm, "Don't lie to me, Paul. Tony told me that he knew you were lying."

"And how would he know? Of course he's going to tell you that, he wants you for himself." Paul fumed.

Laura stood and placed herself in front of him. She took his face into her hands and forced him to truly look at her. "I know you loved Tammy. I could see it every time you looked at her. I tried to ignore my instincts, because I didn't want to believe that you'd be untrue to me. Paul, don't deny it anymore, for Tammy and for me. When did your attraction to her begin?"

Paul took Laura's hands from his face and kissed them. Tears spilled from his eyes as he held her hands to his lips. "Let's sit down and I'll tell you everything."

CHAPTER 30

Paul's Story

P aul called Massimo in from the front porch and asked him to have a seat. "If I'm going to spill the beans, I don't want to have to do it twice." They sat comfortably on the sofa, while Paul paced before the front window and began *his* story.

"Laura . . . when I first met you the night you were hospitalized, I genuinely was interested. As the time passed and we met briefly, my feelings for you grew. When things began getting a bit more serious, after Marlene's battle with cancer, I got my first visit.

"A strange older gentleman confronted me at the hospital one day. He was average height, dark graying hair, mustache, dressed in a dark expensive suit. He wanted to speak in private and so I led us into an isolated hallway. He asked me if I'd treated you for minor injuries. I explained that that was private information, but 'yes' I had treated you. He smiled at me coyly and stated that he knew I'd taken you out. He told me to treat you nicely. Then, he patted my cheek lightly and he walked away.

"At first, I wasn't too concerned. I figured he was a relative or something. I forgot all about him, until the morning of your graduation day. I was leaving my apartment building to come to your house. As I walked toward my car, two vehicles pulled in behind me. Four men casually walked up to me and literally guided me into their vehicle.

"One said, 'We're here to be sure you're following through with Mr. Valente's orders.' I asked them what they were talking about. They refreshed my memory of the visit that I'd received. Apparently, the older man was this 'Mr. Valente' and his orders were to continue dating you and to treat you 'nice', as he put it. They gave me a brief description of what would happen if I screwed things up. That's why I arrived at your house late and a bit frazzled."

"I remember that clearly," Laura reminisced. "You were so nervous. Even John noticed."

"I must admit, I was freaked out by these visits. I didn't like them telling me what to do, even if I did enjoy your company.

"As for Tammy, I always thought she was sweet. The day you came to visit me at the hospital, after the makeover . . . well, I must confess, I felt an attraction toward her that I never felt before. I ignored it the next few days. On that Friday, when you forgot about our breakfast date, Tammy and I actually got a chance to get to know one another. I started to see a side of her that I'd never noticed before."

Paul sat on the sofa chair and rubbed the prickly stubble that grew on his face. "I certainly never meant for it to happen. But each time that I saw her, my feelings grew deeper. I knew she felt the same, but we hid our feelings. The night of the graduation party, I noticed she wasn't herself. I followed her out into the garden and asked her why. That's when I realized that our feelings *were* mutual. Tammy was angry with me. She wanted me to avoid her at all costs. How could I avoid her? She was there every time I came to see you. Somehow, Mr. Valente caught wind of our attraction to one another."

Laura sat back, trying to make herself comfortable. She pondered on his words a moment. "How, Paul? How could they know what you were feeling inside, unless they saw you express it outwardly?"

Massimo agreed. "Laura's right, Paul. Were you and Tammy seen in public together?"

"Yes," he professed. "The night of the graduation party, when I went outside to see if she was okay . . . I kissed her. Tammy immediately pulled away. She was even angrier with me than before. I wanted to set things right with her, so one day I went to the agency where she worked. It happened to be on the day that our friend, Alfonso, came in. I waited until she was finished with him to confront her about our feelings. How could I have suspected that he was going to eavesdrop on our conversation?

"I apologized more than profusely for the kiss. We both made the decision to forget it and move forward—me with you and Tammy with whomever she pleased. Rengali heard it all, I later found out.

"That night I received my first major warning. Before I left to meet you, Mr. Valente's goons met me at my car again. One of the men pulled out a bat and promised to smash my head in if I didn't make our relationship permanent. They let me go, but I wasn't spared the consequences of my actions. My brakes had been tampered with. My mechanic confirmed it for me, when my vehicle was towed in. The message was loud and clear. I needed to propose to you, or risk my life.

"Laura, I was in no way ready. I knew you still struggled with feelings for Tony. I knew I'd never completely have your heart. I think that's why my attraction to Tammy grew. We tried to deny it. We tried to move on. Within the next few days, I received more warnings. This time, they threatened my family. They knew my parents' names, my sisters, their husbands, and even their children's names. I was mortified. If I didn't care when they were threatening me, I most certainly cared when they involved my family.

"That's why I proposed, asking for a long engagement. As time passed, my memory became clearer. I remembered where I'd seen Alfonso before. It finally struck me, that I'd not only jeopardized my family's lives, but Tammy's as well. I'd made up my mind. I'd vanish with Tammy, without a trace.

"On Wednesday night, I disguised myself, borrowed the vehicle of a friend, and went to your apartment. I found Tammy dressed and ready to go out with him. I begged her not to go. She grew angry with me, until I had no choice but to tell her the truth. Alfonso showed up and Tammy broke their date. He left and that's when I filled Tammy in on my plan.

"I knew that for a dark character like Alfonso to suddenly appear, Tammy was in danger, too." Paul sighed before he continued.

"Before I went to her, I made contact with my parents in Detroit. I spared them the details, but told them I needed my money liquidated and put into my account in Albany. They promised to have the money wired to me by Friday. If my plan hadn't failed, Tammy and I would've fled out of New York. I was going to empty my bank account, trade my vehicle in, and leave for Florida.

"Unfortunately, that's not how it happened. Wednesday and Thursday, I stayed at the apartment protecting her. Friday, after I got word that the money was in my account, I made Tammy promise to wait for me at the apartment, while I went to the bank and then the dealership. The rest of the story is true. Tammy saw Alfonso follow me out of the parking lot. She took the keys to the car *I* borrowed and came after us. The rest is history." Paul covered his face, as he cried in grief. "We were so close . . . so close, to pulling it off."

Salty liquid spilled from Laura's eyes, as well. The reality of Tammy's death was still too horrendous. She wiped her face dry and forced herself to ask one more question. "Paul, were you planning on leaving just to escape peril or were you both leaving to be together *and* escape?"

Paul got on his knees before her and took her hands in his. "Laura, as you said about yourself with Tony, I say the same to you about Tammy. I can't deny it anymore. I loved her, Laura, and I wanted to be with her."

"Why didn't you come to me? I'm not going to lie, I would've been hurt. But I would've never denied you and Tammy the chance to share that kind of love. I know what it feels like. There was no need for the lies."

Paul stood and paced some more. "Yes, there was. I didn't like it. In fact, I hated lying to you. But do you understand that the threats were always there? I was scared for my family, for Tammy, for *you*. Who *is* this man demanding *your* happiness?"

Laura stood as well and confronted him. "You know what, Paul? We're gonna find out. Tammy is gone and it's nobody's fault but the gangsters who killed her. The only thing we need to find out now is who this 'Mr. Valente' is and why he wants to see to it that you'd marry me—even if that meant forcing you."

Massimo, who sat quietly and listened, finally spoke. "We also need to see if there's any connection between these gangsters and the mobsters that killed your family, Laura."

"And how do we do that?" asked Paul.

"I'm going to do some research and see what I come up with. I'll put an APB out on Alfonso Rengali and have him in for questioning. In the meantime, I think I have a plan."

Paul and Laura sat at the round dining table of the small cabin, and listened to Massimo's plan. While Paul had explained the true version of his story, Massimo's mind conjured up a plan that could flush out the mobster family and put them away for good.

Paul would return to town and resume life as normal. His engagement to Laura would proceed. In fact, a wedding would be planned, to the tiniest detail. It would have to be believable for the mobsters to fall into the trap. The day of the wedding would surely bring forth the family threatening Paul. For certain, they'd want to witness the wedding take place. At the altar, before the 'I do's', Paul would abandon Laura and call off the wedding. The mobsters would make real on their threats. Undercover agents would be ready. Arrests would be made and everyone would be free.

Laura and Paul both agreed to take part in the plan. It was also agreed upon that Marlene and John would be made aware of the plot. After contemplating the plan repeatedly, they decided to have Paul join them and return to Albany. Marlene and John both listened with interest as Massimo explained his scheme. Neither one was happy about using Laura and Paul as bait, but they realized that it was no longer for them to decide. They were happy that police protection would continue to be provided.

Meanwhile, they told extended family of the upcoming wedding day. Though Uncle Joe and Aunt Bernadette didn't voice their thoughts about her young age, it was evident they were happy for Laura and Paul. They hoped that the wedding would bring joy to the heavyhearted home.

As Massimo had presumed, Valente made his next move and confronted Paul immediately after coming out of hiding. And though the undercover agents were close at hand, Paul felt the threat as never before. They seemed satisfied that Paul and Laura had a wedding date set, but still gave him a small reminder of what might happen if he backed out. Massimo was certain their plan would work. Mr. Valente *and* his thugs would get their just pay.

*   *   *

In the next weeks, Laura's life was active. Between returning to college and her job, planning for the small wedding, and visiting Max daily, Laura was wearing thin. Every night, she fell exhausted into her bed. Paul returned to his job at the hospital. In his spare time, he'd go to the Knight home and work on wedding plans with Laura or sit and visit.

The Knights learned the truth about Paul, but felt no ill will toward him. For Laura, they were the essence of true Christianity. They understood that Paul was hurting for Tammy, just as they were.

Massimo worked on his idea. He turned the plan over to the FBI and explained his plan. They agreed to follow through and help along in the case against Mr. Valente and Mario Galante. Meanwhile, they combed Laura's old cabin thoroughly, but found nothing to link the Mob families to the murders. Nor was there any sign of the money Matt had stolen.

Laura called Uncle Frank Blandino daily. He was recovering well from his wound and was back to work at his store. Undercover agents continued to protect him. So far, all of the mobsters involved were at ease.

Only one thing disturbed Laura more than the threats to her own life and to her family's—her visits with Tony. They were becoming more and more dreadful. Max refused to let Laura reach Tony, despite her continual efforts.

A doctor by the name of Marcus Parnell, who now treated Tony regularly, had dire results for Laura one evening. She stood outside of Tony's room, glaring through the window of his secured door. She watched as Tony's body rhythmically moved with every breath. He slept peacefully in his bed.

"We needed to give him a drug to help him rest," the doctor explained. "The insomnia makes him very edgy." Laura nodded, but didn't respond. She was feeling exhausted herself and was ready to leave. "A specialist was in today to see Tony. I'm afraid I don't have good news for you."

"What is it?" Laura asked, her interest suddenly perked.

"After a series of tests, it appears as though Max has proven to be the stronger of the two personalities. At least, at this time, it's highly likely that Tony may not have the strength to overcome him."

Laura's mouth fell open with a sob. She covered her face with her hands. The doctor urged her to have a seat, but she refused. He excused himself after apologizing for being unable to do more. Laura looked through tear-filled eyes at the sleeping figure in the window. Her heart ached. She wished the earth would open up and swallow her. Hesitantly, she shuffled out of the building and went home.

That night in bed, Laura reached out to God. Her pain was so fierce and her hurting so deep, she felt her heart had been ripped in two.

"Oh God," she prayed. "I have sinned against You. When Tammy died, instead of turning to You in my grief, I was angry with You. When I was with Tony, I didn't resist temptation and broke a commandment. Father, please, forgive me.

"Now Lord, I don't have the right to come to You—especially after the way I've treated You. I simply beg for Your grace and pray that You can overlook my faults. I humble myself before You and pray that You might help Tony. He's trapped inside his mind, unable to find a way out. His alternate personality has gained control and again, my Tony is being held prisoner. Father, he has suffered so much loss, so much pain. The only person who can help him now, is You.

"I beg You, with every ounce of my being, to bring my Tony out. Please heal him of this horrible disorder. God I trust You and I thank You. Amen."

*   *   *

In the next couple of weeks, Laura tried concentrating on the wedding plans. She booked the date with a florist and went shopping with Marlene for a wedding dress. The FBI covered every expense for the falsified wedding.

One evening, after yet another disappointing visit with Max, Laura sat next to Paul on the couch in her home. The trials and tribulations had helped to draw their friendship closer. Paul wrapped an arm around Laura, while she lamented over Tony's condition. Her shoulders shook with sobs and she described how Max had spit at her that day.

"There's no getting through to him. I'm praying for that miracle, Paul. I know that it'll happen, but when?"

"Trust God. He has the right timing for everything."

"But the more time goes by, the more impossible it'll be. It's been over a month and a half and still no sign of Tony."

Paul sympathized with her. He held her until her tears subsided. Looking at the clock, he reluctantly mentioned that he had to go. Laura stood from the couch to help him with his jacket. She lifted the jacket and suddenly felt herself starting to swoon.

"Oh man . . ." she stammered.

Paul noticed her sway and held her steady. "Are you okay? Did you eat today?"

"Yes, I . . . I'm okay. I feel a bit dizzy."

"Are you sure you ate?"

"Absolutely. I've had an appetite like a horse . . ." Paul caught Laura's eyes and read into them her fears. She placed a hand over her mouth and abruptly sat. "No," she whispered.

Paul looked at her more closely and stated, "Laura, please don't tell me, what I think you're about to tell me."

Laura's eyes filled. Panic made her heart race at the possibilities that ran through her mind. "No," she repeated.

Paul sat back down on the couch and rested his hand on her back. "Were you *with* Tony?"

Laura lowered her eyes in shame.

"Oh sweet Jesus. Well, you had better get to a doctor. I can call in a favor from a friend."

"And disgrace you? No. Isn't there another way to find out?"

"No, you need to make an appointment with a doctor. If you're pregnant, you need to decide what to do."

"What do you mean, 'decide what to do'?" she lowered her voice to a whisper. "If I'm pregnant with Tony's baby, I'll carry this baby to full-term and I'll love and raise it on my own, if I have to."

"You just had your 19th birthday, Laura. You're too young to shackle your life down with a child. What about school and your career?"

"Paul, regardless of my schooling and my career, I'd never abort this baby, if that's what you're insinuating."

"No! There's always adoption. Let's face reality. What're the chances of Tony living a normal life? He's mentally ill. He can't be a father to this baby, unless God answers and gives you the miracle you're praying for. If you're going to keep this baby and Tony can't father it, who will provide it with a home, with love, and happiness?"

There was a long pause between them as they searched each other's eyes for an answer. Paul suddenly got down on one knee before Laura. "I know that you don't love me the way you love Tony. But I solemnly swear to you, right here, right now, that if you're pregnant and if Tony can't be a father to the child, then I'll marry you and be the best husband and father I can be. I'll do that for you."

Laura broke down uncontrollably. She whispered, "Oh, Paul, you're so sweet. But why would I sentence you to be a father to a child that's not yours? You deserve someone who'll love you with all her heart. A woman you can feel the same way for. Thank you for the sweet gesture, but I'd never let you do that."

"The offer stands. Find out if you're pregnant and we'll call off this whole charade with the FBI and really get married." Laura walked Paul to the door. "I've one last question for you." he asked. "If Tony remained 'dead' and Tammy was just my sister-in-law-to-be, would you've loved me enough to be my wife?"

"Yes."

"Same here. If that doesn't put your doubts to rest, I don't know what will. For now, until you decide on what you'll do, I'll claim this baby as my own. That is, if you're pregnant." Laura opened her mouth to protest. Paul placed a gentle finger on her lips. "Shh! Just listen to me. You're my friend and I do love you, Laura. I'll do what I must to make this right for you." He embraced her quivering body.

"You're my *best* friend, Paul. I love you, too."

Paul exited the Knights' home and left Laura to her thoughts. Before bed, Laura got on her knees and prayed some more.

* * *

The following day, Laura called Paul and asked for a referral to a gynecologist. Paul gave her the number to one of the best OB/GYNs on staff, Dr. Ben Packard. She placed the call and set up the appointment. Paul promised to go with her.

On the day of the appointment, he accompanied Laura into the doctor's office. As they waited for the results, Laura paced the small examining room.

"Stop pacing, you're making *me* nervous," Paul whispered.

"I can't help it. I know what the results will be."

"Positive?"

"Yes. I've noticed changes in my body that I never had before."

"Like, missing a period?"

"No, my periods were never regular. I've been feeling dizziness, fatigued, and . . . to be frank, my chest is killing me," she confessed.

Paul laughed aloud. "You're so subtle."

Dr. Packard knocked and entered the room. "Miss Knight, Paul. I have the results of your tests and they *are* positive. You're pregnant. We can't go according to your last period, because as you stated, you're irregular, but I'm guessing that by the size of the baby, you're about five weeks into the pregnancy. Congratulations."

Laura sat stunned as the doctor described how the first 12 to 15 weeks of the pregnancy were crucial. He warned her not to lift heavy objects and to avoid stress. When the doctor left, Laura fell into a heap of tears. Paul tried to comfort her.

An hour later, they sat in a restaurant. Paul urged her to eat. "Think of the baby."

"How can I eat when my life is in shambles," she cried. "What am I going to do?"

"I already told you what to do. Marry me and we'll live happily ever after." Paul bit into a juicy hamburger. Ketchup slid down his chin. Laura wiped his face with a napkin. "See, we're already acting like an old married couple. Why not make it official?"

A smile almost fell across Laura's face. "You're impossible," she managed.

"All joking aside, Laura. You need to decide what you want to do."

Laura knew Paul was right. She needed to visit Tony before making any life-altering decisions.

*   *   *

The hospital was quiet, as Laura's heels hit the shiny floors. One of the nurses looked up from her station and smiled upon recognizing Laura. For the past month, Laura visited Tony daily. She'd always bring him something. That particular day, before her visit, Laura purchased a set of baby booties and wrapped them in a gift tote.

She asked the doctor if Max could be restrained so she could enter his room. The doctor agreed that the news of the coming baby might motivate Tony to return. An orderly stood close by as Laura entered his room.

"Oh man," Max complained. "Again! Aren't you tired of coming here? I'm tired of you, even if you're nice to look at. I mean, not only do you come bearing lame gifts, but you ask them to strap me down, too!"

Laura sat on the foot of the bed and rested a hand on his bound leg. "I have wonderful news to share with Tony," she stated cheerfully.

"Oh!" he moaned. "*Tony cannot hear you,*" he sang.

"Well, then maybe you can tell him for me."

"Fine. Anything to get you out of here. What is it?"

"I'll open your gift for you."

"Since I can't?" he sarcastically asked. Laura unwrapped the tissue paper and held up the little yellow booties. "Hello, I think they're ten sizes too small."

"They're not for you, silly. They're for our baby. I'm pregnant."

Max's face grew serious. He looked away and scoffed.

"Max, tell Tony the news. Tell him he needs to come back so he can be a father to his baby." Max didn't respond. He continued to look the opposite way. She kissed his forehead, leaving the booties on his bed.

After she exited his room, the doctor, who had been painstakingly watching, was happy with the response Max had. Laura wasn't. Max's silence wasn't what she'd hoped for. Now it was up to her to make a decision based on the facts. Tony wasn't coming back, and she was running out of time. The wedding was supposed to take place in a less than a month. *Should Laura and Paul follow through with the wedding and call off Massimo's plan?* Laura needed the opinion of her beloved mother and father.

CHAPTER 31

Wedding Bells

Needless to say, John and Marlene's reaction to the news of Laura's pregnancy was exactly what Laura had expected. Laura felt humiliated and ashamed of her actions. But both John and Marlene made it clear that they weren't upset. They were concerned for her future and the future of the baby. Of course, after hearing Paul's appeal to claim the baby as his own and marry Laura, they tried to persuade her to take him up on the offer. But, Laura refused.

With each day that passed, Tony's condition worsened. He became near catatonic, where neither Max nor Tony submerged. Laura visited him religiously on her way home from her college courses and work. She'd sit behind the window of his isolated room and stare at his motionless body. One evening, the doctor allowed an open visit, restraining Tony to give Laura the opportunity to speak to him in person.

The silence in the room was deafening. Tony laid on his back staring blankly at the ceiling. It seemed he was withering away. Laura stood near the bed and looked into the hollow eyes of her lover. Her heart shattered at the emptiness within them. The tears welled up in her eyes and Laura couldn't hold back. She collapsed on his chest and sobbed in absolute grief.

"Tony," she cried out. "You said nothing would come between us again. Yet, you lie there and let Max steal you from your life." She ran her fingers through his hair. Max blinked, but still his face was expressionless. "I know you're tired. I know life hasn't treated you right. But, this baby needs you. *I* need you! We can't help you unless *you* fight. I have two weeks until the wedding. Either both Paul and I go through with the plan, to help convict the Valentes, or I really marry him. I don't want to marry Paul. I want to marry you. But if you continue in this way, I don't have a choice. I have to think of our baby's future. Please come back to me. Fight for me—*for us*. You promised to never leave me. You promised," she stated.

Laura's words seemed to fall on deaf ears. Because he was bound and not responding, Laura caressed his face and gazed longingly at his lips. She hadn't kissed him since before he was hospitalized. Now, Tony's body lay fixed to the bed and the temptation to kiss him was alluring. She wiped the tears from her face and placed a soft peck on his lips. From the corner of his eye, a single tear dribbled downward.

"Tony?" Laura whispered in disbelief. "You *can* hear me." She waited for a response. Tony turned his head to meet her gaze. With growing encouragement, she continued. "Don't give up. You *can* come back. I just know it. I'm not going to stop praying. I'm going to pray with all that I've got!" He turned his head away. Laura kissed him once again and collected her purse to go. "I love you, Tony. I'll be back again tomorrow." She turned to leave.

"Don't bother," Max bluntly stated. "He'll never come back. Not if I've something to say about it."

Laura stopped dead in her tracks. Her heart deflated with disappointment, but she wasn't about to let him see it. Turning back around, she glared at Max. "I know you're losing the battle. Tony's working on coming back. I see the struggle and once he beats you and resurfaces, it'll be the last we see of you."

"Like I said, don't hold your breath."

Laura turned around and exited the room. She found a bench in the hallway and sat, releasing her frustration in tears. Her shoulders shook. A warm hand rubbed her back and Laura glanced up to see Paul's handsome face. Concern and love was in his eyes as he took her in his arms and held her.

*   *   *

From the window of his confined room, Max glared at the couple huddled together. He scoffed at the care and devotion in the man's eyes. The orderly had just left his room after unbinding him. He rubbed his wrists as he looked on. He vowed never to let Tony out. Laura was better off with that doctor, than she was with him.

*   *   *

In the next week, Laura continued her visits, in vain. Max grew meaner than ever. Dr. Parnell encouraged Laura to move on without him. Laura lost hope and John and Marlene were desperate to convince her to take Paul as her husband.

Two nights before the big day, Laura found herself driving around the neighborhood, deep in thought. She was still in time to get in touch with Massimo and call the whole plan off. Even if it meant that Mr. Valente and his hoodlums would go scot-free for Tammy's murder. Laura needed time alone. Any more pressure from her parents would surely agitate her more. She pulled into her church parking lot and stared at its doors. In two days, she'd most likely walk into that church as Laura Knight and exit as Laura Roberts.

A tear spilled down her cheek. She needed comfort. She needed Jesus. She entered the church and stepped into a pew. On her knees, Laura talked to God. She asked that the path be made clear and for her choices to be in accordance to His will.

Father Bill entered the pew and sat next to her in the still of the church. Laura sat back and wiped her tears.

"You're so sad. Anything I can do to help?"

The FBI bound Laura to secrecy, and though her heart ached to tell the priest the truth, she did not want to endanger him, as well. She explained that she had a friend in a mental institution whose condition looked grim.

"Well, I'm not saying that you can't count on a miracle because God's in the miracle-making business. So, if you believe that Jesus can pull your friend through this, then He can and He will. But it must be in God's ultimate plan. That's the hard part. It's hard to know what that is. We have to trust that He knows what He's doing. God sees the whole picture. He knows the outcome already. Laura, you just have to trust Jesus. Take a leap of faith and trust."

After their talk, Laura felt confident about her decision. Before leaving, she used the church telephone and called Paul, asking him to meet her at her home. She thanked the priest and promised to see him on Friday, at the wedding.

Laura drove home in eagerness. She hustled the family together in the living room and sat before them. Paul, John, and Marlene were slightly startled by her sudden gust of energy.

She cleared her throat and began. "If I've ever needed you before, it's never more than now. The three of you are all I have and I don't ever want to take advantage of you. Paul, you've been my friend through so much. I know I can count on you. But I will not," she paused, "No! I *cannot* exploit your goodness.

"Friday, the project will go as planned. You're a wonderful man, and *any* woman would be blessed to have you. But I can't betray my baby, or myself, and certainly not Tony. Even if he never returns, at least I know that I was true to him and true to myself. I love you for wanting to fix my blunder, but it's not yours to fix. After this baby is born, I'd be honored if you'd be its Godfather."

Paul appeared speechless at first. At last, he uttered, "Well, of course I'll be the Godfather. It'd be an honor." Laura embraced and thanked him.

Turning to her mother and father, she reached for their hands. "If I didn't have you, I'd have nothing. I'm sorry for humiliating you."

"Stop right there," Marlene stated. "I don't want to hear that. After the hardships you've endured, you could've easily turned your life upside-down. Instead, you used each hurdle as a stepping-stone. I understand what it feels like to love someone beyond your own control. And even though we need to be responsible for our actions, sometimes love clouds our thinking. People do crazy things in the name of love. We're nobody to judge you. However, we do want to see you safe, happy, and healthy. I believe I speak for both your father and I, when I say that we trust you to make the right decisions."

Laura was moved by Marlene's words. Her eyes filled up and she smiled through her tears. Marlene lovingly soothed Laura's back. Laura caught her hand and kissed it. "Mom, Dad, you've the right to have a say in the major decisions in my life. I'm certain that you believe a life with Paul is definitely more stable than a life with Tony.

"But I ask you, is it fair to marry him, when my heart belongs to some-one else? I can't stand before God and vow to give myself to Paul in *every way*. Because if Tony *ever* comes back, my heart belongs to him. And more importantly than *anything else*, how fair would that be to Paul? He deserves to be loved completely. I can't hurt him that way."

John touched Laura's arm and sighed. "You'll make a good lawyer someday. You're right. I'm very proud that you based your decision on oth-ers and not solely on what is best for you. But you're forgetting one little tiny thing."

"No Dad, I haven't forgotten about my baby. I'm going to keep it and raise it on my own. I don't know how yet, but I won't give my baby up."

"What do you mean, 'you don't know how'?" Marlene asked. "What do you think we're here for? I'll help you. It'll have a loving home, right here. It'll be a new experience for the both of us. But I'm sure between all of us, we'll give your child a loving home to live in."

Laura hugged Marlene. "Thank you," she cried. "Thank you."

*　*　*

The next night, Laura, Massimo, Paul, Marlene, and John sat at the dining room table with the curtains drawn, whispering of their plans for the following day. Laura felt nervous over the possibility of seeing Tammy's murderers. After further briefings, Massimo and Paul left.

Laura rested on her bed and stared at the ceiling. She rubbed her hand over her stomach, looking for any sign of growth. A rap on the door broke her concentration. Marlene entered the room and sat on the bed next to Laura.

She gave her a reassuring smile as she rubbed Laura's flat belly. "Everything's going to be okay. When I got sick, both you and Tammy couldn't give me enough encouragement. You both were my pillars, my rocks. Now I want to return it back to you. I'm not going to lie . . . I'm scared. I saw the fear in your eyes tonight, too."

Laura couldn't deny it. "I'm scared, Mom. For every one of us. How do I know those wackos aren't going to bust in there and kill us all?"

Marlene frowned. "We don't know. We can only pray that Jesus will protect us in His house. Say your prayers and go to sleep. We've a long day ahead of us." Marlene kissed Laura's forehead and left the room, closing the door.

Laura sat up, opened the drawer of her nightstand, and pulled out the engagement ring Tony had given her. She had given Paul his ring back. Now, Laura placed Tony's back on her finger. She loved the sight of the ring on her hand.

On her knees, she prayed . . . again.

*   *   *

It was a perfect day for a fall wedding. The sun was bright and not a cloud dared to form. Laura rose extra early and went to the hospital to have one last visit with Tony. Though she could not actually visit with him, she looked through the window at Tony's figure. He glared out the penned-in window of his room. She knocked on the door to get his attention. Max turned around at the sound. He caught her eye and scoffed. She knocked repeatedly, until he finally came to the door. He talked into the two-way speaker.

"What do you want? Aren't you supposed to be getting married today?"

"As a matter of fact I am. I've come to say goodbye."

"Good riddance," he muttered and walked away.

"Wait!" Laura called back.

Max turned around and came back. He waited for her reply.

"I'm not here to say goodbye to Tony, but to you."

"What're you talking about?"

"Max, I bind you in the name of Jesus. He commands you to no longer torment Tony. Jesus's blood covers him and casts you out! Leave him in peace once and for always!" Laura turned and left Max to stare as she left the hospital.

She rushed home and began preparing for the wedding. After a refreshing shower, she dried and set her hair in hot rollers. Carefully, she applied her makeup. Marlene assisted John with his tuxedo tie and Laura helped with his cummerbund. After removing the rollers from her own hair, Marlene helped, and they set the beautiful veil and crown over the long ringlets.

Finally, Marlene dressed and then helped Laura into her gown. Laura looked radiant in the crème satin-beaded dress.

By that time, the house was boisterous with family and friends. Uncle Joe and Aunt Bernadette, along with their boys, complimented Laura and came to give their love and support. The Apolone family also came to escort the Knights to church. After photos and a bite to eat, they collected their things and headed out into the sunlit yard.

John escorted Laura down the porch steps and into his vehicle. She sat in the backseat, as John drove and Marlene sat up front. Laura longed to have Tammy there. Her eyes twinkled with tears, but she suppressed them. John caught a glimpse of Laura's tear-filled eyes in the rearview mirror. He winked at her and she smiled in return.

"I'm sure you're both thinking what I'm thinking," she admitted.

"Tammy?" Marlene asked.

"Yup, Tams," John replied.

"I miss her so much." Laura's voice crackled. "I wish things could've been different. This should've been her wedding day to Paul. I could picture it so perfectly. She'd have been bouncing off the walls with excitement."

"Oh yeah. Her smile would've lit the whole world," John added.

Marlene sniffled and said, "We've been cheated. We could've had a lifetime with her, but . . ."

No one spoke further. It wasn't fair that Tammy's life had been cut short and that day was the day of reckoning.

*   *   *

Paul paced the small room in the church that he waited in. Father Bill chuckled softly and stated that every matrimony began the same—with the apprehensive pacing of the groom.

"I'm going to have to invest in ceramic tile. The carpet will certainly wear if you continue at this rate."

Paul tried to smile, but his stomach twisted in knots. He said a silent prayer for Laura and the baby's safety.

*   *   *

John's vehicle glided into the church parking lot. He helped the women out of the car. Laura and Marlene made their way into a back room where they waited for the ceremony to begin.

John left to go see Paul. He was to stand as Best Man after walking Laura up the aisle. Marlene was the Matron-of-Honor. She watched, as Laura nervously fiddled with her veil. Someone whistled, startling the women. Massimo stood in the doorway, dressed up in a dark blue suit and tie.

"Hi, handsome," Laura stated.

"Now, don't make me blush. It's you who looks amazing." He entered the room, waved to Marlene, and kissed Laura's cheek. He whispered, "I see the worry in your eyes. Don't worry. I'll die before I let any harm come to you or your baby."

"That's what I'm afraid of."

"Don't worry," he repeated, "Everything is all set. The place is swarming with my men. The priest is now in on it. One of our men is disguised as an altar server, others are mingling as guests. Outside the church, I've got sharpshooters planted in the buildings next door. Valente wouldn't dare strike in the church where your family and friends would be witnesses. He'll wait for Paul to exit the church, if he plans to harm him. Trust me. It's going to be okay. Be strong. It'll all be over soon."

Laura shook her head and gave him a hug. As he exited the room, John and Father Bill entered. They closed the door for a brief moment and joined hands in prayer. Father Bill whispered, "Heavenly Father, we come to You today pleading for protection. We ask that not just a hedge, but a legion of Your heavenly hosts protect this family. We ask that justice and goodness prevail over the evil that has surrounded them. Jesus, Your Almighty strength is needed. Guide us, protect us, and keep us safe. We ask this in Your name."

"Amen," they all proclaimed.

At last, it was time. Laura held John's arm as he led her to the aisle way. In the church, white flowers decorated the altar, pews, and altar tables. The lit candles gave a calming effect. Soon the music began and Marlene made her way toward the altar, holding a small bouquet of roses. Father Bill nodded at Laura and John. As they strolled up the aisle, moving to the wedding march, Laura's eyes met with Paul's. He smiled at her and she thought how truly handsome he was. Tammy should've been walking down the aisle to him, not her.

Suddenly, a lump formed in Laura's throat. Her eyes blurred and she fought the uncontrollable need to cry. She tried to clear her vision and focus on the faces in the pews. Through her veil, she grazed the very small gathering of family and friends. Strange faces blended in the mix. At the furthest end of the pews, a strangely familiar man stood with a hat in hand. His dark graying hair was neatly slicked back. His mustache and dark eyes gave him a Mediterranean look. His eyes linked with Laura's. He smiled and nodded. Laura felt a warm feeling fall over her. His smile unusually comforted her.

She smiled, and then turned her attention to Paul, whose eyes were misty with tears. John placed her hand in his, after the priest asked, "Who gives this woman?"

"I do." John stated. He lifted Laura's veil and kissed her cheek. He then took his place next to Paul.

Father Bill began the ceremony. As the readings were being read, Paul whispered to Laura, asking if she'd seen the infamous Mr. Valente. She asked if it was the man in the far pews and he nodded. Laura slowly turned around, only to find that he'd vanished.

A signal from Father Bill gave them the cue to approach the altar. It was showtime and Laura was unmistakably nervous. He began, "Paul Thomas Roberts, do you take this woman to be your lawfully . . ."

"NO!" A voice thundered. Laura's heart leapt from her chest at the familiar tone. She turned toward the foyer and watched in disbelief as Tony raced into the church, coming to a halt at the very first pews furthest from the altar.

Tony's hands were bound and Dr. Parnell and two large orderlies accompanied him. "Laura, don't marry him," Tony shouted. He ran toward her.

The bouquet of flowers fell from Laura's hands. A smile fell across her lips and she lifted the long gown from the floor, stepped down the altar, and ran to meet him. From the corner of her eye, amidst the guest to her left, Laura caught the glimmer of a raised weapon. Her smile vanished. Terror ripped through her. It pointed toward Tony! Laura ran faster. A piercing, single gunshot echoed throughout the church, in the same instant that she reached out, grasped Tony, and embraced him. Someone screamed. She felt a hard shove and tumbled to the floor. Tony cushioned her fall. Another body fell upon her crushing her to Tony.

Pandemonium erupted in the church. People screamed and ran for safety. Undercover agents tackled the gunman to the ground. Others flocked the area in search of other unwanted villains.

Tony used all of his strength to lift the immobile body off Laura, but his hands were still bound. She lifted herself and rolled the body from her legs. Blood had saturated her dress and she froze. Her eyes were blurred with a mixture of tears and makeup. She blinked to see the face of her savior. Laura screamed.

"No. No. No!" But her eyes didn't lie. Paul had saved her life. His lips quivered, as well as his body. A gunshot wound to his neck spilled blood all over the runner and her white gown.

Laura shouted out for help and used her hand to stop the blood from flowing. Tony tried to assist, while Laura cupped Paul's head in her lap and held the wound. Tears spilled from her eyes and she begged him to live. John, Marlene, and a few other brave souls surrounded Laura, Paul, and Tony. Someone offered Laura a piece of clothing to apply pressure to the wound. Another shouted that an ambulance was called and on its way.

Paul tried to speak, but Laura was too hysterical to hear. She tried to soothe him but could barely control herself. His lip trembled as he tried to talk. The blood loss was great and he was weakening by the second.

"Paul, why did you do this? Why?"

In a hoarse voice, he whispered, "Do . . . to the least . . . you do unto me." He smiled through his tear-filled eyes. Laura recognized the biblical quote at once.

"You saved my life!" she wailed. "Don't let go, Paul. An ambulance is coming. You have to hang on. You're the baby's Godfather."

"Laura . . . baby has . . . its father. You got . . . your miracle." He closed his eyes.

"No Paul! Hang on!"

His eyes suddenly opened bright, "Tammy?" he whispered. His last breath left him and Paul closed his eyes, falling limp.

"No!" Laura screamed out, "No!" She pressed Paul's head to her chest and cried out. "Paul!" she repeated over and again. "Don't die on me! Don't die!"

She suddenly rose to her wavering feet, glaring around the church. Anger fueled her shaken body and the crowd around her let her through as she quickly ran from the church in search of her enemy. Marlene, John, and Tony chased after her.

Outside, Massimo and the team of FBI agents had a handful of suspects, including the gunman. They were handcuffed and being placed in an armored van. Laura raced toward them, holding the hem of her gown. As the gunman was being pushed into the vehicle, she grabbed his shirt collar with force.

"Who do you work for? Who sent you here?" she demanded. But the man didn't speak. He glared at her with a stone-cold face. "You tell your boss to stay outta my life! If he's so concerned with whom I marry, tell him to reveal himself instead of hiding behind you thugs. Tell him to stop killing the people I love!"

Someone tugged at Laura, encouraging her to let Paul's killer go. She reluctantly released his shirt. "You people make me sick! You'll rot in hell!" she screamed. An officer pushed the man into the vehicle. She was guided away from the truck. Laura refused to turn away from the armored vehicle as it sped away, taking Paul's and possibly Tammy's murderers to jail. She finally turned around, letting her grief explode. She collapsed into the waiting arms of John and Marlene.

"Come here, baby," John cried. He held her close. Through his tears, he whispered reassuringly, "It's over, now. We got 'em. We got 'em."

Marlene embraced them both and sobbed with abandonment. The trio held tight, while their family and friends circled them, offering their deepest sympathies and comforting words.

Moments later, Father Bill found his way through the crowd and placed his calming hands on Laura's shoulders. He whispered, "That miracle you were praying for—he's patiently waiting his turn to hold you."

Laura lifted her head from John's chest, focusing on the faces around her. At last, her eyes fell upon him. Tony smiled softly.

Laura slowly released herself from John and Marlene's hold and faced him. He held her loving gaze.

"I knew you'd come back to me," she whispered. Unsteadily, she stumbled toward him.

"I promised never to abandon you." Tony answered. He took her into his arms and held her.

CHAPTER 32

Sicilian Connections

After the shooting, Tony was brought back to the hospital. The morning of the wedding, during Laura's visit with him, a sudden battle transpired within him. The doctor explained how his alternate personality began to lose control to him.

At last, Tony took dominion and prevailed. He begged Dr. Parnell to take him to the church to stop Laura from marrying Paul. Though Dr. Parnell was unsure whether to believe in Tony's amazing recovery, he took the chance and allowed Tony a brief reprieve to stop the wedding, obviously unaware that they'd be interrupting a FBI sting. Still, he assigned two of his trained assistants and had Tony's hands bound together as a safety precaution. After witnessing Tony's behavior outside of the restricted room, Dr. Parnell was confident that Tony had truly emerged.

Now, it would be a matter of taking the right steps to help Tony heal. The doctor explained that after a severe confrontation such as this, it was highly probable that Tony could permanently restrain Max. The idea was to integrate Max's feelings into Tony's, fusing the personalities into one. It would take time. Dr. Parnell promised that if proper treatment was undertaken and completed, Tony would have a normal life. The treatment would include talk-therapy, hypnotherapy, and medication. For the time being, he'd remain hospitalized until the doctor felt that he was stable enough to continue the therapy outpatient.

Tony had a long way to go and the therapy would be trying. But Laura believed that with God's help, he'd succeed. Tony had truly kept his promise and returned to her, despite Max's attempt to extinguish him. Paul was right. She had certainly received her miracle.

Laura was fed this information the day following the disaster at the church. After the ambulance arrived, Paul was pronounced dead, and his body was taken. Laura faintly remembered Massimo agonizing over Paul's death, as well. For Paul had worn a bulletproof vest and still wasn't spared from death. Now, his body would be taken back to Michigan to be buried by his despondent family. The rest of the day was a horrible blur. Laura was taken home and was ordered rest by her doctor. The stress was detrimental to the health of her unborn child.

Meanwhile, Paul's assassin was incarcerated and arraignment dates were set. Laura had every intention of avenging both Paul and Tammy's deaths through the judicial system. She prayed that the system wouldn't fail her. Somehow, she hoped the murderers would crack under law enforcement's pressure and give up Mr. Valente. Unfortunately, it didn't appear that that would happen. If they confessed to doing his bidding, they were as good as dead, and so they'd most likely remain silent. Mr. Valente would get away with two murders now. *Could justice ever prevail?* Laura hoped so.

*   *   *

In the following days, she telephoned Uncle Frank and explained the progress Tony was making. He was thrilled to hear the wonderful news and immediately came to Albany for a few days to see Tony for himself. Frank Blandino had well recovered from his last meeting with the Galante famiglia, and since he was still under the protection of the FBI, the Mafiosos continued to remain at ease. But Laura understood that the dangers were still far from passing. She needed to take matters into her own hands. On the night before Uncle Frank's departure, after a hearty dinner, they sat at the dining room table.

"Mom, Dad, Uncle Frank, I've been doing some serious thinking."

"Laura," warned John, "I don't like the sound of that."

"Dad, I'm not joking."

"Neither am I. What has your brain cooked up now?"

"I need somebody to come with me."

"Where do you plan on going?" Marlene asked.

"Back to Brewerton with Uncle Frank. I have a few things I need to do there."

"Like?" John uttered.

"Dad, I need to go back to my first home—the old cabin. Before Patty was killed on that horrible night, she mentioned something about hiding my mother's locket in our old treehouse. I need to find it."

"Is it for sentimental purposes?"

"Yes and no."

"Well, which is it?"

"On the night my mother died, she finally spoke to my sister and me about her family. They had disowned her because she had eloped with my father, who wasn't in my grandfather's good graces. Anyway, the locket would be proof that I'm who I say I am when I find my maternal grand-parents. They had given the locket to my mom on her 16th birthday.

"You see, my mother mentioned that my 'nonno', grandfather in Sicil-ian, was a powerful and influential man. People within the Sicilian com-munity would take loans from him and so on. I'm sure he's probably involved in illegal activities, as well. Regardless, I want to go to Cicero's Town Clerk office and have them produce a copy of my parents' marriage license for me. I'm ashamed to say, but I don't even know my mother's maiden name. I only know that she was originally from Brooklyn.

"I'm hoping to go to Brooklyn to meet my mother's family. I'll play on my grandfather's pity and ask him to help us pay off the Galante famiglia, thus also using his power to make them keep their word to let us be. Uncle Frank will distribute the half-of-a-million to them. As for the quarter-of-a-million dollars my father stole, well, maybe my grandfather will have a generous heart. I've nothing to lose but my time and energy. I feel that it'll be worth the try. What's the worst that can happen? A door slammed in the face? I think I can handle that after everything else."

Marlene, John, and Uncle Frank shared glances. Uncle Frank picked at his dark brown mustache as he pondered on Laura's next plan. He took her hand and said, "Laura, you can count on my help. I'll do what I can to get us all out of this mess."

John agreed, saying, "If you want to confront your mother's parents, I'll accompany you, too. But I think you should let Massimo know. His men will continue to protect you."

"How quickly can you be ready?" Laura asked, a smile finally falling across her lips.

*   *   *

The next day, before their departure, Laura, John, and Frank went to the hospital to see Tony and explain their little excursion. Tony was now able to have person-to-person visitation rights. They sat at the lounge table and discussed their plan.

In just the few days since his recovery, Tony's color was healthier and his well-being appeared brighter. He sat next to Laura, holding her hand in his. Laura noticed as John stared on at the love that was obvious in Tony's eyes.

"As long as you're not alone. Be sure to have all the security you can get. Uncle Frank, I'm counting on you to keep my future family safe."

"Son, you have my solemn vow."

"And mine," added John. He extended a hand and Tony ardently shook it.

Tony turned his attention back to Laura. He had already noticed that she had replaced his ring on her finger. His finger played with it for a moment. "Laura, we've come so far. I'm tempted to tell you not to go. But I understand at this point that this is our last resort. I'm going to have to trust God. He's gotten us this far, He won't fail us now."

"That's right," John added. "'If God is for us, who can be against us?'"

Laura kissed Tony goodbye and after further goodbyes with Marlene, they departed and drove to Brewerton.

*   *   *

The drive was long, as usual—about two and a half hours from Albany to Cicero. By the time they arrived, night had fallen and they made plans to go to the cabin the following day. At the safe house, John slept in the spare bedroom, while Laura took the bed, which she shared with Tony for so many years. Uncle Frank went back to his own home to rest.

The following morning, he returned and joined them for breakfast at a nearby restaurant. From there, John drove them near the outskirts of town, toward the cabin. They turned left onto Mud Mill Road and Laura began to feel the anticipation of seeing the place where it all began. She pointed out the driveway, nearly choked with overgrown brush, and John directed the vehicle through the narrow pathway. Her heart began to pound profusely at the familiarity of the sites. The woods were denser, despite the fallen leaves. Everything appeared overgrown and abandoned, as they were.

The vehicle moved slowly until, at last, the cabin appeared. John pulled up behind the rusted old pick-up and turned off the engine. They sat a moment and stared at the sinking cabin and abandoned landscape. A deer pounced across the small patch of open land, startling them. Laura gathered her courage and exited the car.

The tall woods surrounding the shaded area made the air feel crisp. Laura quivered, while the silent wind lifted the loose strands of her hair. As if in a trance, she turned in a circle taking in the scene before her. The old orange pick-up was exactly where her father had left it, that cold wintery day. It was covered in dust and dirt. In the bed of the truck, the few packed boxes still remained. They were buried in leaves and twigs from past seasons.

Another shiver ran up her spine. She wondered how her life might have turned out, had they left in time.

Laura slowly approached the cabin. John and Uncle Frank followed closely behind.

"Laura, you're going to go in there?" her father asked.

"I want to."

"Let me make sure it's safe." John turned the doorknob and gave the door a slight shove. The door opened and Laura stared in shock. *What poverty! What heartbreak to see the conditions in which she grew up.* The boxes they had packed still remained near the doorway, where Laura had last seen them. The kitchen seemed untouched from that retched day, yet someone had come in and removed all the evidence of the murders. Even so, dust and cobwebs covered the poor home.

Laura, John, and Frank wandered about the small cabin. Laura stood near the couch. The run-down rug was gone. Sabrina's doll had vanished. Massimo was right. There truly was no evidence of the murders. However, the vision of the day of the murders was suddenly so vivid, Laura felt the need to collect herself. She placed a hand over her mouth, trying to keep from regurgitating.

John noticed the paleness in her face. "Are you okay?"

She nodded, but he insisted she sit down. He pulled out a chair from the kitchen table, dusted it with his hand, and had Laura sit. The severity of it was overwhelming and she burst into unbridled tears.

"Laura, this is too hard for you," John insisted. "Let's go."

Laura agreed and stood from the chair, taking in one last look of the abandoned cabin. She shook her head and said, "I've seen enough. Let's get my mother's locket."

Laura began down the old familiar path to the spring. John and Uncle Frank were at her side as she explained the difficult life she led there. Both men listened. Laura automatically followed the dense pathway through the forest. At the opening near the spring, they spotted the old treehouse. Time and weather had eroded most of the wood and loose boards swung perilously from the tree.

"I need to get up there."

"You're *not* going up there, Laura. You have a baby to think about."

"And how will I find where Patty hid the locket?"

"I'll go up there," John offered.

"Hold up, John," Uncle Frank stated. "It's been a while, but back in my day, I was like a monkey. Let me give it a shot." Uncle Frank steadied a foot on the trunk of the tree and reached up for the closest limb, testing it. The treehouse wasn't more than seven feet from the ground, but the ladder Laura's father had built had long since deteriorated. Frank lifted himself up, until he placed an unsure foot on the floor of the treehouse. The board appeared sturdy, but he still held a large branch for safety. With his other hand, he brushed away fallen leaves and broken twigs. There appeared to be no hiding place in the small house for the locket.

"It has to be there. Do you see any loose floorboards or loose planks where it could possibly be hidden?" Laura insisted.

"Laura, it's not possible. Unless . . . unless it's hidden here, in the trunk of the tree. There's a hole in it. Dare I put a hand in there and feel around?"

"What have you got to lose?" John added.

"My fingers," Uncle Frank cracked. He plunged his hand deep into the hollow trunk. He felt around as Laura and John waited in hope. Frank announced that his hand suddenly fell upon something cold and hard. He grabbed it and pulled it from the hole. It was a small steel box, rusted and dirty. He tossed it down to John and carefully climbed down the tree. John dusted the box off and gave it to Laura.

"This must be it. Go ahead and open it."

Laura took the steel box and held it in her trembling hands. The men gathered around her and waited. With cold, red fingers, Laura lifted the lid. Inside she found another small box, loose change, and a wad of rolled dollar bills bound by a dry-rotted rubber band.

"Where did Patty get this money from," Laura wondered aloud. John held the steel box, while Laura peeled the rubber band that crumbled away from the wad of money. She quickly counted a total of $132 in small bills and loose change on the bottom.

"She probably took a little bit at a time from your father. Maybe Patty had a plan of her own," John said. "Open the little box and be sure the locket is still there."

Laura did as he suggested and opened the small box within the steel container. The golden locket still shone. Laura opened the locket and gazed at the faded pictures of her grandparents. They looked young and vigor. Something in the eyes of her grandfather looked familiar. Perhaps it was the similarity to her own eyes.

They quickly walked through the forest and found their way back to the car. Laura gave one final glance and climbed into the vehicle. She promised herself never to return.

The engine revved and John turned his car around to head back toward town. Laura held on to the locket and studied the picture of her grandparents.

She remembered the day so clearly, when her mother presented it to her and Patty. In the meantime, over nine years had gone by. Still, the pain was ever raw. Tears coursed down Laura's face. John reached over his seat. Laura took his hand for comfort.

"You did better than I expected. It doesn't surprise me that you're upset, though," he stated.

Laura blew her nose into a tissue and tried to stop crying. "If you'd have known my mother, you could better understand my pain. She was a good Christian. She made mistakes in her youth, but more than made up for them in the way she raised us."

Uncle Frank shook his head in sadness. He glanced back at Laura and gave her a reassuring smile. "Don't cry anymore, Laura. From here on, things are going to get better. Tony loves you and is working daily at getting better. Your parents adore you and support you completely. We're going to get rid of these mobsters, and you'll finally begin to live a normal life." His big brown eyes smiled at her.

Laura smiled in return. "Now, it's a matter of finding out what my grandparents can do."

John drove them to the Cicero Town Clerk's office. Laura filled out an application, requesting a copy of her mother and father's marriage license. Needing verification, the woman behind the desk requested a death certificate for either of her parents. After explaining her reasons for not having a death certificate for either, the woman at the office was able to do a bit of research and found the death certificate for one: Cara Santa Marcs. Laura verified her own identity with a copy of her original birth certificate, adoption papers, and her driver's license. The woman was then able to produce the original marriage license and made a copy for Laura.

Gathering the paper in her hands, Laura quickly scanned the sheet for her mother's maiden name. The document read:

This license authorizes the marriage of the parties named below within the State of New York by any person empowered to perform a marriage ceremony under the laws of the State of New York.
This certificate of Marriage,
Dated on the 5th day of September A.D. 1965
Between:
Mr. Matthew Duke Marcs and Ms. Cara Santa Valente . . .

Laura's eyes froze on her mother's name.
"Oh my good God!"

John looked the document over, immediately noticing the coincident in the names. "Your mother was a Valente."

"What?" Uncle Frank shouted. He grabbed the license and quickly scanned it. "Can it be? It certainly would explain a whole lot."

"Like what?" John added, "That her own flesh and blood would put her boyfriend and new family in physical harm?"

"John, my friend, we're not talking about your average people. The families we're dealing with aren't humane. They don't consider others' thoughts and feelings. The question is—does Laura still want to go to them?"

"Of course. Now I have even more questions that I want answered."

"But it might be dangerous," John insisted.

"I can't believe that he'd harm his own granddaughter," said Laura.

"Well, I'm not going to let you take that chance."

"Dad, don't do this to me. I have to go to them, if not for the money, then to find out the connection between the names. I need to know if the family that threatened Paul and killed him and Tammy, is my mother's."

"Laura, if I have to pay off the Galante family myself, then I will. But, I don't think it's a good idea to go to your grandfather's," John still insisted.

"But you can't drain your bank account and be left with nothing, because of me. I won't let you. You've already done enough for me. What if we do as Tony said, and went there with police protection? Would you feel better?"

"Man, I don't know anymore. I know only that I'm scared for you." John walked out of the Town Clerk's office. Laura and Uncle Frank followed. John inhaled deeply and placed an arm around Laura who nestled up next to him.

"Please, don't let me down, Dad. I need you."

"Do you know your grandfather's first name?"

"Antonino."

"Let's go to the police station and see if Massimo can track down an Antonino Valente. I'll take you there first thing tomorrow morning. For now, let's grab dinner and go home to rest. You've had a hard day." Laura thanked him.

They entered the car and sped away toward the station. Massimo was able to locate the whereabouts of an Antonino Valente, who fathered a daughter and lived in Brooklyn. Years ago, he moved from New York City to Long Island, where he now owned a secluded piece of property, off the water. His miniature mansion was kept isolated and heavily secured.

The following morning, when Laura, John, Frank, and two police offi-cers arrived at the gates of Antonino Valente's home, his guards approached the vehicle. John rolled the window down.

"State your business," the older of the two ordered.

"We're here to speak with Mr. Valente."

"Who are you and what's your purpose?"

Laura rolled the window down from the backseat. When the guard's eyes fell upon her face, he instantly paled. "Miss Cara," he whispered, and Laura blushed.

"No, but I'm her daughter, Laura. If my grandfather would allow it, I'd like to speak with him. The men here with me, come in peace. They're my adoptive father, my future uncle, and the officers are here for my protec-tion. I'd . . ."

The older guard interrupted her, saying, "Pull the vehicle through the gates and up the driveway. At the house, my men will have to frisk you all and search the vehicle. From there, Mr. Valente will see you. He has been expecting you."

John pulled the car through the gates and up the driveway. He parked the car in the circle drive before the front doors of the massive house. The guards ordered them to slowly exit the car and to be frisked, one at a time. Everyone cooperated and was announced clean. The officers were asked to remove their weapons, but they refused. Laura promised the guards that the officers wouldn't enter the room where Mr. Valente was. They agreed and everyone entered the huge home.

John held Laura's elbow as they walked up the front steps. She was in awe at the size and extravagance of the home. Its mammoth white columns towered over them, giving the house a grand appearance. The front doors were double the size of any door she'd ever seen. Laura thought of her mother and wondered how she did it, going from riches to rags.

Another guard opened the door and led them inward. The house was surfaced in granite flooring from one end to the other. Laura gaped at the beautiful décor. Nothing she had ever seen was comparable to what her eyes absorbed.

They walked down a short but elegant corridor, stopping before a large double door to the left. The guards stopped the group. The older one, who had noticed Laura's resemblance to Cara, spoke first. "Only Ms. Laura may enter."

"I'm not letting her go in there alone," John responded protectively.

"Mr. Valente's business does not apply to you. You, the uncle, and the cops stay here, or there's no meeting."

"It's okay, Dad. I'll be all right," Laura kissed John, who gave her a worried glance. She raised her eyebrows in a silent question and he nodded, giving her the signal to go in.

The doors were opened to an enormous den. Laura entered and glanced around the room. The curtains of the shadowy room were drawn and Laura's eyes needed to adjust to the darkness. In the far-left corner of the room, behind a grand cherrywood desk, she noticed the frame of a man. As she slowly sauntered toward him, a desk lamp turned on and Laura looked into the face of the same man who stood in the far pew of the church on the day of the wedding. He *was* the same Valente.

CHAPTER 33

Redeeming Cara

"It's you," she whispered. "You were there the day of the wedding."

The man rose and walked around the desk. He stood a few feet from Laura and gazed at her. Tears filled his eyes and he shook his head in wonder. "I knew you'd come. Now that I stand before you, I see the remarkable resemblance to my daughter." He nodded in dismay and cried, "Oh, Cara *mia*. Why?"

Laura fought to keep her tears in check. "She realized a little too late, that you were right," Laura sniffled. "My father never deserved her."

"You say the truth," he agreed, speaking with his heavy accent. "So why, after all these years, do you come to me, Laura?"

Laura cleared her throat and spoke more firmly. "Mr. Valente . . ."

"I am you *nonno*. I expect to be addressed as '*Nonno*'!" he exclaimed. "Come." He pointed to a burgundy leather couch, insisting they sit down. Laura did as he requested.

"Okay, Nonno Nino, you're a smart man. I don't need to insult your intelligence by telling you why I'm here. You already know." Antonino Valente said nothing. Laura waited a moment and replied with frustration. "I want to know why you were terrorizing Paul Roberts. I want to know why you were threatening his life and the life of his family."

"I can no lie to you. It's obvious that you have put two and two together and come to this conclusion. But, before you begin throwing accusations my way, I must tell you my version of the story."

"Your thugs, killed my adoptive sister—my best friend," Laura stated calmly. "What can you possibly say to me that can explain that?"

"No thing, I'm afraid. I see you hurt and I see you anger. I know that you do not know me, but I want you to understand me."

This time it was Laura who shook her head. She rose from the couch and paced in turmoil. "I look at all you have here and it sickens me to know that my mother died in a poor, pitiful shack, because you couldn't forgive her for being an ignorant teenager. She was a naive little girl, taken advantage of by a con artist. You've no idea what my mother endured for 13 years of her marriage."

"I do. I was keeping the tabs on her all the time."

"To no avail, Nonno! You never saved her from the horrible life she lived. The suffering she went through having you disown her was enough to break her. Then she had to live with the pain of knowing that … *you were right*. The day my mother gave birth to Sabrina, he could've saved her. He was too drunk to even stand. If you knew all of this, why did you let her suffer?"

Antonino Valente looked down at the floor in shame. His forehead wrinkled, as he drew his eyebrows together. Tears filled his eyes. "I was full of the pride and anger. I know that I was wrong. Because of my pride, I no only lost my daughter, but my wife, too. My Vita became ill after Cara left. Losing our daughter, left her with no hope. When we heard that she die, you grandmother died only two months after. And because I had wronged her, I brought her back to the old country to be buried with her family."

Laura was disappointed to find that her grandmother had passed away. "I'm sorry. I wish I could've known her."

"Oh, she would have loved you. You're Cara's spitting image. When I saw you for the first time, walking down the church, my heart broke in two. For one: because I did no have the honor of walking you momma down the aisle, and two: because I never make my peace with her. Seeing you was like seeing her ghost."

Laura stopped the conversation a moment to rustle around in her purse. She pulled out her mother's locket. Nonno Nino squinted as he gazed upon it. Laura placed it in his leathered hands. He gasped after recognizing it. "We gave this to Cara on her 16th birthday."

Laura nodded as she sighed. "The day my mother passed away—just before she went into labor—she took Patty and I into her bedroom. Underneath a floorboard, she hid this from my father. Momma made Patty promise to take care of it and hide it from him, if something ever happened to her. That same day, she told us all about you and Nonna. She finally confessed everything. She told us how she tried to get in touch with you many times and you wouldn't hear of it."

"It's true, I'm shame to say. I had her letters torn in two, before Vita even had the chance to read them. I did not want her to become more depressed."

"How could you keep a mother from her daughter? Are you trying to ease your conscience now by forcing love into *my life?*" Laura shouted.

"I said I'm no proud of my behavior. But I have changed. When Vita died, I realized that I was wrong. I'm sorry that I wronged you momma! That is why I have taken the special precautions to see that you have been taken care of."

"How, by killing the man I was going to marry and my sister?"

"Tammy's death was no mean to happen!"

"But it did. She was my best friend. She was the sister I always wanted, but didn't have because of people like you."

"I did not cause the death of you father and you sisters."

"I know that. The Galante famiglia did." Laura stopped pacing and sat back down next to her grandfather. "Nonno Nino," she continued. "I'm no one to come in here and accuse you, because I'm a sinner too. I see that you're sorry for never forgiving my mother. The past can't be rewritten, but the future can. Do you know why my father and sisters were killed?"

Nonno Nino wiped the tears from his face and looked into Laura's questioning eyes. "Yes, I know everything. You father pilfered a quarter of a million dollars from his boss, Mario Galante, my arch *enimigo*. He was going to leave town with you, but it never happened. Thank God, somehow you were spared when the murders happened, and after you were taken in by that punk, Giacalone, and Blandino."

"Be careful how you speak of my future husband."

"What? Are you *pazza? Crazy? He's mad*! You can no marry him."

"You're right, I won't be able to marry him, because the Galantes want us both dead. Either that or pay them three quarter-of-a-million dollars that we don't have. Tony will be turning 24 on Dec 4, this year. He won't be able to come into his inheritance to pay off the half a million dollars until he's 25. They doubled the amount that his father borrowed! That's what they're demanding! The other quarter of a million is the amount my father stole from them. They're also demanding that money now and there's no possible way for us to pay it back. We've searched everywhere for the money. But it's nowhere to be found."

Nino looked at his granddaughter firmly. "I know all this."

"You do? How?"

"I found out that that bum of you father was working for them. He did that to spite me, you know. He know that Mario Galante is my enemy! That . . . bum! My men keep a close eye on you and you sisters because we knew that he was no intelligent enough to stay out of trouble. After he stole the money, our connections told us that the Galantes were going after him. When my men go to the cabin to protect you girls, it was too late. They believed you all to be dead."

Laura stopped a moment to consider this. In a matter of those five fate-filled minutes, everyone was drawn to the old cabin. The Galantes—to murder her father and whoever got in their way, Nino Valente—to protect his family, and Max—to do whatever he'd intended. God had truly spared her.

Nino distracted her thoughts and continued, "Later that night, we returned so we could give you girls a proper burial. That is when we discovered that you had not perished. We took Sabrina and Patty's bodies and buried them, before Galante could destroy the evidence of the murders."

"You buried my sisters," Laura whispered, near tears.

"Yes. One day, I hope to move them next to your mother's grave."

"Thank you," she uttered. "I would like to visit their graves one day."

Nino nodded. "Of course. I will take you. You know, I searched for you for years. When you finally left that Giacalone, and the Knight family adopted you, I found you again. It was then that I made a solemn vow to take care of you."

"What happened after your men found my family dead?"

"They arrived immediately after the killing. My men see Gino Galante when he was leaving the cabin. He was looking for the money. My men try to kill him. They failed and he got away. After finding that they had arrived too late, my men searched the area. Behind the driver's seat of you father's truck, they found the briefcase with the money. They take it."

"*You* have their money?" Laura questioned dumbstruck.

"Yes, we keep it as a compensation for the death of my *nipote*, my granddaughters. When I found you, Laura *mia*, I was overjoy! I had a chance to make right the wrong I had done in the past. That is why I try so hard to help you. I was so happy to see that that nice man, John, adopted you. I know it may no mean too much to you, now. But what I have here— is yours. I want to fix my mistakes and take care of you. I will protect you from Mario Galante and anyone who try to hurt you. You all I have left," he confessed.

"Nonno, all I really need is to give Mario Galante back that money or I won't be around for us to be able to have any kind of a future. Would you give them the money back for me?"

"I'll do better than that. If you will forgive me for my mistakes, I will pay off the entire loan and you may go you own way. Giacalone will get his inheritance next year and live a wealthy life of his own."

Laura sat stunned by his offer. She scoffed at it. "In other words, you'll pay off the debt if I promise not to marry Tony?" The old man didn't verbally answer, but merely nodded his head. "Nonno, do you have any idea how hard I've fought to keep Tony?"

"You think you love him. Laura, you young. Don't be like my daughter. Listen to me, I'm old and I know the ways of this world."

"You don't know him, Nonno. He helped me when my family was killed and I had no one. He is my life."

"I see that he stopped you from wedding that nice Dr. Paul. You would've been well off with the doctor. I see that this Tony is broken inside and if this problem returns, he'll kill you. Do you blame me?"

"Then why did you threaten to kill Paul and ultimately make good on your threats?" Laura began to grow frustrated with his impossible thinking. "Nonno, Paul didn't love me. He was in love with my sister, Tammy. But, because he was scared to death of your goons, he was forced to propose to me. I never really had his heart and he never had mine. You can't force love."

Nonno Nino stood from the couch and peered out the window of the den. He turned to her suddenly with a finger pointing in the air, matter-of-factly. "That is no true. I forced you Nonna Vita to admit her love for me. I convince her! Anyway, Paul and Tammy was no supposed to get hurt. Their deaths were accidents and the person who made that fatal mistake, paid with their life."

Laura's eyes bulged in disbelieve. "More pointless deaths? Where does the bloodshed end? Nonno, if you don't change, you'll burn in hell."

"Perhaps you right. In my defense, I say that my motives were pure. I could no save my daughter from the life she chose, but I try to help you with yours."

"And you can. Please, pay the balance owed to the Galantes and make them keep their word to let us be! Tony has suffered so much at their hands." Laura rose and stood before the husky old man. "I don't know if you already know, but I'm with child and Tony is the father. When he's better, I'll marry him, and make a home for my baby, *if* you help me."

He touched her cheek tenderly. "So many dreams, but dreams are no the reality. My offer still stands. I'll pay the Galantes off, if you and your child start a new life, without this crazy character."

Laura pushed his hand away. Her anger boiled. "Nonno, it's obvious you've learned nothing from your past experiences. I'll pray for you and I hope you come to see the truth. But I'll not be blackmailed into leaving Tony. I don't need you or your money. Even if you did steal it from the

Galantes, the same way my father did. Think about it, you're no different than him, if you don't do the right thing."

"I'm sorry that you feel that way," he whispered. "My intentions were never to bring pain to you."

"Jesus says, 'You will know them by their fruits'. Show me your heart is true by your actions, Nonno."

"I am simply looking out for you best interests!" He clasped his wrinkled hands together and shook them. "Please, try to understand."

"Nonno, you can't try to run everybody's life. If my mother made a mistake in marrying my father, she learned that soon enough. That's how people grow, by making mistakes and bettering themselves from them. You ought to know that by now. If I want to take the risk of marrying Tony, that's my decision. Now you need to trust my judgment and respect it. If I make a mistake, I'll count on God to help me through it."

"You like you momma. You look to God for the help?"

"That's right. She taught me that. God has helped me through the hardest times in my life. I can count on Him and so should you. But first, I suggest you get right with Him and correct your errors. Turn away from sin. Even if that means you have to give this all up." She waved her arms around the room.

"I don't know about this stuff," he huffed, crossing his arms over his chest.

"There's nothing to know, Nonno. You need Jesus to forgive you and you need to follow Him, not the almighty dollar. If you love money first, you can't have God. But if you love God first, your blessings will be far greater than any riches money can buy."

"But will Jesus forgive a man like me? I have sinned far more than I care to admit."

Laura clasped his hands in hers and smiled. "Nonno a sin is a sin, big or little. No matter what, we all need a savior. What counts is your heart. Are you sorry for your sins? Do you want God's forgiveness?"

"It's a good thing God is no like me, ehh? Because if I was Him, I'd strike me down for even thinking of coming to Him to ask for *pardono*."

"Nonno, as long as you're sincere, He'll forgive *and* forget."

A knock on the door interrupted the conversation. Laura looked deeply into her grandfather's eyes. "I'm counting on you to do what's right. Perhaps that *could* lead us to having a closer relationship. Otherwise, I'll have my answer. Thank you for your time." She leaned forward and kissed his smooth cheek.

Laura opened the door and found John and Uncle Frank standing behind it. "Are you okay?" her father whispered.

Laura nodded and they left.

*   *   *

In the next few days, Uncle Frank got word from the Galante famiglia that the loan was paid off in full. Laura's grandfather also sent word to her, thanking her for the visit and insisting she come visit with him soon. Two weeks later, Laura made another visit to Nonno Nino's home and tried to convince him to come to Christ. He said the sinner's prayer and promised to do his best to turn from his old ways.

He retired from his vague business, making promises to Laura, and to God, that he'd no longer involve himself in illegal activities. Still, he didn't feel that he should pay for crimes he didn't actually commit, despite the order given to warn Paul that ultimately killed Tammy. As for the bullet that was meant for Tony on the wedding day, Nino claimed that there was never a plan to use force. The orders were only to witness the matrimony.

According to Massimo, no charges against him would stick in a court of law. Of course, Nino felt justified in his actions because he was doing it all in Laura's best interest. He said that he wanted to be a true grandfather to her and the upcoming baby. Laura was skeptical, but was called by God to forgive.

Meanwhile, Massimo Desanti continued to work with the FBI to find just cause to incriminate the Galante famiglia. All the while, the gunmen who were arrested at the wedding were tried and convicted. Though, they refused to give up the name of the man for whom they worked. The man who pulled the trigger that killed Paul, *was* found dead in his cell—a supposed suicide. Nevertheless, a few less Mafiosos on the street was certainly a good start.

Over the course of the next few weeks, Tony's recovery was slow but effective. His therapy sessions would prove to be trying. At last, the courts released him to continue his therapy on an outpatient schedule.

Tony was set free, in many ways. He was free to love Laura with no restraint, free to become the man he wanted to be, and free from Max's hold over him. Upon his release, he asked John for Laura's hand in marriage, for by that time, Laura's pregnancy was obvious and well underway. They'd marry as soon as Tony could gather his things together and get himself settled. He purchased a small home near John and Marlene's in Albany. Uncle Frank, feeling too far away, uprooted his life and moved into town, as well.

Everyone was excited about the coming wedding and the arrival of the new baby in May. Marlene, having been given a second chance at life, remained in remission and looked forward to helping to raise her future grandchild.

Laura understood too well that John and Marlene could've easily felt nothing but contempt for the man who set the stage for Tammy and Paul's deaths—even if the deaths were supposed accidents. Nevertheless, they displayed amazing Christian attributes and forgave Nino.

At times, even Laura wondered how she was able to forgive him for Tammy and Paul's deaths. Somehow, God had provided her with mercy in her heart. Her grandfather's fruits proved to be noble, for the time being. In reuniting with him, Laura felt a sense of belonging. She found her roots and was happy to be a part of her mother's family.

As for Laura and Tony, their love was immovable. Nothing could break the bond that formed back in the midst of the old 'abandoned' house. Their marriage and the birth of their child could only strengthen that bond even more.

EPILOGUE

Looking back, I can only say that it had to be God's omnipotence to have pulled us through those dark and perilous times. I could see that with every hardship—there was a reason, with every dark cloud—a silver lining. If my family hadn't been killed, I wouldn't have met Tony. If Tony wasn't ill, I wouldn't have found Tammy, Marlene, and John. If Marlene hadn't gotten sick, Paul would've probably never given me a second glance. And through it all, no matter the heartache, I was able to come to know the most extraordinary souls. God, in his infinite wisdom, brought me through every trial.

Recently, while sitting in the nursery of my future home, holding my mid-section starting to round in form, I was moved to tears. For, even in my sin God had blessed me with so much: Tony's love, our child, and our new home—small, but cozy. We will live only five blocks from my adoptive parents and two miles from Uncle Frank.

Prior to the holidays, we took a trip to the house in Cicero, and made some renovations to it. John and Marlene both loved the old house. Uncle Frank joined in, simply happy to be a part of our little family. We turned the home into a quiet 'get-a-way'. There, I hope to spend summer weekends at our little lake, swimming, playing, and watching my family grow.

The property I grew up on was another issue. Since my father never wrote a 'will', it made it hard to claim the property and the cabin as my own. After much deliberation, the courts ruled in my favor and appointed me the sole landowner. Yet, too many ugly memories made it difficult for me want to keep it. Therefore, we placed the property on the market.

To make up for some of the heartache, Nonno Nino erected a memorial, next to my mother's grave, for Patty and Sabrina's bodies. I finally felt closure and peace when going to visit them.

As for my fiancé, he's everything I could ever want in a future husband. I pray for him daily, just to be sure the Lord keeps his evil alter at bay. He continues with therapy, eager to find a way to merge his feelings into one personality. He toils greatly to overcome his fears and his pain. There's more to his anguish than he cares to admit. Dr. Parnell says we must dig deeper to find the core of Tony's torment. We knew it wouldn't be easy.

Yet, I couldn't be more proud of him. He has stood the test of time and still triumphed. His strength is rock solid. His determination—*resilient!* In addition to getting his life back in order, he has taken the position of the management of John's rentals.

Meanwhile, despite *my* valiant efforts, I decided to put school on hold, as both work and college had become too much for my pregnant body to juggle. Mr. Stone kept his promise. My position at his firm remained available. And so, I'll continue to run his office until I ultimately leave to stay home and raise my baby. Eventually, if it's God's will, I plan to return to school, though I'm not quite sure what God calls me to. I simply pray He will use me and my experiences to help others.

I can honestly say that I've seen His mighty hand at work.

It's true what the apostle Paul said to the Romans, "And we know that all that happens to us is working for our good, if we love God and are fitting into his plans." I know this because, even though I've had my share of angry moments with Him, He still worked everything out for my own good. He gave me my heart's desires.

Last night, I crawled up next to Tony on John and Marlene's couch. I didn't want him to leave to go home. I fell exhausted into his arms, seeking some affection, after helping Marlene with Thanksgiving clean-up.

It had been two long years since the nightmare began, when Tony lost control to Max. Too long a period of pain and sorrow. I look forward to peace and happiness, for a change.

Tony wrapped his arms around me and held me tight. His touch will forever send shivers down my spine. I don't know if it's possible, but I pray my heart will go aflutter every time I look into his beautiful eyes. He rubbed my tummy and whispered that he couldn't wait to see our baby. He also said he couldn't wait to become my husband. I shivered with excitement!

At last, we close the chapter on the hardest times of our lives. Now, we start anew with hope, faith, and love to guide us. 'And the greatest of these is love'.

CPSIA information can be obtained at www.ICGtesting.com
Printed in the USA
BVOW08s2229290915

420255BV00001B/1/P